# A Change of Key

Part II of *The Sideman*

By Howard Bruce Weiner

**A CHANGE OF KEY**

This is a work of fiction. As a novel with a historical context, some of the characters are actual personages from the period depicted. Others are purely the product of the author's imagination. Some of the events are out of chronological sequence to fit the overall pattern of the narrative. All the dialogue by real figures is the invention of the author.

Copyright 2021

Dr. Howard Bruce Weiner

All Rights Reserved

**A CHANGE OF KEY**

# ALSO BY HOWARD B. WEINER

*The Caltrap Murders: A Bradley Davison Mystery*
*Here Lies Arthur: A Bradley Davison Mystery*
*The Robin Hood Horde; A Bradley Davison Mystery*
*Heir to the Pendragon: A Novel of King Arthur*
*Remains to be Seen: A Novel of Vietnam*
*An Eternity to Weep" A Novel of Elizabethan England*
*The Sideman: A Novel of the Big Band Era*

# A CHANGE OF KEY

Dr. Howard B. Weiner

1973

**A CHANGE OF KEY**

Once again for Carmela

My Muse and Inspiration

For Annmarie

The Real Fran Michaels

For Chris

The Technological Wizard

## AUTHOR'S NOTE

The period following the Second World War was one of the most interesting eras in American music history. Post-war recession and the toll of the war essentially led to the demise of the Big Band or Swing era. It is true that some big bands both survived and thrived, such as Les Brown, Tommy and Jimmy Dorsey, Woody Herman, Stan Kenton and Tex Beneke—first as the leader of the Glenn Miller Orchestra and then leading his own band. But America faced new challenges after the war and the music industry reflected those challenges. American music became fragmented into numerous musical styles like bebop, progressive jazz, combo jazz, Avant Garde jazz, rhythm and blues, rockabilly and ultimately rock n' roll. The emergence and evolution of these styles is the substance of *A Change of Key: Book II of The Sideman*.

The novel follows the story of Buck Fisher, one of the most famous big band leaders of the 1940s as he attempts to find his place in this new world of the American music scene. His rise to fame was depicted in *The Sideman* which traced his life from local sideman to world-wide fame. Now in the post-war musical maelstrom as a rising music executive, his impact on developing new musical talents and genres is the substance of *A Change of Key*.

I have thoroughly enjoyed chronicling Buck Fisher's rise to stardom in *The Sideman: A Novel of the Big Band Era*. I hope you will enjoy following his continued success in *A Change of Key: Book II of The Sideman*.

Dr. Howard Weiner

2021

**A CHANGE OF KEY**

# CHAPTER ONE
### *Board Meeting, January 1946*

New York City's Rockefeller Center was a huge complex of Art Deco buildings constructed of steel and Indiana limestone in the heart of the city between 48$^{th}$ Street and 51$^{st}$ Street. The twenty-two-acre assortment of commercial buildings included such landmarks as Radio City Music Hall, the ice-skating rink in Rockefeller Plaza, the huge statues of Prometheus commissioned in 1934 which presides over the skating rink and Atlas commissioned in 1936 which is situated in front of the International Building. Built by over 40,000 workers in the height of the Great Depression, it was one of the greatest construction projects of that troubled time.

One of the most notable structures in the entire development was the RCA building which opened in Mid-May of 1932. Located at 30 Rockefeller Plaza, it was the home of RCA Victor's radio and record divisions as well as recording and broadcasting studios. It was to '30 Rock' that Buck Fisher made his way on the chilly morning of January 3$^{rd}$, 1946. He had taken the subway from Main Street, Flushing and transferred to the F train which took him to the 47$^{th}$-50$^{th}$ Street stop on the IND line. It was a short walk to the entrance to the building but he was moving slowly taking in the brisk winter air and enjoying the sight of the 75-foot spruce Christmas tree in Rockefeller Plaza that attracted tens of thousands of tourists each year.

Buck Fisher's name was almost synonymous with the Big Band era. His meteoric rise as a musician and leader had brought him international acclaim and a great fortune, putting him in the same class as Glenn Miller, Benny Goodman and Tommy Dorsey. Unfortunately, a critical and almost fatal injury he suffered in England while leading his Army Special Services band had put a hold on his performing career. But his friend and mentor, Jack Merrill, formerly the head of the Artist and Development Department, now president of Bluebird Records, had offered Buck an executive position with Bluebird once the war ended.

## A CHANGE OF KEY

That morning Buck kissed his wife Carrie and his two children before heading out to Manhattan. Carrie had been the vocalist with the Johnny Blair Orchestra when Buck first met her and it was almost instantaneous love. Carrie had gladly given up her singing career to raise Edward and Laura, the couple's two children. Buck reluctantly yet realistically accepted the fact that because of his injury, performing might never be an option again, but with Carrie's encouragement, he was ready to begin a brand-new chapter of his life. She called it 'a change of key.'

"This is going to be great for us, darling," said Carrie. "No more touring, no more struggles making it to the top---and plenty of time for me and the kids."

"I know you're right, love," said Buck, but there was a twinge of sadness in his voice. The lure of performing and creating was still strong within him.

Jack Merrill wanted Buck to meet the CEO and other top executives of RCA Victor as he embarked upon his new career as Vice President of New Artist Development. Buck had had only a few days since his discharge from the Army to crystallize some of his plans and ideas for his new position, but he was confident that he could present them in a way that they would be approved and implemented.

Buck took one of the eight express elevator cars to the 25$^{th}$ floor and he found Jack Merrill's office. He introduced himself to Merrill's secretary who buzzed him on the intercom to tell him that Buck Fisher had arrived. The door to Merrill's office opened immediately and Jack came out, saw Buck and embraced him in a bear hug.

"Lemme have a look at you!" said Merrill. "Jesus, you look like shit, my friend! I see Carrie and your mom haven't been able to fatten you up—yet."

"Give it time, Jack. My plumbing still isn't quite back to normal yet," said Buck.

Buck's war injury in a buzz bomb blast in London had severed his intestine, nearly killing him, and causing an Army surgeon to remove over two feet of it. His recovery had been gradual and his diet would be carefully monitored for the rest of his life. But day by day he felt his strength growing and though he could no longer walk quickly and he tired rapidly, he felt that in time he would be back to himself and hopefully be able to play his tenor sax again.

Merrill ushered Buck into his office where the two friends caught up on everything from Buck's health to his two children to how glad he was to be home with Carrie and his family. As president of one of RCA's most profitable divisions, Merrill wielded great power and was in a position to see to it that Buck was as successful in his new role as he had been as a band leader of almost legendary stature.

"Here's my advice, Buck. In just a few minutes you will be meeting with some incredibly important and impressive people. Don't hold back. Don't bullshit them. Tell them what you want, how you will go about doing things and what you need. They will respect you for that—and by the way, they already respect you for the millions of dollars you made for them in record sales. But they are for the most part suits—and what they used to call during the war 'bean counters.' Money is important to them and they can smell when there's money to be made. But they also pride themselves on how they treat everyone like family and want to see their people succeed. So now, tell me what you've got."

For the next twenty minutes, Buck laid out his plans, and how he would go about scouting out new talent and developing them into recording artists. He was specific about what he would need to get the job done and Jack jotted down notes on a yellow fool's cap pad as Buck spoke.

When Buck finished his spiel, Jack nodded and said, "This is great stuff, Buck. It's different, but Victor isn't opposed to any kind of innovation. I think they'll go for this in a big way. And by the way, I'm impressed. Now let's go sell this."

They took an elevator to the 65$^{th}$ floor where there was a boardroom and the office of the Chairman of the Board of RCA Victor. When they entered the boardroom, there were already a dozen executives seated at a huge table. At the head of the table

## A CHANGE OF KEY

sat David Sarnoff, the Russian-American corporate chairman who was a legend in the communications industry. His recognition of radio as a means to reach massive audiences on a national scale led to the promulgation of radio as the chief entertainment format in America from the 1920s through and past World War II.

"General Sarnoff, may I introduce you to Colonel Buck Fisher," said Merrill.

David Sarnoff was a part of General Dwight Eisenhower's communication staff and in 1945 he received his star as a Brigadier General in the Army Reserves. His staff frequently used his title of 'general' when addressing him, and Sarnoff for his part, had no objections.

As for Buck, he began his Army career as a buck private shortly after Pearl Harbor, but he was advanced rapidly to the rank of First Lieutenant and ultimately Major, as his contributions to the war effort, particularly in selling War Bonds, were recognized by the Army and the War Department. By the time he returned from England on convalescent duty at Fort Hamilton, Brooklyn, he had been made an Acting Lieutenant Colonel. But the war ended before his rank became permanent; nevertheless, he was entitled to use his rank of colonel for the rest of his life.

All the executives at the table rose as one and applauded loudly after Merrill's introduction of Buck. Sarnoff himself came around from the head of the table and shook Buck's hand. He then found a seat in a chair that had been reserved for him in the middle of the table with Merrill seated next to him.

"Buck," Sarnoff began, "I can't tell you what an honor it is to have you with us at Victor. You made us a ton of money with your civilian band, and your Army band was a godsend to so many of those kids overseas. As for your injury, well, the front lines weren't the only place an American serviceman could be hurt. We all know how dire your wound was and we're just glad you made it home safely. I wish I could say the same for Glenn Miller, but our country will feel his loss for decades to come."

"Thank you, general," said Buck. "Glenn was a good friend and I mourn his loss every day."

## A CHANGE OF KEY

"As do we all," said Sarnoff. "Now, tell us what your plans are for the new division you're going to head up."

"Well, general, one thing I learned in the Army was that there are fantastic musicians all over this country just waiting for a break. They are skillful, creative and deserving of a shot. One thing I want to do is 'beat the bushes' in search of new talent. I want to hear them perform and whenever possible, bring them in for auditions. But this is a big country and I can't do that alone. I will need a few assistants—willing to travel and frankly, more capable of traveling than I am at this point in time. I have several in mind—men I worked with in the Army and who are geniuses in organization and logistics."

"How do you see them traveling, Buck," asked Sarnoff.

"With the end of the war, general, commercial air travel will become enormously popular in America. If they have to go to the west coast, a plane ride would be a lot better in terms of hours spent doing nothing while riding a train cross country."

Some of the executives at the table nodded in agreement; others kept their poker faces. Sarnoff said, "What else, Buck?"

"You know how Arturo Toscanini leads the NBC Symphony Orchestra—one of the great orchestras in the world with some of the world's most renowned players? I think we need that on the popular side as well. A cadre of top-notch musicians to do all the studio backings of singers or groups that we sign, rather than relying upon free-lancers. And, Jack, it might sound like heresy coming from me, but I think we should add a string section like Shaw had and later Glenn had in the Army Air Force band. It would enable us to produce a lush sound on ballads that could become the 'Victor Sound,' easily recognizable as our own."

Jack Merrill then spoke up and said, "It won't be hard to put out the word that we're looking for players. There are lots of unemployed sidemen who are looking for steady work, and we could make them part of the Victor family."

Sarnoff was silent for a few minutes and then he dropped a blockbuster announcement that even Jack Merrill was unaware of. "Within the next few months, we will be putting the Bluebird

## A CHANGE OF KEY

label to sleep. It served its purpose and made us a lot of money. But we're reorganizing our recorded music divisions. Jack, you're going to head up the RCA Victor label, complete with its 'His Master's Voice' trademark. All classical recordings will be issued on the RCA Red Seal label and Bruce Baldwin will be in charge of that including signing new talent."

Buck, who was stunned by the announcement said, "General, all the Buck Fisher Orchestra material that we recorded for Bluebird—what happens to that, and not to sound mercenary, but what happens to the royalties from those tunes?"

Sarnoff smiled and said, "I figured that would get your attention, Buck, so let me explain."

Evidently everyone else at the table was equally surprised at the reorganization because they all leaned in closer at the table to hear Sarnoff's explanation.

"Gentlemen, 78 RPM recordings are soon to be a thing of the past. Truth is, they aren't very practical and new recording techniques will eclipse them quickly—and we need to be in on the ground floor. Very soon, artists will be releasing individual songs on seven-inch 45 RPM discs. They are less expensive to produce and we can sell them for thirty-five to forty-five cents apiece. Maybe even less. They will pair nicely with a new line of Victrola record players specifically designed for 45 RPM records."

Bill Totten from Marketing said, "General, you expect every American to go out and spend money on these Victrolas when they have perfectly serviceable record players already?"

"Ah, Bill, good point—but not at all. We are also manufacturing a small plastic adapter that fits right over the spindle on a turntable. The 45s will slip right onto them."

"And I assume they will only cost a few cents?" said Totten. "Exactly, Bill. But that's not all," said Sarnoff. "The future of recorded music lies in albums of 33 RPM Long Playing discs. These LPs can hold as many as fourteen songs, seven to a side. So for a relatively small investment, record buyers will be able to hear a whole selection of music by their favorite artist without having to change a record every three or four minutes.

## A CHANGE OF KEY

These record albums will have beautiful cover photos or artwork and extensive liner notes on the back explaining what the music is all about—complete with backgrounds on the artists, times of the tracks, and other recording information."

Sarnoff could read the surprised expression on Buck's face. Laughing, he said, "So Buck, another of your responsibilities will be to help assemble these LPs. You'll be combing through our lists of artists and tunes they recorded and then selecting which ones will go on a disc and in what order. You'll be doing the same with all the discs your band recorded for Bluebird as well. And don't worry, Buck, you and the members of your band will still be collecting royalties on anything they recorded."

There were some technical questions from some of the assembled executives which Sarnoff addressed, but at length he said, "Buck, I like everything you've presented to us today. This isn't a democracy so I'm ready to get started on your ideas as soon as you are ready. How soon can you start?"

"How's Monday morning, general?" said Buck.

"Excellent. I like a man who can hit the deck running. When you get here on Monday, I will have an office set up for you and I'll assign a secretary to you. As you assemble your staff, you'll have them go to personnel for all the paperwork—and you have to do that too."

Sarnoff looked around the table one last time and said, "All right, gentlemen, let's make all this happen—and quickly."

The meeting adjourned and Buck and Jack returned to Merrill's office. When they got there, Jack said, "Wow! He went for the whole thing! Honestly, Buck, I never expected him to buy into half of what you want, but what the general wants, the general gets. Now what about these assistants you told the general about. What's the story with them?"

"I have two men I would love to have as my scouts and assistants. They were with me in the Army and they are the best at what they do. I need to know what I can offer them by way of salary since at least one of them is going to have to move here from the Midwest."

## A CHANGE OF KEY

Merrill thought for a moment before saying, "I think we can offer them 25,000 a year plus some perks when they are out of town and some fringe benefits thrown into the mix."

"That's more than fair, Jack, but what about the sidemen for the studio orchestra? I only want top players."

"We're talking about maybe twenty-eight players Buck?"

"Yes, the seventeen big band players plus the augmented string section. In time, maybe a few more."

That took some more thought and scrawled calculations on Merrill's pad. "Does 15,000 a year sound OK with you?"

In his civilian band, at ninety bucks a week, his players were making a little over 4,000 a year, plus any royalties the band made. A payday of 15,000 bucks a year was more than fair. "That should get me some top players, Jack. That works for me."

"Good. I can clear these figures down at Finance, but there shouldn't be a problem. Like I once told you, we're a worldwide company with deep pockets and plenty of resources."

"There's one more thing, Jack," said Buck.

"Uh oh. Am I going to hate this?"

"No, I don't think so. We can use many of the charts I used in my civilian band, but with Johnny gone, we need a staff of arrangers to integrate the string section into the arrangements. I imagine Jerry Gray and Bill Finnegan are spoken for, and Henry Mancini was doing charts for the Army Air Force band. Maybe he's around. Other than them, I don't have too many contacts in the arranging business. That's how vital Johnny was to what we did."

"All right, Buck, let me put out some feelers and I'll get back to you. Let's go have some lunch and kick around some more ideas. Good thing about midtown Manhattan is there's no shortage of great places to eat. I know you still have some limitations, but don't worry. Wherever we go, I'm sure you'll find something that won't rattle your innards too much."

They went to a Schraft's restaurant in Rockefeller plaza where Benny had scrambled eggs and some dry toast. Merrill shook his head at the paltry plate in front of Buck and said, "When do the docs think you'll be back to normal, Buck?"

"It's hard to say, Jack. Six months, maybe. But some foods will be strictly verboten for a long time to come. Things like broccoli, cauliflower and beans—anything that could load me up with gas. Don't feel bad for me, Jack. Carrie and my mom have figured out lots of things that I can eat without causing too many problems."

They discussed some more details and figures over lunch, both of them growing eager to begin the new chapter in Buck Fisher's life. At the conclusion of the meal, Jack said, "You still driving that Oldsmobile, Buck?"

"My sisters probably use it more than I do. Carrie still has her Cord."

"Well, we're going to do something about that. But until then, no more subways for you. You'll have a reserved space in the garage. Hell, you're a big executive now, Buck. So take advantage of it."

They shook hands and Buck said, "See you Monday morning, Jack."

…..

Buck arrived home at about three that afternoon. As soon as he opened the door, he was attacked by both Eddie and Laura, each one wanting to be picked up and held. Even with his diminished strength, he picked them both up at the same time and kissed each one of his children.

"All right, you two, let your mother get a hug and kiss from the boss, yeah?"

Buck opened his arms and embraced Carrie, kissing her tenderly and holding her tight. It was still difficult for him to believe that he was home alive, was recuperating, and was with the people he loved most in the entire world.

"I have a nice dinner for you, sweetheart. We'll eat, then put these two rugrats to bed and we'll have time for you to tell me everything that happened today. I want to hear every detail."

## A CHANGE OF KEY

In the nearly seven years that Buck Fisher had known Carrie Collins, he could not imagine loving any other woman with the intensity he still felt for her. Yes, there had been a slight bump early in their relationship, but other than that, they were equally delirious about each other. Carrie had lost none of her radiant beauty and it wasn't hard for Buck to remember how he had longed for her when he was overseas during the war.

Dinner was at six and by a quarter to seven, both children were yawning and ready for sleep. Buck tucked Laura into her bed, pulled the covers up to her chin and sat on a chair next to her. There was a storybook on the small nightstand and he picked it up to read a few pages to her. That is all it took; after only three pages, his daughter was sleeping soundly. Carrie closed the door to Eddie's room, leaving a small night light on and then she came into the living room and sat on the sofa. When Buck joined her, she opened her arms and they hugged and kissed. Then Carrie pushed him back gently and said, "OK, colonel, spill. Tell me what happened."

Omitting no details, Buck explained how he had outlined what he thought his job would entail—to none other than David Sarnoff himself. This impressed Carrie who said, "Oh darling, this all sounds so wonderful—but tell me, and be honest—how much traveling will you have to do?"

"I'm going to be hiring assistants, darling. They will do most of the legwork. I can't promise that I won't have to do some traveling, but I already told Jack that it has to be kept to a minimum. I didn't exactly tell him that my health was an important limitation on traveling; I didn't have to. He brought it up himself and promised to keep me local as much as possible."

"So this studio band, honey, will you reach out to some of the guys from the civilian band or look for all new players?"

"Of course I would love to have some of them with me, but it really wouldn't be me they'd be working for. I'll put the band together, but someone else will have to lead it. I wouldn't mind if I could also track down some of the guys from the Army band. They were superb players too."

# A CHANGE OF KEY

"What about vocalists, Bucky?" asked Carrie.

"I foresee having backup singers for the out-front performers. Once I get a staff of arrangers, we can discuss how best to integrate them into the studio sound. Why? Are you volunteering?"

Carrie laughed her infectious laugh and said, "Loved one, I've already got a full-time job. Your son and daughter keep me on my toes from sunrise to the time they go to sleep." She thought for a moment before adding, "But I wouldn't mind coming down and watching on occasion if Mom and the girls can watch the kids."

"I had a feeling that's what you were thinking," said Buck.

He then reached up and gently touched her on her breast. "I know you had a long day, darling, but maybe if you aren't too tired, we could—"

"Say no more. I'm never too tired for that," said Carrie, rising from the sofa and leading him to the bedroom.

**A CHANGE OF KEY**

# CHAPTER TWO
## *Reunions, January, 1946*

When Buck arrived at 30 Rock on Monday morning, he met briefly with Jack Merrill who then escorted him to his office on the 20th floor. By any standard, it would have been considered opulent—a huge open-spaced waiting room with a secretary's desk and sofas and a private office that looked down on Rockefeller Plaza where already skaters were doing axels and leaps beneath the shadow of the eighteen-foot, eight-ton statue of mighty Prometheus. The crystal-clear day enabled Buck to have a spectacular view of the many skyscrapers along 6th Avenue, renamed Avenue of the Americas by Mayor Fiorello LaGuardia in 1945.

"Buck, let me introduce you to Kelsey Burton, your secretary and all-around Gal Friday," said Jack.

Kelsey Burton rose from behind her desk and came around to Buck and Jack. She extended her hand and said, "It's an honor to meet you, Mr. Fisher."

"Rule number one, Kelsey—it's Buck. I might wear a suit every day, but in my bands it was always a first-name basis. It made us feel more like a family than employer-employee, if you get my point."

"All right, Buck, that works for me," said Kelsey. "Anything you need, you can count on me to get it for you."

Kelsey Burton was a beautiful brunette of about twenty-four. She had a knock-out figure that could have propelled her to a modeling career rather than the somewhat stuffy world of corporate America. She had a million-dollar smile to go with her eye-popping shape. She also had a husband who had recently returned from a naval hospital after losing half a leg to a kamikaze attack on the USS Intrepid (CV11) during the Okinawa campaign—a battle that cost the lives of over 12,500 Americans, the costliest battle of the entire war.

## A CHANGE OF KEY

"We hired Kelsey right out of the Katharine Gibbs Secretarial School," said Jack, "but don't kid yourself, before she went there, she got a degree from NYU in Fine Arts—so she's a smart cookie."

Buck, who had gone no further than a diploma from James Madison High School in Brooklyn, was suitably impressed by his new assistant's credentials. He was sure she would be an invaluable addition to the team he planned on putting together.

"I'm going to leave you two to get to know each other and let you start getting the wheels rolling," said Jack. "Let's touch base at about two this afternoon and you can give me a progress report."

When Jack left, Kelsey said, "OK, boss, where do we begin?"

Buck laughed and said, "That's a good question. I'd like you to track down the phone numbers of two people for me. The first is Bill Dwyer out in Erlanger, Kentucky. The second is Al Rovitz. He's up in the Bronx. I'll be in my office playing around with some numbers. When you find them, just let me know. In time I might want you to track down some other names."

"Got it, Buck."

Ten minutes later, Kelsey knocked on Buck's door, entered and handed him a slip of paper with two telephone numbers on it. "Thanks, Kel, that was pretty quick. Thanks very much."

"Piece of cake, Buck. Can't wait to sink my teeth into something more challenging."

When she left, Buck picked up the phone on his desk and asked the operator for an outside line. When he heard the dial tone, he dialed the Erlanger, Kentucky number.

"Good morning. May I please speak to Bill Dwyer?"

"Yes, one moment," said a young woman. "Bill? Phone."

A minute later, "This is Bill Dwyer. How can I help you?"

## A CHANGE OF KEY

"Well, Major, to begin with, you can get your ass to New York City where I have a job waiting for you—unless you still have your heart set on being a Kentucky State Trooper again."

"Buck! That you?"

"It sure is, buddy. And I'm not kidding. I would like you to come work for me at Victor."

"Holy Jesus, Buck! This is unbelievable!" said Dwyer.

Bill Dwyer had been Buck's company commander in Basic Training at Camp Polk, Louisiana. He was the man responsible for getting him to start the Army Special Services band and getting him commissioned as a First Lieutenant. They had served every day together during the war and they rose up through the ranks at the same time. They also had become best friends. When Buck had been injured and was taken to the London Free Hospital, Bill Dwyer sat by his bedside every evening through his coma and several subsequent surgeries. He was more than a friend; to Buck, he was the brother he never had.

"Level with me, Bill. If you get your job back with the KSP, how much would they pay you?"

Dwyer thought for a few moments and then said, "When I left for the Army, I was making 3600 a year."

"How does twenty-five Gs sound to you, Bill?"

There was an audible 'gulp' on the line before Dwyer said, "You're shitting me, right?"

"Nope. This is the straight poop."

"But Buck, how would this work?"

"OK, here's how I see it playing out," said Buck. "You fly into New York City. I explain what we're going to be doing. If you're interested, you stay with me in Queens. We have a finished basement that is actually its own apartment. Someday when the kids are older it will be their playroom. We then go house-hunting, or apartment hunting for you and your family. Remember when you told the guys in the band about the GI Bill and low-rate mortgages? That applies to officers too, and this could be the right time to buy a home. We have great schools in Queens and really nice neighborhoods. I'll put my secretary onto finding you a selection of homes to look at. Once you close a deal, you can bring your family east. Victor will pay the moving costs."

"Christ on a crutch, Buck, this is a lot to take in. I have to run it by Cathy. Can you give me until tomorrow?"

"Of course. Jot down my number. And Bill? There's one more thing: should all of this work out and I move up in the company, you'll move up right with me."

Buck gave Dwyer his office number and said, "I hope you'll do this, Bill. It could be great to be working together again. But let me know ASAP, because we've got a ton of work to do."

"You got it, Buck," said Dwyer as he rang off.

Buck's next call was to Al Rovitz. Buck first met Al when the Special Services Band got to England. Rovitz was a wizard at logistics, organizing scheduling, billeting, travel arrangements and all the other details of making the band's tours a success. Rovitz had been a supervisor for the Borden Dairy Company in charge of hundreds of employees. Now, Buck wanted him for his team at Victor.

The phone rang three times before Rovitz answered with a cheery, "Hello!"

"That you, Al?" asked Buck.

"Holy shit! Bucky! Well hell, how are ya, fella?"

"I'm good, Al, real good. How about yourself?"

"Taking it easy for a bit before I get back to the grind," said Rovitz.

"Let me tell you why I called, Al. But first, I have to ask you a personal question."

"Shoot, Buck. You know I'm an open book."

"How much was Borden's paying you before the war?"

"Oh, 11,000 bucks plus a year-end bonus of another 500 or so. They had to take me back because of the GI Bill and I was told that in time I'd be making a few G's more."

## A CHANGE OF KEY

"Nice. What would you say to making 25,000 a year plus a bonus for Christmas?"

Rovitz's response was similar to Bill Dwyer's. "Holy shit, Buck! You go into the bank robbing business or something?"

Buck took twenty minutes to explain what was going on with him at RCA Victor and where he would fit in with the plans for the division. Then Buck said, "I've also asked Bill Dwyer to come on board and be part of the team. He'll let me know by tomorrow."

"Wow. And here I thought this was just a friendly social call, Buck. But I tell you what, this sounds great. I'm in."

"Don't have to run it past your wife?" asked Buck.

"Still single, Buck. Haven't found the right woman who's willing to put up with my antics, so no, I don't need anyone's approval."

"Nah, you were a pretty straight shooter over in England, Al. But if you two guys work with me, we can do some tremendous things," said Buck.

"Well you tell Bill this Bronx kid'll kick his ass if he turns you down!"

"OK, Al, so when I hear back from Bill, we'll set up a meeting here at 30 Rock and go over all the details. And buddy? I'm thrilled you'll be back with me again."

Like Bill Dwyer, Al Rovitz had stayed by Buck's side every day he was in the hospital. The two of them had stepped up and directed the band's operations in Buck's absence and later when they all returned to America and continued their duties in and around Fort Hamilton. He, too, had become a dear friend to Buck.

At the conclusion of the calls, he buzzed his secretary and said, 'Kel? Can you come in here for a few minutes?"

"Right there, Buck," she said. Kelsey came into Buck's office, steno pad in hand, and sat in the chair opposite his desk. "Need to dictate something, Buck?"

## A CHANGE OF KEY

"Not right now, Kel. What I need to do is pick your brain about something."

"I'll tell you what I can. What's up?"

Buck then explained about forming a studio orchestra modeled on his civilian and Army bands but with an added string section. "I want to put the word out to get the names of available musicians who have had big band experience. Jack Merrill has some contacts and I have some names also. But I've never worked with strings before so I don't even know where to begin to get them. I need you to find me a way to gather the players we need."

"No problem, Buck. I'm all over this," said Kelsey.

"And Kel?"

"Yes?"

"By tomorrow."

Buck knew that was probably an impossible demand and it would take at least a few days for Kelsey to come up with some advice, but at least it would show her the urgency of what he was trying to establish at Victor.

The rest of Buck's day was spent at Personnel filling out forms for the Internal Revenue Service, medical information, a lengthy employee profile, contact information and half a dozen or so internal forms for the company.

On the ride back to Queens, Buck thought about an even bigger problem: how to put together a staff of arrangers for the new orchestra. Jerry Gray, Glenn Miller's chief arranger in his civilian and AAF band was now leading a Miller-styled band of his own. He had snapped up a bunch of Miller sidemen like Wilbur Schwartz, Trigger Alpert, Bernie Privin, Johnny Best and Jimmy Priddy. Henry Mancini was now arranging for Tex Beneke who was leading a band in the Miller Style complete with a string section. Bill Finnegan, another of Miller's arrangers, and Eddie Sauter, a product of Columbia University and Julliard School of Music, were thinking of starting their own band so that ruled them out.

## A CHANGE OF KEY

Buck was reluctant to use free-lance arrangers because he wanted them to be a permanent part of the new orchestra. But he was afraid he would have no choice if he didn't come up with something quickly. It was at times like this that he really felt the loss of his friend and partner, Johnny Blair.

When he got home, Carrie and the two children embraced him, Carrie giving him a particularly tender and hungry kiss. He saw that the dining room table was set for five with two high chairs placed near Carrie's end of the table. "Dinner guests, sweetheart?" asked Buck.

"Mom and the girls are coming over. I hope you don't mind, Bucky, but now and again it gets a little lonely and I need some company—we need some company."

"Of course I don't mind, darling. I love to have them over. What time is dinner?"

"Sixish, so you'll have time to shower if you'd like."

"Ok, good, maybe I'll lay down a little unless you need me to help with the cooking."

Carrie laughed loudly at that. "My darling, don't you know I've become a perfect little *balabusta?* I love to cook and Mom and the girls have given me so many tips. So no. No help needed."

Buck's mother Rachel and his two sisters, Arlene and Beverly lived two doors down in a house that he had originally rented for them but eventually bought and placed in his sisters' names. He always had a very strong sense of family and it was a great comfort to him to have his mother and sisters so close to Carrie while he was in the Army.

At six o'clock the doorbell rang and Carrie answered it hugging Rachel, Arlene and Beverly Feinstein with great affection. When Buck came out of the bedroom and saw his mother, she said, "*Nu* Benjamin? You don't have a hug for your mother and sisters?" Rachel Feinstein had never quite gotten used to the fact that Buck Fisher was in fact Benjamin Feinstein, not quite understanding why a nice Jewish boy would need a new name. Even his two sisters called him Benny as they had for his entire life, but they had a better grasp on the reason for the name change. Benny hugged and kissed the three of them and accepted a box of cookies from Rachel which she had brought for dessert. "These are more for the kids than for you, Benjamin. They have this gooey chocolate all over them"

Just then the two children spotted their grandmother and aunts and little Eddie cried out, "Nana!" as he ran to hug her legs. Laura too was eager to hug and kiss her aunts and grandmother. The girls never showed up without some kind of toy for each of the children and tonight was no exception.

The dinner conversation mostly revolved around Buck's new job which he talked about at length. But he was equally interested in what his sisters had been doing. Beverly had a new job at Queens General Hospital and was thinking about going to nursing school. She was also dating one of the residents—a neurologist.

"Wow! A doctor! Nice going, Bev. And how about you, big sis?" he said to Arlene who was older than Buck by two years."

"Nothing yet, Benny. A few dates here and there but nothing to get excited about. Still waiting for the right man to come along. Too many of them want only one thing from a girl, and that's the one thing I'm not giving them. Some of the others, well, they're either weak or they think women are inferior."

Rachel helped feed the children and by eight o'clock, with work the next day, the dinner came to an end and the girls and his mother went home. While Carrie cleared the table and did the dishes, Buck put his two children to sleep after reading to each one for a few minutes until their eyes closed. Then he went into the kitchen and hugged Carrie.

"Bucky?"

"Yes love?"

"Can we make love tonight? I need you so badly!"

## A CHANGE OF KEY

"I think that can be arranged, sweetheart, and by the way—I need you just as badly."

Buck and Carrie had become experienced and proficient lovers. They knew just how to please each other and though they did not make love with wild abandon, each one brought the other to spectacular climaxes---Carrie many times over—until they fell asleep entwined in each other's arms.

.....

The next morning, Buck drove to Manhattan and parked the Olds in his reserved space in the 30 Rock garage. Kelsey Burton was already there and had brewed a pot of coffee, handing a cup to Buck as soon as he entered his office. "You have a meeting with Jack Merrill at one, Buck, and I have lots of stuff to tell you about. Oh, and Bill Dwyer called and said he'd call you at about ten our time."

"That's great, Kel. Come into the office and let's hear what you have for me."

In his office, Kelsey once again sat with her pad on her lap, pencil in hand and was ready to provide the information she had gathered.

"OK, let's have it," said Buck.

"First, I called Local 802, the musician's union. I explained what we're looking for and they said they would have a list for me in a few days. I mentioned your name and that really greased the wheels. 'Anything for Buck Fisher' is what the woman I spoke to said. On my way home last night I stopped off at this really great newsstand in Times Square. They carry newspapers from all over the country, including some trade papers. I'm thinking we could place a big ad in one or more of them announcing auditions with a number to call to confirm. By the way, having access to those newspapers will be a big help when it comes to seeing who's playing at what clubs or concert halls. Oh, and I also picked up a copy of this week's *Cue* magazine. There's nothing better for finding out who's playing in New York City and the Metro area. They list every club and concert venue in three states along with what musicians are playing there along with the dates, times and prices."

*Cue* had been published since 1932 founded by Mort Glankoff. For both residents and tourists, it was the bible for anyone looking for any kind of entertainment in the city. Buck had never even thought about using it and was glad Kelsey Burton was so on the ball.

"That's great work, Kel," said Buck. "Anything else?"

"Yes. I hope you won't be angry, but I took it upon myself to call Manhattan School of Music, Julliard and NYU's Music Department. I wanted to put out the word in case they have some very talented musicians that might fit in. I also called some of the other local colleges that have music departments."

"I'm not mad at all, Kelsey. That was good thinking. I know they probably don't have much experience, but hell, the beginning of my career wasn't exactly overnight stardom either. I just needed someone to give me a break. Maybe some of these kids need the same chance I had."

"That's what I have for now, Buck, but I'll keep looking around to see what else I can find,"

Just a few minutes after Kelsey left the office, the phone rang and it was Bill Dwyer.

"Buck? Bill. Deal me in, buddy. I haven't seen Cathy so excited since she was elected prom queen in senior year. Tell me how we're going to work this."

"This is great news, Bill. I'm going to have my secretary make reservations for you to fly into LaGuardia Airport—let's make it next Monday. She'll arrange to have a car with a driver waiting for you. The car will bring you to my home in Queens where we'll settle you in. Then on Tuesday, you, me and Al Rovitz will meet at 30 Rock and we'll talk over the whole deal. Believe me, there's a lot to discuss. I'm also going to have my secretary check out homes in the area that are in good shape and reasonably

## A CHANGE OF KEY

priced—homes big enough for you, Cathy and the kids. You'll stay with me until you find something."

Dwyer thought for a minute and said, "You know, Buck, this is a terrible imposition on your family. I fear I'll be in the way."

"Nonsense. It will be great having you. Come to think of it, I'm going to call Al and tell him the meeting will be at my house instead of 30 Rock. We won't be disturbed. Then we'll all have dinner there. I'll get Carrie to make something special and I'll invite my Mom and sisters too."

"Sounds like an awful lot of trouble for your wife, Buck," said Dwyer.

"Leave it to me, Bill. It will be fine."

"OK, boss, see you then!"

As soon as Dwyer rang off, Buck got on the phone to Al Rovitz and told him about next Tuesday's meeting at his Queens home. As a bachelor, Rovitz gladly accepted the offer of a nice home-made dinner. He got driving instructions to Buck's home and said, "Imagine this, Buck. The three of us back together again. Who would even think it could be possible?"

"Maybe there will be some other surprises by next week, Al. We'll see."

At the lunch meeting with Jack Merrill, Buck reviewed what he had done so far and what was in the works. "Jesus, Buck," said Merrill, "you military guys jump in with both feet, don't you? I'm impressed. You keep up the great work and you'll own this company someday!"

"Let's just hope I can make this department a success before we worry about me owning the company!"

At home that night, Buck went over every detail with Carrie who was also impressed and proud of her husband. "As far as dinner goes, darling, I'll do something extra special for your friends and maybe Mama can help out a little. Don't worry about a thing."

**A CHANGE OF KEY**

For the first time in a long while, Buck slept through the night without interruption, holding Carrie and smiling as he drifted off.

A CHANGE OF KEY

# CHAPTER THREE
*Big Plans and Unexpected Sparks: The Following Week*

Buck's week at 30 Rock passed quickly. Working closely with Kelsey Burton, he started to get a feel for what the big-name clubs were in New York City and who some of the featured performers were regulars at those jazz venues. He was surprised to see the names of some well-known sidemen now playing in tiny bars and restaurants in Greenwich Village and the west side of Manhattan. But as Jack Merrill had explained to him, the post-war economy had more or less killed off most of the big bands so musicians took whatever gigs they could find. Some of those gigs paid very little, but at least it was work.

Bill Dwyer flew into LaGuardia Airport at four o'clock Monday afternoon. He was met by a limousine provided by RCA and driven to the Fisher home in Flushing where he arrived at half past five. When the doorbell rang, Buck answered it and showed Bill in. The two men embraced like long-lost brothers.

"Jesus, you look great, Bill!" said Buck. Dwyer was still the ramrod straight ex-state trooper and former Army major who had entered Buck's life so long ago. "Carrie! Come meet Bill!" said Buck. Carrie came out of the kitchen, apron in hand and gave Bill an equally affectionate hug.

"You don't remember me, Mrs. Fisher, but I surely remember you from that awful night in Erlanger when your band got shot up and that young man was killed," said Bill.

"Oh my God! You were there?" said Carrie in amazement.

"I was a state trooper back then and I answered the call after the shooting. You looked fabulous then and you look fabulous now," said Bill.

Carrie laughed and said to Buck, "Wow, this one's a charmer. And who's this Mrs. Fisher? It's Carrie." Then she said,

"Bucky, why don't you settle Bill in downstairs and I'll have supper on the table in about a half hour."

Buck took Bill to the downstairs apartment and gave him the tour. He sat on the loveseat against one corner of the basement wall and Bill sat in an armchair across from him. He frowned and said, "What's up with you, Buck? You look like shit warmed over."

Buck laughed and said, "Jack Merrill told me the same thing. I'm all right, Bill. It's just taking me a little longer than I thought it would to get my full strength back. It's hard for me to eat a lot and fatten up, but the docs all tell me it'll take time."

Bill nodded and said, "Buck? You sure you're up to this new job? It sounds like a lot of responsibility for one person."

"It's not one person, Bill. It's me, you, and Al Rovitz—and anyone else I need to make this new music division a success. Jack's pretty much given me a free hand and a big budget to make it work, so it's going to be hard—but I have no doubt that we can make it happen."

"Kind of sounds like the Army when we had a huge budget to put that band together and make it the great outfit it was. Al and I are going to make this as easy for you as we can. I can promise you that."

"That's good enough for me, Bill. Now let's go see what Carrie has whipped up for chow."

Bill, who had three children of his own, was a natural with Eddie and Laura. "Eddie? This is your Uncle Bill and you're going to be great friends with him," Buck said. "Laura, give Uncle Bill a big hug, OK?"

At dinner, Carrie had dozens of questions for Bill about the Army, his family, the new job and his move east. There was instant chemistry between the two of them and even when Bill described how close they had come to losing Buck in London, she felt that as long as this man was around, Buck would have the support he needed.

**A CHANGE OF KEY**

Over dessert, Carrie said, "Bucky, you know the house at the end of the block on the corner? That old lady, Mrs. Kakanakis lives there?"

"Sure, I've passed it a hundred times. What about it?"

"A 'For Sale' sign went up on the front lawn today. Maybe Bill would like to take a look at it. There's a realtor's number on the sign."

"That's great! I was going to have my secretary start to search out properties tomorrow, but first I'll have her get the details on this house. I'll still have her check out some others so Bill can compare. You think Cathy will trust you to pick out a home, Bill?"

"I know she will. She is so excited about sight-seeing; she can hardly wait to get here."

"Bucky?" said Carrie, "Your meeting here isn't until mid-afternoon. Why don't you let Bill get some sleep now and first thing in the morning, you can check out that house. Your friend Al should be here by two and you'll have a few hours for your meeting until Mama and the girls get here for dinner at six. Bill can get a feel for the neighborhood at the same time."

"See Bill? Who needs generals when I have Carrie to boss me around?"

Dinner ended and the children hugged their 'uncle' Bill. Carrie took them to their rooms and Bill said, "That dinner was wonderful, Carrie. How about I clear and do the dishes?"

"Out! Out! My guests don't do manual labor. Bucky, get this ex-GI out of my kitchen before I attack him with a skillet."

Buck took Bill downstairs and the two friends talked for another hour before he said, "Bedtime for me, buddy. We have a big day tomorrow, so first call is about eight. That suit you?"

"Everything suits me fine, Buck. And again, thanks for this chance."

"See you then."

"Oh, by the way, Carrie left you towels and toiletries in

case you forgot to bring some things."

The next morning after a light breakfast, Buck and Bill got into his Oldsmobile and drove to the end of the block. They jotted down the name of the Realtor, Nicholas Brothers, and the address and phone number. It was located on Northern Boulevard only a half mile away. After giving Bill a tour of the neighborhood showing him where the market, the bakery, the cleaners and the Woolworth's were, they arrived at the realtor as it opened at ten o'clock.

They were greeted by an agent who introduced himself as Stavros Nikolaides. Buck said, "We are interested in taking a look at the house on 187$^{th}$ Street and 47$^{th}$ Avenue—the corner property."

"Ah!" said Nikolaides. "The Kakanakis home. She's my aunt. My uncle died five years ago and the house is just too much for her to take care of. She's nearly eighty, you know. She's going to be moving in with my other aunt—her sister, but first she has to sell the house."

"Tell me about the house, Mr. Nikolaides," said Bill.

"Well, it's forty years old and in excellent shape. I've helped look after the home for my aunt for years. There are three bedrooms, three baths, a big kitchen, a dining room, a living room, a parlor and a basement that is the complete size of the home. It's not finished, but it has heat and plumbing. If you're handy, it could be a perfect family room or playroom. The backyard is fenced in and it's big. It also has a pair of apple trees in it."

"Let's hear the down side, Mr. Nikolaides," said Bill.

"OK, it needs a complete paint job inside. The outside is fine. The carpets are old and worn and you might want to rip them up and replace them. The stove is old as is the refrigerator. You might want to replace them too. I have a brother who owns a furniture/appliance store in Long Island City. He has great stuff at great prices. I make a call, he takes care of you. Also, there had been a leak in the roof a few years back, but I fixed that myself. It was just some loose shingles that blew off in a big storm. It's fine now."

"What kind of price are we looking at, Mr. Nikolaides?"

"She wants 8400, but I know she'll take 7700. We handle all the details with the bank for the mortgage. Are you a veteran by any chance?"

"Yes, I am," said Bill. "I was recently discharged from the Army as a major."

Nikolaides whistled and said, "*Ekpliktikos!* Oh, sorry, that means 'wonderful.' With the GI Bill you are going to get a great mortgage rate."

"How much would I have to put down?" asked Bill.

"Ten percent. That's pretty standard."

Dwyer's mustering out pay from the army could easily handle the down payment—with plenty left over to fix up the home if they liked it. "When can I see the house?" he asked.

"Let me call my aunt and make sure she's up. If she is, how about right now?"

"Perfect," said Bill.

He placed the call, exchanged some words in Greek and then smiling, said, "She's been up for hours. Let's go take a look."

Nikolaides opened the front door and called out, "*Thee-a Sofia? Tikanis?*"

"*Kala, kala!* I'm fine, Stavros."

Sofia Kakanakis was no more than five feet tall and as shriveled as a raisin. Stavros introduced Bill and Buck to her. Looking at Buck, she said, "You live up the street, no?"

"Yes ma'am. On the other corner."

"Beautiful wife. Beautiful children."

"Thank you, Mrs. Kakanakis. You have a lovely home."

"Eh, time to move on," she said.

Nikolaides then took Bill on a complete tour of the house, inside and out, showing him every closet and cupboard in the home as well as the fuse box in the basement, the pipes under the sinks, even flushing the toilets to show Bill that they were in working order.

Walking down the stairs from the second floor, Bill said to Buck, "Jesus, boss, compared to this, we live in a shack back in Kentucky. Cathy will love this place."

"Then let's do a deal," said Buck.

They sat at the dining room table and Bill said, "Mrs. Kakanakis, I would like to offer you 7700 dollars for your home."

Buck, who was used to his mother Rachel *hondling* over a sack of potatoes at the produce market was stunned when Mrs. Kakanakis said, "I take this."

"Whoa, pardner," said Buck. "You sure you don't want to check out a few more places first?"

"No, Buck. This is the place. This is the one. I'm pretty handy with tools and I can fix it up real nice for Cathy and the kids."

Buck looked at Nikolaides who shrugged and took a contract from his suit jacket pocket. "We'll sign this now, have a lawyer draw up the formal papers and go back to the office to fill out the mortgage application. With your service, it shouldn't take but a week or so to get a commitment from the bank. When do you want to move in?"

"Soon as possible," said Bill.

"Unless you want any of the furniture, I can have the Salvation Army pick it up in just a few days. Oh, and my other brother is a house painter. He can have this place painted and cleaned up by early next week. I can get you a great rate. I got lots of family in the trades in case you need other things done."

"Maybe you should take him up on the offer, Bill," said Buck. We're gonna be awfully busy over the next few weeks and you want it in shipshape by the time Cathy and the kids arrive."

"Yeah, good idea Buck. Mr. Nikolaides? As soon as we get the mortgage commitment, hook me up with your brother so we can get the whole house painted."

## A CHANGE OF KEY

"It's a deal. And don't forget about my brother and his furniture store," said Nikolaides.

By noon, Buck and Bill were back home, all the paperwork having been completed, and they had lunch with Carrie and the kids. Carrie was thrilled about the prospect of a mother with three children moving on the block. Two of them, Michael and Dorothy were the same age as Eddie and Laura. Bill's third child, April, was nearly twelve and as Bill described her, "Twelve going on twenty."

At two o'clock sharp, Al Rovitz arrived and the reunion of the three Army buddies moved Carrie to tears. Carrie, who could cry over almost anything, hugged Rovitz and thanked him for looking after Buck in the Army.

"Don't kid yourself, sugar, Buck looked after all of us. He and Bill made quite a team and believe you me, not only was he a great musician, but he was a great leader too. The guys in the band would have walked through a minefield for him."

"OK, guys, enough frivolity. Let's go into the office and talk about the jobs you'll be doing and how we can get all these plans rolling."

Buck's office was large enough for three chairs and a large desk that was strewn haphazardly with papers. They drew the chairs close and Buck said, "For the most part, guys, we are going to be talent scouts. We're going to beat the bushes for new artists offering new material. Your job is to find them and offer to sign them with Victor. My job is to take raw talent and polish it up so we can get them on wax."

"You know, Buck, neither Al or me are musicians. But you want us scouting out musical talent. That make sense to you?" said Bill.

"It is exactly why I want you," said Buck.

"Explain," said Al.

"Bottom line is, it's all about the bottom line. RCA is in this to make money. They want to develop stars who would appeal to the every day record buyer. They don't necessarily have to be a Sinatra or a Dick Haymes. They're stars already. They want new talent who people will hear and appeal to what Jack Merrill calls the 'everyman' factor. What's more American than a rags to riches story? A rise from obscurity to stardom? Our job is to find the rags and turn them into Cinderellas. I'll be honest, guys, I'm going to do a lot of listening in and around the city. But you guys? You're going into the tall grass and even the west coast. I hear there's a lot of good things happening out in San Francisco in jazz. You listen, you write up your opinions, and you bring them east if your opinions are strong enough. You're going to spend a substantial amount of time out of town. Bill? How big a problem is that for you with Cathy and the kids?"

"I've already discussed the possibility with her, Buck. She knows what an opportunity this is for me—for us—and to be honest, neither of us ever believed we could make this kind of money, so yeah, we'll be fine."

"And you, Al?"

"You know me, Buck. No ties that bind. The folks are gone and they left the house to me, so I don't have a lot of expenses. The money from this job is great and hell, it'll be like old times touring the country. Don't worry about me at all. I'm chomping at the bit to get going."

"OK, tomorrow we meet again at 30 Rock. Jack Merrill will want to meet you guys but Bill, I think you already met Jack when the band was cutting those V-discs during the war."

"Yes, I did. He was always looking out for you which was a big plus," said Bill.

"Buck, let me ask you a question," said Al.

"Shoot."

"Do you think you'll ever play again? You know, I mean when you're all better?"

A shadow passed across Buck's face and an unmistakable look of sadness was evident in his eyes. He sighed and said,

"Honestly, Al? I haven't picked up my horn since the injury. I'm afraid I'll tear something up inside if I try."

"Buck, Buck, you know the doctors would have told you so if that could happen. "You're Buck Fisher—and I just know you have a lot more to say musically."

"Thanks, Al. We'll see. Maybe I'll pick it up one day. Noodle around with it a bit. But for now, we're business 'executives' and we're going to make our mark in a different way."

They talked for another hour and Buck outlined what they would have to do at Personnel the next day at Victor. Carrie came into the study and said, "Mama and the girls will be here in a half hour. Maybe you guys want to get cleaned up before they get here?"

"Good idea. I'll be right up, said Buck."

.....

Because she would be feeding three grown men and the rest of the family, Carrie had gotten a six-pound standing rib roast from Buck's old employer, Katz's Quality Meats. The wonderful aroma of the roasting meat permeated the entire first floor of the house. At a quarter past six, Rachel and Buck's sisters Arlene and Beverly arrived—with two pies and a *shtollen* for dessert.

After hugs and introductions were exchanged, Carrie had everyone come to the dining room where dinner was almost ready. "Sit anywhere you'd like," said Carrie, who noticed with curiosity that Arlene maneuvered herself to sit next to Al Rovitz. Buck noticed the same thing and stifled a smile.

"So, Benjamin, why don't your friends tell us about themselves," said Rachel.

A stifled smile became a grin as Buck said, "You first, Al, give everybody the lowdown—and don't leave out your criminal record!"

Rachel's jaw fell open, and laughing, Buck said, "Just kidding, Ma. He's as pure as the driven snow."

**A CHANGE OF KEY**

As Al talked about himself, Buck was amused to see that Arlene's eyes never left him. When he finished, she said, "No wife or kids, Al?"

Buck, who had taken a sip of water, spat it out onto his plate.

"Nah, nothing yet, but you know, I always have my eye open," said Al.

As Carrie served matzoh ball soup to everyone, Bill Dwyer talked about how he met Buck in the Army and their adventures at home and abroad. Then he told everyone about his purchase of the Kakanakis house that morning.

"Fantastic!" said Arlene. "We can all be neighbors!"

Carrie shot Buck a look and he subtly shrugged. But then Arlene added, "And where do you live, Al?"

"I'm up in Eastchester in the Bronx. I have a house right on the water," said Al.

"Wow, that must be something," said Arlene. "I'd really love to see that some time."

This time, both Carrie and Buck stared wide-eyed at each other with an expression of undisguised astonishment.

"Great! I'll have to show it to you someday," said Al.

After dessert, Bill said, "Buck, would you mind if I called home to Cathy? I want to break the good news to her and tell her to get things rolling for the move."

"Sure, Bill. Use the phone in our bedroom. Take as much time as you need."

Then Al said, "Well boss, gotta head home. I'll meet you at 30 Rock by nine tomorrow morning."

Arlene quickly said, "I'll walk you to your car, Al."

Beverly giggled and Al said, "Why thank you, my lady. I wouldn't want to get lost or anything."

"Oh, in that case, maybe I *better* walk you to your car if you're afraid of the neighborhood," said Arlene.

"Nah, that's all right. I'm a big boy," said Al.

**A CHANGE OF KEY**

Rachel said to Buck as she was putting on her coat, "Benjamin? He's Jewish, maybe?"

Buck shook his head and said, "Yes, Mama. He's Jewish. Bar Mitzvahed and everything. You don't have to worry."

When everyone left, Carrie burst out laughing and said, "Oh my God!"

"I know, I know. She's smitten. I've never seen her like that in my entire life."

"You know how much I love her, Bucky. It would be great for her to have someone in her life. Besides, I want to be an aunt someday."

"Whoa! Whoa! Whoa! We've got a cart before the horse problem going on here, sweetheart. They just met."

"Darling man. So blind. You only saw how Arlene was looking at Al, but I saw how he was looking at her. We girls get a sixth sense about these things. Just wait, you'll see."

"Uh huh. Right now, Mrs. Feinstein, what I want to see is you lying next to me in bed—preferably the way God sent you into the world."

"I thought you'd never ask," said Carrie.

# CHAPTER FOUR
## "Sometimes it stays with you"

At three o'clock that morning, Buck started screaming in his sleep. He sat bolt-upright, soaked with perspiration staring wide-eyed into the darkness of the bedroom. Carrie awoke instantly and hugged him. "Darling, darling, it's all right. Nothing's wrong. Shh. Shh."

Al Dwyer had heard the shouting and bolted up the stairs. He knocked on the bedroom door and said, "Carrie? Buck? Everything OK?"

"Bill! Come in, please!"

When Bill entered, he saw Buck still sitting upright in bed, frozen in place staring in horror at—at something that had terrified him. Carrie was soothing him and easing him back against the pillow. She kissed him on the lips and said, "You sleep, darling. Everything is fine." Moments later, he was fast asleep, breathing heavily, Carrie put on a robe and led Bill to the kitchen table. She made coffee and placed a cup in front of Bill along with a server of milk and sugar.

Tears were welling up in her eyes. "What was that, Bill. What's happening to him?"

"Carrie, dear, try to understand something. In England when we were playing hospitals after North Africa and D-Day, we saw young kids maimed in ways I don't want to describe. Their lives had been altered completely and some would never recover—even if they survived. The nurses and doctors we met talked about what these young men went through—some every night as the incredible memories of what they saw and did haunted their sleep. Buck has been through something that neither I nor you can fully grasp. It's over now, so it can't hurt to tell you just how close to dying he was. Lying there in the gutter torn open, bleeding out in the street. Sometimes it stays with you and you

## A CHANGE OF KEY

relive it—mostly at night. That's what happened tonight, Carrie. You have to be patient with him. He's a man who thought he was witnessing his own death. In time it may all just fade away, or at least that's what the doctors say. But if it comes back, you have to do just what you did tonight: soothe him and ease him back to the current reality of where he is. Chances are he won't even remember what happened tonight."

"Oh Bill! Of course I can be patient. I love him so much and I just don't want anything bad to happen to him—ever."

"Well, that bad has already happened to him, but with you, the kids, the family—and pretty soon my family, we'll all help him get beyond this. I promise you he's going to be fine. After all, he's Buck Fisher and like it or not, he's a national treasure."

Carrie came around the table and hugged Bill. She wiped away her tears and said, "You better get some sleep. Bucky says you have a busy day tomorrow."

"You get some sleep too, Carrie. See you in the morning."

.....

Just as Bill had predicted, Buck awoke refreshed with seemingly no recollection of the night terrors he suffered mere hours earlier. He dressed, knocked on Bill's door and the two of them sat to breakfast while Carrie served them and fed the children. The only indication that something was different was evidenced by Buck's ravenous hunger. He usually only ate a light breakfast, but today he ate everything he could get on his plate.

"Hon? Today's a pretty full day, so we probably won't get home until about six," said Buck.

"That's fine, darling. I have a lot of roast beef left over and I'll make some other things to go along with it," said Carrie.

In the car, Bill said, "How you feeling today, boss?"

"Pretty good, Bill. I think I ate too much last night, but I'll go easier on my stomach today."

"So what's the plan, Buck?"

## A CHANGE OF KEY

"To begin with, you and Al have a shitload of paperwork at Personnel this morning. Hopefully by around eleven you'll be done and we can get to work."

Al Rovitz was already waiting in Buck's office by the time he and Bill arrived. Buck introduced the pair to Kelsey Burton. "Kelsey is my secretary—but as far as that goes, she also works for you Bill, and you Al. Whatever you need, you tell her. She can handle anything. Kel? Take Al and Bill down to Personnel so we can get that out of the way. I've got some papers to go over and I hope to be done by the time they get back."

Seated at his desk, Buck took out a yellow pad and started to jot down names. He also sketched out a tentative model for an ad for trade journals and newspapers seeking musicians and arrangers. One after another, he crossed the designs out, knowing they weren't attractive and were poorly laid out. This came as no surprise to him since he knew he had zero artistic skills. Maybe Kelsey could do better. He checked in with Jack Merrill who had some good news. "I've got some names for you, Buck. Really good sidemen looking for work—and even better, I may have a line on some string players.

"Oh? How'd you manage that?"

"An old friend of mine, Manny Wishnow. We met back in the early '30s. He's a professor in the music department at the University of Nebraska—and he was also in the string section of Glenn Miller's Army Air Force Band. He's a helluva violin player, but he's really set up out west and doesn't want to relocate. But he gave me some names of a few of his students who he said would fit in any symphony in the world. But since almost all of those chairs are filled, these youngsters are looking for work. They might be just what you need."

"That sounds terrific, Jack. I'll send Kelsey to pick up the names and we'll start the ball rolling."

Kelsey knocked and entered Buck's office holding a sheaf of papers. Buck's hunch was right: Kelsey's degree in Fine Arts really paid off. She had designed three or four sample ads in different sizes for trade mags and newspapers. "Once we have the date for auditions, Buck, we can just plug it into the layout and it will be ready to go to press."

Buck soon came to realize that this was no mere secretary. Kelsey was going to become a vital part of the management team. Al and Bill had returned from Personnel and they came into Buck's office. They sat with pads awaiting their marching orders from Buck.

"Al, when we left England, you said you had permission to make calls to the families to let them know we were coming home. Do you still have those numbers?" asked Buck.

"They're probably in my duffel bag with some other papers I brought home with me," said Rovitz.

"OK, try to dig them out. I want Kelsey to start making calls to see if any of the boys are interested in coming to work for us. I've got the business ledgers from the civilian band, you know, payroll information and tax forms. I'm going to bring those in and Kelsey can see if any of them want to come on board too."

"How big a band are we talking about, Buck?" asked Bill.

"Well, the core of the orchestra will be seventeen pieces, a 5-4-4-4 configuration: five reeds, four trumpets, four bones and four rhythm. Then there's the strings. Glenn had twenty-one strings in the AAF band. That group was gigantic and I can't even imagine the logistical problems they had. I don't think we need that many strings, but we have to have enough to give us that orchestral sound. Oh, and I think I'd like to have a French Horn player as well, so Kelsey's gonna have to contact Julliard or local colleges to see who's available."

Bill and Al exchanged glances and it was Al who said, "Buck? Where are we going with this?"

Buck laughed and said, "I'm not quite sure, guys. I have ideas rolling around in my head but they haven't quite solidified yet. It's not that important that we swing like we did in the civvie and Army band. I hate to say it, but I know that era is just about dead. No, this studio orchestra isn't here to make records. As I see it, our job is to enhance the talents of the vocalists with terrific backgrounds to their singing. And that, guys, is the major problem we have."

"What's that, Buck?" asked Al.

"Where the hell are we going to find arrangers who can write for this type of group? All the great ones are already working."

Bill took the layouts Kelsey had worked up off of Buck's desk. "OK, how about this, Buck. Kelsey's ads talk about musicians. How about we add arrangers to the ads—but put that first. Musicians, while not exactly a dime a dozen, are gonna be a lot easier to find than skilled arrangers. If we put that first, we might get somebody that we can use who'll crawl out of the woodwork."

Buck nodded and said, "Let's put all these ideas together and keep our fingers crossed."

"By the way, Buck," said Al, "How much are we offering these guys? I was a numbers guy at Borden's before the war and I had to keep track of every nickel and dime."

"Jack and I already came up with a figure of 15,000 a year."

Al whistled and said, "Jesus Buck, that's about ten times what an average Joe makes a year. I guess you weren't kidding when you said RCA has deep pockets."

"The trick is, Al, to make the job so appealing, so secure that these guys will stay with us. Remember, these are all experts in their field and I want to offer them careers complete with pensions and fringe benefits. You know, in my civilian band for as long as we were together, we only lost five players: Bump Barnes, my pianist, just couldn't take the wear and tear of touring any longer. Then I lost my fourth trombone, Hal Hausman, to the Cincinnati Symphony. Kenny Ferraro left when his mom died and

## A CHANGE OF KEY

of course Jimmy Jones was killed in Kentucky and Bobby Landers nearly lost a leg in that shoot-out. Other than them, everyone in the band was happy with their salaries—especially when royalties kicked in. And we came to love each other as family. That's what I want to create here, so if it takes money to get that feeling, then we'll spend it."

"I get it, Buck. You're the boss and you know best how to make this work. I just hope that down the road, some accountant downstairs doesn't tell us our checking account is overdrawn and we have to let people go. That would be terrible."

"I agree, Al. I'll handle it. OK, let's talk about some other details now."

…..

Two weeks later, Cathy Dwyer and her three kids came to New York City. Bill had closed on the house three days before their arrival and Stavros Nikolaides was true to his word: his brother had done a great job putting a new coat of paint inside the home. Kelsey had gotten a company car for Bill so he could meet the family at LaGuardia Airport.

The TWA flight landed on time at two in the afternoon on Sunday, January 27th. It was a joyous reunion for Bill and his family. He was as much of a family man as Buck and he treasured his kids. They got their luggage, loaded it into the car, and got on the Grand Central Parkway headed towards Flushing. Bill got lost on the way home and almost crossed the Triboro Bridge into the Bronx before catching his error. Cathy Dwyer was amazed at how many buildings there were in such a small place. Coming from semi-rural Kentucky, it was a lot to digest.

"Cat, we're going to drop off the bags at the house, I'll show you around and we can get cleaned up. Buck is having us all over for dinner tonight and I know you're going to love his wife. Carrie is very special."

"Hope she doesn't make fun of this ol' country girl, Billy," she said.

## A CHANGE OF KEY

"No chance. She's warm and loving and she's going to make you feel right at home. And Buck's sisters will be there too. They're just as terrific as Carrie."

"And the kids, Billy?"

"I predict they will be great friends. Oh, and by the way, don't be surprised if they call you Aunt Cathy. I'm already Uncle Bill to them."

"Do you think I'll like it here, Billy? It's going to be so different for all of us."

"Honestly, hon? This is the most exciting place in the world. You got here too late for Christmas at Rockefeller Center this year, but wait until the next time. You and the kids are going to go crazy when you see how they deck it out."

It took almost an hour to get to Flushing. It was well worth the wait. When Cathy Dwyer stood in front of her new home, she stared at it and said, "Good Lord, Billy, this place is gigantic!"

"Wait till you see it in the spring with the trees in bloom and the lawn green. It's fabulous. It's got just about everything we ever wanted in a house."

"Let's get the kids inside. It's freezing out here," she said.

Her reaction to the inside was everything Bill hoped it would be. They had sent on the furniture they planned on keeping a week earlier: beds, a dining room table they had inherited from Cathy's family, and an easy chair that was Bill's favorite. Other than those few pieces, the house was devoid of furnishings which was fine with Bill. He wanted Cathy to pick out the living room furniture and other pieces that she liked so she could make the home her own.

They all rested for a while and at six that evening, Bill said, "Hon, we have to be at Buck's for half past six. We can all just walk up the block and you can see what some of the other houses look like."

"Billy, it's pitch black out there. Winter, remember? I'll have to check them out in the light," said Cathy.

**A CHANGE OF KEY**

The greeting at the Fisher house was as warm and effusive as Bill said it would be. Carrie introduced Rachel, Beverly and Arlene to Cathy and the children immediately took to each other. "I hope everyone likes pot roast," said Carrie. I got the recipe from Mama and she tells me its even better than the way she makes it." Carrie kissed Rachel and hugged her.

Benny had put two large leafs in the dining room table so that it could seat everyone. Both Eddie and Laura were old enough now so that they no longer needed high chairs, but Arlene still tied bibs around them to minimize the stains from food which missed their mouths.

As usual, the meal was splendid in every respect. Cathy couldn't praise the cooking enough. Carrie was almost as excited as Cathy at the prospect of new friends and neighbors and Beverly was over the moon with the prospect of taking Cathy to the city for shopping at Macy's and Gimbels.

Cathy said, "Can I be honest with you all? I was sort of afraid to come to New York City because all my friends back in Erlanger said how mean and cold everyone was—especially to strangers. Boy, did you all prove them wrong!"

"Not so fast!" cautioned Arlene. "It's not so much that New Yorkers are mean, but the pace in the city is full speed ahead all the time so people don't have time to engage in idle conversation. Don't expect something out of a scene in *"The Egg and I"* with folks driving by shouting, 'Howdy neighbor.' That would be unusual. But I can tell you this: Despite their icy facades, New Yorkers would strip naked and give you their clothes if you needed help."

"See Cat?" said Bill. "I told you everything's going to be great here."

"Now folks," said Arlene, "I hate to eat and run, but I have a date."

Buck looked at Carrie who shrugged as if to say, "Beats me who it's with."

## A CHANGE OF KEY

Arlene grabbed her coat and scarf and exited the front door. Unable to resist, Carrie left to the table and went to the living room window where she surreptitiously pulled back a corner of the curtain. "Oh my God!" she said. "It's Al Rovitz!"

"What!" said Buck.

"He just got out of the car to open the door for Arlene."

"That snake. I just may have to fire him," said Buck jokingly.

"I'm glad for her, Benny," said Beverly. "Arlene is such a wonderful person. She's smart, beautiful and she'd be some catch for the right guy."

Rachel, who had not reacted to any of this said at last, "Please God he should be the right one for her."

The evening moved to its close with Cathy and Bill thanking Carrie and Buck for their hospitality and friendship. The children also said goodbye and promised that they would play together very soon.

"OK, Bill, lots to do tomorrow, so let's be ready to go no later than 9: 15."

"I'll be there, Buck. I got my parking pass form Personnel, so I'm good to go in the morning."

In bed that night, Carrie went on and on about how lovely Cathy Dwyer was and how beautiful her children were. "I want us all to be friends, Bucky. I could use another friend for when Bev and Arlene are at work every day."

"Well, now you'll have one. So come on over here and let me take a look at that spectacular body of yours."

"Why Mr. Feinstein, I certainly hope your intentions are honorable," said Carrie.

"They most certainly are not," said Buck.

"Good! Just what I wanted to hear." She switched off the night lamp and moved into Buck's arms.

**A CHANGE OF KEY**

# CHAPTER FIVE
*Not Exactly Auditions, February, 1946*

Kelsey Burton had gotten the ads into the 'trades' by the beginning of February. She had included a number to call to confirm and, in the meantime, Buck had secured rehearsal space at 30 Rock for February 15th at ten in the morning. Buck had explained to Jack that mostly he wanted to see who would show up and what they had. "It's not exactly an audition, Jack, because I know what most of these guys can do. It's more to see who wants to sign on for the long run." Just in case, Buck intended to bring along a number of Johnny Blair's arrangements to see what they could do—minus strings, since none of the charts were written for them.

Kelsey was typing on her Royal Arrow portable typewriter when the door to the office opened and a hulking figure entered. He put his finger to his lips indicating that she should say nothing, and he nodded at the inner office door with an unasked question on his face. She nodded and was going to protest his barging in when the man knocked ponderously on the door. Then he opened it, stood in the doorway and said, "You don't write, you don't call! Get over here, you sonofabitch colonel!"

It was Chuck Fein. When Buck had joined the Johnny Blair Orchestra, it was Chuck Fein who first befriended him. They had become fast friends over the years and when Buck organized the Army Special Services Band, Chuck was the first player he brought on board. He, too, sat at Buck's bedside every night in the London Free Hospital as he recuperated from his wound.

"Holy Jesus! Chuck!" Buck came out from behind his desk and the two friends hugged.

"Let's have a look at you," said Chuck.

"I know, I know, don't say it. I look like shit," said Buck.

# A CHANGE OF KEY

"Well, yeah, but I'm not surprised. Sit down and tell me everything."

For an hour, the two men caught up with Buck laying out his plans at Victor. "Sorry to see the old Bluebird label go under," said Chuck. "We all made plenty of money from those sides."

"Don't worry. Once those LPs are released, you'll still be getting checks."

"That's great, Buck. Now tell me how that beautiful gal of yours is doing. And the kids too."

Buck filled Chuck in on Carrie and the children and at that moment, both Bill Dwyer and Al Rovitz entered the office.

"Holy crap!" said Al. "We back in the Army again and someone forgot to tell me?"

The three men shook hands, embraced as only fellow soldiers could, and it was Bill who said, "So what brings you here, Chuck?"

"I hear you might be looking for a bull fiddle player," said Fein.

"You're in," said Buck. "No questions asked. And I hope some of the other guys will show up as well."

"Pays a helluva lot more than the Army did," said Al. "You might even get rich," he added.

"Eh, that's the Jew in me. I go where the bucks are. But mostly, the chance of working again with this character—that's better than a big paycheck any day," said Chuck, nodding at Buck.

"OK, then. How 'bout you get the hell out of here and let us three get some actual work done. And Chuck? Better bring your bass on the 15th. We're gonna air out some charts and see what it sounds like," said Buck.

"Got ya covered, boss. And give a big hug and kiss to my girl Carrie, OK?"

When Chuck left, Buck said, "I've been looking over the names of those players who confirmed they would be here on the

## A CHANGE OF KEY

15th. I've been playing around with what the sections might look like, but I still don't really know what to do with these strings."

"Can Kelsey track down Jerry Gray?" asked Bill. "He arranged for Artie Shaw who had a string section and also for Glenn's Army Air Force band, with that whole mob of strings. Maybe he can offer us some tips. I can give him a call."

"Great idea, Bill, but he's leading his own band now. I'm not sure he's gonna give away any trade secrets," said Buck.

"Nah, we're not his rival, Buck. He's touring just like in the old days. We're staying put, plus, we're not doing the same things as him. Can't hurt to try."

"OK, Bill, check with Kelsey and see what you can get done. For now, you and Al figure out who we're going to listen to in some local spots. She's got all the trade magazines and *Cue* at her desk so you can see who's around this week and next."

Bill and Al left the office and went down the hall to their own which they shared. It wasn't nearly as big as Buck's, but then again, it was fully equipped and comfortable enough for them to work together without falling all over each other.

When they had gone, Buck tilted back in his desk chair and let his mind wander back to all the touring, all the one-nighters he had played with Chuck and the Johnny Blair Orchestra, which later became the Buck Fisher Orchestra. The bus rides, the tank towns, the great crowds—the not-so-great crowds. It all came back to him in a rush.

Then the Army tours with the USO performers, the war bond drives, the harrowing plane ride through Iceland and Greenland to England. It all came back to Buck as he played over in his memory his rise from a kid from Bensonhurst, Brooklyn to the top of the musical pyramid as one of America's top saxophonists and band leaders. So much of it was unbelievable. Long ago, his music teacher and friend Freddy Constantine had told him it just took one break, one person to hear him play and his career would take off. He had been right. So many other great players never got that break. Why him? Why was he so lucky? His journey into nostalgia was interrupted by the buzzing of his desk intercom. He turned the switch and said, "What's up Kel?"

"Buck, I have a Mrs. Pete McCormack here. She says she knows you."

Pete McCormack had been Buck's lead alto player in both his civilian band and the Army Special Services band, but he had no idea that he was married. "Send her in, Kel," said Buck. He was eager to see who Pete married.

The door opened and in walked Mrs. Pete McCormack. It was Fran Michaels, his vocalist from the civilian band. Fran had replaced Carrie as vocalist when Carrie's pregnancy was too advanced for her to keep performing. A trained operatic singer, Fran Michaels was also the most beautiful woman Buck had ever seen. Tall, slender, flowing black hair, a body that might have been sculpted by Praxitiles and a mezzo-soprano voice that could have charmed a cobra from its basket, Fran Michaels was one of the reasons his band had had such great success.

"Oh my God! Franny! It's you!" Buck came to her and embraced her with the great affection he felt toward her.

Her smile soon devolved into tears as she eyed Buck up. "Oh, God, Buck—are you all right?"

He laughed and said, "Wow, everyone asks me that. Yes, Franny, still recovering but really, I'm doing fine. Now, mind telling me what all this Mrs. Pete McCormack is all about?"

Fran laughed and said, "We got close in the last few months of the band before it broke up. When Pete left for the Army, I wrote to him all the time. I was so relieved when he became part of your Army band rather than having to be on the front lines. He kept me informed of everything that went on in the band and—" Here she stopped and dabbed at her eyes. "And he told me about your injury. Oh Buck, I was so frightened for you— and for Carrie. Pete said how serious it was and that we almost lost you. Everybody in the band was so worried and I was frantic at the thought of losing you." By this time, tears were streaming down Fran Michael's cheeks.

"Franny, I'm here, I'm alive and everything's going to be fine. But thanks for the concern. Now tell me, what brings you here?"

"Well, when Pete got his discharge, it didn't take long for him to pop the question. He's a wonderful guy, Buck, and we have a nice place in Sheepshead Bay. In case you couldn't tell, I'm very happy."

"I'm glad, Fran. For both of you. Any little ones in the future?"

"Nothing yet, but we're trying."

"Franny? Can I assume you're here because Pete is looking for a job?"

"It's been tough since he got out, Buck. The big bands are gone and there's just not a lot of free lance work around. He saw your ad in one of the trades, but he was afraid to contact you."

"Jesus! Why?" said Buck.

"Pride, mostly. He didn't want it to seem like he was begging for a job. And by the way, Buck, he has no idea that I'm here. None. I'd appreciate it if you wouldn't tell him."

"You know, Fran, in both bands, every reed player—including me—said the same thing about Pete: he was the best lead alto player they had ever played with. He set the tone, kept the blend tight, and his articulation was perfect. Why the heck wouldn't I want him with me again?"

"He's proud, Buck. So proud. He's never had to look for work before."

"OK, I tell you what I'm going to do. You leave me your phone number. I'm going to personally call Pete and tell him I need him to be in this orchestra. I'm going to tell him I can't do this without him. That sound good to you?"

"Oh, Buck, you're just the greatest. I don't know what to say or how to thank you."

## A CHANGE OF KEY

Fran started to stand and get ready to leave when Buck motioned her to sit. "Franny, let me tell you what my job is here. Over at CBS, they're preparing a radio show for Arthur Godfrey called 'Talent Scouts.' Each week his talent scouts will bring a performer to the show and they'll compete with each other for prizes—and I assume recording contracts. Think of me as a talent scout. Jack Merrill wants me to scout out new talent, develop it and turn them into stars."

"That sounds great, Buck, but—"

"Lemme finish. The very first time I heard you sing, I knew you had star written all over you. You proved that again and again with the band. What would you say to letting me develop you into the star you deserve to be? You'll cut records with the orchestra we're forming here and we'll get your voice onto LPs that will be distributed all over the country. If they're as good as I know they'll be, we'll sign you to a contract at RCA Victor and you'll be on your way."

"You really think that's possible, Buck?" asked Fran.

"Of course I do. The big bands might be gone—but look what happened to their singers: Doris Day, June Christy, Anita O'Day, Betty Hutton, Peggy Lee—they're all stars now in their own right. I want Fran Michaels to be just as successful as they are."

Fran rushed to Buck and hugged and kissed him. "Yes! I'll do anything you want, Buck. And if you need me to sing backups for other singers, count me in."

"Do me a favor, Franny, wait outside for about five minutes while I make a call," said Buck.

When she left, Buck called Jack Merrill. "Jack? Get me 40 Gs."

Merrill laughed and said, "Well good morning to you too, Buck. What's this all about?"

"I have Fran Michaels in my outer office. I want her to be the first star we develop. If her sides are good enough for LPs, I want you to sign her to a contract. But aside from that, I want to hire her and three other girl singers to do backup vocals behind the other talent we're going to develop. I would want to pay each of them ten thousand a year. They'll work every day, so you'll get plenty of return on your investment. And believe me, you've heard Fran sing. Victor is gonna make a ton of money off of her."

"She's a beauty, all right. And yes, I love her voice." Buck could tell that Jack was hesitating.

"Tell you what, Jack. I'm going to keep the number of strings to the bare minimum. We don't need the New York Philharmonic, so you'll save money that way and give you the leeway for me to hire the backup singers."

"OK, OK, but let's start them at 8 Gs and see how they work out. If they are good, we can always bump them up down the road."

"Done. And Jack? Thanks."

Buck called Fran back into his office. "Here's the deal, Franny. I would like to hire you as a back-up singer in a group of four girls. We don't have the other three yet, but that's not a problem. This is exclusive of any contract we may sign you to if your recording tracks are good enough for LPs. It pays eight thousand a year."

Fran looked at Buck like she had just seen a strange creature. "Is this for real, Buck?" she asked.

"It's as real as New York City traffic jam. We're not going to say anything until after I speak to Pete and get him on board. Is that OK with you?"

"It's better than anything I could have hoped for, Buck. When I came here this morning, I never thought this would happen."

"You know, Fran, the first time I met you, Carrie was hysterical because she was afraid I would fall in love with you and leave her. I did fall in love with you—as did every guy in the band

and everyone who has ever heard you sing. You deserve every break you can get and I aim to see that you get them."

Fran hugged Buck and thanked him again. Then she wrote her phone number down on the pad on his desk. "I'm going to call Pete tonight—but don't worry, it's hush-hush that you were ever here."

Fran thanked Buck yet again and left.

First Chuck, then Fran and soon Pete. It had been a great day, thus far, thought Buck. But at three o'clock that afternoon, he got yet another surprise—and perhaps the most important one of the day.

Kelsey buzzed Buck and said, "Buck, I have a young man here whose name is Kip Roman. He'd like to speak to you."

The name wasn't familiar to him, but he said, "Show him in, Kel."

Kip Roman was a young man of about twenty-one. He scarcely looked old enough to shave. He was carrying a small leather-handled case in his left hand. Buck shook hands with him and showed him to the sofa.

"What can I do for you, Mr. Roman?"

"Well, Mr. Fisher, I'm from Pawnee City, Nebraska, and before I enlisted, I was a student at the University of Nebraska. Professor Emmanuel Wishnow was my teacher."

"Wait, wait, you were in the Army?"

"Yessir. Eleventh Airborne Division. I know, I'm older than I look. Professor Wishnow told me about a new orchestra he heard was being formed at RCA. I'm trying to make it in the music business, but every year conservatories and universities are graduating dozens of violin players. That's not really what I want to do."

"Oh? And what exactly is it you'd like to do, Mr. Roman?" asked Buck.

"My interest—and I hope my talent—is in arranging."

## A CHANGE OF KEY

That got Buck's attention and he leaned forward, elbows on his desk. "Go on."

"Professor Wishnow used to tell all his students of his time with Glenn Miller in the AAF band and once I heard them, I went out and bought every 78 I could find of that band. They were just terrific, and I loved the way they integrated strings with brass and reeds. Once I heard that sound, I knew that was what I wanted to do: arrange for that type of group."

"You know, Mr. Roman—"

"Kip. It's Kip. It's really Karl, but I grew up with it as Kip."

"OK, then it's Buck. You know, Kip, when I led my civilian band, Johnny Blair was our arranger. He could turn out four, maybe five charts in a day or two. How fast are you? Because you see, we are going to need a lot of material—quickly."

Kip Roman opened the brief case had handed Buck six charts: "Darn that Dream," "Sentimental Journey," "It's Been a Long, Long Time," "Five Minutes More," and "Dancing in the Dark." Buck perused the parts and saw that the writing for the reeds was melodic and yet rhythmically complex. The string parts for first and second violins, viola and cello were lush and primarily scored beneath a vocal lead line.

Buck was impressed but he didn't want to play his hand too quickly. "Here's the thing, Kip. These look good, but you understand that all these songs have been recorded before and were hits for other singers. No one's going to do a better job with "Sentimental Journey" than Doris Day did with Les Brown. And just about everybody has recorded "Five Minutes More.""

That was all true, but from the looks of the charts, Kip Roman showed a lot of promise. "Let me ask you a question, Kip. Do you want to be a free-lance arranger or do you want to be a part of what we are trying to create here?"

"Well, Mr. Fisher—"

"Buck. Please, it's Buck."

"Well, Buck, RCA Victor is about the biggest label there is. Yes, Columbia and Decca are also big, but Victor? No one compares. I want to be a part of this orchestra."

"As a violinist? Is that what you're aiming for? A chair in the string section?"

"Hell no! I want to be your arranger! You'll have more than enough fiddle players. Playing would only take time away from arranging."

"I see. Well, look, Kip, I'm going to make you the same offer I will make to anyone who joins this group. The pay is 15,000 a year—and for that money, you're going to work harder than you ever worked in your life. Eventually, you'll supervise a staff of arrangers—if we can find anyone else—and you'll grow with the company."

"Buck, during college I was working at a filling station for twenty-five cents an hour. Fifteen thousand dollars seems like all the money in the world to me. And I just want to tell you what an honor it is to work with Buck Fisher. Everyone in America knew how great your band was—and even in the Pacific we knew what happened to you in England. Believe me, I understand. I took a bullet in the leg in Manilla in the Philippines and spent a month in a hospital on Guam. You were a hero and an example to so many of us."

Buck had trouble believing that the young man standing before him was a combat veteran with a Purple Heart, but he knew no person with a conscience would ever lie about that. He saw it as a chance to give a helping hand to another veteran.

"So you're in?" said Buck.

"Darn right I'm in!"

"Good. Now I want you here on February 15$^{th}$ to meet everybody. Hopefully we have the right personnel to put this orchestra together. In the meantime, I want you to keep writing charts. Keep them in a range for a female vocalist with a mezzo-soprano to alto range. Be creative. Be inventive. I don't want them to just be a knockoff of Harry James or Artie Shaw. I want something new."

"You got it, Buck. I won't let you down."

.....

That night, Buck had so much to share with Carrie. She was so excited to hear that Chuck Fein would be back with him and when Buck told her about Fran Michaels, Carrie said, "She's a fabulous singer, darling, and she's so beautiful, I predict that someday she'll be a movie star."

Buck also told her about Kip Roman. "You know, Bucky, you have to give that kid credit. He comes here all the way from Nebraska on the outside chance he'd land a job. That takes guts. And if he's as good as you say he could be, well, Johnny had to start somewhere too. It took him time to develop, so maybe this young man will be another Johnny Blair."

"Hon, I have a call to make before dinner. Is that OK?"

"Sure sweetheart. I made us a London broil, and franks and beans casserole for the kids."

"Great. Be back in a few," said Buck.

He went into the bedroom and dialed Pete McCormack's number. When he answered the phone after the fourth ring, Buck said, "That you Pete?"

"Yes, who is this, please?"

"Well hell, you don't remember your old boss?"

"Jesus Christ! Buck! Is that you?"

"It sure is, buddy. How you doing?"

For a half hour, the two friends caught up, Pete telling Buck of his marriage to Fran, and Buck talking about the job at Victor and his plans. "Let me cut to the chase, Pete. I'm looking for first class players in every chair in the band. I want you on lead alto. No, that's not quite right. I need you on lead alto. The job pays 15,000 a year and there are all kinds of fringe benefits. It's a full-time gig, so you wouldn't have to scrounge around on weekends for peanuts. What do you say?"

## A CHANGE OF KEY

"What do I say? I say yes! This is a godsend, Buck. Jobs are like hen's teeth these days. Franny and I are trying to save enough money to be able to afford a kid. This could just put us over the top."

"You know I'd do anything for you guys, Pete. Tell you what. You be at the RCA Building at ten on February 15$^{th}$. Bring your alto and we'll get everything going then."

"I'll be there. And Buck? Thanks again."

Buck found Carrie and told her the good news—that Pete McCormack would be coming to work at Victor. "Jeez, darling, it's going to feel like old times," she said.

"Not quite, honey, we're not going to be a jazz band anymore. Our job is to back up new talent and make their recordings a success. We're just the background—but I aim to make us the best backup studio orchestra in the country."

"Whatever you do will be great, Buck. I guarantee it."

"Well, we'll find out next week what we have. So keep your fingers crossed."

**A CHANGE OF KEY**

# CHAPTER SIX
*"So Here's the Pitch," February 15$^{th}$, 1946*

When Buck Fisher walked into the rehearsal studio at 30 Rock on Friday morning of the fifteenth, he was immediately met by several familiar faces who swamped him with hugs and pats on the back. Noni Furillo, his 4$^{th}$ tenor player in the civilian and Army band, Kenny Ferraro who had to leave the band when his mother died and he had to return to New York City, Tony Tancredi, his drummer who propelled both bands to new rhythmic heights, and Gus D'Amico, his always reliable baritone sax player were overjoyed to see their old friend and leader.

There were a lot of other players who he did not recognize, but who had answered the ads and were looking for work. Buck introduced himself and explained what this new orchestra was going to do. He talked about salary, commitment to the group, the kind of music they would be playing—anything and everything prospective players might want to know. When he asked for questions, there were several.

"Boss? You going to be playing tenor in this group?" asked Noni Furillo. Noni had been in both bands and when Buck was injured during the war, he took over the 2$^{nd}$ tenor book for the rest of the band's dates.

"That's not part of the plan, Noni," said Buck. "We're not here to show off the solo skills of the sidemen. We're a backup band to singers who we hope will become superstars. Solos might just distract from the singing and we don't want to upstage them in any way."

Some of the players in the hall had been stars with big bands before and during the war. They even had fan clubs, but this was a whole new thing. No one would get to shine except the singers. Buck felt that despite the money he was offering, this would drive away a lot of those who had shown up. He could understand this. Money wasn't everything and musicians had an innate desire to be heard and be creative.

Another player who was holding a trumpet case on his lap asked, "Will we be touring with this band?"

"No. We're a studio band and this is our home. We might have to move into one of Victor's state-of-the art studios downtown when it comes to actually cutting discs, but no, we're not busing and trucking anywhere like the old days." That seemed to please the musicians.

Ken Ferraro said, "Any royalties involved, Buck?"

"Not this time, Kenny. Your salaries should make up for that. But I'm not discounting the possibility of year-end bonuses. That's more up to the accountants than me, though."

"Gus D'Amico then asked, "Buck, will we be under contract with Victor?"

"Yes, Gus. It's an exclusive. If someone over at Capitol or Decca wants you for a session, you have to decline the offer. In a sense, you belong to Victor and your talents are restricted to this label."

"Now, you string players, I don't know any of you so if you don't mind, tell us a little about yourselves, where you studied, where you've been playing."

Most of the players were in their early twenties and each one recited his musical background—several from Julliard, one from the New England Conservatory and one from the Curtis Institute in Philadelphia. "No symphony jobs available for you guys?" said Buck.

A young man named Terry Turner who played viola said, "Truth is, those guys stay in their chairs until they die. A lot of my classmates took off for California where they hoped to get work in motion picture studio orchestras. Half of them are gonna wind up selling shoes or something."

It was no exaggeration. It was just another reality of the music business.

## A CHANGE OF KEY

A violinist who looked to be about twenty years older than the other players stood up and introduced himself as Mendel Cohen. "I spent two years with Jascha Bunchuk and his Swing Symphony. We were the studio orchestra on the Major Bowes radio program. It was steady work, but it paid *bupkis*. I'm hoping to do better here."

"Where'd you play before that," asked Buck.

"I was first violin in the Vienna Philharmonic back in '30-'31. When that *momser* Hitler came to power, every Jew in the orchestra was fired—or worse. I got out with my family just in time. Came to New York and made a life for myself and my family here. Believe me, I was one of the lucky ones. Anyone ever says to you 'it can't happen here,' don't listen. That's what we all said back then and we were as wrong as we could be."

Chuck Fein stood up and moved to Mendel Cohen, extending his hand. "Mendy, I'm Chuck Fein and I'm a *lantzman*. I hope we'll be working together."

The door to the studio swung open and a man walked in carrying a guitar case. He looked around and laughed heartily. "Well, this sho' ain't the Count Basie Orchestra, in'it?" He was a Negro with skin the color of espresso with a dash of cream. "Ahm Walker Scaggs, and this here guitar? I can play the shit out of it like no one you ever heard."

Most of the players exchanged surprised looks at each other. Chuck Fein stifled a grin and just shook his head. A Negro player with a white band was a rarity. Benny Goodman had taken a big risk when he hired Teddy Wilson for his trio and later quartet in the mid-1930s, but he took a lot of abuse for it. Artie Shaw had hired Billy Holiday as his vocalist, but when she was subjected to intolerable bigotry when he took his band south, she quit and headed back home. Bigotry was nothing new to Buck. When the Johnny Blair Orchestra played a job in Georgia, Chuck Fein wasn't even allowed to register at the hotel that had been booked because his name sounded 'Jewish.' The entire band had to find

# A CHANGE OF KEY

another hotel rather than patronize such a small-minded institution that judged people by their names.

"Grab a chair, Walker," said Buck. "Can I ask you a question?"

"You go right ahead there, boss man. 'Ahma tell you anything you needs to know."

"OK, well, we're going to be a studio orchestra backing up vocalists. All the music is charted and there are very, very few opportunities for soloists to strut their stuff. So basically, you'll be doing little more than chucking chords fitting in with the rest of the rhythm section. Do you read chords?"

Walker Scaggs laughed loudly and said, "They ain't made the chord that I don't know and can't read. And I transposes at sight."

Buck nodded and Chuck gave him a surreptitious thumbs up."

"You Buck Fisher, ain't ya?" said Scaggs.

"Yes, I am."

"Heh, heh, you don't say. Coupla years back, I did some work with Prez. He said, 'Buddy—that's what everyone calls me—Buddy, there's this kid named Fisher. He gonna blow me outta da water.' Dat's what 'ole Prez said. Pleasure to meet you, Massa Buck."

"It's just Buck, Walker."

"Dat case, it's just Buddy."

"All right, Buddy, we'll be starting real soon."

"OK, fellas, lets make some noise. Take about fifteen minutes to get warmed up and tuned up. Kip will pass out some parts to some charts he's penned and we can see what we have."

Buck stepped out of the rehearsal hall and Chuck Fein followed him. "Buck, far be it from me to tell you what to do, but lemme say this: we shouldn't be like the people we've come to hate. We've been on the wrong end of things too many times. Let's not put anyone else in that position. If he can read and sound good, you've gotta take him. Color be damned. Anyone who doesn't like it should walk."

"You're right, Chuck. Victor has no color policy as far as I know. Believe me, if it did, I would never take a job here. Let's see if he can play. If he's good, he's in."

Chuck slapped Buck on the back and returned to the hall to tune his bass fiddle.

Buck had selected six charts from the Buck Fisher Orchestra book to see what the players could do. He chose them because they were structured on riffs with great section work—with no tenor solos which normally Buck would have played. One chart had a brief eight measure ride which Noni Furillo could easily handle. Other than that, it was all about the blend.

"Strings? You lay out for a bit. We'll get to all of you soon enough."

It didn't take long for Buck to realize that he was dealing with prime musicians, not just the ones that he knew, but the sidemen from other outfits as well. An original that Johnny Blair had written for the band called "Riffin Away," sounded just as good with these players as it had with his civilian and army bands. Pete McCormack's alto drove the section with Gus D'Amico anchoring it at the other end on baritone sax. Two other ballads and two more swing charts convinced Buck that he had struck gold. But that was with the jazz charts. What about the string arrangements? That was the question.

"OK, strings, lets try 'Dancing in the Dark' and follow that up with "They Say that Falling in Love is Wonderful."

Buck nodded at Tony Tancredi who clicked his sticks four times and the orchestra was off on the Dietz and Schwartz song that was introduced in a show called "The Band Wagon" by John Barker. Bing Crosby had the first recording of the song in 1931 and Artie Shaw had a massive hit with it in the early '40s. Kip Roman's arrangement was terrific, capturing the romantic intonations of the entire string section. In his mind, Benny could hear the lyric to the song with the strings and clarinets providing the backdrop.

The Irving Berlin song, "Falling in Love," was just as lush. Bill Dwyer, who had listened to the entire rehearsal whispered to Buck, "This kid's really got something." Buck merely nodded.

Kip's arrangement of "White Christmas" struck the exact note of nostalgia and longing that Buck would have wanted to write—if he knew how to arrange. After all the charts were played, Buck, said, "OK, now, anyone who has not yet played, switch with someone who has and we'll play through everything again."

It was, at the same time, laborious and yet pleasurable to hear so many expert musicians ply their craft. By the time they had done the second run-throughs, it was one o'clock and Buck said, "All right. Take an hour for lunch and be back here at two."

Pete McCormack came up to Buck and said, "You know what's missing, boss? The vocals that go over all these backdrops we're doing. What would you think about asking Fran to come in and sing with us? Buck turned away and smiled. Then he said, feigning total innocence, "Gee, Pete, do you think she'd want to?"

"I don't know, but it couldn't hurt to ask."

Buck pretended that he was pondering the proposition deeply. Then he said to Pete, "Tell you what. We're going to start again on Monday at ten. Why don't you ask her if she'd like to come in and sing with us? If she isn't interested, I won't take offense, but like you said, it can't hurt to ask."

Pete nodded and left to grab a bite to eat at Child's over on 6th Avenue.

When he left, Bill came up to Buck and said, "You're a clever sonofabitch, Buck, I'll give you that."

Buck laughed and said, "Maybe someday I'll tell him that the fix was in. For now, though, let's let Pete think it was all his idea. I just hope that Fran catches on and plays along. I think she can pull it off, but we'll know for sure on Monday."

## A CHANGE OF KEY

When the band came back at two, Buck pulled up a chair and spoke to them. "The good news, fellas, is that you are all fantastic musicians. Your skills were apparent in every measure you played. But the bad news is I can't hire all of you—though I wish I could. I need five saxes, four trumpets, four trombones, four rhythm, six violins, two violas and a pair of cellos. That's going to leave about fifteen of you out in the cold. It's just the way the business works, guys. I'm sure you all realize that you don't always get every job you go for, but in this case, it's not because you aren't good enough. I would be proud to work with each and every one of you."

Then he said, "So here's what we're going to do. Bill, Al and me are going to go over all our notes and make our final selections by Sunday. We'll call all of you, both the ones who made it and the ones who didn't. Those of you who didn't, deserve that courtesy from us. But just in case some of you turn the gig down, all of you have to be ready to come back here Monday morning at ten to start work. You'll all spend a few hours at Personnel filling out forms, but I hope by eleven, we'll be making music. Any questions?"

There were none. Buck had laid it out as clearly as he could and everyone understood that saying yes to some and no to others was never an easy task. But they all had respect for Buck Fisher and they appreciated his honesty.

The players packed up their horns and left the rehearsal hall. When only Buck, Bill and Al were left, they sat down at a small bridge table to talk things over. "Wow," said Al. What are we gonna do, Buck?"

"I want you guys to give me your honest impressions and opinions. It'll be good practice for when you're out there beating the bushes looking for talent. It was Bill Dwyer who started. "What about the old guy, Buck. He's gonna stick out like a sore thumb. He's got twenty, twenty-five years on the next oldest player who showed up."

## A CHANGE OF KEY

"No, Bill. He's in. He's probably the most talented string player here. The Vienna Philharmonic, for Chrissake. Besides, he deserves a break. And he'll steady the section. Don't forget, Bill, we're not performing in public, so looks don't matter very much. It's not like we're gonna fit these guys for slacks and blazers. That's one advantage of studio work—you come as you are."

"OK," said Al. "Mendy's in. Who's next?"

One by one they reviewed each player's background and the impression they made. Buck excused himself and went to the wall phone in the studio. He dialed his office and said, "Kel? Could you have the commissary send us a couple of pots of coffee? I think we're gonna be here for a while."

"I'll get right on it, Buck. Do you need me down there?"

"No, no, we have things covered here, but it's been a grueling day and we need something to keep us awake."

The coffee certainly helped because it took another three hours of back and forth to come up with the final personnel list for the RCA Studio Orchestra.

"We better pick some alternates in each section, Buck," said Bill. "Money aside, some of these guys might want to be in an outfit which really highlights their abilities, so they may turn us down."

"That's a good idea, Bill. Let's get two backup reeds, two strings and one each trumpet and trombone."

"What about Buddy Scaggs?" said Al.

"What about him?"

"Do we really need him, Buck? I mean, he's a character and all, but honestly? I could barely hear him over all the other instruments. That guitar just doesn't carry."

Bill said, "We can see if the engineers can come up with some kind of a small amplifier and a mike. That could help a lot. Nothing too big, but something that will get his sound out there."

"You take care of that Monday morning, Bill. See what the tech whizzes can come up with. But he's in. You guys weren't with us when down south—and even some place further north, people complained that we were playing too much 'jigaboo' and 'nigger' music. That's never going to happen here. Teddy Wilson was in small Goodman combos. If Buddy Scraggs is the first Negro in a major studio orchestra, then good for us."

"OK, Buck. I understand," said Al.

"Now I have to saddle you guys with the shit detail. Take this list, divide it in half, and tomorrow, start making calls. Each of you take some yesses and nos so neither of you has to come across as the hatchet man. Probably I should be doing it, but I know how I would feel being rejected so you guys are going to do my dirty work."

"No problem, Buck," said Bill. "We'll handle it."

"You want to come to dinner tonight, Al?" asked Buck.

That took Al Rovitz by surprise and he stammered an answer, "Oh, well, uh, umm, thanks Buck, but umm, I've got a date tonight."

"Say, that's great, Al." Then he added with a wink, "Just make sure you treat my sister right. She's very dear to me."

Bill and Al left, and Buck gathered the papers to take them back to his office. When he walked out of the rehearsal space, Buddy Scraggs was sitting on the floor in the hall, his back leaning against the wall.

"You OK, Buddy?" asked Buck.

"I'm good, but lemme ask you somethin'. You really gonna pay us all that money, Mr. Buck?"

"Of course I am, why would you think I wouldn't?"

"I's a Black man, Mr. Buck. I'm gonna get the same as all them white boys?"

"You certainly are. This isn't Mississippi, Buddy. You're as much of a man as anyone in this group. Where do you live?"

"Up in Harlem. Lenox Avenue. I gots me a nice little place. Nothin' special but I keeps it clean and it suits me fine long as the cockroaches and rats stay away from it."

# A CHANGE OF KEY

"Near the Savoy Ballroom?"

"Three, mebbe four blocks away. Played there manys a time back in the '30s. Place could hold four thousand people and when they's was jittebuggin' the whole building shook."

"Really!"

"Subbed in the Chick Webb band a number of times. He was the main house band up there, ya know." Scraggs grinned and said, "Even dated Ella a few times, but she was too young for me and her mama watched her like a hawk. Also played with Cootie Williams up there and once or twice with Lucky Millander. All good men. Fair men. I hopes you gonna be fair wid me, Mr. Buck."

"You work hard for me, Buddy, you do your job, learn your parts, be on time, and you'll get nothing but fair from me. You have my word on that."

"You needs to understand, Mr. Buck, there's black man's word and white man's word. Sometimes they don't always means the same thing."

"Wait. You're a black man? I hadn't noticed. All I saw was a musician."

That earned Buck a horse laugh. "Awright, Mr. Buck. I'ma trust you and like you gives me your word? I gives you mine. I'll give you the best playing I got inside me. Always."

Buck extended his hand which Buddy Scraggs shook. Then Buck said, "Welcome aboard, Buddy. We're gonna make a lot of music together." He patted him on the back and walked towards the elevator to return to his office.

"You still here, Kelsey?" said Buck when he entered the office.

"Just finishing up checking out who's playing where over the next few weeks. I'll be leaving soon."

"No, you're leaving now. You've put in a long enough day. Have a great weekend and I'll see you early Monday morning. Oh, say, how's your husband doing?"

## A CHANGE OF KEY

"It's been a challenge, Buck. They are fitting him with a wooden leg at the VA hospital and he's going to need a lot of training to learn how to use it. But he's a brave man and he'll lick this."

"With your help and love, I'm sure he will. I hope to meet him someday. For now—get out of here and go home."

…..

That night over dinner, there was so much to tell Carrie about. He spoke of the auditions, the caliber of the players, the new charts that young Kip Roman had written, the reunion with Pete, Noni Tony, and Gus. He replayed the whole day for her, but Carrie could tell that there was something bothering him.

"I'm waiting," she said.

"Waiting?"

Carrie sighed. "Buck Fisher, I know every square inch of your body—you don't think I can read your face like a map? Tell me what's wrong."

Buck shrugged.

"I'm still waiting," Carrie said.

"It's just that I feel bad, Carrie. I can't hire them all. They're all so good—every one of them. And I feel like a real louse to boot."

"Why?"

"Because I gave Bill and Al the job of telling them they didn't get the job. What a coward I am!"

"No, darling. Not a coward. Like it or not, you're the boss. You delegate jobs and responsibilities. It comes with the title."

"Yeah, but no one ever likes hearing 'no.'"

"Bucky, my love, you are probably the only musician on the planet who never flopped at an audition. You think every star on Broadway started that way? Jeez, babe, they probably did a dozen auditions before they landed their first job—and then it was probably as an extra. No one goes into this business thinking they'll be an instant success, so don't feel bad. If they're as good as you say, they'll find work. Otherwise, they'll do something else with their lives. Honey, don't forget, if you didn't get a break, you'd be back slicing lamb chops for a living."

Buck nodded in agreement, but Carrie, who could read his every emotion and expression knew that there was something else eating at him. "There's more, isn't there, darling?"

There was no use in hiding it, and he knew she'd get it out of him eventually. "I listened to the band today, Carrie, as they ran through the charts---some from my old band."

"And?"

"I miss playing so much. It was—is—such a part of me, and now what am I? A suit? An Executive? I feel like part of me is missing—cut out of me like those two feet of my guts I lost in the war. I think giving up playing just might be the toughest thing I've ever done."

"So tell me, love. What's stopping you?"

"Fear, mostly. Hell, I don't even know how long I could hold a horn, no less blow into it for hours at a time."

"You could try, Bucky. There's no harm in trying," said Carrie.

"I had a crazy thought on the drive home today, hon," said Buck.

"Let's hear."

"I thought maybe I could switch to soprano sax. It only takes half the air and it's only a bout a quarter of the weight of the tenor. But maybe I could start with one of those and work my way up to the bigger horn."

"Darling, I'm no expert in these things," said Carrie, "but does anyone use one of those things anymore? They're kind of old-fashioned, no?"

It was true. In early jazz, the soprano sax was a good alternative to the clarinet. It didn't have nearly the range, but it had a bolder, ballsier sound. Jazz legends like Sidney Bechet used both the clarinet and soprano in recordings.

## A CHANGE OF KEY

"I was thinking I could give Francois Boucault over at Selmer a call. Maybe he can get me a good deal on a horn. We're still getting endorsement checks from them, right?"

"Yes we are. Every month. But Bucky, do I have to show you one of our bank books? Even with no 'deal' from Francois, we can easily afford to buy you a horn if that's what you'd like to do."

That much was true. Buck had been one of the highest paid musicians in the country. When he broke up the band after being drafted in 1942, he had been averaging twenty-eight thousand dollars a week for more than a year, so indeed, he was a wealthy man.

"Maybe I learned it from my mother, darling, but I'm always looking for a bargain. I'll call him Monday and see what he says. Now, enough of my pissing and moaning. Tell me about your day."

"It was great! I went with Cathy and we registered April at the local junior high school and Mikey at the elementary school right down the block. Next year Dorothy will start kindergarten there. Then we went to the local A & P on 46th Avenue and we stocked up her refrigerator and pantry with everything she needs. She's such a sweet girl, Buck! And next month they are opening a huge H.C. Bohack market on 46th Avenue and Utopia Parkway. It's what they call a 'supermarket' and it's about five times as big as the A & P. I can't wait to shop there! And there's talk that Bloomingdale's is going to open a gigantic store in Fresh Meadows in 1948 or 1949. Can you believe it? We won't have to schlep to 59th street in Manhattan to shop anymore."

Unlike most men, Buck never objected to tagging along with Carrie on one of her shopping sprees because it always made her so happy—and she was more concerned about buying things for others than for herself. If she took such joy in so simple an activity, then it made him happy as well.

"Bucky?"

"Yes, darling."

"Don't be afraid. You'll take it slow and see how it feels to play again. If it works, it works, but there's no shame in it if you can't make it happen. Not after what you went through. And I'll love you just as much whatever you decide to do."

Buck hugged Carrie and said, "How about you feed your husband and children and we'll put them to bed together. Maybe we can go to bed early and you know, see what comes up."

Carrie laughed. "I know exactly what will come up, love. And believe me, I plan on enjoying every moment of it."

# CHAPTER EIGHT
## *"Meet Our First Star," Monday Febuary 18$^{th}$ 1946*

Buck had to hand it to Fran Michaels. Not only was she a superb singer, but she was a terrific actress as well. When she walked into the rehearsal hall Monday morning with Pete McCormack, she cried out, "Buck!" and ran to him, throwing her arms around him as if she had not seen him for years—rather than less than a week.

"Oh my God I'm so glad to see you! When Pete told me that you wanted me to sing with you, I could hardly believe it. I thought you had forgotten about me long ago."

"Franny, no one who has ever met you would or could ever forget you."

Proof of that came when Chuck, Gus, and Tony and Kenny surrounded Fran, each one of her former bandmates hugging her—with Chuck almost crushing the breath out of her. "Well look at you, gorgeous," said Fein, "how'd that skinny-assed horn player get so lucky to land you?"

"Aww, Chuckie, don't be jealous. You know I'll always love you," said Fran.

The rest of the players who had been selected had gathered and were in the process of assembling their instruments and getting them tuned up. Bill Dwyer and Al Rovitz reported that of all the players they contacted, only one opted out—a trumpet player named Danny Donaldson who had played with Al Donahue's band.

"I went down the list and replaced him with Gerry Koch. He's our new 4$^{th}$ trumpet."

"Good, that's great work, guys. I'm glad everyone else is eager to be a part of this orchestra."

Then to the band he said, "Fellas? A moment please. Before I send you all down to Personnel to do the required paperwork, I want you to meet our first star—Fran Michaels. Franny, come on up here."

Fran came forward and stood by Buck. "As you can see, she's about the most beautiful girl any of you jokers has ever seen, but besides that, her voice is going to knock you on your asses. She was my vocalist in the civilian band, so if you bought any Buck Fisher 78s on Bluebird, you probably have already heard her voice. She's going to be the first in a long line of talent that we will sign to a contract with Victor and if all goes well, our first project will be getting one of those new LPs you've been reading about laid down with her on the vocals. If all goes well, you could be looking at the next Margaret Whiting. Oh, and one more thing. It's hands off. She happens to be married to our lead alto player, Pete McCormack."

The band 'booed' good-naturedly, but Buck could see that all eyes were riveted upon this magnificent girl. Kelsey Burton had just come through the door and Buck said, "Kel, would you take these guys down to Personnel and get all that paperwork rolling? Stay with them to answer any questions and get them all back here as soon as you can so we can start work. Process Kip and Kenny Ferraro first because we can at least start looking over the charts with them even before the rest of the guys get back."

"Sure thing, Buck. I'll take care of everything," said Kelsey.

When the band members left for Personnel, Buck sat with Kip and Fran and discussed the charts that Kip had written. "What we need, Kip, is an instrumental break in between the bridge and the final chorus. I want that on every song, otherwise, it's like reading straight through a piano lead sheet and the songs will last two minutes. Sherman Kaufman, our new lead trumpet, has a really sweet tone. I'm thinking you can feature him on an eight-bar solo during that instrumental break, maybe on cup mute. Nothing too loud. I don't want it to overpower the mood of the ballads."

## A CHANGE OF KEY

"Nothing for sax, Buck?"

"Tell you what. Let's give Pete McCormack on alto some obligatos behind Fran. Solo alto isn't exactly the warmest of tones, so if it doesn't work, we can move it over to tenor. Noni can handle those."

"You'll never be playing with us, Buck?"

"I don't think so, Franny. I don't have my wind back and besides, I'm little more than a suit now," said Buck.

"Then who will conduct the orchestra?" asked Fran.

Buck hadn't given any thought to that, but it was a good thing Fran brought it up. Kip said, "Buck, I took four conducting classes at Nebraska and I got to conduct the university's orchestra and symphonic band. I don't think it would be very hard to conduct this orchestra—especially since I wrote all the charts and I know every note in them."

Buck thought about it and said, "It would solve the problem, Kip, but the thing is, I can't offer you any more money right now for taking on the additional job. Maybe I can make it up to you in a year-end bonus."

"That's no problem, Buck. You're already paying me plenty of money—far more than I ever expected to make right out of school. So don't worry about that."

"I never asked you, Kip, but you're here from Nebraska. Where do you live?"

"Right now I'm renting a small place in Williamsburg. It's just about big enough to turn around in, but that's fine for me. I've got my eye on a nice house in Glendale, Queens. I banked most of my Army pay and with the G.I. Bill, I think I can pick it up for a song."

"Well, if you need any help, I know a very good realtor. He helped Bill get his house."

"Thanks, Buck. I'll keep it in mind."

By this time the band had returned and was ready to work. Kip had written a chart on the Ellington tune, "I've Got it Bad and that Ain't Good," that he recorded with Ivey Anderson. It was perfect for Fran's husky alto voice. It was a slow, melancholy song about unrequited love whose lyric plumbed every emotion of heartbreak. But Fran Michaels took the lyric to a higher level. She made it sound sultry, the crying out of a soul wrapped in sadness. It was enough to make a listener weep in empathy with the singer.

When she completed the song, Chuck Fein called out, "Jesus, Bucky, that gal has a million-dollar set of pipes. Just as good when she sang with the old band. She's gonna sell a million records for this company."

Buck was certain that the rest of the band was thinking, 'yeah, to go right along with her million-dollar body.' They finished the charts that Kip had written and then Buck said, "OK, strings, lay out for a bit. I want to hear how Fran does on some of the up-tempo swing charts we did in my civilian band."

Buck knew that if they were going to produce LP 'albums' featuring one singer's voice, it would be necessary to provide the listener a variety of song tempos and moods. "Let's try 'Nice Work if You Can Get It.' Then we'll try 'You're the Top.' I'll fill in on the vocal for that one until we find someone better."

The Gershwin tune was one of the show-stoppers with Buck's band and he always sang it with Carrie when she was the band's girl singer. Again, Fran made the songs come to life. She never was just a singer; she was a performer. Perhaps it was her operatic training, but Fran Michaels never just stood behind a microphone and sang. Each number became a vignette with her as the lead actress. Every player in the orchestra had, at one time or another, seen other singers ply their trade. But never had any of them seen anyone like Fran Michaels. She was a young woman destined for greatness and RCA Victor was going to do everything in its power to see that end realized.

The orchestra rehearsed for three more hours making slight changes and improvements in Kip's charts. At the

## A CHANGE OF KEY

completion of the rehearsal, Buck said, "Great work, guys. We're back here tomorrow at ten. See you all then."

As everyone was leaving, Buddy Scraggs came up to Buck and said, "Mistah Buck, that chile can sing like an angel outta heaven. Reminds me of how Ella sings. Leastwise, her tone is just as good. But I saw Ella when she was jes a kid. Dis girl, well, she already top of the heap. Just thought I'd tell you dat."

Then Buck had a thought and called Fran and Kip over. "You know, Fran, if we're going to make an LP all about you, I want you to be comfortable with the material we record. You have to sing songs that really speak to you. So for tomorrow, I want you to make a list of those kinds of songs you'd like to sing and Kip, then I want you to write charts for them."

"There are two I've been thinking about for a while, Buck. I'd really love to do them."

"OK Frannie, let's hear."

"There's a Johnny Mercer song the Pied Pipers did back in 1944, 'Dream.' I would love to cover that song. It's got this really neat tenor obligato part. I always think of you when I hear it. And I also love 'A Nightingale Sang in Berkeley Square.' Oh, and also the Cole Porter song, "What Is This Thing Called Love." I think these are terrific songs that will work perfectly in my range."

"Do you know them, Kip?"

"Absolutely. I'll have them for you by tomorrow's rehearsal."

"You're kidding me," said Buck.

"Nah. This is easy stuff, but don't worry, I'll make it sound great."

"OK, then see you both tomorrow."

.....

As soon as Buck saw Carrie that night, he knew that something was wrong. She looked pale and drawn and seemed listless.

## A CHANGE OF KEY

"Darling, what's wrong?" he asked, alarmed at her appearance.

"It's nothing, sweetie. Just a long day is all. I'm fine. Go get cleaned up and we'll eat."

He didn't buy the explanation, but in time he'd get the truth out of her. At dinner, Carrie said, "I was so tired today, I called Mama to ask if she could watch the kids for a few hours. Arlene came over instead and she was great with them. Then we had a long talk."

"Uh oh, why don't I like the sound of that," said Buck.

Carrie laughed and said, "You should be thrilled, darling. Your big sister is in love. Deep."

Benny's fork paused halfway to his mouth and he said, "Give me that again."

She laughed again and said, "Want me to spell it for you, Bucky? L-O-V-E!"

"Al?" said Buck.

"Who else. They've been seeing each other every night for two weeks, closer to three, actually."

"This is too soon, Carrie, way too soon."

"Calm down, darling. You sound like a teenager's father rather than a kid brother. After all, how long did it take you to fall in love with me?" asked Carrie.

"About twelve minutes," said Buck.

"See? Maybe it runs in the family. She went on and on about him, about what a gentleman he is, how he treats her, their plans together."

"Yeah but what about—"

"I didn't ask, Bucky. That's way too personal and it's between Arlene and Al. But she knows if she wanted to talk to someone about it, I'm the one she could come to. I have the feeling that Arlene has zero experience in that area, but I also sense that she's eager to find out all about it."

"Does Mama know?" he asked.

## A CHANGE OF KEY

"Didn't you once tell me that mothers know everything about their children—even before they knew it themselves? I'm sure Mama has figured it out on her own."

"And Beverly?"

"If Arlene confided in me, don't you think she'd talk it over with her own sister? Look darling, Arlene only has one fear and she's willing to call the whole thing off if it's going to be a problem."

"What kind of problem?"

"She's concerned that there will be a problem because Al works for you. She doesn't want it to be any kind of a conflict of interest. So if it's going to be, she'll end it in a second."

"That's ridiculous. Al and Bill are both like brothers to me. He's a great guy and I'd trust him with my life—and with my sister. My only concern is that she'll be happy."

"Why don't you talk to her then, Bucky? She thinks the world of you and she would respect anything you have to say."

"Yeah, maybe I will. Maybe I'll also talk to Al."

"Good idea. Now finish eating."

Buck took a few more bites, then got up from the table.

"Look, darling, I'm going to clear and do the dishes. I'll put the kids to bed too. I want you to go inside and rest. Sleep if you can. I'll be there as soon as I finish up."

"Thank you, Bucky. Maybe I will."

When Buck got to the bedroom, Carrie was already asleep, so he held her and spooned against her until he too drifted off. But by the following morning, it became apparent to him what was wrong with Carrie. At five o'clock he was startled awake by the sound of Carrie heaving uncontrollably into the toilet in their bedroom. He jumped out of bed, ran to the bathroom and held her head as she voided her stomach of all she had eaten the night before. She was so weakened from the voluminous retching that she could hardly stand. He stayed while she gargled with Listerine and then helped her back to bed.

## A CHANGE OF KEY

"I'm calling the doctor, Carrie. We have to get you to a hospital."

She smiled and said, "No, no, darling, it's all right. It's nothing I haven't been through before."

"What do you—" And then it hit him. "Carrie?"

She smiled and nodded. Then she opened her arms and he came to her. "Don't be angry, Bucky," she said, immediately beginning to cry.

Bucky held her at arm's length and raised her chin so he could look her in the eyes. "Sweetheart, didn't you ask me that when you found out you were pregnant with Eddie? I wasn't angry then, I wasn't angry for Laura—and I am absolutely ecstatic about us having another child. You think I don't have enough love inside me for another one?"

"No, but—" she began.

"Right—no buts about it. But I have to tell you something, darling. This time it seems to be taking more of a toll on you, and that worries me a lot."

"I'm older, Bucky. Maybe it gets harder the older you get. But I'll be fine."

"When can we tell Mama and the girls?"

"I was thinking we could have them over for dinner Friday night. I'll make something nice."

"No. I'm taking half a day Friday and *we'll* make something nice. I want you to take it easy this coming week. Promise me."

Carrie laughed. "Yessir, colonel sir," she said, offering a mock salute.

"You go back to sleep. I'm going to make pancakes for the kids. We still have any Corn Flakes left? I'll give them that too. And if you need anything from the market, just make me a list and let me know. I'll pick up anything we need."

"The Corn Flakes are in the cupboard by the left of the sink, darling."

## A CHANGE OF KEY

"OK, don't worry about a thing. I'll bring you breakfast in bed if you'd like," said Buck.

Carrie sighed. "Bucky, I am not an invalid. Of course I can get up. And I'll be fine with the kids all day. If I need help, I'll call Cathy. I tell you, it's a godsend having her right down the block."

"All right, but we're making an appointment with Morris Teitelbaum to give you a check-up."

"No dice, darling. Dr. Teitelbaum finally retired. He was almost eighty, after all. But he turned his practice over to Dr. Meyers. As in Catherine Meyers. She's the only female OB/GYN at Queens General Hospital and she has a list of letters after her name that look like alphabet soup. The letter Dr. Teitelbaum sent to his patients said that she went to Yale and during the war she was based at one of the Naval hospitals in Pearl Harbor. Can I tell you something, Buck?"

"Of course you can."

"Well, this is a bit embarrassing, but I'll feel a lot better with a woman looking up there. Not that Dr. Teitelbaum wasn't completely professional and all, but you know, it's just easier for me," she said.

"If that's what you want, then I want you to call Monday morning and make an appointment soon as possible."

…..

The only thing that spoiled the serenity of the weekend was Carrie retching again on Sunday morning. As before, Buck steadied her over the bowl in the bathroom and helped her clean up after the episode had concluded.

"You say this has been going on for over a week now and I didn't know about it?" said Buck.

"At first it wasn't violent. It was more like gagging. But then on Saturday, well, you saw what it was like and that happened again today. I'm going to ask Dr. Meyers about it. Can you come with me on Friday?"

## A CHANGE OF KEY

"Yes. I'll call Kip and have him do the rehearsal. It will give him more experience with leading the band and the guys need to come to trust him and his decisions," said Buck.

"He's a really special kid, isn't he?" said Carrie.

"He's to this group what Johnny was to the other. One day maybe Kip will be as famous an arranger as Finnegan or Gray or even Fletcher Henderson. When that happens, I hope we'll still be able to keep him when greener pastures beckon."

"Bucky, RCA Victor is about as green as pastures get. But let's not worry about the future just yet. There's a long way to go and I imagine he's still got a lot to learn."

Buck knew Carrie was right. For now, his major concern was Carrie's health.

On Monday morning, the band assembled by ten and Kip was already there handing out new parts to the orchestra. Fran Michaels arrived with Pete shortly thereafter and she scanned the vocal sheets, noting the keys and the bridges.

Kip looked at Buck who merely shrugged and said, "Your show Kip. You're on."

"OK guys, first up, let's run 'A Nightingale Sang in Berkeley Square.' Fran? Do you need the vocal sheet?" asked Kip.

"No, I've had the lyric down for a long time," she said.

It turned out to be a perfect song for Fran. There was a longing to the lyric, perhaps because the real Berkeley Square in London's Mayfair section, was where so many American servicemen took their dates. No doubt for many of them, it would be the last time they would see those girls in their lives.

Buck remembered Glenn Miller's recording of the song with Ray Eberle on the vocal, but that version had nothing on Kip Roman's—or Fran's delivery. She turned the song into a tone poem—a miniature drama in which every syllable was nuanced.

She did even better on "Dream." The Johnny Mercer lyric was another of those songs that promised hope out of gloom, light out of darkness.

## A CHANGE OF KEY

The Pied Pipers' recording used a celeste on the obligato, but Kip had noted on the piano part, "ad lib beneath the vocal." Kenny Ferraro, a masterful player, did just that. His counterpoint figures worked perfectly under Fran's delivery. It was a thing of beauty and as soon as Buck heard it, he knew it would have to be part of Fran's LP.

Kip had also written a brand-new chart on Cole Porter's "You'd Be So Easy to Love." On the first run through, Kip had to stop the orchestra several times to make corrections on their parts. During one of the instrumental bridges, he had mistakenly written a harmony line in parallel fifths—and it sounded awful. He quickly corrected his error and on the second run-through, it was much improved. Fran was a perfectionist and when she finished the song, she said, "Buck? That's no good. I wasn't comfortable with what I did on the lyric. I was missing something. Can we run it again?"

"Ask Kip, dear. He's the boss at these rehearsals," said Buck.

"Kip?" she asked, looking at him.

"Of course we can. Fellas? Let's take it from the edge, please. Wait, I tell you what. Let's run it with just the orchestra and you follow along pairing the lyric in your head. Then we'll run it again with you singing."

The third run-through was much better. Fran changed the phrasing of the lyric to emphasize the warmth and sincerity of the emotions of the song. Every time she sang, Buck was impressed at how she could extract such feelings from black ink on a page. He thought to himself that Julliard must have really drummed perfection and precision into her head because she always seemed to know how and where to take a song.

Over the next four days, Kip provided a wide variety of arrangements for the band: up-tempo swing, ballads and even a few novelties. After the rehearsal on Wednesday, Kip said, "Buck, can I speak to you for a minute?"

"Sure, Kip. Come into the office and we'll sit down."

Buck sat behind the small desk in the rehearsal room's office and Kip sat in the chair across from him. "What's up Kip?"

The young man hesitated for a moment or two before saying, "Buck, I need help."

"Oh? How so?"

"See, I have all these ideas in my head for charts—and I can knock them out by the dozens if that's what you want. But Once I write the score, it takes me hours to transfer each line to the individual parts for the band. What I need is a skilled—and fast—copyist. That way I can put all my energy into the chart without having to do the tedious copying job."

The idea of a copyist had never occurred to Buck. Johnny Blair had never mentioned using one and Buck was sure he would have wound up on the payroll sheet if he hired one on. That was part of the genius of Johnny. Not only could he create the music, but he could lay it down on paper just as quickly as his brain produced it. Buck only recollected a few occasions when corrections were needed on a part or two. When he realized he had made an error, Johnny would say, "Only Mozart was perfect. There's not a single correction on any score he ever wrote."

"I have no idea how we'd go about finding one, Kip." Said Buck.

"You said that Friday you'll only be here for half a day. Let me end the rehearsal by noon and I'll go over to Julliard and speak to the chairman of the Music Department. I'll tell him what we are looking for and see if he has anyone in mind. But what can I tell him we can pay?"

That was a good question and Buck had to think about it. "Tell you what: offer a hundred bucks a chart or 4,000 a year, whichever is more. But one way or another, it's got to be his full-time job. To get it right and done quickly, it'll need his undivided attention."

"I'll make sure he knows that," said Kip.

## A CHANGE OF KEY

"All right, Kip. See what you can find out over at Julliard and I'll check with Jack Merrill to see if he has any ideas."

…..

Friday was an exceptionally busy day for everyone. Again Carrie spent the early hours in the bathroom voiding her stomach of the previous night's dinner with Buck carrying her back to bed and pulling the covers over her. "You sleep for a few more hours, darling. I'll take care of the kids and when Mama comes over, we can leave for the doctor. The appointment's not until ten."

"Thanks, babe. I just need a little more sleep," said Carrie, who closed her eyes and fell out instantly.

Buck went into the kitchen and was getting ready to prepare breakfast when the doorbell rang. It was Rachel. "Mama! You didn't have to be here until after nine."

"Benjamin, I don't want you to have to *potschke* around the kitchen when you have to take Carrie to the doctor. You have enough on your mind. I'll make breakfast for the children and you just take care of her."

Buck sat at the kitchen table and Rachel kept glancing at him as she prepared the breakfast. She stopped what she was doing and sat down across from him at the table. "Tell me, Benjamin. What has you all tied up in knots?"

"I'm fine, Ma."

"No, you are not fine. And I'm your mother so you can talk to me."

Buck sighed and said, "It's Carrie, Ma. I've never seen her so weak, so sick. It's like every morning it's worse and worse. I'm scared."

There was a twinkle in Rachel's eye. "So tell me, Benjamin, this dinner tonight is when you're going to announce that I'm going to be a grandmother again?"

Buck was floored. "How could you know?"

"Oy, Benjamin. She's sick every morning. You think it's just indigestion maybe? I assume your sisters have no idea, so don't worry. Your secret is safe. I'll even act surprised when you tell us. Now, how can I help?"

"No, Ma. Carrie is adamant about wanting to make this dinner. I told her I would help with the preparations and the cooking. She really wants to do this. Maybe if you want to bring a cake for dessert and some cookies for the kids, that would be fine with her."

Rachel put her hand on Buck's cheek. "Benjamin, God has watched over you through tougher times than this. He's watched over all of us. You're in His eye, so don't worry. All will be well."

Buck kissed his mother's hand and then said, "Let me get the kids ready for breakfast, Ma. Then I'll get Carrie up and about."

Buck returned to the bedroom and gently nudged Carrie awake. "Time to get up, sweetheart. Ma's here and feeding the kids."

Slowly, Carrie got out of bed, showered, did her hair and make-up as Buck watched her every move. "You don't have to watch me, Bucky, I'm not gonna fall down or anything."

"I know, darling, I just love to look at you. I figure after the doctor we can go do the food shopping for tonight—unless you're not up to it and you make a list and I'll do it for you."

"Nothing doing, Feinstein. This dinner's a big deal in case you forgot, and I want it to be extra special. I just don't know what to make," said Carrie. "But don't worry. I'll come up with something."

"I have an idea," said Buck.

"Give."

"How about we get six of those baby chickens—what do they call them—Cornish hens or something like that. They're real small so everybody gets their own—with the kids splitting one. We can get some wild rice and we'll stuff the birds with that. They're so small, they'll all fit into one pan to cook. Easy peasy."

## A CHANGE OF KEY

She thought for a moment and then said, "You're a genius, Bucky. That sounds great. We'll figure out the rest of the meal when we get to the supermarket."

Carrie came out of the bedroom, saw Rachel, and embraced her. "Oh Ma, thanks so much for doing this. It's such a big help."

Rachel kissed Carrie and said, "What, I have to be thanked for looking after my grandchildren? Carrie darling, it's a pleasure to look after them. What else would an old lady do—wash the windows? Mop the floors?"

"You'll never be old, Mama. You're too feisty."

After breakfast, Carrie and Buck left for Dr. Meyers, whose office was on Sanford Avenue in Flushing. Her office was close to Parsons Hospital, but as a female gynecologist, the demand for her services gave her hospital privileges at Flushing Hospital and other New York City institutions. In the waiting room, Carrie had to fill out a lengthy medical history to create a profile of her health and previous pregnancies. As her spouse, Buck was asked to fill out a similar, but much shorter, medical history including any surgeries and chronic conditions.

"Well, I've got plenty of those," said Buck.

After waiting for over half an hour, Dr. Meyer's nurse ushered Carrie and Buck into an examination room. Five minutes later, Dr. Meyers entered. She was a handsome woman in her early 40s, with gray hair intermingled with a rich brunette. "Mr. and Mrs. Feinstein, this is a real pleasure," said the doctor. "Or may I call you Buck?" she said with a smile.

That shocked Buck.

She laughed and said, "More Americans can recognize your face than they can President Truman's. Everyone knows who you are. Fully recovered I hope?"

"I'm getting there. Slower than I'd like, I'm afraid. But in time I hope to be one hundred percent," said Buck.

"I'll make sure of it, doctor," said Carrie.

## A CHANGE OF KEY

"Well, your injury was very serious. I bet most of the country was praying for your recovery. Now, Carrie, time to have a look. Buck? Maybe you could wait outside for this part of it."

"Yes, I'm sure Carrie would like that," he said.

When he left, Dr. Myers had Carrie change into a hospital gown and then get onto the examination table. She had been through this twice before, but it was never a comfortable experience, having her feet in the stirrups and feeling helpless. Dr. Myers blew on the speculum to warm it up slightly and then said, "OK, this won't hurt. Just try to relax."

The actual internal examination lasted for only a minute or so. "OK, Carrie, you can hop down now. I'm going to have my nurse draw some blood and we'll have the results back from the lab in about three or four days. Let's get Buck back in here and have a chat."

Buck returned and sat down next to Carrie, holding her hand. "I'd say you are about a month pregnant," Dr. Meyers began. There's a little bit of redness inside and to prevent infection, I'm going to prescribe antibiotics and a vaginal cream you'll use three times a day. I also will write a prescription for vitamins that you must be diligent about taking—no skipping, Carrie."

"Doctor, we have two children," said Buck, "but I have never seen Carrie so sick in the mornings or for so long. Why is that happening?"

"Well, Buck, every woman is different and every pregnancy is different. Some women have morning sickness for two or three days, but believe it or not, some have it for several months—and that can really be a problem. The fetus is sucking out the hormones and nutrients from Carrie's body and it's causing an imbalance that brings about the retching."

"Carrie, let me ask you something. When you vomit, is there any blood in it?"

"No, none at all."

"How about when you urinate or move your bowels? Any bleeding there?"

"No, doctor. None."

"Good, that's good—but I want you to be very aware if that changes. You must notify me immediately if that starts happening."

"Doctor, Carrie has been losing a lot of weight recently. Is that unusual?" said Buck.

Dr. Meyers laughed and said, "No, Buck, and in time that's going to reverse and she'll start to gain weight as the baby grows. The trick is not in the gaining weight, but in losing it after a baby is born. Too many women don't lose that baby weight and it's very unhealthy, particularly because of the strain it puts on the heart. How did you do after the first two, Carrie?"

"I didn't have any problem losing the weight after my son and daughter were born."

"That's great—but be very careful, Carrie. You're older now and the older you get, the harder it is to lose weight. As we get closer, we'll talk about dietary issues once the baby is born. For now, I'm going to see you every two weeks. I want to make sure that possible infection doesn't bloom inside you."

They thanked the doctor, paid the bill and left the office. In the car ride home, Buck said, "What do you think of her, Carrie?"

"I like her. She's no-nonsense, but kind at the same time. I don't know if she has kids of her own, but she sure acts like she's been through this before. That's something Morris Teitelbaum could never say."

"We'll stop on 46th Avenue at the pharmacy and get those prescriptions filled for you, darling," said Buck.

"There's a King Kullen on Northern Boulevard I would like to try. It's ten times bigger than the A & P. I've heard it's such a great place to shop—the whole store is divided into departments and they were the first market to provide shopping carts instead of those hand baskets that don't hold very much. We can get everything we need for the big dinner tonight right there."

"Suits me, babe. But remember, I'm helping with the dinner. I don't want you knocking yourself out," said Buck.

They did their shopping, went to the pharmacy and waited in the car for twenty minutes until the druggist filled the prescriptions. Even though Dr. Meyers had explained how to use the medicines, Dr. Talbot, the pharmacist who had owned the store at the corner of 46th Avenue and Utopia Parkway had been there for twenty years, went over it again with Carrie. He cautioned her not to skip any doses and let her doctor know if there was any adverse reaction to the drugs.

When they got home, Buck unloaded the shopping bags and sent Carrie inside ahead of him. Rachel was sitting on the couch watching Eddie and Laura play. Eddie was coloring and Laura was serving tea to some of the many dolls Arlene and Beverly had bought for her.

"How were they, Mama?" asked Carrie.

"How should they be? They were perfect. They both are growing like weeds. They're going to need new clothes every month, I think," said Rachel.

Buck kissed Rachel and said, "OK, Mama, you're off-duty. We'll take it from here. See you tonight at six."

At about four that afternoon, the phone rang. It was Jack Merrill. "Buck! How's Carrie?"

"The doctor is going to watch her closely, but she says that everything is going as expected, so that's good news."

"Great, great! Listen, here's why I'm calling. Would you mind if I stopped down to rehearsal on Monday to see how things are going?"

"Sure, Jack. You've got a great ear so feedback from you would be welcome."

"Terrific. See you at about ten or so. Have a great weekend," said Jack, ringing off.

## A CHANGE OF KEY

Carrie and Buck made all the preparations for dinner and by half past five, they had set the table with eight places. Carrie even brought out the good china they hadn't used but twice since they were married. Rachel and the girls arrived promptly at six. Buck took their coats, kissed his sisters and said, "I sure hope you're all hungry because we made a very special meal tonight."

"Listen to this," said Beverly. "My brother the chef. So don't keep me in suspense. What's for dinner?"

"It's a surprise. Come to the table and we'll get started," said Carrie.

It was Beverly who noticed the extra place setting. "Who's coming to dinner, Bill or someone else in the orchestra?"

"We don't know—yet," said Buck.

"What do you mean you don't—" Beverly stopped short in mid-sentence.

Arlene started to laugh and said, "You mean you're—"

"Yep. You're going to be aunts again. Next September," said Carrie.

The girls squealed and came around to hug Carrie and Buck.

"Benjamin, it's going to get pretty crowded in this house, no?" said Rachel.

"No problem, Mama. "I'm going to move my office to the basement and that will free up a room on the second floor so all the kids can have their own rooms."

"Come here *mamala* and let me give you a hug," said Rachel to Carrie.

"Surprised, Mama?" said Carrie.

"Oh yes, very much so," said Rachel, winking at Buck over Carrie's shoulder.

The meal was everything Carrie hoped it would be. The girls were impressed by the individual Cornish hens and the wild rice stuffing was cooked to perfection. Carrie had bought some asparagus and wrapped them in bacon before baking them. "Good thing none of us keep kosher," said Arlene—because these things are delicious. A mixed salad and whipped potatoes dusted with paprika completed the menu.

"You weren't kidding about Benny being a chef," said Arlene to Beverly. "I don't think he learned how to do this in the Army."

"Hey, what about me?" said Carrie.

Arlene laughed. "Sweetheart, we already knew you were a *balabusta*. It's Benny who's the real shock."

Over dessert, Beverly said, "Tell us what you need and we'll get it for you."

"We're in good shape, sis. We still have all the baby clothes from Eddie and Laura. We were going to donate all of it to ORT America. Good thing we kept all of it."

ORT was an organization founded after the First World War to provide relief for Jews in Eastern Europe who had been impacted by the conflict. During and after World War II, it helped displaced Jews from all over Europe come to America or Israel and provide them with life's basics after what so many had endured in Hitler's death camps. Two million Jewish children had perished during the Holocaust, but there were still plenty alive who were in need of all the help they could get.

"No, no. You donate those things, Benny," said Arlene. "We've got this covered."

"Not too much, girls! Some day you're going to have kids of your own, so you better start saving your money now," said Benny, looking directly at Arlene.

Carrie almost spit her coffee back into her cup and Arlene blushed, turning away from Buck's knowing look.

Soon Carrie said she had to get the kids ready for bed and so Rachel and the girls cleared the dishes, got their coats and left. When Carrie came back into the kitchen she said, "Well Bucky, I guess Arlene now knows that you know."

"Knows what?" said Buck, all innocent.

## A CHANGE OF KEY

Carrie punched him in the shoulder. "Have you spoken to Al yet?"

"No, but next week for sure. And anyway, what am I supposed to say to him, treat my sister right or I'll have some gunsel rub you out?"

"Of course not, silly. Just tell him how welcome an addition to the family he would be—and then tell him he better treat Arlene right or you'll have him rubbed out."

"Uh huh," said Buck. He still didn't know quite how he could even approach the topic with Al, but he'd figure it out. Arlene was not as experienced with men as Beverly. For that reason, Buck was very protective of her, but he knew the quality of man that Al Rovitz was and if he could make Arlene happy, what else mattered?

They finished with the dishes, went to the bedroom where they undressed each other, and then nestled in bed until they both fell asleep, having had a busy but productive day.

# CHAPTER NINE
### *"She's the One:" Monday Morning*

Buck arrived at the rehearsal hall first thing Monday morning. Kip and most of the musicians were already there warming up. There was a young woman who Buck had not seen before standing with Kip. He brought her over to Buck and said, "Buck, this is Pamela Wendorfer."

"It's Pam or Pammy, Mr. Fisher. Only my professors ever called me Pamela."

"Nice to meet you, Pammy. What can I do for you?"

It was Kip who answered. "I spoke to the Music chairman at Julliard and told him what we were looking for. He immediately recommended Pam."

The girl was carrying a portfolio and she opened it and handed Buck a few sheets of music. The musical notation was absolutely exquisite. It looked like it had been printed by a commercial music publisher. He leafed through sheet after sheet and each one looked perfect.

"What did you major in at Julliard, Pammy?" asked Buck.

"I was a flute major. I had hopes of playing in a symphony some day but every inquiry I made---from Boston to San Francisco—the answer was the same: sorry, but the chairs are filled. I never even got to do an audition, which is pretty sad considering I've been playing since I was seven years old."

"Yeah, I know how tough it is out there for long-hairs. But I must say, your musical penmanship is amazing, Pammy," said Buck, "but I don't know if Kip explained that time is of the essence for us. He needs the parts copied from the scores he writes almost on a daily basis because the orchestra is in constant need of new material."

"Give me a try, Mr. Fisher. You won't be disappointed," said Pam.

## A CHANGE OF KEY

"Buck. It's Buck. Did Kip tell you about the money situation? Do you want to be freelance or come to work for us here at RCA?"

"Thing about freelance, Mr.—um, Buck—is that there just aren't that many bands around that are looking for a copyist. So if it's all the same to you, yes, I'd like to be a full-time employee."

Buck had an idea. "Kip, we're an orchestra rather than a band. Do you think in some of the ballads you could work some flute lines into the arrangements? None of the guys in the sax section triples, though they all play clarinet, of course."

Kip's eyes lit up. "I sure could, Buck, and it would really add something to the charts—a new tonal dimension."

"What do you say, Pammy? Would you like to do double-duty and play on some of Kip's arrangements?"

"Oh gee! That would be fantastic, Buck," said Pam.

"It might mean you have to stay up late doing the copying if you're here all day for rehearsals," said Buck. "Sometimes they run later than that."

That made Pam laugh. "They worked us so hard at Julliard, Buck, I never got to sleep before one, two in the morning. So staying up late is what I'm used to," she said.

"Ah to be young again," said Buck. "OK, you're not going to be on every chart, but I'm going to get an extra thousand bucks out of Jack Merrill for you. How does that sound?"

Pam Wendorfer threw her arms around Buck and said, "I'm going to work my butt off for you, Buck. That's a promise."

By this time, Al McCormack and Fran had arrived. As Al was putting together his alto, Buck said to the orchestra, "Fellas, can I have a moment with you please?"

The band settled down and everyone took their seats.

"I just wanted to tell you that I have some news." There was a pregnant pause as some of the players leaned in closer. "I'm going to be a father again."

## A CHANGE OF KEY

"Holy shit!" said Chuck Fein. "I'm gonna be an uncle again!" He laid his bass fiddle down and came down to wrap Buck in his massive arms. "When's all this happening, buddy?"

"Next September. We saw the doctor on Friday."

As the orchestra members applauded, Fran Michaels came up to Buck and kissed him. "Send our love to Carrie, Buck. And congratulations."

"Got the new chart, Kip?" asked Buck.

"Right here, boss."

Buck had asked Kip to write an arrangement of "I Know Why (And So Do You)," a Glenn Miller song that first appeared in *Sun Valley Serenade,* one of two Twentieth Century Fox movies made specifically for the Miller band. The film starred John Payne and Lynn Bari. On the soundtrack, Lynn Bari lip-synched the Mack Gordon lyric but the actual singer was Pat Friday. Buck thought it was one of the most beautiful songs his friend Glenn Miller ever recorded. The melody by Harry Warren was romantic and emotional. Buck could hear the 'Miller Sound' in his head. Whenever he heard the song or that sound his heart ached for his dead friend, another casualty of World War II. The song also featured the Modernaires with Paula Kelly doing the background vocals., but in Kip's arrangement, Fran would have to carry the whole song since as of yet, there were no background singers on board.

Kip handed out the parts and he said to Fran, "Do you need the lyric sheet?"

"No thanks, I know the song very well. I love it."

Fran didn't just love the lyric; she simply made love to it. Kip's arrangement provided that lush string sound behind her vocal, and the reeds who had switched to clarinet also contributed to the beauty of the chart. Unbeknownst to Buck, who was concentrating intently on the song, Jack Merrill had slipped into the rehearsal hall behind him. When the song ended, Jack said, "Oh my God, this girl is perfect!"

## A CHANGE OF KEY

Buck turned around, saw Jack and shook hands with him. "She's one of the main reasons my band was so successful, Jack. Anyone who heard her sing fell in love with her voice instantly."

"She's the one, Buck. We have to get this girl onto an LP right away. How are you doing with repertoire for her?"

"We've got five ballads for sure—six with this last song. But we have to mix some up-tempo tunes into the mix. We're going to need a couple of weeks of rehearsal before we finalize the playlist. If you'd like, we'll invite you down to hear her sing the whole list."

"Yes, fine, that's fine, Buck. We also have to have the art department get to work on a photo shoot for the front of the album. That'll take at least a full day. And I want you to think about writing the liner notes for the LP. Who better to do that than you?"

"Buck?" said Fran, "I have an idea for a song I think is perfect for me. As long as Jack is here, maybe we could see what he thinks too."

"Bing Crosby had a big hit with it in 1943. "I'll Be Home for Christmas." During the war while Pete and you were in the Army, every time I heard the song, it made me cry," said Fran.

It was no wonder. The song by Kim Gannon and Walter Kent was written from the point of view of a G.I. overseas during the war, longing for the simple pleasures of a Christmas at home. Certainly the song resonated with the soldiers during the Battle of the Bulge in that freezing Christmas at Bastogne. The song touched the hearts of all Americans and since Crosby's recording, other artists had tried their hands at the song.

"Kip, come on over here," said Buck. He explained what Fran wanted to do.

"It's a beautiful song, Buck, and I know she could absolutely kill it, but I just have one little doubt," said Kip.

"What's that?"

"Do you think it's too much of a downer on the LP? I know we have a lot of sentimental ballads, but is this one too much? Oh, and another thing: if Fran's album is a success, maybe we should give some thought to an entire album of Christmas materials."

Jack Merrill who was listening to the exchange of ideas said, "You know, Buck, I think maybe Kip is onto something here. If Fran hits it big with the first LP, yes, we can do a whole Christmas album and have it ready for November or December of this year. Fran? What do you think?"

"I'm thrilled that you guys have so much confidence in me, but one question. If it's recorded now, can't it be pieced into another LP at a later date?" asked Fran.

"Absolutely," said Jack. "Just as long as we have a good master, we can use it at any time."

"OK, it's settled then," said Buck. "Kip? You've got some homework."

"No problem, boss."

"Now, how about this orchestra play some of the new arrangements for me so I can hear some more of Fran's singing. And just to mix it up, can they do some of your swing charts too?" asked Jack.

"I think the band would like that, Jack," said Buck. "Grab a chair and you can be our one-person audience."

Buck called out the songs in the book that he wanted the orchestra to showcase for Jack Merrill; some were Johnny Blair's.

For the next hour, the RCA Studio Orchestra strutted its stuff for the president of the division. When they had finished and Kip gave them a break, Jack Merrill said, "Jesus, Buck, that was tremendous. You've done wonders in such a short time. I had a time frame in mind of about five or six months to make it all happen; you did it in a matter of weeks. How much are we paying Kip?"

"Fifteen thousand a year," said Buck.

"Let's bump him up another ten. This kid's got a talent and I don't want to lose him."

**A CHANGE OF KEY**

Jack then told the orchestra what a great job they were doing and he returned to his office and his duties of running a huge component of RCA Victor.

When Buck told Kip about his raise, he could hardly believe it. "I haven't really done that much yet, Buck. But I sure am grateful."

"Then I want you to really get on the stick and start grinding out materials for this outfit. See if you can get some flute writing into it for Pammy and huddle up with Franny and see what other songs she would like to do for the LP. Remember, we need some up-tempo songs as well as ballads."

"You've got it, Buck. Every day I'll have new arrangements."

"OK, keep rehearsing for another few hours and then send them home. I need to talk to Bill and Al."

…..

Back in his office, Buck huddled up with Bill and Al to discuss further plans for his division. "We need to start scouting out new talent, guys. I want you to get together with Kelsey, see who's playing in clubs in the city and check them out this weekend. Monday you'll let me know what you've heard and if there are any prospects I should give a listen to."

"Do you want us to talk to them, Buck?" asked Bill.

"Not just yet, Bill. Not till I've had a chance to hear them. Then maybe I'll do the talking or Jack wants, he'll have someone from legal show up with contracts to sign them to the label. Eventually, you'll be able to sign them up yourselves."

"Kel? What do you have for us? Anything coming up this weekend? "said Buck.

"According to *Cue,* Buck, there are a lot of jazz clubs on 52$^{nd}$ Street. That seems to be where a lot of bands are playing these days."

"Sure, it's been that way since they repealed Prohibition. They call it 'Swing Street.' That used to be 133$^{rd}$ Street up in

## A CHANGE OF KEY

Harlem, but I guess they all moved downtown. So who's playing?"

"This weekend at the Three Deuces, there's a sax player who a lot of people are talking about. You might want to give him a listen," said Kelsey.

"What's his name?" asked Buck.

"Charlie Parker. He's there with a quartet this weekend through next weekend," she said.

"OK, Bill, I want you to catch his act and see what you think," said Buck.

The rest of the week passed with Kip providing more arrangements and finding ways to give the orchestra different sonorities. He had a knack for orchestrations that was surprising for someone right out of college. No wonder Jack Merrill wanted to keep him.

…..

Monday morning, Bill Dwyer met with Buck at ten. "Hey, Jack, how was the weekend. What's with this Parker guy?" asked Buck when Bill had sat down. Al Rovitz joined them a few minutes later.

Bill's expression was hard to read. "I tell you Buck, I never heard anything like this in my life."

"Meaning?"

"He's got high octane in his fingers. I never heard anyone play as fast as this guy. No one's even close. But I don't understand what he's doing," said Bill.

"How so?"

"Remember, Buck, I'm not a musician. But here's the thing: take a song like 'April in Paris.' He plays the melody line or close to it. Then he takes off on this endless solo—and you can't identify any part of the melody again. It just disappears totally. If you came into the club a minute after the song started, you would never have any idea what song he was playing."

## A CHANGE OF KEY

"I've been asking around, Buck," said Al. "They call this kind of music 'be-bop' but don't ask me what that even means."

"I talked to some people at the Three Deuces, Buck. They obviously were fans of this Parker guy and they say this is the wave of the future. They tell me half the clubs on 52$^{nd}$ street feature be-bop players," said Bill.

"Anybody notable backing him up," asked Buck.

Bill took a piece of paper from his suit jacket and said, "Tommy Potter, Miles Davis, Max Roach and Duke Jordan. This Davis guy on trumpet was doing the same thing as Parker. A mile a minute on his solo."

"Is he just playing on weekends or is he there mid-week, Bill?" asked Buck. "Both," said Bill.

"OK, thanks Bill. See who else is on the street and keep checking them out. I think I need to hear this Parker for myself," said Buck.

When Bill and Al returned to their office, Buck picked up the phone and called Carrie. "Hi, hon. Just me. Don't hold dinner for me tonight. I have to hear a sax player over on 52$^{nd}$ Street. I'll stay for a set or two and then come home."

"I'll leave a plate in the oven, darling, just in case I'm asleep when you get here," said Carrie.

Next, he called the Three Deuces and made a reservation for the night's show. Buck left 30 Rock at about six that evening and drove to 52$^{nd}$ Street. He parked in a lot off of 8$^{th}$ Avenue and walked in the cold night air to the club.

The Three Deuces was a smallish venue that held perhaps a hundred people. The tables were small and close together and a cloud of blue smoke hovered over the entire interior. At the back of the club was where the band set up. It was not a bandstand as such, but there really wasn't enough room for that.

At about eight o'clock, the musicians took their places. Charlie Parker was the last to emerge from what was evidently a back stage area with dressing rooms. He welcomed the crowd and

## A CHANGE OF KEY

kicked off the set with the 1939 Rogers and Hart Standard, "I Didn't Know What Time it Was." Buck immediately understood what Bill Dwyer was saying in his assessment of Charlie Parker. To begin with, the song, a natural ballad, was played at least three times as fast as anyone else did it. The melody sped by so fast that a listener couldn't even fit the words to the music. Then Parker was off on his ride—which lasted for over five minutes. His speed and dexterity were both phenomenal, but like Bill had said, where was the melody? It seemed that Parker was playing the chord changes with no regard for the need to return to the melody of the tune. Leaps, runs, glides into notes off the natural range of the horn, no repetition of any figure he had played—it was an amazing performance.

Parker then announced a tune called "Ornithology," which evidently the crowd was familiar with because they roared with approval as they did the following tune, "Yardbird Suite." Four songs later, the set came to an end with the audience as exhausted as the quartet.

Buck got up from his table and went to the bandstand where he introduced himself to Charlie Parker, giving him a business card with the RCA trademark on it.

"Well, well!" exclaimed Parker. "Buck Fisher! This is a real honor. Come to my dressing room and have a drink with me."

The dressing room was tiny but there was a vanity with a mirror on the wall above it, and a collection of bottles on its surface. Parker poured three fingers of Gordon's Gin for himself and offered a glass and the bottle to Buck."

"Oh, no thanks. Doctor's orders. Still a little bit banged up inside," said Buck.

"Yeah, I heard about your injury during the war, Buck. Hell, everybody heard about it. As I recollect, I was playing at Clark Monroe's Uptown House in Harlem when we heard the news. You were a national hero, you know, and Coleman Hawkins once said to me, 'If I was white, I'd want to play like Buck Fisher.'

## A CHANGE OF KEY

There's no one like him.' Lots of people praying for you back then, Mr. Fisher. I can tell you that."

"Buck. It's Buck."

"So what brings you to this little night spot, Buck?"

"I heard amazing things about you and wanted to hear for myself."

"Well, what do you think?"

"I think I never heard anyone play alto like you before. What kind of horn do you use?"

"My horn is a King Super 20. When I play, I feel like it's part of my body. I blow into it and it does just what I want it to do. But what about the style, Buck? What do you think of it?"

'It impresses me; it confuses me; it angers me—all at the same time."

Parker laughed. "Good! That's what we're trying to do, Buck. You were a great tenor player. Right up there with Prez, Ben Webster and Hawk. But what you've done has been done. Again and again. We're looking to do something different musically. No offense, Buck, but we be-bop musicians call your style of play 'moldy figs.' You probably felt the same way about Louis and Kid Ory's music. It was dated. Don't get me wrong. The music you made, people will be listening to it a hundred years from now. But our kind of music is just getting started. We're finally getting airplay. Ever hear of a DJ named Symphony Sid? He loves our stuff and gets it on the air whenever his program director lets him."

"So you think this is the wave of the future, Charlie?" asked Buck.

Parker knocked back the gin and poured himself another. "There are some great players who play be-pop. Miles Davis—you heard him tonight, Dizzy Gillespie, and there's a tenor player who just got out of the Navy name of John Coltrane. He plays a lot like me, but on tenor—but he goes even further."

"How so?" asked Buck.

## A CHANGE OF KEY

"He's experimenting with a lot of modal stuff. You know, Dorian, Lydian, Mixolydian, Phrygian."

Buck laughed and said, "Charlie, you could be talking Chinese to me with that stuff. I never went to college or studied music formally."

"Neither did he, but you'd be amazed what you pick up along the way," said Parker.

"So you think this is the future of jazz?" said Buck.

"Put it to you this way: it's my future in jazz. We're gonna push the envelope as far as we can. See, key word is 'experimenting.' Music gotta keep moving forward, Buck, if you know what I mean."

"I guess that makes me a fossil in a museum," said Buck.

"Not at all. I got me some of your 78s. Had 'em for years. I'll tell you this: I never heard a sweeter tone come out of anyone's tenor that could match yours. Ole' Ben Webster uses that subtone. I don't dig that. Sounds like he's blowing through a comb and tissue paper. And those long-ass rides you took on some of those swing charts? Prez never did anything like that. Frankly, some of his solos, he kept repeating the same figure over and over again—like in that 'Lester Leaps In' chart he did with Basie. See? You constantly created on every ride you took. You're not that different from me, except you did it to the melody and I'm doing it to the chords. In the second set, I'm gonna play a song called 'Moose the Mooch.' The melody is my own—but the chord progression?" Here he laughed. "It's nothing more than the chords from 'I Got Rhythm.' Listen carefully and you can superimpose that melody over what I'm playing. That's what be-bop is all about, Buck. Chords and the scales associated with those chords."

"Let me tell you why I'm here, Charlie," said Buck.

Again Parker laughed, "Had me a feeling you didn't just drop in out of nowhere."

"I'm now vice-president at RCA Victor and my job is to find talent, sign it up and develop it into a marketable commodity that will appeal to the public and make the artists rich. Are you currently under contract to a label?"

"Well, Buck, we record for the Savoy label. They're small, but I'll tell you why I like them. They leave me alone. I can play what I like the way I like and no executive who don't know beans about music looks over my shoulder and says to do it differently. I'm not saying your that kind of guy, but big labels like Victor are all about money. They have it in their minds what music should be like, and they don't like it when you leave the reservation, so to speak. Fact is, once my contract with Savoy is up, I'm thinking I'll go independent—record for any label that'll give me studio time."

"I respect that, Charlie. But let me leave you with this thought. You have my card. If you ever change your mind, or even want to just talk things over, give me a call. From what I heard tonight, I can tell you're right on your way to the top of the pyramid. I think we could be a big part of that, but I'll leave that up to you. I'm going to listen to some of the second set; then I have to get home to my wife and kids."

Charlie Parker extended his hand and said, "Someday, I'll tell my own kids that I met the great Buck Fisher—and he offered me a job! Gotta get back to the band now. Great talking to you."

Buck stayed for three numbers in the second set: "Ko-Ko," "Moose the Mooch," and "April in Paris." His reaction was the same as it had been to the first set. Utterly amazed at Parker's speed, but dumbfounded at what he was hearing and trying to understand. If the chords to "I've Got Rhythm" were the same as "Moose the Mooch," you could have fooled him, because he heard nothing that he could recognize.

If Charlie Parker was correct and this was the future of jazz, Buck seriously wondered how he could possibly fit into that world.

A CHANGE OF KEY

# CHAPTER TEN
*"How Can We Help?" March, 1946*

After weeks of rehearsal, polishing and adjusting Kip Roman's charts, Buck felt that the orchestra was ready to lay down the tracks for Fran Michaels' LP. There were over thirty charts from which to choose the playlist and when Buck asked Jack Merrill if he wanted final approval, Jack said, "This is your show, Buck. You're the musician so I trust you to put this package together the best way possible so that it sells."

The photo shoot for the cover of the LP jacket took almost an entire day. Jack had brought in a hair and make-up specialist and that took nearly ninety minutes to get Fran's look just right. Buck thought that such preening and primping was unnecessary because she was so beautiful even without a stitch of make-up.

Paul Gennet was the photographer for the session. He was a free-lance photographer whose work had appeared in *Life, Look,* and *Time* magazines. When he saw Fran, he said to Buck, "She's quite something, isn't she?"

"She sure is, so treat her with kid gloves," said Buck.

"Leave everything to me. We'll do right by her."

There was no reason for Buck to stick around for the photo shoot so he told Paul to forward the glossies to him when he was finished processing and printing them.

Back in the office, Buck met with Bill and Al to discuss where they would be scouting for talent. Buck described his experience listening to Charlie Parker. "I don't get this be-bop jazz and I don't care for the sound—but there's so much buzz about it that maybe we have to keep our eyes and ears open and sign up some of these players and groups."

"The trick is, Buck, to find players that haven't already signed with these two-bit labels that have them locked in for years," said Al.

## A CHANGE OF KEY

"Yeah, well, that's what we're here for. OK, Al, I want you to get up to Harlem to the Lafayette Theatre. There's a stage show up there and I want you to check out a group called The Bluebirds. I think there's a big market out there for Negro singing groups. Look at how successful the Ink Spots have been."

The Lafayette Theatre was located on 132$^{nd}$ Street and 7$^{th}$ Avenue. It could hold 1500 people and was notable because as far back as 1923, Duke Ellington made his New York debut there when he was working in Wilbur Sweatman's band. It hosted plays as well as variety shows. The Bluebirds were on that weekend's bill along with Bill 'Bojangles' Robinson, one of the world's greatest tap dancers, and Chick Webb's band, moonlighting from its regular gig at the Savoy Ballroom.

"Check them out, Al, and see what you think. Find out if they're contracted to a label yet."

"Got it. You'll have a full report Monday morning," said Al.

"Bill, I've got news for you too," said Buck.

"I'm open to anything, Buck, you know that."

"Good, you better be, because you're going to San Francisco this weekend, said Buck.

"Huh? Why San Francisco?"

"I was talking to Jack and he's heard that there are some amazing players out there doing really unique stuff. I need them checked out and if they're good enough, maybe get them to come to New York. I know it's going to be tough on Cathy and the kids, Bill, but it's part of the job."

"Don't worry about Cathy, Buck. She got to be very independent when I was in the Army and she can do well without me for a while. By the way, how long are we talking about me being there?"

"I figure a week out there should do it. And I'll have Carrie check on Cathy every day. I can't guarantee that you'll find anything we can use out there, but it's worth a look."

## A CHANGE OF KEY

Buck then called Kelsey into his office. "Kel? I need you to make flight reservations and hotel arrangements for Bill in San Francisco. I want you to arrange for a car and driver for him for as long as he's there."

"Leaving when, Buck?" asked Kelsey.

"See if you can get him an early morning flight out of LaGuardia for Thursday morning. And Bill? You're on an expense account. You make sure you don't skip any meals—just bring me receipts for everything you spend."

"OK, Buck, let me go call Cathy and tell her to start packing a bag for me."

…..

When Buck got home that night, Carrie said, "You better call Mama, darling. I think something is going on."

His initial thought was that Al had proposed to Arlene, but the expression on Carrie's face indicated that it was something else. "OK, how about I wash up and you give Mom a call and tell her to come over. She can stay to dinner if she'd like."

Carrie called and five minutes later, Rachel, Arlene and Beverly came into the house. "Let me have your coats," said Buck. "Did you all eat yet?"

"We ate Benny," said Beverly. "But thanks."

"All right, then, let's hear what the problem is," said Buck.

"Arlene, maybe you could explain better than me," said Rachel. "You're better with words," said Rachel.

"Benny, I want you to think all the way back to 1938—that K*ristalnacht* thing in Germany. Remember?"

"Hard to forget," said Buck.

"Right after that, they started rounding up Jews all over Europe and putting them in camps. Mama was terrified when she heard the news because we still had some relatives in Poland."

"OK, I'm with you so far," said Buck.

## A CHANGE OF KEY

"We got a call today from a representative of the United Nations Relief and Rehabilitation Administration. These people try to get the survivors of the death camps back to their countries, but with anti-Semitism still running through Europe, many survivors don't want to go home. They want to emigrate to other countries. Most want to go to Palestine where so many other Jews live."

"But?" said Buck.

"Some want to go to other countries—especially if they have relatives there," said Arlene.

"President Truman has changed some of the immigration rules and giving precedence to widows with children," added Beverly.

"First of all, who are these relatives? I've never heard of them before," said Buck.

Here Rachel said, "My cousin Mila Sadowsky and her two children Zofia and Agnieska. My aunt Magda's children."

"Where did they live before Hitler started rounding up Jews?" asked Buck.

"They lived in Krakow. Mila was a doctor. So was her husband, but he died early form a heart attack," said Rachel.

"The man from the U.N. said they were all at Bergen-Belsen," said Arlene.

"Which is?"

"Was. A death camp. One of Hitler's murder factories. Along with places like Auschwitz and Treblinka. Now it's a Displaced Persons camp. There are tens of thousands of people there—all survivors of the camps," said Beverly.

"I see," said Buck. "How can we help?"

"The U.N. representative said that if a relative will act as a sponsor, it could really cut through all the red tape and get them over here pretty quickly," said Arlene. "There are requirements that have to be met," she added.

"What's involved in being a sponsor," asked Buck.

"We'd have to set them up in an apartment, get the kids registered for school and help Mila get a job. The UNRRA will provide a stipend to help until they get on their feet."

"Do these people speak any English, Ma?" asked Buck.

"Some, Benjamin. Like you studied Spanish in school, in Poland they study English."

"Well, heck, I was so bad at Spanish I wouldn't last ten minutes in Spain," said Buck.

"You didn't try very hard, Benjamin. The girls did much better than you," said Rachel.

"True. Well, look, money's not the problem. This is family. Did the man from the U.N. leave a call back number?" asked Buck.

"Yes, it's back at the house," said Arlene.

"Call him first thing in the morning. Bev? There's a new apartment building over on about 168$^{th}$ Street across Horace Harding Boulevard. Call them in the morning and see if they have any apartments for rent. Has to be two bedrooms. If they say yes, I'll write a check for the first month's rent and any security deposit they need."

Buck's two sisters hugged him and Rachel said, "Benjamin, you are such a good boy. How can I thank you?"

"Thank me, Ma? How many years did you do my laundry, clean up after me, cook for me? I'd say I'm the one who should thank you. And remember, you always taught us there was nothing more important than family."

When Rachel and the girls left, Carrie said, "This is going to be great for Ma, Bucky. It's the only family she has and the kids will have cousins. I was never close with mine growing up and I missed that."

"And she was a doctor. I'm impressed," said Buck.

"I don't think she can practice in America unless she went back to school, but I'm not sure. It would be great if she could practice again," said Carrie.

"Now that we have that all settled, Mrs. Feinstein, do you plan on feeding me tonight?"

"Since you asked nicely, of course. Let me get the kids and we'll have dinner in about fifteen minutes. Then after we put the kids to bed, you can put me to bed—and make love to me until I howl like a banshee."

"In that case, let's skip dessert."

…..

A week later, Jack Merrill called Buck to his office. "Buck, we have to move quickly on Fran's album. Columbia is going all in on these LPs and we're pretty far behind them. You need to get together with our A & R people and pick some of our big names. Then from their repertoires, pick about 14 songs we can get onto an LP album."

"Jack, I don't know anything about these LPs. How they work or anything," said Buck.

"That's why I set up a meeting for you with our engineers. They'll go over the whole process with you. It'll probably sound like gibberish to you, but that's OK. What's important is that you get those selections made soon as you can."

"Got it," said Buck.

"And Buck? One more thing: One of our first LPs is going to be 'The Best of the Buck Fisher Orchestra,' so you pick out your fourteen best tracks."

"Come on, Jack, you think anyone remembers any of that? Hell, I feel like some old-timer you're hauling out of retirement or something."

Merrill laughed and said, "Bucky, only Glenn Miller had more million selling records than you. He had the very first one with 'Chatanooga Choo Choo,' and had about a dozen more—but you were right behind him. People followed your career in the Army and the whole country prayed for you when you got hurt, so simple answer? Yes. Most of America remembers you—fondly. The chance to own a whole album of your songs instead of fourteen separate 78s? We're banking on that LP really taking us off and putting us in the game with Columbia."

Down in the Audio Engineering Department, Buck met with Phil Flagler, one of the technical whizzes at RCA. For the next hour he extolled the virtues of Long-Playing records in terminology that went completely over Buck's head.

"It's all about speed, Buck. See, the 78s, as their name indicates, were recorded at 78 rotations per minute—that's damned fast. The new LPs only rotate at 33 1/3 RPMs. But the trick is to avoid the distortion that happens at a slower speed. I won't bore you with how we handle that; it's pretty complex."

The last thing Buck needed was a scientific excursus on sound distortion.

"Another thing, Buck, is high frequency hiss," said Flagler.

"See, the slower the speed, the more apt a recording is to pick up any extraneous sounds. So we had to come up with a method to filter out a lot of that noise to keep the recordings clean."

"And you succeeded?" asked Buck.

"Not entirely, but we're getting a lot closer. Most of that high frequency noise is too high for the human ear—but there's still a little that bleeds in. Given enough time, we'll figure out a way to filter all of it out. We've got some of the best sound engineers in the business working right here."

"Will it diminish the overall sound and make people not want to buy these LPs?" asked Buck.

"Not unless they're Superman with super hearing. Unless you're specifically listening for it, you probably won't even notice it," said Flagler.

"How much time can we get on a side of an LP?" asked Buck.

"Right now, about 40-42 minutes. In time, we might up that by about 6 or 7 more," said Flagler.

## A CHANGE OF KEY

"So a total of about an hour's worth of music to an LP," said Buck.

"I'd leave myself some leeway there. Keep it closer to 50 minutes."

"That works out to about 7 songs per side, 6 if they run over three minutes. That's going to be tight and we might have to adjust the arrangements to fit that time limitation."

"Well, Buck, that's your department. I'm sure you'll figure it out," said Flagler.

"Let's hope so. Thanks for the tour, Phil. If I have any more questions, I'll drop by," said Buck.

"Anytime. We don't get too many visitors down here," said Flagler. They shook hands and Buck returned to his office.

.....

Al Rovitz was waiting for Buck when he returned from Engineering. "Morning, buddy. What's going on?" said Al.

"Ugh. Just had a seminar on the finer points of LPs—how they're made and what their problems are. My head's swimming. I never was terribly good at science in high school. The stuff the guy downstairs told me was way beyond that."

"Yeah, well he probably can't play saxophone. Now, let me tell you what I heard last weekend when I saw the Bluebirds."

"OK. Let's hear."

"First, I hate their name. It's just a little bit wishy-washy. Maybe if we sign them, we can get them to change their name. I spoke to Ty Terrell and Billy and Roy Richards. They're twins. The fourth member of the group is fella named Bobby Nunn."

"What's the second thing," asked Buck.

"Well, boss, they ain't the Ink Spots. Tell you the truth, I never liked the Ink Spots. All they sang were these syrupy ballads and I thought the lead tenor's voice sounded fake to me. It's like they could never sing anything up-beat."

"Thank you, Deems Taylor, for that incisive analysis. What about these guys?"

## A CHANGE OF KEY

"I talked to a bunch of people at the Lafayette Theatre. They're singing in a style called Rhythm and Blues—and it's a real up and coming sound for Negro musicians. In fact, there's a separate hit chart for what's being called 'race music.' It's exclusively for Negro performers. There are a lot of groups out there singing in this style, and I don't know why, but they love bird names—The Orioles, The Crows, The Ravens., all pretty much in the same style."

"So what is it about this style? What's different?"

"For one thing, they aren't locked into slow stuff like the Ink Spots. Those guys musta been allergic to up-beat music. These guys, well, they could swing. Lots of up-beat songs, and a totally different blend than say the Mills Brothers. Totally different harmonies and they often use a bass lead instead of a tenor."

"Jesus, Al, you're starting to sound like a musician instead of a milk company exec."

"Well, let's just say I've been doing my homework."

"What about signing them?" asked Buck.

"Most of these groups record for really small labels. Except the Ravens. They're with Columbia. But, Buck, the whole 'race' thing. You think the execs at Victor will go for that?"

"If I convince them that there's a huge market for this kind of music, they'll go for it in a flash. Look, I want you to go back to the Lafayette, see them again and try to get one of them to come in to see me. In the meantime, I'll make the pitch to Jack and let's see if we can get them on a contract and start recording them."

"I'm telling you, Buck, this stuff is brand new. It's gritty, edgy. The Mills Brothers were smooth as a baby's ass compared to these guys—but their singing sure won over the crowd at the Lafayette."

…..

That night, Carrie made a big dinner for Buck and the children, but it took its toll. The following morning Carrie had her worst bout of morning sickness and she threw up some blood mixed with bile and the remnants of what she ate. Buck insisted that the following morning she call Dr. Meyers and he would not leave for work until she spoke to her.

"Bring her right in and we'll check her out," said Dr. Meyers.

"Bucky, it's not necessary. I really feel all right now," said Carrie.

"Nothing doing, sweets. You're going to the doctor."

An hour later they were in Flushing waiting to be seen. The nurse ushered them into an examination room and since it was not a vaginal examination, Buck could stay with her.

The examination was thorough but Dr. Meyers said, "This isn't that unusual, but to really see what's going on, she would have to see a specialist who could look down way past her throat into the lining of the esophagus. She'd have to be put under for that. I think we can wait awhile before we do that, though. I'm not fond of general anesthesia for pregnant women. For now, let's try this: I want Carrie to be on a fairly bland diet. Nothing too hard to digest."

"I know a good deal about that, Dr. Meyers," said Buck.

"Yes, I'm sure after your wartime injury, you were on just such a diet for quite some time," said Dr. Meyers.

"Actually, I still have to be reasonably careful about what I eat," said Buck.

"Good, then you can help Carrie with picking things that are healthy for her. Let's have her back here in two weeks to see if things settle down."

Buck drove Carrie home and settled her in; then he left for the city arriving at 30 Rock by half past eleven. He stopped by the studio where Fran and the orchestra were making adjustments to Kip's arrangements. Buck had explained to Kip the time limitations for one side of an LP. To fit in eight songs per side, they could be no more than four minutes in length—slightly more if they dropped down to seven on a side. Still, to be able to cue up one LP and hear the better part of an hour's worth of music was a vast improvement over having to change records seven or eight times. These vinyl LPs represented a huge leap forward in recording technology, but RCA was still playing catch-up ball with Columbia. For that reason, Buck would do as Jack had suggested and examine every RCA's performer's catalogue to see if there was enough good material to fill an LP.

The easiest to examine was his own band's work. For the LP entitled, "The Best of the Buck Fisher Orchestra," he chose thirteen cuts. Some of them featured extended solos that he had played, so there would be fewer songs on his LP.

"Here's what you have to remember," Jack Merrill had said, "you don't want to shoot your whole load on one LP. You've had eight million-selling records. But if you put them all on one record, what do you leave for a follow-up? Every album inevitably has some 'filler' songs on it. That's how it works from the marketing point of view—not the artistic point of view. But we're here to make money, so sometimes we have to bow to the wishes of those people who have to sell the products."

"But is it really a 'best of' album, Jack?" Buck had asked.

That made Jack laugh heartily. "Buck, are you kidding? The way your Bluebird discs sold, everything was a hit, even if it didn't hit the gold record mark. I wouldn't worry too much about the numbers you put on an album."

That made the task of picking songs easier for Buck, but he was adamant about the nature of the 'filler' numbers. Every one of them had to be high quality. If he was going to run this division, it was going to be based on excellence, not throw-away crap.

Al Rovitz knocked on Buck's door at about noon and said, "Boss? Let's do lunch. I've got some news for you."

"Great. Where do you want to go?" said Buck.

"Well, the Rainbow Room is out," said Al. The world-famous restaurant on the 65$^{th}$ floor of the RCA Building opened

**A CHANGE OF KEY**

in 1934, but because of World War II, it was closed and wasn't scheduled to reopen until 1950, after a full renovation.

"Let's go to the concourse. There are a bunch of places to eat down there," said Buck.

The concourse of the RCA building was accessed via banks of escalators. There were dozens of retail shops, eateries and specialty boutiques which made it a shopper's paradise. It also had a direct entrance to the 47$^{th}$-50$^{th}$ Street subway station on the F Train which made it very convenient for shoppers and tourists alike to get to the building.

Buck and Al found a coffee shop that was very crowded since it was the lunch hour, but they scored a table in the rear of the dining area and settled in as a waitress brought menus to the table and took drink orders.

Al ordered a double cheeseburger with fries and onion rings and a chocolate malted. Buck ordered a cheese omelet with a side of ham and coffee.

"I hate you," said Buck when Al's mammoth order was delivered. "You eat like a pig in a sty but you never gain an ounce. How the hell do you do that?"

Al laughed and said, "Dunno. I've been this way all my life. I guess I have a really high metabolism or something. Buck's order looked tiny in comparison.

"OK, so what's the news?" asked Buck.

"Next Tuesday I've got Ty Terrell of the Bluebirds coming in with his group. He'd like to audition for you. We can use a small studio and since they do a lot of *a capella* stuff, they don't need any backup. When I saw them at the Lafayette, all they had backing them was drums, a bass and a guitar. You can get a pretty good idea of what they sound like."

"That's great work, Al. Do they have enough stuff for an entire LP?"

"Maybe not yet, but their small label—it's called Spark— has been releasing their songs on those new 45s. They seem to be selling very well, especially with Negro buyers. That's the target audience for this rhythm and blues stuff. I think we can lure them away and onto Victor which could open up a whole new customer base for RCA."

"Thing is, Al, like it or not, RCA is kind of a white company. True, we have under contract Negro artists from Duke Ellington to Etta James to Fletcher Henderson and a dozen or more in between. But now we're asking them to take a chance on a new group with ground-breaking material. But I tell you what, I'll be there to give a listen and if they are good as you say, I'll push Jack to sign them."

"Fair enough," said Buck. "What else is going on?"

"Not much, really. Been keeping busy working with Bill and I'm going to marry your sister."

Buck spit a piece of omelet back onto his plate. "Run that by me again, Al."

"C'mon Buck, don't tell me you didn't have a hunch about this," said Al.

"Well, yeah, but—"

"Listen, Buck, I love Arlene."

"Did you tell her?"

"Many times."

"And?"

"She says she loves me too. Look, Buck, I have a good job, I have tons of money saved up—advantage of being a bachelor for years—I have a home free and clear—and we love each other. I don't see a problem."

"No, no, don't get me wrong. I'm happy for you and I'm really happy for my sister. So when does the big announcement come?"

"Not until I get her a ring. I know absolutely *bupkis* about diamond rings," said Al.

"I've got a guy, Al. Morris Horowitz, over on 47th Street. He's the one that fixed me up with Carrie's engagement ring. I'll get you the address. You tell him I sent you and believe me, he'll give you the deal of your life. But here's the thing: whatever price he gives you, you must make a counter-offer."

"What if it's a great deal?"

"Makes no difference. *Hondling* is a big part of that industry. It's expected, so if you don't want to sound like an amateur, you have to bargain with him. I'm telling you, he'll respect you for it."

"If you say so, but I warn you, I'm not very good at that kind of thing."

"Well, whenever it happens, you make sure the two of you get over to my mother's to show her the ring. And don't be upset if she starts *cheppering* you about giving her more grandkids," said Buck.

"Fact is, Buck, we've talked about it already. Both of us want kids. Don't forget, neither of us are kids anymore and the longer we wait, well, I want to be a young enough father to play with my children without the aches and pains of old age."

"Does Bill know?"

"Yeah, I hope you don't mind. I talked it over with him before you. Bill's a real family guy. He told me when he was a State Trooper back in Kentucky, his shifts kept him from really being around for his kids. Then there was the Army, which did that in spades. So now with a regular job, he really wants to make it up to his children. He says there's nothing like having children. I guess you know that too."

"Shit. Now I feel like a real louse sending him all over the country scouting talent," said Buck.

"No, don't feel that way. You were right up front with what his job entailed and he was more than willing to do what it takes. But whenever he's home, he takes full advantage of his time with his kids. I want that too, Buck."

Buck extended his hand across the table and said, "I couldn't ask for a better brother-in-law, Al. Welcome to the family. I do see one problem, Al. I might as well get it out in the open now."

"What's that, Buck?"

"Well, Mom, Arlene and Bevvy have been in the same household since we were all kids. Ma tries to be independent, but she really relies upon the girls for help. With you all the way up in the Bronx, that could make things difficult for her. And with Bevvy real serious with the doctor she's dating, it's only going to get harder."

"We talked about that too, Buck. Here's the thing: I own my house free and clear. It's big, it's waterfront and I could get a shitload of money for it. I'm more than willing to sell the house, take the money and buy one closer to your mother in Queens. Tell you the truth, it's quite a haul form Eastchester to midtown Manhattan every day. Queens would be a lot easier for me—and certainly for any job Arlene has."

"That makes me feel a lot better, Al. Once again, congrats and welcome to the family."

They finished their lunch and returned to their respective offices. When Buck entered his, Kelsey handed him a thick manilla envelope.

"What's this, Kel?"

"Those are the proofs from Fran Michaels' photo shoot," she said.

"Oh! Great. How bout you come into the office and help me go through them?"

"Sure. Be there in a sec."

There were over a hundred 8 x 10 glossies. "Wow, no wonder the shoot took all day," said Buck.

"How about we make three piles, Buck. One for yesses, one for maybes and one for definitely nots."

"Good idea. Let's do it."

For the next hour and a half, Buck and Kelsey studied every photograph. Paul Jennet had captured every angle, every

## A CHANGE OF KEY

mood of Fran Michaels from innocent to vampish. One photo depicted her with a come-hither look and a lit cigarette close to her lips. Buck said, "Absolutely no to this one. This is not the image of Fran that we want to project. Never this one!"

"Jeez, good thing I quit a while back," said Kelsey.

"Don't tell me you smoked!" said Buck in horror.

"I started when my husband shipped out for the Pacific. I was nervous every day, mail came infrequently and it helped settle my nerves. Then one day I realized what a jerk I was being and I just stopped. Hope it doesn't kill my image with you, Buck."

"Not at all. The important thing is you stopped. I made Fran stop when she was in my civilian band. I thought it would damage her voice. I'm surprised she agreed to take this picture."

"Photographers can be pretty persuasive, so don't be too hard on her."

They kept sifting through the glossies until they had three piles on Buck's desk. "OK, now we have to go through the 'yesses' until we find the one photo that says it all."

"She's an unbelievably beautiful girl, Buck. Any of these photos does her justice," said Kelsey.

"Do you think we should ask Fran what she thinks?" said Buck.

"No."

"Really?"

"You're the boss, Buck. You have to make the tough decisions," said Kelsey.

"Yeah, I guess you're right."

They settled upon a beautiful picture of Fran where she was leaning forward on a desk, her hands propping up her chin and her million-dollar smile illuminating the entire photograph.

"You have great taste, Buck—that's the exact same picture I would have chosen."

Having completed that chore, Buck finished up some progress reports for Jack Merrill and then went back to combing

## A CHANGE OF KEY

through the A & R catalogue of RCA recording artists. After another two hours, he had narrowed the list down to fifteen who had enough material to fill an LP. He would leave it to Bill to book studio time for each of them so they could get new cuts on their records and not rely upon just rehashing old materials. At a little after five, he buttoned up the office and headed for home.

## CHAPTER ELEVEN
*"Let's Make One:" April 15th, 1946*

On Monday, April 15th, Al Rovitz brought the four members of the Bluebirds to Buck's office. Ty Terrell was the spokesman for the group and he was extremely well-spoken. In preparation for the meeting, Kelsey had Maintenance bring four more chairs into the office which because of its large size, easily accommodated the group, Al, Kelsey to take notes, and Buck.

"Gentlemen, it's a real pleasure to meet you," said Buck. "Al here has told me great things about your group."

"Pleasure to meet you too, Mr. Fisher. Even amongst us black folks, everyone knows who you are. Lotsa folks preferred your style over Prez or Hawk. Me? I'm partial to Johnny Hodges." said Terrell.

For the next hour, Buck laid out what he wanted to do for and with the group. Roy Richard, one of the twin brothers in the group said, "Missa Fisher, we kinda have an audience with Negroes. That's who this rhythm and blues be aimed at. How come Victor be interested in a group like ours?"

"That's a good question, Roy. Is there any reason why white people can't appreciate your kind of music?" asked Buck.

"They ain't never heard anything like what we do," said Billy Richard, the other twin."

"What about the Ink Spots?" said Buck.

"Shee-it," said Bobby Nunn, the fourth member of the group. "They ain't nothin' like us, Missa Fisher. They closer to the Mills Brothers than what we do. Don't get me wrong—I like both them groups, but they ain't us."

"What if we could make your music universal?" asked Buck.

"Meaning?" said Ty Terrell.

"Don't underestimate how powerful RCA Victor is as a marketing force. We make you universal by getting your name out there. Getting you on tours so you can be heard all over the country. Placing you on radio stations. That's how my band got to the top of the heap," said Buck.

That made Roy Richard laugh. "Missa Fisher, ain't no white radio station gonna play our kinda music. Shee-it, they even got separate best seller lists for white and black musicians."

"Let me ask you fellas this: what label are you with now?"

"We with a label called Whippet," said Billy Richard.

"OK, and how do they promote you?"

"Promote us? What you mean?"

"How exactly did they get your music out to the public?" asked Buck.

They thought for a few moments with no one responding to the question. Finally, it was Ty who answered. "They press a couple a hundred copies and send a few to every Negro record shop in the area. That's about it. Nothing else that comes to mind right away."

"See? That's just what I mean. That 'it' isn't anything," said Buck. "I'm talking about publicity campaigns, articles in papers and trade magazines, air play. When RCA signs a new group, it's big news in the music world. That's what we can do for you," said Buck.

Here Al interjected, "Buck, before we get too far ahead of ourselves, maybe you should give these boys a listen. I've got them in a small studio down on twenty-seven. Guys? I have a drummer, bass, guitar and piano to back you up. Don't worry, they can follow anything you do."

"They better," laughed Buck, "they're all part of the RCA Studio Orchestra I've put together and they're a very able bunch of guys."

"That suits us fine, Mr. Fisher. Let us show you what we can do," said Ty Terrell. Me and the boys playing together so long, there isn't much we can't play. "Anything in particular you would like to hear us sing, Mr. Fisher? We're ready to do a variety of our

## A CHANGE OF KEY

songs for you." "No, it's your choice—and it's Buck. We're very informal around here."

They took the elevator to the rehearsal studio where Chuck Fein, Kenny Ferraro, Tony Tancredi on drums and Buddy Scraggs were waiting for them. After introductions and a brief discussion of keys and tempo with the four musicians, the group was ready to perform.

They had four songs prepared: "My Baby Done Told Me," "Courtroom Blues," "Around About Midnight," and "You Sure Look Good to Me." The tunes each had a different feel, a different tempo from dirty blues to up tempo rhythm. Kenny Ferraro provided the chordal background and Tony Tancredi and Chuck Fein propelled the tune forward and especially on the "Courtroom Blues," Buddy Scraggs' blues guitar fills were the perfect accompaniment to the voices.

When they were done, Ty Terrell said, "Well, Mr. Fisher, what do you think?"

"I think I have never heard anything like this in my life-- and it's great! This is just brand-new stuff, guys. I predict this style of music is going to be huge and I'd like to get you guys in on the ground floor. When can you break away from that Whippet label?"

"We owe them two sides. Then we're on our own," said Tyrell.

'Would you like to record for RCA Victor?" asked Buck.

The four members of the group looked at each other and it was Billy Richard who said, "Sho' nuff, Missa. Fisher. Where we sign?" said Roy Richard."

"Let's go back to my office and we'll go over the details. But there's one thing," said Buck.

"What's that?" said Tyrell.

"I hope you won't take offense guys, but I hate the name of the group. Bluebirds just doesn't cut it for me. How about we give you a fresh start and call you The Robins?"

## A CHANGE OF KEY

"Doan see much of a difference," said Bobby Nunn, "but you the boss, Missa Fisher."

Back in Buck's office, he explained, "I can't sign you until you are free from Whippet. That would open up a real can of legal worms that I'm sure we all want to avoid. But how about we do this: here's my card. The moment you aren't under contract, you contact me and you'll become RCA's newest recording group."

The four newly-named Robins agreed, shook hands with Buck and left with the promise of a successful recording career on the horizon.

When they had gone, Buck said, "Now for the hard part. I have to sell Jack on this." He buzzed Kelsey and said, "Kel, call up to Jack Merrill and ask if I can have ten minutes of his time." A few moments later, Kelsey said, "Jack says to come up in a half hour."

Jack invited Buck into his office and said, "Grab a seat. What's doing, Buck?"

Buck spent far more than the ten minutes he had asked for explaining about the Robins and the entire rhythm and blues movement. Jack was skeptical. "Buck, I don't know if this is the kind of stuff we handle over here. Negro quartets?"

"We handle a lot of Negro singers, Jack. Hell, Etta James isn't exactly Doris Day the way she sings and she sells plenty of records for us. I'm thinking of making a whole album of her songs."

"What if this rhythm and blues thing is just a flash in the pan?" said Jack.

"It's always possible. You don't hear too much about the Merry Macs anymore, but when they were hot, they sold a lot of records. They even recorded with Bing Crosby. But I don't think that's what will happen with these guys and with this style. I think it's going to grow into something even bigger."

Jack Merrill still wasn't sold.

## A CHANGE OF KEY

"Jack, you've trusted me this far. You've given me a free hand with my division and I haven't let you down yet. Trust me on this. If it doesn't work out, you can fire me."

"No one's firing you, Buck, and you're right. I did give you a lot of leeway. So OK, soon as you can, get these boys signed up. Now tell me what's going on with Fran's LP."

"I'll send you the playlist with times that we've picked. I think it's a terrific mix and next Monday we're moving everything down to 26$^{th}$ Street and we'll start recording her tracks."

"Careful, Buck. Watch out for this 'we' stuff. Let the pros do what they do best. You don't want to mother hen the whole production. You're an executive now."

"I'll be there strictly as an observer, Jack. "I've got Tommy Taylor on board as producer and Whip Elliot as the sound engineer.

"Great, they're two of the best. Keep me posted on how those sessions go, Buck—and keep up the great work," said Jack.

…..

The following Monday, the entire RCA Studio Orchestra assembled at the 26$^{th}$ Street Studio. Since Buck recorded there before the war, there were tremendous changes. He was baffled by the variety and number of recording devices, microphones, amplifiers, speakers and a bank of dials and gauges more appropriate to a physics laboratory than a recording studio.

Tommy Taylor came up to Buck and said, "Good to see you, Buck. How are you feeling?"

"Much better, Tommy. Almost back to normal. We all set to go here?"

"Just about. Let me get Whip over here and we'll go over the details."

Whip Elliot joined them and shook hands with Buck. As the producer, he had overall control of the session, but he worked hand-in-hand with Tommy Taylor and Kip Roman as the director of the orchestra. "Here's how I see it going," said Whip. "It's going to take some time to get the right balance so I'll be checking levels on every track. Once I have the orchestra in balance with the vocalist, we will do a few run-throughs. When everyone is happy, we'll make some masters. In essence, it's not all that different from the way you recorded before the war except we have a lot more gadgets these days."

Buck had a feeling that Tommy and Whip were deferring to him. He needed to correct that immediately. "Look guys, I'm just here as an observer. You've got a fantastic orchestra and a singer who will just break your heart with her voice. I'm leaving everything in your hands. I trust you to give us the best product possible. Remember, we're in direct competition with Columbia and they have the jump on us, so we have to turn out A-1 products to keep up."

"OK, Buck. How about you take a seat in the booth and you can watch the whole dance," said Whip.

Fran's first song was "I Got it Bad and That Ain't Good." But it was necessary to get the orchestra down first and add Fran's vocal over it. Kip's arrangement captured the longing in the lyric and the strings interplaying with the reeds was a perfect blend—especially since he had Noni Furillo playing bass clarinet on the chart which added depth to the sound.

Whip sat in front of a huge board which seemed to have a slider for every instrument in the orchestra, each one labeled with a piece of masking tape. As the orchestra ran through the chart, he moved the sliders up and down until he was satisfied with the mix.

He pressed a button on the intercom and said, "OK, Franny, how about we check your microphone. Run through the number with just piano and bass and we'll see how it sounds."

Fran nodded, Kip counted off the intro and they ran the song with the lyric. Whip adjusted the slider for her microphone and when she finished, he said, "Holy Jesus Christ, Buck! She is phenomenal! Best I ever heard."

"Wait, Whip. She's got a lot more to show you."

## A CHANGE OF KEY

Next they put the orchestra together with Fran's singing and again he adjusted all the sliders until he was satisfied with the overall sound. It took three run-throughs to get it perfect.

Finally, when Tommy, Whip and Kip were satisfied, Tommy said, "All right, folks, let's make one."

Kip silently counted off the free measure and the orchestra began. But about sixteen bars into the song, Pete McCormack's metal mouthpiece cap fell out of his pocket and clinked on the riser. "Cut!" said Tommy Taylor.

"Sorry, guys. Won't happen again," said Pete.

"Nice of my husband to sabotage the recording session," said Fran.

"OK," said Kip. "Let's take it from the edge."

He counted off the intro again and this time, the song came out perfectly. When the song ended, Tommy poked his head into the booth and said, "That million-dollar voice matches her million dollar looks. I don't think I ever heard anyone that good."

"She's a great girl, Tommy. She was fantastic with my band, but I think she's gotten even better. Maybe the war-time experience of missing Pete when he was overseas with me gave her singing a new dimension—a sadness that only that kind of an experience could create."

Then Tommy said, "I think we're going to make one more track and call it a day. I don't want to burn out her voice." Then to Kip he said, "Kip? What's up next?"

"Let's go a little more up-beat. We'll do "Nice Work if You Can Get It," said Kip.

The Gershwin song was in the perfect alto range that fit Fran's belting style on faster numbers. As he listened to the song, Buck remembered how when Fran replaced Carrie in the band, she had taken Fran aside and told her to loosen up her elocution a little. Fran was a Juliard trained opera student; with Carrie's help, she transformed into an amazing pop singer. It showed in her delivery of the Gershwin tune.

**A CHANGE OF KEY**

After an additional two run-throughs, Tommy said, "Let's lay it down and then go home."

Tired though everyone was, they delivered a perfect performance which met everyone's approval. Kip then said, "OK, fellas, back here at nine tomorrow morning and we'll aim for another couple of numbers."

.....

At home that night, Carrie wanted to hear all about the recording session. "How was Fran, darling," asked Carrie.

"She was amazing. But you knew that, didn't you?"

"I had a feeling. You know, Bucky, now that she's a real solo act, you don't want to waste all that gorgeousness just making records."

"Meaning?"

"She could probably carry her own show at Carnegie Hall someday if she has enough material for ninety minutes plus an encore. There, or maybe some of the major theaters in Manhattan. That do live stage shows. She'd be great live."

Buck hadn't even thought of Fran in terms of carrying a one woman show, but it certainly was worth exploring. For just an instant, a look passed across Buck's face, and then vanished, but not before Carrie noticed it.

"What's wrong, darling?" she asked.

"Oh, nothing. Nothing, really."

"One of the few smart things my mother ever said was that 'nothing means something.' So give. What's troubling you?"

"I watched Franny singing today and I just wondered, how much do you miss it?"

Carrie reached out and touched Buck's cheek with her palm. "Look at me, sweetheart. Then look around. We have two wonderful little kids, a beautiful home, family next door, friends, plenty of money in the bank, and more importantly than anything else—I have you. You really think I'm missing out on something? I had my shot, darling. I got the wolf whistles, I played to big crowds. I felt the excitement of performing. But that's just not my life now, honey. This is," she said, motioning with her hands to their home. "So this is my life now—and I swear to you, I wouldn't trade it for anything in this world." She leaned in and kissed him on the lips. "So no more worrying about that, ok?"

"Do you have any idea how much I love you, Carrie?" asked Buck.

"I've got a pretty good notion. And I hope it's as much as I love you—and by the way, I plan on showing you a few hours from now. Now you go play with your kids while I get dinner ready. Oh, and there's one more thing."

"Yes?"

"Arlene called. She's invited us all out for a dinner Friday night at the House of Chan on Horace Harding Boulevard in Fresh Meadows."

"What's the occasion?" asked Buck.

Carrie looked at the ceiling smiling and said, "Oh, I don't know. Must be something big, I guess."

"You guess?"

She couldn't contain her laughter as she said, "You can't be that blind, angel. I think there's going to be an announcement Friday. Oh, and if you didn't figure it out, she said she's invited Al to join us."

"Uh oh," said Buck. "I have a feeling my friend paid a visit to 47$^{th}$ Street."

"We'll know Friday," said Carrie, with a wink.

A CHANGE OF KEY

# CHAPTER TWELVE
### *Celebration: April 22, 1946*

The House of Chan occupied a double store front on Horace Harding Boulevard. It was nestled in the major shopping center for Northern Queens, with dozens of stores for shoppers to choose from. The owner and chefs had emigrated from China right before Japan invaded. In fact, all three hailed from Nanking, the city where massacres and rapes were perpetrated against the Chinese population. Estimates of those murdered were anywhere from 50,000 to 300,000. The Rape of Nanking began on December 13, 1937. Martin Wong, his family and his two friends who were his chefs in his restaurant in China left the city on December 1st and made their way to the United States via a dangerous and torturous route. By early next year, the Nanking War Crimes Tribunal would meet to try the perpetrators of the massacre for crimes against humanity.

Martin Wong had built his business from scratch and through hard work and by serving authentic Cantonese cuisine, he had built a comfortable life for his wife and two sons in America. The restaurant had two private rooms and Arlene (or maybe Al) had booked one of them for a party of thirteen which included Buck, Carrie and the kids, Rachel, Arlene and Beverly, and the Dwyers—all five of them, and of course, Al Rovitz. Bill had gotten back from San Francisco two days earlier and had not yet had time to sit with Buck to tell him what he heard. That he would do at the beginning of the following week.

Martin Wong had prepared a veritable feast equal to the magnificent one he prepared for the Chinese New Year. It consisted of nine separate dishes served in four courses. Cantonese cooking tended to be blander than other Chinese regional dishes like Hunan or Szhezuan, so Buck was able to sample all of the dishes in moderation. Even Rachel, who had probably never tasted Chinese food in her life, remarked at how tasty every dish was.

Right before dessert, which consisted of fried candied bananas, almond cookies and of course fortune cookies, Wong brought out two bottles of champagne—one pink, the other white. Al Rovitz stood up and clinked the inside of his water tumbler with his spoon. A hush fell over the table.

When Al nervously announced, "I suppose you're all wondering why we're all here tonight," everyone at the table laughed. "It's simple, really. I want to tell you that I've fallen in love. But more than that, I've fallen in love with the woman I plan on spending the rest of my life with. Arlene? Wanna stand up, hon?"

A smiling Arlene Feinstein stood up at her end of the table. "I think you have something you would like to show everyone," said Al.

Arlene held up her left hand and displayed a two-carat pear shaped diamond surrounded by baguettes. She wiggled her finger for everyone to see, and then she ran to Al who she hugged and kissed passionately to the cheers of everyone at the table. Carrie and Beverly ran to Arlene and embraced her and Buck gave her the biggest hug of all.

As Arlene circulated around the table showing off her ring, Beverly came to Buck with tears in her eyes. "What's wrong, Bev?" he asked. "Don't worry, your time is going to come soon enough."

"Benny, I'm just so happy for her. She's such a good person. When you were away during the war, she held everything together. Mama counted on her and she always came through. She deserves all the happiness she's feeling, and Al seems like such a right guy."

"If I had any doubts about Al, Bev, I would have discouraged this from the start. But I know him very well. Soldiers learn to rely on each other and when I got hurt, Al took over and really kept the band going. I can't tell you how many hours he spent at my bedside—because I was unconscious for a good five days. He was a true friend. That's one reason why I wanted to offer him the job with me. Now, let me go congratulate him."

Buck and Al embraced and Al said, "When I told Morris Horowitz that you sent me, well, he took care of me real good. A great ring at a terrific price. Thanks for that, Buck."

"So any idea when the wedding will be? I'd hate to send you out of town that weekend and have you miss it," said Buck.

"We're thinking about mid-November, maybe early December. I want to give Arlene time to plan the wedding of her dreams. She's a wonderful girl, Buck. I don't know how I got so lucky."

The meal came to a close and when Martin Wong brought the check, Buck grabbed it and said, "It's on me. Consider it an early engagement present," he said.

Everyone gathered up their kids and their coats and headed for home.

…..

Day after day, week after week, work progressed on Fran's album. Buck couldn't be at every session to observe, but Kip would come up once the orchestra had gone home and filled him in on what tracks were laid down and how he thought things were going.

"I'll tell you this, Buck: we talked about filler songs on the album but the truth is, every song Fran sings is just a gem. Today we laid down 'Dream.' She loved the sound of the orchestra behind her and her vocal was perfect. I even gave Noni a short obligato that I wrote out for him and that worked well. We also put down 'I'll Be Home for Christmas,' even though I know we're not going to use it on this LP. I've been working on a number of other Christmas songs that I think will fit her voice, but first things first; let's get this album done."

## A CHANGE OF KEY

Buck finally cleared a two-hour block of time to meet with Bill Dwyer to find out what he heard on the West Coast. "So what did you hear, Bill?" asked Buck.

"Jeez, Buck, where do I begin? First, the good news. I heard a Latin band and got to speak to the leader for some time. His name is Perez Prado and he's from Cuba—same as Desi Arnaz. His specialty is music for a dance called the mambo. You can't believe the reaction from his fans. They simply go crazy dancing to these rhythms. He leads a big band but his rhythm section has all kinds of drums—timbales, congas, bongos. And his rhythm players also play what look like native instruments called gourds, which they scrape with a wooden rod and something called an *afuche cabasa* which sounds like no instrument you've ever heard. Add to that wood blocks, metal bells, something called a slap stick, and I'm telling you, Buck, it's wild. You can have some research done, but I bet you that census statistics show that there's a considerable Latin American population in America. His music would really be a hot seller with them."

Buck could feel the enthusiasm in every word Bill said.

"Did you give him a card and pitch him?" asked Buck.

"That's the even better news. He's bringing his band east and they have a series of concerts in Spanish Harlem. He invited you to come listen to the group. If you like what you hear, he would gladly sign with RCA as long as we give him a three-album deal and a promise to promote his music."

"I'll clear that with Jack, but if I like what I hear, I'm going to push for us to sign him. RCA has an entire International Division and he might have more success with the distributing LPs in Central and South America. I'll leave that up to Jack."

"It's not like he'd be the first with this kind of music, Buck. Xavier Cugat and Desi Arnaz both had successful bands in the '30s and '40s, and ninety percent of their music was strictly Latin. But Prado? He takes it a step farther. His rhythms are really infectious."

"You sound pretty enthusiastic about this band, Bill. You think they're that good?"

"Buck, remember how you told me over in Europe how your civilian band would play a conga and you once had 2000 college kids doing the dance?'

"Sure. We played the conga a lot. It was a big favorite, even amongst the dress-up crowd."

"Well now imagine an entire ballroom of people doing this mambo thing. It was amazing to watch the energy they put into that dance," said Bill.

"OK, we'll make sure we get up to see him. What else is doing out there?"

"Well, first of all, nobody dances out there. I went to a number of jazz clubs like the Black Hawk and the Band Box. Everybody just sits and drinks and listens. In fact, the stuff I was hearing, it's not even possible to dance to it."

"I noticed the same thing when I heard Charlie Parker play. Everyone listens, applauds—and sits."

"I just don't understand the music I was hearing, Buck. It's so different. I'm not a musician, but to my ear, much of it sounds ugly. But the audiences—mostly college kids from what I saw—eat that stuff up."

"Anyone in particular you had your eye on?" asked Buck.

"When I was at the Black Hawk I heard this trio. Dave Brubeck, Paul Desmond, and a Negro bass player named Sam Saxon. Desmond was on alto sax and his tone was unbelievable. Brubeck was all over the piano playing changes that no one has ever heard before. He's obviously talented but he's way out of the mainstream of what we know as jazz."

"Think there's any future to what he's doing?"

"Buck, the way those kids reacted to him, I would bet on it. He's going to be a major voice in jazz."

"That's what Charlie Parker told me: this is the future of jazz. Who else did you hear?"

## A CHANGE OF KEY

"Get this: I heard this eighteen-year-old kid named Pepper Martin. He's playing this same confusing music—but on baritone sax! Jesus, Buck, who ever heard of a baritone sax as a lead instrument? Then I heard another young saxophonist---also on baritone—and he was even further out there. His name is Gerry Mulligan. Next I heard an alto player named Art Pepper. I got to talk to him a little and told him who I was. He played with Benny Carter and then with Stan Kenton until he got drafted. Jokingly I said, whatever happened to melody? He laughed and said, 'Who needs melody when you understand the chords?' That could have been Chinese to me. All I know is it sounds nothing like what we've been doing for years."

"Well, Bill, if Swing is dead, maybe it took melody to the grave with it."

"They call their style 'bop,'" said Bill.

"Yeah, on the east coast they call it bebop. Two sides of the same coin. How long is this Brubeck trio going to be at this Black Hawk club?"

"He's kind of the house band there so it's open-ended," said Bill.

Buck sighed and said, "I think I'm on a plane for the coast. I'm going to have to hear this stuff in person. No offense, Bill, but I need to hear it from a musician's point-of-view."

"No offense taken, Buck. Should I have Kelsey get you a flight?"

"Let me check my calendar and break the news to Carrie."

"She gonna be OK with this?"

"She's been having some terrible bouts of morning sickness and I've helped her through it. I hate to leave her alone."

"I'll have Cathy check on her every day. She went through the same thing with April. She was our first. The other two things went a lot easier. Don't ask me why."

"Thanks, Bill. I'll talk it over with Carrie tonight. For now, let's call it a day."

"OK, boss, I'm going to check downstairs and see what's going on with Fran's LP. It should be wrapping up any day now."

"Thanks, Bill. Keep me informed."

…..

That night Buck explained to Carrie about the trip to California. At first there was a brief look of panic that flitted across her face, but she quickly composed herself.

"How long will you be away, Bucky?"

"It will take the better part of a day just to get there and another day to get home. So I figure if I stay for five days out there, I can see the groups I need to see. Unless something unexpected happens, about a week then."

She opened her arms and Buck came into her embrace. "It's your job, honey, and you have to do what you have to do. The last time you were away from me was when you left for the Army. It was terrible then because you were going to war. This is nothing like that, so don't you worry. Now, Laura wants to show you what she colored today, so you spend some time with her and dinner will be ready soon. It's meat loaf. Hope you don't mind."

At four years old, Laura was a real chatterbox. She was also precocious. When she took out her coloring book to show Buck, she said, "You see, daddy, the trick is to stay in the lines when you color. Here, watch." She took a brown crayon and carefully colored two paws of a dog she was diligently working on. "I'm going to frame this and give it to mommy for her birthday," said Laura.

All Buck could do was shake his head in wonderment, thinking, 'where does she get this stuff—framing her picture?' At that point, Eddie, two years Laura's senior, came in and said, "Daddy, look what I'm working on." Buck had bought Eddie a huge Erector Set the previous Hanukkah. The toy, which had been around since 1913, was supposed to challenge the minds of youngsters by giving them miniature construction projects which they had to figure out how to build. The kit had hundreds of metal pieces that served as beams, plus a motor, gears and dozens upon dozens of miniature bolts and nuts. "What do you think, daddy?"

Eddie's project looked like nothing native to Earth. Beams jutted out everywhere and what should have been the ceiling was attached at the side of two long metal strips. Every hole in the strips had a bolt and a nut—for no apparent reason. Carrie, who had seemingly read every book on child-rearing, had told Buck, "Always compliment them, no matter what they do. The psychologists call it positive reinforcement."

Buck, ever mindful of Carrie's advice, said, "Wow, Eddie—this is really amazing! It looks to me like you're building a spaceship."

"Daddy, you're so silly. It's a steam shovel!"

"Oh, of course! How silly of me. Now I see it," said Buck, barely containing his laughter. "And look what your sister is drawing. I think we have an artist in the family."

Eddie leaned in and looked at Laura's coloring book. He pulled a face and said, "I'm not so sure, daddy."

"Hey!" said Laura, whacking Eddie on his arm.

Carrie, who unbeknownst to Buck had been monitoring the whole scene, began to giggle. Buck left the children and went into the kitchen with her.

"Benjamin Feinstein," she said, "you are as incredible a father as you are a husband. Those kids love you as much as I do." She kissed him on the lips and said, "Bring the kids in. It's dinner."

.....

The next morning, Buck had Kelsey make travel arrangements for him for a five day stay in San Francisco starting on April 30th. Always efficient, fifteen minutes later, Kelsey came into Buck's office and consulting her pad said, "OK, Buck, you leave out of LaGuardia Airport at 8 AM flying American Airlines Flight 1223. Better bring a seat cushion, because the flight makes a few stops and is going to last close to ten hours total. Then I have you booked for five nights at the Fairmont Hotel. It's pretty ritzy, but I figure your expense account should handle it with ease. I also have a list of good restaurants not too far from the hotel, also on your expense account. Remember to bring all receipts home with you, Buck. Gotta keep the folks down in accounting happy. You'll be coming back Sunday afternoon."

Kelsey Burton was absolutely indispensable to Buck. Her efficiency and attention to detail was what elevated her from the steno pool to the secretary for a vice-president of RCA Victor. He'd see to it that her year-end bonus was a large one. She was the sole money-earner in her household and even though her husband was on full disability from his loss of a leg in the Navy, it still must have been difficult for her. There was no guarantee that her husband would ever work again and there were times when Buck thought she was struggling with it.

Buck took the photo of Fran Michaels he had selected and went down to the rehearsal studio to see how the album was progressing. He got there just in time to hear Fran sing "Someone to Watch Over Me." It was a Gershwin tune that she never got to sing with Buck's civilian band. She turned it into an emotional tableau of bittersweet longing. It was perfect.

When she finished the song, she noticed Buck and came to him and kissed him. "You look great, Buck. What brings you down to this cave?"

"Got something to show you," said Buck. "Take a look. This is what's going on the cover of your album."

She took the photo, stared at it and said, "Wow, do I really look like that?"

"Do you mean gorgeous? Yes. Definitely."

"Pete, come take a look at this," she said, calling her husband over.

"What do you think, hon?" said Fran.

"I think I married the most beautiful woman on the planet. That's what I think," said Pete McCormack.

## A CHANGE OF KEY

"I've been toying with album titles, Franny. I think I want to keep it simple. What I've come up with is 'Love, Fran.'"

"That sounds great, Buck. But you know, after all this work, this album sure better sell," said Fran.

"Franny, when the world hears you sing, this will be the first of many albums you'll be making, so start thinking of a follow up soon. I still have to write the liner notes, but that's just a couple of hundred words. Shouldn't take me that long. Once we get a mock-up of the artwork, I'll show you the whole package."

"Love you, Buck. Thanks for having faith in me," said Fran.

With all the travel arrangements made, Buck headed home to spend the weekend with the family, pack a suitcase and get ready for the jaunt across country to hear some revolutionary new musicians.

A CHANGE OF KEY

# CHAPTER THIRTEEN
## Golden Gate City, April 1946

It was with a sense of anxiety that Buck boarded the American Airlines DC-3 at LaGuardia Airport on the morning of April 30th. He couldn't help but remember the harrowing ride in the belly of a B-24 Liberator bomber that ferried his Army Special Services band to England—and had lost an engine between Iceland and Greenland. The cabin aircraft had filled with smoke and everyone on board was certain they would crash into the sea. The ride home from England on a Douglas DC-3 was luxurious by comparison and it was this same type of aircraft that would carry him to San Francisco.

A pretty Air Hostess in a blue uniform with red, white and blue trim seated him and offered him a pillow for the flight. After announcing the safety procedures for the aircraft (just in case) the pilot got on the intercom and announced the flying time and altitude they would fly at to their first stop—Chicago. By anyone's standards, the flight was grueling. The seats were not overly wide and reclined no more than six inches. Drinks were served shortly after take-off and the hostess walked down the aisle carrying copies of the latest issues of *Life, Look* and *Time* magazines which she distributed to passengers eager for a distraction from the long flight. In Chicago, the plane had to be refueled, so everyone had to disembark from the plane as per the Civil Aeronautics Administration guidelines.

Buck grabbed a coffee in the crowded terminal and sat at the gate huddled in his overcoat trying to keep warm in a Chicago winter that didn't seem to want to segue into spring. He closed his eyes and was just at the point of dozing off when he heard," "Holy shit! Is that you, Buck?"

Standing before him was Paul Tanner, the lead trombonist in Glenn Miller's civilian band from its beginning in 1938 to the time it disbanded in 1942. Buck had met him several times at Webster Hall where both groups had recording sessions and at the Bluebird studio in downtown Manhattan. He was easy to talk to and was an expert in music theory.

"Paul! How the hell are you!" said Buck.

"Jeez, it's great to see you. What brings you to Chicago?" asked Tanner.

Buck explained he was on his way to San Francisco to scout out talent for RCA Victor and Chicago was one stop along the way.

"How 'bout yourself, Paul?"

"I've got a studio gig in Hollywood. The money's great and I don't have to move around. It was fun when I was younger, but now I like being in one place."

"Lemme ask you, Paul, how come you weren't with Glenn in the Army Air Force Band?"

"It's a funny thing, Buck. After Glenn enlisted and the band broke up, we all went our separate ways. I enlisted in the Army Air Force. I wound up in the 378th Army Service Forces Band. We were based at Fort Slocum, New York and didn't do much else but parade around to Sousa marches every time a Basic Training class graduated. I tried to transfer into Glenn's outfit, but my CO said I was too important to the group to let go. Bullshit. He was a real prick who just liked throwing his weight around."

"That's too bad, Paul. That AAF band was really something," said Buck.

"Yes it was—but everybody knew about your Army band too. The zillions in war bonds you sold, the tours to so many bases—and then your entertaining the troops in England. It's funny. We lost Glenn to that war and nearly lost you too. Yeah, everybody in the Army knew about your injury, Buck. Lousy luck—but at least you made it home."

"True, I was one of the lucky ones. We entertained a lot of kids who weren't nearly that lucky."

## A CHANGE OF KEY

"Goddamned war," said Tanner. "You still playing?" he asked.

"No, not right now. Still recovering. Now I'm just an executive. Vice-president at RCA in charge of finding new talent and turning them into stars."

"How's that going?"

"We have a few already and I'm out here to see if I can pick up some more. It's interesting work—a real challenge—but I miss being out in front of a band and playing. I guess you never really lose that love of performing."

"I tell you, Buck, you and Tex were the two best tenor players I ever heard. Tex went Navy, I think. Well look, I have to catch my flight to L.A. I hope you get better soon and pick up that horn again. The music world needs you."

They shook hands and Tanner said, "Great to see you, Buck. Have a safe flight."

Twenty minutes later, the gate agent announced over the loudspeaker that Flight 1223 would be reboarding immediately. The passengers got back on the aircraft and nestled into their seats for the next leg of the flight which would be in Denver. By the time the aircraft landed in San Francisco, Buck felt like he had been traveling for a week. He got his single suitcase and hailed a cab at the curb to take him to the Fairmont Hotel.

"First time in Frisco?" asked the driver.

"Yes it is," said Buck.

"Well, don't call it Frisco. Only natives can call it that. They'll know you're a tourist and then they'll screw you six ways from Sunday."

"Thanks for the tip. Say, ever hear of a club called the Black Hawk?"

"Yeah, I heard. I don't dig that shit though."

"Oh no? What do you like?"

"I'll take Crosby and Astaire over that crap any day," said the driver.

## A CHANGE OF KEY

"I see. Do you know how far that club is from the Fairmont?"

"Coupla maybe three miles. Don't try to walk it. Hills in this city'll give you a heart attack."

The cab pulled up in front of the hotel and the driver took Buck's suitcase from the trunk. Buck gave him a nice tip and thanked him. Then he entered the hotel and went to the registration desk. He got his key and found his room. It was spacious and comfortable with a queen-sized bed. All Buck wanted was a good night's sleep. By the time he got to his room it was close to 8 PM and he felt that was too late to call Carrie, with the time difference of three hours now separating them. Instead, he undressed, showered and put on the pajamas that Carrie had packed for him. He fell asleep almost immediately.

The next morning, he awoke at almost nine which was absurdly late for someone used to being out of bed by six. He dressed and asked the desk clerk where he could find a breakfast place. He was directed to a luncheonette two blocks from the hotel. It was very similar to his friend Eddie Holberg's place on 86th Street in Bensonhurst. Eddie had been his closest friend since first grade and all through high school, but once he moved to Queens, he rarely got back to Brooklyn to see him. He promised himself he would call him once he got back home.

He picked up a copy of the *San Francisco Chronicle* and perused the first few pages which covered international news. The paper made much of the fact that the day before marked the one-year anniversary of Adolph Hitler blowing his brains out in the *fuhrer* bunker in Berlin, effectively meaning that the war was virtually over. Was it really just a year ago? Even in so short a time, memories had faded making it feel like the war was decades in the past.

San Francisco was considerably milder in climate than Chicago and New York so Buck decided to walk around the city a bit, getting as far as a park with a view of the Golden Gate

**A CHANGE OF KEY**

Bridge, the Bay and The Presidio, the Army base that served as the gateway to the Pacific during World War II. Since 1847 it had been occupied by the United States Army and it still served as a major military installation on the western coast of the United States. From his vantage point, Buck got to share the spectacular view that every soldier serving at the base had from anywhere on the post. Soldiers stationed there were also close to the major entertainment section of the city.

He got to ride a cable car which took him to a retail district of the city. He grabbed a light lunch at a burger joint and then returned to the Fairmont where he could nap a bit before he headed out to the Black Hawk that evening. But first he called Carrie.

"Babe? It's me," he said when she picked up the phone.

"Bucky! How was the flight? I miss you like crazy already!"

"It was long and boring, but I got here in one piece. I took a tour of the city. It's a very beautiful place, but there's something about these West Coasters that feels different from New York. Not quite sure what it is, but I can sense it. I'm going to see this Brubeck trio tonight, then maybe catch a few other players, and then come home."

"Are you eating, darling?" said Carrie.

Buck laughed. "You sound like my mother, sweetheart."

"Gotta make sure my man stays healthy," she said.

"I am. Promise. Now I'm going to lay down for a bit before I head out. I love you, darling. Kiss the kids for me."

"Love you too. Hurry home to us, Bucky."

After he hung up, he took off his shirt, flopped down on the bed and fell asleep instantly. At six he awakened, dressed and asked about a nice restaurant where he could get dinner. He showed the desk clerk the list Kelsey had drawn up for him.

"Oh! This one for sure," said the clerk. The Tadich Grill. It's the oldest restaurant in the city; it dates back to 1849 and the seafood is fantastic. They also have great steaks and chops if you aren't crazy about fish. It's in the financial district. Would you like me to call a cab for you, Mr. Fisher?"

"That would be terrific. And thanks," said Buck.

The cab arrived ten minutes later and Buck was ushered to a seat in the historic restaurant. It's art deco interior, elaborate moldings and dark woodwork bespoke of an earlier age, but it was comfortable, warm and homey. The menu was extensive and Buck decided to ask the waiter what he recommended.

"One of our house specialties is called *cioppino*. It's a mixture of shrimp, crab, clams and mussels, scallops plus pieces of the catch of the day all served in a rich tomato-based broth with a touch of wine added. It's an authentic Italian-American dish that originated right here in San Francisco. Believe me, you won't regret it."

"Not exactly kosher cooking, is it?"

"Sir?"

"Never mind."

"Not too spicy, is it?"

"Oh, no, no, no. Too much spice would mask the taste of the fish. Would you like something to drink with your meal?"

"OK, lets go with what you suggested, but just water for the time being."

The waiter thanked Buck, took his menu, bowed slightly and brought the order to the kitchen. Twenty minutes later, the waiter brough the dish in a bowl as big as a wash basin. "Holy cow! This is all for one person?" said Buck.

"Take your time—and enjoy," said the waiter.

Since the Brubeck trio wasn't scheduled to start its first set until 9 PM, Buck took his time to savor every morsel of seafood in the dish. He could not remember a single occasion when shellfish had been served in the Feinstein household when he was growing up. It wasn't that it wasn't kosher or anything, but it was costly. Now and again Rachel would broil filet of flounder or even sole. And of course, there was the pike and whitefish when she made gefilte fish. Buck's experience with shellfish came at the many places he had eaten at when his band toured. But nothing compared to the *cioppino* he was now relishing. At the end of the meal, the waiter brought a finger bowl and hand towel to the table, a necessity since the crab legs were eaten with the hands.

Buck declined dessert, asked for the check, which was surprisingly reasonable, and left a handsome tip for his waiter. He asked the seating hostess to call a cab for him. When it arrived, he asked the driver to take him to the Black Hawk Club.

The Black Hawk nightclub located on Hyde Street in the Tenderloin district of the city was one of the most popular jazz clubs in San Francisco. It had an intimate atmosphere perfect for a small combo such as the Brubeck trio. He sat at a small bistro table near the band and ordered a martini. At nine, the trio members came out from behind a curtain and they took their places at their instruments.

It only took two songs for Buck to understand what Bill Dwyer was trying to explain to him. The first thing that he noticed was that Paul Desmond on alto sax was almost the exact opposite of Charlie Parker. Whereas Bird could fit more notes into a single measure than would seem possible, Desmond's playing was almost spare. And yet, it sounded completely different from the kind of jazz Buck had grown up with. When Desmond laid out and Brubeck took his piano solos, the chords seemed outrageous. They were dissonant, and yet they fit the character of the piece he was playing. As any musician would, Buck tried tapping his foot to the songs, but he found it impossible to find a consistent downbeat. That was something he had to ask about.

At one point while Brubeck was playing and Desmond laying out, the alto sax player made eye contact with Buck and his eyes opened wide in recognition. Each song featured extended solos with even Sam Saxon on bass taking an extended ride and so the entire first set consisted of only four tunes. At the break, Buck approached the group and it was Desmond who said, "Holy

## A CHANGE OF KEY

Mother, Buck Fisher?" The two men shook hands and Desmond said, "Hey Dave, come on over here and meet a genuine legend."

Brubeck also recognized Buck and vigorously shook his hand. "Well, Jesus, what the heck are you doing in this sinful city, Buck?"

"I came to hear you guys play. That set was really something," he said.

"Come on into the dressing room and let's talk," said Brubeck.

They sat on folding chairs in the tiny space and it was Desmond who said, "You know, Buck, Dave and I met in the 253$^{rd}$ Army Band. I was in the group and he was trying out. He got sent to Europe but I profiled out and stayed stateside. We got back together after the war and here we are."

"Let me ask you about your music. It's very different, isn't it?" said Buck.

"It's very *avant garde* if that's what you mean," said Brubeck. "See, the kind of music you played in your band—and don't get me wrong, that band and most of the rest of the swing bands were terrific with great sidemen—with your tenor being about the best of the lot, but why does jazz have to be in 4/4 time or cut time? Who wrote that in stone? We're experimenting with new time signatures. Here, let me show you."

Brubeck picked up some piano sheets from a small vanity and showed them to Buck. He was amazed to see time signatures like 13/4, 7/4, 5/4. "How can you dance to this, Dave?" asked Buck.

"Ah, that's the trick. We're not a dance band. We're a lot more cerebral than that. We want our audiences to really listen to the music and try to hear the complexity of the chordal structure."

Buck wasn't an expert at theory, but a glance at the piano chart showed that Brubeck had intentionally written chords with some very odd and unmusical intervals like seconds and fourths, which made them intentionally dissonant. Desmond saw the look

## A CHANGE OF KEY

of confusion on Buck's face and laughing, he said, "Yeah, I know, it took some time before I figured out how to improvise over those chords without sounding like a junior high school band hitting all the wrong notes."

"We're going even further than this, Buck," said Brubeck. "I have this tune rolling around in my head which does something very different in 9/8 time."

"Seriously?" said Buck.

"Think of Bach's 'Jesu, Joy of Man's Desiring." It's in 9/8, but its divided into threes; 123, 123, 123 and so forth. What I'm thinking about is doing it this way: 12, 12, 12, 123. It's got the same number of counts in each measure, but it's just subdivided in a different way. I haven't put it down on paper yet, but I will someday."

It was a masterstroke musically, and very sophisticated stuff, so different from traditional jazz. "Let me tell you why I'm here. I work for RCA Victor now. I scout out new talent to sign to our label and then develop that talent so they and Victor make a lot of money. We're moving into the area of LPs now. 78s are as dead as Marley's ghost. This is all new to us and we want to offer a catalogue which features a wide variety of styles and performers. Are you currently with a label?"

Brubeck and Desmond exchanged glances. "We signed a deal for three albums with Columbia. They've given us a year to produce the first one, but we still have to find a drummer who can handle all these new time signatures. No luck yet," said Brubeck. Know anyone who might fit the bill?"

"Nah, but damn. That's too bad. We would have signed you in a heartbeat. Well, how about I leave a card with you. If Columbia doesn't do right by you, give me a call and we'll see what we can do together. Our aim is to be number one in the LP business so we'll promote the hell out of our artists."

"You know Buck, there's a bunch of other players out here on the coast that you might want to listen to. Chet Baker on

## A CHANGE OF KEY

trumpet, Art Pepper on alto, and Gerry Mulligan on bari sax are all out here. Try to catch some of them," said Brubeck.

"Yeah, Baker's a real comer. He's still in the Army over at the Presidio but on weekends, you can catch him at Bop City. He's an interesting guy and I think you'll like him," said Desmond.

"Thanks, I will," said Buck.

Then Desmond said, "I was at Fort Meade in First Army when I got the word you were forming a big band and were looking for players. But right after that, I hurt my back in a godamned PT test and they gave me a profile. I had to stay with the 253$^{rd}$. They never would have sent me to England, but I sure as hell would have loved playing in that band."

"Thank you, Paul. That's very flattering. I'm going to listen to the second set and then head out. It was a real pleasure hearing you and getting to talk to you," said Buck.

On his way out of the dressing room, Desmond said, "Check out a kid named Sandy Adams. He's at the Boom Boom Room. I think you might be impressed by him."

"Will do—and thanks again," said Buck.

The second set proved to be just as interesting as the first set—defying every musical principle Buck had grown up with, yet fascinating nonetheless. He knew that the group would one day achieve stardom and he was saddened by the fact that Columbia had already snapped them up. He returned to the Fairmont, jotted down some notes and went to sleep early.

The desk clerk informed Buck that the Boom Boom Room was located in the Pacific Heights section of the city and was in the clerk's words, "kind of a dive." Benny wasn't put off by that since he had played his share of such establishments as a rising sideman in Brooklyn.

"How about another restaurant recommendation?" asked Buck. "The Tadich Grill was fantastic last night. One of the best meals I've had in ages."

## A CHANGE OF KEY

"If you aren't tired of seafood, you might consider The Old Clam House. It's not quite as old as the Tadich, but it's been in the same place since 1861. They have fantastic prime rib, if you feel like meat."

"That sounds good. Can you have a cab ready for me at about six this evening?" asked Buck.

"Certainly, Mr. Fisher. It will be waiting out front for you." Then the young man looked sheepishly at Buck and said, "Mr. Fisher? Do you think I could have your autograph?"

Buck laughed and said, "Here I thought I was anonymous."

"Oh, no sir. My mom has a whole collection of your 78s on Bluebird. She said you were the greatest tenor player of all time."

"Well, I think she might have exaggerated a bit, but thank her for me. Sure I'll give you an autograph if you have a piece of hotel stationery. By the way, what's your name, son?"

"It's Bobby Tenant."

Buck wrote on the paper, "To Bobby: Thanks for all the good advice on eating and the great service at the Fairmont. Best always, Buck Fisher."

"This is great, Mr. Fisher! Anything else you need, you just ask and I'll get it for you."

"It's a deal, Bobby. Call me at about a quarter to six and I'll come down to the lobby to get that cab."

"Sure thing, Mr. Fisher."

It was only four in the afternoon, so Buck wanted to call Carrie. It was seven on the east coast and maybe the kids would still be awake.

Carrie answered and was thrilled to hear from Buck. "Darling! How's it going there?"

"Pretty well, hon. Hearing a lot of music and checking someone else out tonight. Are the kids still awake?"

"Yes, both of them."

**A CHANGE OF KEY**

"Can I say hello to them?"

"Sure let me round them up. Eddie! Laura! It's daddy. He wants to say hello."

Buck spent the next ten minutes talking to his children who were so excited to speak to him. He suddenly realized that he couldn't go home without bringing them something—Carrie too. The next day he would spend several hours shopping for them.

"How is everyone there, hon?" asked Buck.

"Just fine. Arlene, Bevvy and I get together every night and kick around ideas for the wedding. She's so excited, Buck. We're going to make this so special for her."

"How about Mama?"

"We talk every day and when I go out to the supermarket, she watches the kids and I pick up anything she needs. She sends her love and says to make sure I tell you to eat."

"Figures," said Buck.

"I'm counting the days, Bucky. Three to go and you're home to me," said Carrie.

"Be there before you know it. Hugs and kisses to everyone," said Buck before he hung up.

He showered and shaved, changed his clothes and by that time, the phone rang and Bobby Tenant said, "A quarter to six, Mr. Fisher. Cab will be here soon."

"Thanks, Bobby. Coming right down."

The Old Clam House was located on Bay Shore Boulevard and the cab driver knew it well. The ride took about a half hour to maneuver through traffic to get there. The interior of the restaurant was a step back into the 19$^{th}$ century. Patterned floors, solid oak bar, checkered table cloths that resembled those at Peter Luger's in Brooklyn where Carrie once took Buck to dinner for his birthday in the very early days of their dating relationship.

The hostess offered him a choice of table or booth and Buck opted for a booth. As with the Tadich Grill, the menu was

## A CHANGE OF KEY

oversized with numerous fish dishes. One entrée that caught his eye had the odd name of Surf and Turf. When his waiter came to the table to take a beverage order, he asked him what that meant.

"It's a combination of an eight-ounce piece of prime rib and a ten-ounce lobster tail. It sounds like a lot of food, but don't forget, the weight of the lobster tail includes the shell so it's not as much as you think. It's one of the house specialties and lots of people order it."

"That sounds good. I'd like that," said Buck.

"How would you like your prime rib cooked?"

"Rare as possible, if you don't mind."

"Certainly. I'll bring your drink right away."

When the waiter brought the enormous plate of food, Buck wondered if he should be more careful about eating too much. Though mostly healed from his wartime injury, he could not deny the fact that he had lost over two feet of his intestines. Now and again, his belly reminded him with shooting pains which he tried without luck to hide from Carrie. She had been his watchdog, preparing easily digestible meals that would put minimal strain on his innards. And now, he was looking at a side of beef and a lobster tail plus sides of a baked potato and string beans.

"Eh, what the hell, it's not like I eat this way all the time," he thought.

After eating to the bursting point, he once again declined dessert and asked for the check. The hostess called for a cab for Buck and he told the driver he was looking for the Boom Boom Room.

"I know the joint," said the driver. "It's kind of small, but there are a lot of regulars who go there just to get sloshed. They have live music, but those alkies aren't really interested in it."

A smallish sandwich sign outside the club advertised 'Live Music,' and beneath is, was scrawled in black crayon, 'Terrell Chance Quartet featuring Sandy Adams.'

## A CHANGE OF KEY

If possible, the Boom Boom Room was even more of a dive than Bobby Tenant had intimated. Buck entered the club and was enveloped in a cloud of blue smoke. The entire room was redolent with the smell of old beer and greasy burgers.

As he looked around the club, he wondered how a quartet could possibly fit in it. But the piano was an old upright which took up less room than a baby grand. The trap set was minimal and a string bass lay on its side next to the drums.

Buck ordered a martini and spent the next half hour until the band began watching the crowd. Dancing was out of the question in such a small room so anyone who came for the music came just to listen.

The group chose as its first song, "How High the Moon," a song that had made its debut in 1940 in a Broadway revue called "Two for the Show" and Broadway star Alfred Drake introduced the tune. Sandy Adams on baritone sax looked like he was no older than fourteen. He had a baby face which no razor had ever had need to touch. He was slender and had he been in the Army with Buck, his platoon mates would have dubbed him "Stringbean."

After the exposition of the melody, Adams began his ride, which to Buck's ear sounded bizarre on a baritone sax. Even in the upper register, the instrument had a distinctive throaty sound never as pure as the tenor or alto saxes. The kid obviously had chops. His improvisation was not as harmonically wild as Paul Desmond's, nor as blazingly fast at Charlie Parker's. It lay somewhere in between. There was no question about Sandy Adams' creativity. He had an inventiveness that was startling in someone so young. He was playing figures that Buck had never heard—even in Charlie Parker's playing. His improvs never strayed too far from the melody, which was close to Buck's own style. But the chords gave those episodes a totally different sound.

Next from the group was an original which Terrell Chance at the piano announced was called "Flamin' Blues." This composition was in a more Parkeresque tempo, Adams' fingers

# A CHANGE OF KEY

flying over the keys in both registers. Was it bebop? Perhaps—but maybe West Coast bebop would be a more accurate description.

Two more numbers completed the first set: a 1923 chestnut, "Who's Sorry Now?" and a down-tempo ballad by the Gershwin brothers, "The Man I Love." Buck wasn't sure if it really worked on baritone sax. The melancholy lyric was much more suitable for a tenor or even an alto. Nevertheless, Sandy Adams was able to find its emotional core and his improvisation after the exposition was a thing of beauty.

After the set ended, Buck went up to the band and said, "Sandy Adams? I'm Buck Fisher. Can I have a word with you?"

The young man's expression was priceless. "THE Buck Fisher?"

Buck laughed and said, "I don't know any others of that name, so yeah, I'm THE Buck Fisher."

"Wow, this is really something," said Adams, pumping Buck's hand like he was jacking up a car. "My mom used to tell me a story about how she snuck out one night to hear you and your band when you played in Boulder at the University of Colorado. She said there's never been anyone like you."

"That's very kind of her. Listen, Sandy, can we go someplace and have a chat?"

"Sure. There's no dressing room, but it's not too crowded tonight so we can get a table near the back of the room."

For the next twenty minutes, Buck explained why he was there and what he was offering. "Gee, Mr. Fisher, Terrell and the other guys all have families and they live here in San Francisco. I don' think they want to move back east."

"That's understandable, Sandy, but it's not a problem. RCA has studios in Los Angeles and San Francisco. You could stay right here, but there are some things you might want to know. Your type of jazz is a whole new scene in America. It's very different from Swing era jazz. I think it's in a very experimental stage right now. If you accept a recording contract from us, you can play the same way you're playing tonight. But there might be a few less originals and more standards that we want to hear so record buyers can get used to what you're doing. Once we can see if your records sell, you can get a little more daring."

"So you want the final say as to what goes into an album, is that right, Mr. Fisher?"

"That's about the size of it. But it's how Victor works with all our artists."

"What if the other guys don't want to do it?"

"It's up to you, Sandy. If you want to stay with them, we'll shake hands right here and no harm done. Or, if you want to leave them, I can always find studio musicians to back you up. I think you should know that from what I heard tonight, you're the star of this group. People will buy records to hear you, not the bull fiddle player or the drummer. There's a lot of money to be made in this business, Sandy, and RCA has the muscle to promote you and get you to the top."

"Jeez. Can I have a couple of minutes to talk to the guys, Mr. Fisher?"

"Sure. I'm going to stay for another set anyhow," said Buck.

"Good. Talk to you later, Mr. Fisher."

The second set mimicked the first. It combined jazz standards with original compositions. Though Buck preferred the standards, he did find the originals, very modern in sound, fascinating. But would they sell to more than a small segment of the listening public?

When the set finished with a vivace version of "You'd Be So Easy to Love," Sandy Adams spent a few minutes talking to his band mates. Then the four of them came to Buck's table and introduced themselves.

"A real pleasure, Missa Fisher," said Tyrrell Chance. "Ya know, I'm from back east. Harlem, up on 136th Street. I come out here five, mebbe six years ago. Time was I used to play a lot at the

Savoy. Once subbed at the Cotton Club and I was the piano accompanist at the Apollo Theater's talent nights."

On a hunch, Buck said, "Ever run into a guy named Buddy Scraggs?"

"Heh, ole' Walker? What he doin' these days?" said Roland Fish, the bassist in the quartet.

"Actually, he works for me. I've formed an RCA studio orchestra to back up all the singers and other acts we're signing to our label. He's a really fine player," said Buck.

"Long as he stays sober, ain't none better," said Edgar Ruwan, the quartet's drummer.

"Nah, he on the wagon fo' years now," said Fish. "He had 'is troubles, but he over them now, I figure, or you wouldna hired him."

"So what do you guys think about signing with RCA for a couple of albums?"

It was Tyrell Chance who said, "Missa Fisher, you say this young white boy here is going places—maybe even to the top. I sho' would like to take that ride wit 'im."

"Me too," said Edgar Ruwan.

"An' me three, said Roland Fish."

"Good. Sandy explained about how we put together the sessions, have input into the material but give you enough artistic freedom to be creative."

"You gonna do all you say, Missa Fisher? I mean to make us famous? And you sayin' you always gonna be fair with us?" said Tyrell.

"It's Funny, Tyrell, but Buddy Scraggs asked me the same thing. He wanted to know if he could trust a white man to do everything he said he would. Well, I can get you his number and you can call him. He's been cashing a pretty fine paycheck every week—to the tune of fifteen thousand bucks a year," said Buck.

"Shee-it, ain't no black man makin' that kinda dough 'lessen his name is Basie or Ellington," said Ruwan.

## A CHANGE OF KEY

"That's what all my musicians make—and there's about thirty of them in the orchestra. Look, fellas, RCA is big—really big. We want you to succeed as much as you do—because let's be honest, it's all about the bottom line in a ledger some egghead accountant is keeping. You make money, we make money, and it's as simple as that."

"You a famous guy, Mr.—"

"Please, it's Buck."

"Awright, Buck, you a famous guy. You were the best and maybe you work in an office instead of in front of a band, but I know you did great things. You say you can make things happen for us, I trust you. Fellas?" he said, looking at the three other musicians.

Each one nodded indicating that they were in.

"Great. Tyrell, you're the leader of the band so you're going to be on point for the contracts. Give me your address and I'll have contracts drawn up and sent to you. Everybody has to sign them and then you send them right back to me. I'm going to have one of our producers fly out here to work with you on putting together recording sessions. His name is Phil Flagler and he's worked with everyone from Sinatra to Jimmy Lunceford. He's great at what he does. So let me have phone numbers and addresses for all of you. Here's my card, Tyrell. Any questions, any problems, any doubts, you call that number and I will take care of them. I'm the vice-president of this division and my word is pretty much the way it's going to be."

"You got yo'self a hot quartet, Buck. Thissa real special night for us. But now, we got two more sets to get through so we better hit the downbeat," said Tyrell.

Buck shook hands with the group and hailed a cab back to the Fairmont for much needed sleep. He put in a call at the desk for nine the following morning. It was too late to call Carrie and that saddened him because he missed her with every fiber in his body. He hoped he would dream about her as he fell asleep.

## A CHANGE OF KEY

.....

Buck had one more day in San Francisco and he wanted to hit what everyone said was the most famous jazz club in the city—Bop City. The club was located in what was known as Japantown, but when FDR ordered all Japanese on the coast sent to internment camps as a matter of national security, the population shifted from Japanese-American to Negro. The club itself had played host to virtually every famous name in the jazz world.

At the front desk, Buck said to Bobby Tenant, "Bobby, does Bop City take reservations?"

A look of panic crossed the young man's face. "Well—"

"Is there a problem? They can't be closed on Fridays," said Buck.

"No, but Mr. Fisher, Bop City doesn't even open until 2 AM!"

"Holy shit! Seriously?"

"I read in a local magazine that the owner of the club, Jimbo Edwards, doesn't want to open until all the other clubs have closed for the night. That way, his crowd is made up of real jazz fans and musicians coming from other jobs. The article said that admission is only a dollar and musicians get in for free. I can call and see if I can get you a reservation, but I hope you won't be upset if they're fully booked."

"No, that's OK, Bobby. See what you can do."

"Can you give me about twenty minutes, Mr. Fisher?"

"Take your time, Bobby. I don't have anything on my schedule for today."

The young man went into the inner office behind the registration desk. He came back in fifteen minutes and said, "Well!"

"Good news, Bobby?"

"I'll say. Mr. Edwards was at the club early cleaning up from the night before. When I told him Buck Fisher wanted to come to the club tonight, he said he'd have to roll out the red carpet for such a famous player."

"Well, Bobby, that throws a wrench into my plans, but let me ask you, is there any movie theater close by?"

"Oh sure, there's an RKO about five blocks from here. It's showing *The Best Years of Our Lives* and boy, has that picture got some great reviews."

Indeed it had, and it resonated with Buck. Veterans returning home from the war trying to adjust their lives to new realities, some coming home in one piece, one not so much. It also starred Myrna Loy who Buck had been crazy about ever since he saw her in *The Thin Man* and its sequels. It also starred Dana Andrews who had already made six World War II movies. Because he had fathered three children in the 1930s, he was exempt from the draft. But so convincing an actor was he, that one would never guess that he was not a veteran himself.

"I guess I'll get some breakfast and maybe lunch after the film. Then I'll come back here and sleep till about midnight. You can get me a cab so I'll make it to the club by two?"

"Absolutely, Mr. Fisher. I'll take care of everything. Oh, and you know that list of restaurants you gave me? Since you're here one more night, you might try Fior D'Italia. It's another one of those places that have been around forever—I think around 1886. If you like Italian food, it's the place to go."

"Say Bobby, I need to buy gifts for my kids and my wife. Are there any department stores you would recommend?"

"Well, there's a Bloomingdales not far from here, but I would take a cab if I were you. There's also a Nordstrom's and they're both on Market Street. But If I could make a recommendation, Mr. Fisher, go to Fisherman's Wharf. There's a chocolate factory there--Ghirardelli's. They have everything chocolate you could imagine. Maybe your wife would like that."

"Good idea, Bobby. Want to get me a cab?"

"Coming right up, Mr. Fisher."

# A CHANGE OF KEY

When Buck got into the cab, he said to the driver, "How would you like to make twenty bucks plus tip today?"

The driver, whose name, Herman Katz, was posted on his hack license on the visor of the windshield, spoke with a distinctive Bronx accent. "What, I'm driving Rockefeller or somethin'?" he said.

"No, no, but I have a number of places to go today and rather than having to call a cab after each stop, I'd like to hire you for the day."

He pulled away from the curb and said, "Fella, for a double sawbuck, I'd drive you to Seattle. Name's Herman Katz—from the Grand Concourse in the good ole' Bronx, USA. Came out here after the war. Third Infantry Division—Marne Division. Hiked all over goddamned Europe. Just another dogface soldier, like the song says."

"Pleasure to meet you, Herman. My name is Buck Fisher. Just call me Buck."

The cab screeched to a halt and Herman Katz turned around to look in the back seat. "Yer shittin' me. You're Buck Fisher?"

"Yes I am."

"Well dip me in shit and fry me," said Katz. "Wait till I tell Selma—she's the missus—who I drove today. Tell you somethin'. I got wounded shortly after D-Day. Took one in the hip and they sent me to some godamned shithole hospital in the north of England. Well I'll be damned if it wasn't your Army band that came to entertain us dogfaces. I remember this little girl you had singing with your band—a real looker. Sang like a canary or some goddamned bird, but I tell ya what, we all were glad you came. Lot of those boys never made it. I was one of the lucky ones---but then again, so were you. I was still up there in the hospital when news got to us about what happened to you. Tell you this, Buck, wasn't a dry eye in that hospital when we heard. Sure am glad to see you're home in one piece."

165

## A CHANGE OF KEY

"That's real nice of you to say, Herman. After that happened to me, I don't remember all that much. I got shipped home with my band and rode out the war at Ft. Hamilton in Brooklyn."

"Well, Uncle Sam takes real good care of me. I drive this hack just to keep busy. My wife—I tell you her name was Selma? She's a teacher, so money's no problem. That don't mean I won't take your twenty, Buck, but if I'm your driver for the day, just tell me where you want to go."

"Great. Fisherman's Wharf is first—that chocolate factory."

"Ah, sure. That's easy."

Buck got lucky. He found a large box of hand-dipped chocolates in a variety of shapes with different fillings. Carrie would love them, even though she was watching her weight carefully during her pregnancy.

Then Herman drove him to the wharf itself. He strolled along it inhaling the salt air of San Francisco Bay. In the distance, he could see Alcatraz Island—the infamous prison that had housed notorious criminals like Al Capone, Machine Gun Kelly, and Alvin 'Creepy" Karpis of Brooklyn's Murder Incorporated. He found a large store that sold everything from antiques to cooking utensils and everything in between. There he found the perfect gift for Eddie: a set of Lincoln Logs. Buck had a set when he was growing up and since Eddie loved his Erector Set, he thought he'd have fun with Lincoln Logs. The toy was invented by John Lloyd Wright, second son of the famous architect Frank Lloyd Wright, in 1916, so it was just a few years younger than Erector Set.

With two gifts taken care of, he still needed something for Laura. He said to Herman, "I'd like to find a doll or a set of dolls for my daughter. She plays with them all the time—tea parties and such. Any ideas, Herman?"

"Easy enough, Buck. I have three daughters and all they do is have tea parties all day with their dolls too. It's pretty cute to watch. I know a store over on Market Street that sells nothing but dolls. From all over the world. Hop in and I'll show you."

Hopper's was everything Herman Katz said it would be. Thousands of dolls in every size and shape, costumed in garb native to the countries they represented. It was a treasure trove. He wished Laura could be with him at that moment so she could look with a child's wonder at the amazing collection. After close to an hour in the shop, Buck settled on three miniature dolls, each one about seven inches tall and exquisitely dressed like princesses. Laura would love them.

Back in the car, Herman said, "Where to next, boss?"

"I tell you what, let me take you to lunch," said Buck.

"Selma packed me a sandwich, but I'll save it for tomorrow. Say, you like tacos?"

"Never had one," said Buck.

"Jesus, guy, you don't know what you're missing. I know a place over on Pine Street in the Tenderloin, 'Rufio's.' You're in for a real treat, boss."

Herman parked the cab and they were ushered to a booth and given menus. "I think you better order for me, Herman. I know *bupkis* about Mexican food. But nothing too spicy. Not good for my plumbing," said Buck.

"No problem. There's some Mexican food that'll burn your *gotkis* off, but I'll go easy on you."

When the waitress returned, Herman ordered two hard shell tacos and two soft shell—both with beef. Buck picked up his knife and fork and Herman said, "Uh uh, Buck. With your hands—like a Coney Island hot dog at Nathan's—but this one's form south of the border."

Buck enjoyed both types of tacos and washed them down with a Golden Glow beer, one of the popular brands in California. But even more than the food, Buck enjoyed the company of Herman Katz—two veterans who shared the common denominator of war. As an infantryman, Katz's exploits were a lot more heroic than Buck's. North Africa, Salerno, Sicily—the Marne Division had been in the thick of it for the entire war. "Yeah, we were one of Patton's favorites. He threw us into the shit every chance he got," said Herman.

"After my wound," he said, "they made a mistake. They sent me back too soon and it really screwed up my hip, which is why the Army is on the hook and has to pay me for the rest of my life. But I was there in time for Augsburg."

"What happened there, Herman?" asked Buck.

Herman paused mid-bite and stared at Buck. Then he said, "Dachau."

"Oh shit, no!" said Buck.

"Oh shit, yes," said Herman. "We were there. We saw the stacked corpses, the pits filled with bodies, the walking skeletons who barely looked human anymore."

"My God!" said Buck.

"God? Sorry Buck. God went AWOL in Europe. You think I still don't have nightmares about what we saw? Or what we did?"

"What do you mean what you did?"

Herman was silent for a minute, as it came back to him.

"Buck, the corpses were everywhere—thousands of them. The division doc was afraid of an outbreak of typhus or cholera or some shit. So the general ordered an Engineer Battalion to come into the camp and open up a trench. Then a front-end loader came in and just plowed the bodies into that ditch. They fell into that hole like falling leaves, Buck. It was enough to make grown men cry—and believe you me, lots of us did. Some things you just can't erase from your mind, Buck. I'll take those images to my grave."

"It embarrasses me, Herman. You guys on the line, what you had to do. And me? Never fired a gun in anger except when I was pissed off in Basic at the range. Makes me feel like I was a big nothing with my wound."

## A CHANGE OF KEY

"Oh, bullshit, Buck," said Herman with surprising vehemence. "You think we didn't know about that fucking buzz bomb that got you? About how you almost died? Shit, it was all over *Stars and Stripes,* same as it was when Glenn Miller vanished. You think every injury is the result of combat? We were training for the invasion of North Africa and a guy in my company was on the obstacle course. He got to the tower—you know the one, you probably did it in Basic. Well, he fell off. Broke his back. He'll never walk again and the government has to take care of him forever. You don't think that was a war injury?"

"I guess. But I think it was more like I was in the wrong place at the wrong time. Just lousy luck," said Buck.

That made Herman laugh. "You think you make a reservation to get shot, Buck? Bullets find the guys on either side of you but leave you untouched. You don't think that's luck? They even got a name for it: survivor's guilt. It's all luck. Thank God you were lucky enough to live."

"Too bad you live 3000 miles away from me, Herman. I think we could be really good friends," said Buck.

"Hey, you ever get out to the coast again, you look me up Buck. My Selma still makes a mean brisket. Old family recipe. So, let's finish up and tell me where you want to go next."

"There's a movie I want to see at 2:15. It's at the RKO not far form the hotel. It's almost a three-hour movie. Can you pick me up at six and we'll go to dinner?"

"You're spending a fortune on me, Buck. Sure you can afford it?"

"It's all on my expense account. What do you know about Fior D'Italia?"

"I know I'm not dressed for it," said Herman.

"OK, so while I'm in the movie, go home and change. And if you want to bring Selma to dinner, it's fine with me."

"For real?"

"Most definitely."

## A CHANGE OF KEY

"But first, I need to find a jeweler. I want to bring Carrie something really nice," said Buck.

"Nicer than chocolate? Got it. I know just the place. It's over on Haight Street. It ain't cheap, Buck," said Herman.

"That's OK, she's worth it."

Whitney's was a corner store with display windows on two sides. The black velvet tiers of jewelry showed every type of gem set in every kind of piece. Buck entered the store and was met immediately by a stately gentleman who was either the owner or the senior sales representative. He showed Buck dozens of pieces until finally, he selected a bracelet made of alternating diamonds and sapphires set in gold. It cost $125 dollars. A small price to pay to make Carrie happy. Back in the car he showed it to Herman who said, "Shit, Buck, I picked the wrong line of work! It's beautiful. She'll love it."

"Now take me to the theater, and don't forget to pick me up at six."

.....

*The Best Years of Our Lives* was everything the critics said it would be. At the conclusion of the film, there were very few dry eyes in the theater. There was still a half hour until Herman picked him up and that gave Buck a lot of time to think about the war. Even a year after it had ended, Buck found himself thinking about it an inordinate amount of time. He kept thinking that he ought to be able to do something for veterans. Maybe he would talk to Jack Merrill when he got back to the city.

Buck and Herman talked about the film on the way to Fior D'Italia. Unfortunately, Selma had a migraine so it would just be the two of them for dinner. Once again they traded stories, Herman about the Army, Buck about his musical travels.

"Did I tell you Buck that I knew Audie Murphy?"

"Get outta here!"

"No, really. He was my platoon leader when he got his direct commission. Soon thereafter he got hurt badly. He was slated to go to West Point, but that injury profiled him right out of the service. Everyone in the Third ID was proud that the most decorated soldier in American history started out like a plain old dogface soldier like the rest of us. I was his staff sergeant and he was a real righteous guy. He was absolutely fearless. Threw himself into every combat situation like he had some kind of a death wish."

Then Buck talked about his friendship with Glenn Miller and how he had subbed for Buck when he was in the hospital in London. "His death over the English Channel was a terrible loss to the music world," said Buck.

"You know, Buck, I'm not a musician. Never was, but I want to tell you something. Glenn Miller's band had such a distinctive sound. I guess it was what he did with those reeds. But your band, yours also sounded like no other band. See, that's the thing. If you took Goodman, Shaw, Herman, Barnet out of their solos in their bands, they'd all sound alike. Same number of instruments, same type of songs. Only you two were different. You should be proud of that."

"I am, but I can't take credit for it. Johnny Blair who first hired me was our arranger. He created the sound of the Buck Fisher Orchestra. He was a genius."

"What became of him?"

"Cancer. Ate him up from the inside," said Buck.

They finished up and Buck said, "OK, pal, time to get me back to the Fairmont and I'll grab some sleep before I head out to Bop City. At the hotel, Herman helped him get his packages out of the car and into the lobby. Buck then handed him a hundred-dollar bill.

"Shit, Buck, I don't have change for this C-note."

"Don't want it, don't need it. This has been great Herman. If you ever get back to the city, you look me up, hear?"

The two men embraced, then Herman slapped Buck on the back and said, "You're the greatest. Good luck, Buck."

**A CHANGE OF KEY**

At the desk, Buck told the clerk to give his room a call at midnight. Then he brought the gifts to his room and, undressed, and fell into a sound sleep.

…..

The day had been excruciatingly long, and it was about to get longer as a cab brought him to Bop City on Post Street. When he arrived, he told the fellow at the door who he was and that he had a reservation. That fellow turned out to be Jimbo Edwards himself. "I can't tell you what an honor this is, Mr. Fisher, to have you at our club," he said.

"Please, it's Buck."

"Come on in and I'll get you a great table. Drinks are on the house for you," said Edwards. He snapped his fingers and immediately a waiter came to the table to take Buck's order for drinks. "You need anything else, you just call me. We serve some good food here if you're hungry," said Edwards.

"I heard that Chet Baker is playing tonight. Is that right, Jimbo?"

"It sure is, and I think you're going to like what he does."

"Great! Can't wait to hear him.

Jimbo Edwards was not only the owner of the club, but he was also the emcee. At 2 AM, with the club amazingly jam-packed, he took the microphone of the stage and said, "Now all you cats and kittens, before we get started tonight—and I hope you'll drink yourselves silly—I'd like to announce that in our audience tonight, we have the greatest tenor man who led the goddamned best band this country ever heard—Buck Fisher!"

At first the crowd was quiet—then it jumped to its feet and applauded long and loud."

"Stand up for us, Buck—let everyone here see that you're home in one piece from the war and doing well."

Dutifully, Buck stood, waved to the crowd, and with a red face, resumed his seat. Several of the patrons immediately came to his table to shake his hand. Buck was flattered by all the attention, but he knew this wasn't exactly a 'swing' crowd there at two in the morning.

Chet Baker was everything Jimbo Edwards said he would be. He was movie star handsome with wavy black hair and a face that could have been chiseled from stone. His playing wasn't very different from Sandy Adams'. He had a total command of his instrument and he never approached the speed of a Charlie Parker but was inventive in how he utilized the chord structure of a piece. He could also sing. His rendition of "My Funny Valentine" from the 1937 Rogers and Hart musical *Babes in Arms,* was a masterful piece of emotion, phrasing and delivery. When he was hearing it, he immediately wanted Kip Roman to write an arrangement for Fran Michaels. It would be perfect for her.

At the break he introduced himself to Chet Baker who said, "Jeez, this is really great! How did you like the set?"

Buck proceeded to tell Baker why he was there. "You know, Buck, I'm on the hook in the Army until 1951."

"Really?"

"Yeah I enlisted in '46 and got assigned to the 298th Army Band in Berlin. I was there when that Cold War thing started to get a little warmer, but I ETSed the same year because the Army was shrinking after the war and they said they didn't need me. There was nothing much doing for jobs when I got out, so I re-upped for five years and got assigned to the 6th Army Band here at the Presidio. They said I'd make rank quickly if I re-upped. The Army's not going to let me sign a contract while I'm government property—you know how it works."

"When's your hitch up?" asked Buck

"Late 1951."

"Well, Chet, let me leave you with a card. When you ETS again, give me a call. I think RCA would really like to have you with our label. We're big and getting bigger in the area of popular music. We've got some terrific people lined up already and I think you'd be a perfect fit for the direction we're moving in."

## A CHANGE OF KEY

"Thanks, Buck. I'll definitely do that."

"I'm going to stay for another set and then head out. Great to meet and hear you, Chet."

The next set again showed off Baker's technique and voice. What a coup it would be if he could sign him—in 1951.

By 3:30 that morning, Buck was in a cab headed back to the Fairmont. He remembered little of what he did when he got to his room. He fell asleep instantly and slept until eleven the next morning. As soon as he woke up, he called Carrie and told her he would be leaving early the next morning.

"Tell that plane to fly fast, love, I can't wait to have you home with us," she said.

Once he was up and about, Buck spent the rest of the day just wandering about San Francisco for a final look at the city. It had been a very successful trip but home was home, and he couldn't wait to get there. Bobby Tenant woke him at nine and had a cab waiting for him by ten. Buck handed Bobby a hundred-dollar bill and said, "Thanks for all your help, Bobby. You made my stay here a real pleasure. Next time I get out to the coast, I'll be sure to book my stay right here."

Bobby stared at the bill and stammered, "Th-thank you, Mr. Fisher. I was just doing my job, you know."

"You did it very well, Bobby."

"This will help pay for a semester of college, Mr. Fisher. Thank you again."

They shook hands and Buck grabbed his bag, his other bag full of presents, and headed for the cab and the airport. Knowing he would soon be with his family again made the trip endurable.

# CHAPTER FOURTEEN
## *Fate Deals the Cards*

Buck's reunion with his family was all he hoped it would be. Once Carrie was in his arms, he didn't want to let go of her. Their kiss had all the warmth and love of two people who even after years together were still passionately in love. The children shouted in joy when they saw Buck, Laura insisting that he look at her latest coloring book masterpiece and Eddie chattering on about how he had lined up his toy soldiers.

He had arrived home in time for a simple dinner of roast chicken. During the meal, he filled Carrie in on all the details of the trip, who he had met, who he had potentially signed, how different the jazz was on the west coast, where he ate. Everything. Carrie wanted all the details.

When it was her turn, Carrie talked about how she spent the week. "Darling, I know it was only a week but it seemed so long without you—more like a month," she said. She talked about helping Arlene plan the wedding, checking up on Mama every day, having dinner at her house with the kids, getting together almost daily with Cathy Dwyer, how well the kids were all getting along. She went on and on and Buck enjoyed every word.

"Sounds like you didn't have time to miss me, Mrs. Feinstein," said Buck.

"Give me a few hours and you'll see just how much I missed you. For now, I'm going to get these two scamps ready for bed. Just put the dishes in the sink. I'll do them later," she said.

Everyone got up from the table and Buck opened his arms to Carrie, who came to him and kissed him tenderly on the lips.

"Ewwww! Dad!" said Eddie.

"Oh, sorry, buddy. It's an adult thing."

Laura looked at her brother and just shook her head like a wise old woman would. Then she said, "Don't mind him, daddy, he's just silly. And mommy missed you lots."

## A CHANGE OF KEY

"OK, brats, come here and hug your old man and then hit the sack. Pleasant dreams to you both."

That night in bed Buck and Carrie made love again and again. Slow, sweet, giving love. They shared their bodies, pleasured each other and Carrie kept murmuring how much she loved him. After their third coupling, Buck thought to himself that he hoped he'd never have to leave her again. Not even for a few days. They fell asleep spooning together with Buck holding Carrie's breasts, his nose nuzzling her neck, and both of them smiling contentedly.

…..

The next day back in his office, there was much to accomplish. He called Jack Merrill who asked him to come up right away. Jack wanted to know who he had heard and what the prospects were for signing them. Buck told Jack who he had seen and who he wanted for the label.

"It's a pity we couldn't get Brubeck, Jack. He's really doing incredible stuff," said Buck.

"Well, we don't want to get too far out of the orbit we move in, Buck. I mean, he sounds really great and all but very *avant garde* stuff."

"That's exactly what Brubeck called it. But I tell you Jack, Paul Desmond is one incredible alto player. Like no one I ever heard before. He kind of wanted to move to RCA, but they're tied up in that contract with Columbia. If he ever leaves that group, I'm sure we can sign him."

Buck then told Jack about Perez Prado and as he surmised, Jack said, "We're going to get him on our International label. We'll distribute mostly south of the border but maybe we'll release a few singles here and see how they play. Then we can cut an album with him."

"Speaking of albums, Jack, where do we stand with Fran's? asked Buck.

He buzzed his intercom and said, "Margie, would you bring in all of the Fran Michaels PR materials so Buck can take a look at them? Thanks."

## A CHANGE OF KEY

Jack's secretary then came in with a life size cut-out of Fran, a mock-up of the album cover, glossy posters for every record store in the tri-state area and more for shipment throughout the country. There were also several different tent cards that could be put on counters and tables in clubs, bars and restaurants. "We also have some thirty second radio ads prepared for local stations—especially WNEW," said Jack.

"You've been busy since I was gone," said Buck. "This is all great stuff, Jack."

"We think she's going to be one of our biggest stars, Buck, so we're giving it the full-court press to get her name and albums out there. Hopefully by May 1$^{st}$, the albums are in the record stores all across the country. Did you bring a copy of the liner notes for the album?" asked Jack.

"Right here." He handed a typed sheet to Jack who perused it:

*When you talk about the voice of the century, you think Crosby, Sinatra, or Ella Fitzgerald. I'm proud to say that you can now add another voice to that list: Fran Michaels. I first met Fran when she auditioned for my civilian band when my vocalist (now my wife) Carrie Collins went on maternity leave. Fran was right out of college back then, a trained opera singer out of the Juliard School who had just done a local performance of Puccini's Tosca. As soon as I heard her, I knew she was going to be a big star and once her voice was heard on our Bluebird 78s, sales took off like no one expected. My band became a huge success and Fran Michaels was a tremendous part of that. When I got back from the war and began working for RCA Victor, her voice was one of the first I wanted to be featured on the new LP format. The disc you are holding is a collection of wonderful songs sung by an amazing stylist. Watch for her name, because you're going to be seeing it a lot. And when you play this LP, you'll know why and recognize her for the phenomenal singer she is.*
*Buck Fisher*

## A CHANGE OF KEY

"That's good, Buck. It's got that personal touch that I was looking for. OK, I'll get this down to production and we'll start pressing albums in about a week. In the meantime, let's think of a follow-up for her," said Jack.

"You know, Jack, since this LP is coming out in May, sales will go on all through the summer and hopefully into the early fall. Maybe we should think about a holiday album for her as a follow up?"

Jack Merrill thought for a few moments before saying, "She's too classy to be singing 'Jingle Bells' or any nonsense like that, Buck. But if you can put together a playlist of songs to fill an album, I'll consider it."

"Thanks, Jack. Anything else?"

"No, I'll take it from here. I'll have legal draw up contracts for Sandy Adams, Tyrell Chance and Perez Prado. And by the way, you did great work out there, Buck. Proud of you."

.....

Back in his office, he found Kelsey Burton perusing the new copy of *Cue* magazine and jotting notes on a yellow pad. As her finger traced down the listing of clubs in the city, she paused and looked at Buck.

"Got something, Kel?"

"I may." She hesitated and Buck said, "What gives?"

"Buck, what did you say was the name of that girl soldier who sang with you in the Army band?" she asked.

"Cindy Kay. Well, Cynthia Kowalski, actually. We changed it when she joined the band. How come?"

"Don't hold me to it, Buck, but there's a Cynthia Kay playing at a club in the West Village on Jane Street called 'Tony's.' Think it could be the same girl?"

Buck smiled and said, "It's possible. When is she there?"

"She has a two-week run. First show is at 8 PM and then another at 11."

"Get me a reservation for two for this weekend. I want to bring Carrie to see her," said Buck.

"Got it."

## A CHANGE OF KEY

Buck then met with Bill Dwyer and Al Rovitz and reviewed everything that he had done on the coast and got a report of what they had been doing in the city. "Were those groups as good as I said they were?" said Bill.

"Definitely. Especially Brubeck, but Columbia grabbed him first so that's a no-go. But I got several others to go with us. Anybody check downstairs with Kip and the orchestra?"

"Not today," said Bill.

"OK, let's all go down and see what they're working on."

They took the elevator to the floor with the rehearsal studio and Buck shook hands with Kip and hugged Fran. "Doll? We've got huge things going on for you. I'll fill you in later, but oh boy are you going to be surprised."

Then he said to Buddy Scraggs, "Hey Buddy, I bring greetings from Tyrell Chance."

Scraggs' eyes lit up and he said, "Well, ah'll be. Me and Ty goes back lotsa years. How'd you run inta him?"

"He's backing a baritone sax player we're signing and we're bringing his quartet on board. They're a pretty good group," said Buck.

"Sho' would be with ole Ty at the helm," said Buddy.

Then Buck went over some charts with Kip and he told him, "We're thinking of a Christmas album for Fran, so start thinking about songs and how you're going to arrange them. Let's limit the corn."

"Already been giving it some thought, Buck. By next week I should have some things down on paper."

"Good. Keep me posted."

Back in the office, Buck took the issue of *Cue* from Kelsey and went into his office to see if he recognized any names playing locally. After a few hours, he called it a day and headed for home.

.....

"A package came for you, darling," said Carrie after hugging and kissing Buck when he entered the house.

"Were we expecting something?" he asked.

**A CHANGE OF KEY**

"Nothing I know of," said Carrie. Did you order anything from work?"

"No. Let me take my coat off, and let's take a look."

The package was about two and a half feet long and weighed maybe twelve or thirteen pounds. Carrie gave Buck a knife and he slit the outer packaging open. Inside was an instrument case that had in its upper left-hand corner a silver plaque that said Selmer. Buck released the two hasps and within the case was a brand-new, exquisite straight soprano sax with a rose lacquer finish. He stared at the instrument and Carrie noticed that his hands started to tremble.

"Bucky? Are you all right?"

He shook his head as if to clear it and said, "Oh, yes. I'm fine sweetheart. I guess Francois Boucault came through for me and sent me this horn." There was a small card in the accessory compartment of the case which said, "Use it well—F.B."

But Buck wasn't all right and Carrie knew it. She hugged him and said, "Come have dinner, darling."

Buck didn't say much at dinner but Carrie noticed that he kept looking around the dining room furtively, as though he expected to see someone or something. She also noticed that Buck was perspiring profusely. She came around the table and put her hand on his forehead. "Honey? Do you think you have a fever?"

"Huh? What? Oh, no, it's just very warm in here is all." Except it wasn't. "Sweetheart? I think you should go to sleep early tonight. I think maybe the trip from the coast has taken a toll on you. You need to rest."

"Huh? Oh. Maybe you're right, babe." He opened his arms to hug the kids, kissed them both goodnight and headed for the bedroom. At one point, Carrie would have sworn he had lost his way to the staircase to the second floor. She was frantic with worry. Once she was sure Buck was asleep, she called next door and got Beverly on the phone.

"Bevvy? I think there might be something wrong with Buck."

"What? What's wrong, Carrie?" said Bevvy.

**A CHANGE OF KEY**

"I'll be right over." Two minutes later, there was a light knock on the front door and Carrie opened it. Bevvy kissed Carrie and said, "Come sit down and tell me everything."

"It started when he opened the saxophone case from Selmer. He took one look at the instrument and he started to shake. At dinner he just wasn't himself. Something's not right, Bevvy, and I don't know what it is."

"OK. First thing, we're going to stay calm and try to figure this out. Something about seeing that instrument triggered something in Benny's head. What could it be?"

"I know he misses playing—a lot, but I also know he's afraid to touch his sax for fear that he'll get all torn up inside. I don't think that's going to happen or the doctors would have warned him," said Carrie.

"It's in his head, honey. You need to give him time to work through it."

"But how can I help him?"

"Patience, babe. Patience. Love him, support him and it will all turn out all right," said Bevvy.

By this time tears were streaming down Carrie's cheeks. Bevvy took a tissue from her purse and wiped them away. Then she hugged her and said, "Just watch him carefully, but don't let on that you're eyeballing his every move. Be subtle. If you need me or Arlene, just call. It's going to be all right."

But it wasn't. In the middle of the night, Buck started screaming incoherently in his sleep. He was flailing with his arms as if trying to ward off something repeating "No! No! No! He was crying as he called out, "Carrie! No!"

Carrie awoke horrified at what she was seeing. She hugged him and cradled his head against her breasts, stroking his hair, soothing him, saying, "My love, it's all right. Nothing can hurt you now. I'm here and we're all safe."

There was a look of abject terror of Buck's face, his eyes staring into some unknown oblivion. Suddenly, Buck stared straight at Carrie and looked as if he recognized her. Then he opened his mouth to scream until Carrie put her fingers on his lips, hugging him tightly saying, "No, my darling, no, I won't let anything happen to you—ever."

Buck was panting, almost gasping for air. Carrie eased him back onto the bed, still holding him tightly. Slowly, very slowly Buck's breathing returned to some semblance of normalcy. Before he closed his eyes, she heard him whisper, "Doc, pull it out of me!" Then he fell into a deep sleep.

Carrie got up and put her robe on, walking into the kitchen and sitting at the table. Out loud she said, "God, I need a cigarette," but that was never going to happen again. Instead, she poured herself an inch of Hennessy and sipped it trying to make sense of what had just happened. It really wasn't very hard to figure out. He was back in the gutter in London, dying, and he was in brutal pain. He was reliving the agony and something about seeing the new saxophone had triggered the whole thing. Maybe because that injury had robbed him of the thing he loved most—his musical life.

All right, she thought, if his mind keeps traveling back to that horror, maybe I should suggest that he see a psychiatrist to help him. She knew Buck would bridle even at the suggestion of him seeing a 'shrink,' and if this was like the last episode, he wouldn't even remember it in the morning.

She was right. Buck awoke the next morning with a fierce headache—but no recollection of what had occurred during the night. He showered, shaved and dressed for work with Carrie surreptitiously watching his every move. She brought him a cup of water and two aspirin for his headache. The whole thing was so sensitive, Carrie didn't know how she could bring it up, but then she thought there was no time like the present.

"Bucky? Can I talk to you, before the children wake up?"

"Of course, love, you look upset? What's wrong?"

"Come sit by me on the sofa," she said, leading him into the living room.

"Wow, this looks serious," he said.

"It is," said Carrie.

"Did I do something to annoy you, darling?"

# A CHANGE OF KEY

That scared him and for an instant, he thought Carrie was going to tell him she was leaving him. He took her hand and said, "Are you leaving me, Carrie?"

She immediately started to cry and said, "Oh my God! How could you think that, Buck? I love you with every cell in my being. I will never, ever leave you."

"Then what's wrong, darling? You look positively miserable," said Buck.

She took a deep breath and said, "Bucky, do you remember anything about last night?"

He thought for a moment and said, "Well, I think I got up to pee, but I'm not sure."

"No darling. You had a horrible nightmare. A shrieking, awful nightmare—and it's not the first time it's happened. You just went away, Buck. You were somewhere else and I couldn't bring you back right away. You had this look of terror on your face like I've only seen once before—when it happened to you before."

Buck looked confused. "Last night?"

"Yes darling, and it's terrifying when it happens. You mean you don't remember the nightmare at all?"

"I'm sorry, sweetheart, but I can't remember it. Don't be mad at me."

Carrie took his hand and kissed his fingertips. "Oh, Bucky, I'm not mad at you. I just want to help you."

"Help me how, Carrie?"

"Can I tell you what you said while you were having the nightmare?"

"You remember?" asked Buck, surprised.

"I don't think I'll ever forget it," she said.

Again Carrie took a deep breath. "Well, first you started screaming 'No, no, no! Then you shouted, 'Carrie, no!' And right before I finally got you to get back to sleep, you said, 'Pull it out of me doc.' Then it was over and you were back to a deep sleep."

For a moment, that look of terror she saw the previous night was back on his face.

## A CHANGE OF KEY

"Shh, shh, darling. It's all right now," she said, hugging him tightly.

Buck hugged her and said, "Why can't I remember any of this, hon?"

"Listen to me Buck—and listen to what I say coming from someone who loves you to the moon and back. Honey, there's something locked up inside of you. Those awful memories of what happened to you in London. You've never gotten over it completely and even though outwardly you seem perfectly fine, its buried deep in your mind and now and again it surfaces. I think when you saw the new saxophone that Francois sent you, it triggered those memories. I feel utterly helpless when it happens and I don't know how to help you."

"I'm so sorry, sweetheart," said Buck.

"No, no. This isn't about being sorry. It's about helping you to get rid of the demons inside you."

"You sound like I need a priest—a what do you call it, an exorcist or something."

Now for the hard part. "No, darling, not a priest, a doctor."

"Carrie, I—"

"No, wait."

"Bucky, in all the years we've been together, how many times have I asked you for something?" said Carrie.

"Not many. Almost none that I can remember. I just like doing things for you," said Buck.

"That's because you're the best man I could imagine. Damned near perfect. But now I'm going to ask you to do something for me. It's the only thing I want from you, darling."

"Which is?" said Buck.

"See a doctor. A doctor who will listen to you and help you. Please, Buck, do this for me," she said.

"Maybe these things will go away on their own, Carrie. You never can tell."

"It's possible, but why take a chance if you can get help now?"

"I'm not crazy, Carrie."

**A CHANGE OF KEY**

She hugged him again. "Of course you're not, darling. But you are troubled and I want to see you get past this. Will you do this for me?"

"Things are pretty busy for me now and—"

"Buck?"

He could sense defeat. "All right. I've never denied you anything. I'm not going to start now," he said.

Carrie smiled and kissed him ardently on the lips. "Thank you, my love. Thank you." Then she said, "I'm going to call Dr. Meyers and see if I can get a referral for us."

"Us?"

"Yes, I think at least at the beginning I should be there to explain what's been happening. Then you can go on your own. Sound fair?"

He kissed her and said, "For you, the world, darling. Now feed me and let me get to work before I lose this cushy job. Oh, and one more thing, hon. Maybe let's keep this just between us for now. I don't want the family to worry—or think I'm a wacko or something."

She saw no point in telling him that she'd already spoken to Bevvy, so she merely said, "Of course, darling. Anything you want."

"Oh, by the way, could you call Mama and ask if she could watch the kids Saturday night? You and I are going out. It's a surprise I think you're going to like."

"Wow. Man of mystery! All right, I'll call her this morning."

A half hour later, Buck was off to work wondering why Carrie thought a doctor could help him.

.....

Tony's in the West Village wasn't the seedy place Buck imagined it would be. It was located in one of the brownstones on Jane Street that had been converted to a nightclub that attracted the well-to-do crowd that lived in the Village. Buck introduced himself at the small reception desk and the gentleman who was manning it said, "I'm Tony Forlenza and this is my club. I hope you enjoy the show. Anything you and your wife want to eat, it's on the house. Drinks too."

"Thank you, Tony. Actually, I've come to see your singer perform."

"My wife?"

Buck looked at Carrie. "Your wife?"

"Yep. Almost three months now. She's quite a gal. I think you're going to like her. She can really sing," said Tony Forlenza.

He ushered Buck and Carrie to a table off to the side of the stage. The house lights dimmed and another young man, evidently the piano player in the quartet, welcomed the crowd and then said, "Ladies and gentlemen, Miss Cynthia Kay!"

And then there she was. Little Cindi Kay, the little girl with the huge voice and even bigger heart.

She opened with "Wrap Your Troubles in Dreams," and her delivery was perfect. Buck remembered a Glen Gray version of the song back in the early '40s with Gray's scratchy voice on the vocal. But Cindi's voice was like warm maple syrup. She followed it up with "On the Acheson, Topeka and Santa Fe," an upbeat song written by Johnny Mercer and Harry Warren. It had just won the Academy Award in 1946 and though it was more or less a novelty tune, Cindi turned it into a charming, yet swinging number. Eight more songs comprised the first act. Everything from Jerome Kern to the Gershwins to Cole Porter to Irving Berlin. Each song performed with a polished professionalism. Private Cynthia Kowalski had become a spectacular singer.

Carrie, who had met Cindi several times when the band was stationed at Fort Hamilton and even sang with her on one occasion, turned to Buck and said, "Darling, she's fabulous!"

When the set was over, Buck stood and walked toward the small band riser. Cindi saw him and said, "Oh! Oh!" She ran to Buck and threw her arms around him. "Buck! Oh My God, Buck! I can't believe you're here!"

Tony Forlenza witnessed the scene and came over and said, "Something I should know about?"

Buck laughed and said, "it's not what you think,"

## A CHANGE OF KEY

"Darling, this is Buck Fisher! My CO in the Army Band—and the best damned tenor sax player in the world!"

Tony then said, "Jesus Christ, what an idiot I am. I took the reservation and never made the connection with the name. Buck Fisher—in my club!" Cindi saw Carrie and ran to her to give her a big hug. "Carrie! You look fantastic! Come and sit. I want to hear everything," she said.

They sat at the table and Cindi took a pack of Chesterfields from a tiny purse. She lit it and offered one to Carrie. "No, babe, I'm done with those. You should be too."

"You're right," she said, exhaling a long stream of smoke towards the ceiling. "Soon."

"Cindi," said Buck, 'tell me how you got back to New York."

"Well, after my discharge, I went back to Nebraska and stayed there for a few weeks with my family. But there was just something missing. I tell you Buck, I was never happier than when I was singing in front of thousands of G.I.s, so I made up my mind to give it a shot in the big city. I met Tony by chance, more like fate, really, and we started dating. In a month I knew I was completely in love with this man. He encouraged me to keep singing and then he made me the headliner in his own club. No, it's not a brigade of screaming, whistling troops, but I'm happy, Buck. So happy to sing for people."

"Cin, do you remember what I told you the day we said goodbye at Hamilton?" said Buck.

"I'll never forget it. I was crying like a baby and you said I was going to be a star someday and that in your new job with RCA, you might be able to make that happen."

"Well? What do you say?" said Buck.

"Say? About what?"

"Would you like to be a star?"

Then Buck explained what his job was and how he was in the process of making Fran Michaels a musical superstar. "I'd like you to come to 30 Rock and audition for us. You'll be singing with the RCA Studio Orchestra that I've put together—and you'll see some of your old pals from the Army band. If it works out—and with a voice like I just heard I know it will—I'd like to sign you to a contract for several albums and start promoting your solo career."

All this time, Tony Forlenza had been silent, listening to Buck talk about what he wanted to do with Cindi. She turned to her husband and said, "Tony? What do you think?"

"Well, hon, if Buck can do what he says he can do, I say go ahead. It's what you've always wanted, and this could be your big break. Besides, Cin, you don't want to spend your entire career singing in front of fifty or sixty people—not with that voice." Then to Buck he said, "I don't know how you found my place, Buck, maybe it was just fate—but I'm glad you did."

Cindi lit another cigarette and said, "So what do I have to do, Buck?"

"Monday morning, come to 30 Rock. Here's my card. I'm up on the twenty-seventh floor. We can go over some details and then I'll take you down to the rehearsal studio and we'll have you sing for our arranger. He's also the conductor of the orchestra and I'm thinking of giving him the title of Music Director. Then we'll go back upstairs and iron out everything. How's that sound to you?"

"I love you Buck! Sorry, Tony, sorry Carrie—but this man, he gave me the opportunity of a lifetime and now he wants to do more for me. How do you thank someone like that?"

Buck smiled and said, "You can start by getting back up there and knocking my socks off in your second set."

"Just watch me!" she said.

By the second set, Cindi Kay was really showing her versatility. She did a scat version of "It Don't Mean a Thing if it Ain't Got That Swing," that was even more impressive than when Fran sang it in Buck's band. She followed the swing number with "You'll Never Walk Alone," from *Carousel*. The Rodgers and Hammerstein show had run for 890 performances on Broadway with John Raitt and Jan Clayton in the leads. Cindi turned it into an emotional soliloquy. When she completed the number, Carrie whispered to Buck, "This gal is a powerhouse, Bucky. That is some voice!"

That gave Buck an idea. He would bill Cindi as "Little Miss Powerhouse." RCA was going to make a ton of money off of Cindi Kay—and she would too. Buck and Carrie enjoyed every moment of the performance. When it was over, hugs and kisses were exchanged all around.

"Come back anytime you'd like, Buck," said Tony Forlenza. I never heard Cin sing better than she did tonight. Must've been you in the audience."

"See you Monday morning," said Cindi.

"Bright and early, I hope," said Buck.

"Count on it!"

Buck and Carrie drove back to Queens with Buck content in the knowledge that he had just found Victor's next star.

**A CHANGE OF KEY**

# CHAPTER FIFTEEN
*"You Have to Let it Go" May 17th, 1946*

Dr. Martin Engelhardt's office was on Park Avenue and 79th Street on one of the toniest blocks in the entire city. Buck found a parking space three blocks away and he and Carrie walked arm in arm to the office. It was 8 PM and Buck was evidently the last patient of the day. The office receptionist had Buck fill out five or six pages of medical history before leading Buck and Carrie into the doctor's office.

"Buck Fisher—and Carrie Collins! Welcome, welcome."

The two looked confused and Dr. Engelhardt laughed. "1937, Scheutzen Park in New Jersey. The Johnny Blair Orchestra on New Year's Eve. I heard the two of you way back then and have followed your career, Buck, ever since. When it became the Buck Fisher Orchestra, I felt you deserved that break and I was thrilled at your success."

Dr. Martin Engelhardt was a distinguished looking man in his early fifties with steel gray hair and piercing blue eyes. He wore horn rimmed glasses which gave him a marked professorial look. The expensive three-piece suit with a precisely tied blazer-striped tie completed the image of a successful, competent physician.

"Now, tell me, what brings you here?"

When Carrie started to speak, Dr. Engelhardt held up his hand and said, "Wait. Let me tell *you,* why you're here. But first, let me tell you a little about myself. I was a Marine. Not originally, but I was drafted in 1942 after Guadalcanal. So many of those boys were mentally shattered after that battle, the Navy Department felt they needed psychiatrists to help them deal with the horrors of what they saw and did, even doctors as old as I was. You know, the expression, the 'Thousand Yard Stare' was born on the Canal. I followed the Marines through every horror show in the Pacific: Tarawa, Peleliu, Saipan, goddamned Iwo and then Okinawa. Jesus Christ, Buck, the men I had to treat., first at Guam, then back at Pearl. I got out like you—a colonel. I'm still a

# A CHANGE OF KEY

reservist, you know, so I still treat so many of those Marines right here or at a Veterans Administration Hospital. Honestly? Some of them I just can't help. They're gone, Buck. Their minds lost in the mud and the blood and the stink of those jungle death traps. But I do what I can. OK, you're not paying me to hear me yap on and on. Let's hear from you."

It was Carrie who spoke. "I have to describe what's been happening, doctor because Bucky doesn't remember any of it. His nightmares—"

"Night terrors, Carrie. One step beyond a mere nightmare," said the doctor.

"All right, then night terrors." She then recounted every detail of what had been happening to Buck. She even talked about how the arrival of the new sax seemed to trigger what happened that night.

"That's exactly the word, Carrie—trigger. Think of it like opening up a valve in the brain. An image, an object—even a single word can open that valve and bring out what's been submerged for a long time. Sometimes for years, sometimes less."

"Aren't there any pills you can prescribe for Buck, doctor?"

"Oh, I can give him sleeping pills, but that's not treating the root of the problem. Take my word for it, it goes a lot deeper than just prescribing a sleeping pill or some other sedative. Your turn, Buck. I need to hear from you now."

"But like Carrie said, doc, I don't remember it."

"Sure you do."

"No, I—"

"Sure you do!"

Buck said nothing at first. He was taken aback by the vehemence of Dr. Engelhardt's tone. He stayed silent staring at the wall filled with the doctor's diplomas—and his framed commission in the United States Marine Corps.

"You do remember, Buck. Let me ask you, have you ever talked about it? What happened over there? Have you ever fully discussed it with Carrie or anyone else in your family?"

## A CHANGE OF KEY

"I didn't think anyone needed to hear the gory details, doc. Besides, I was unconscious for much of it. Maybe most of it."

"Then tell me what you do remember. Tell Carrie, Buck."

"I—I—"

"You have to let it go, Buck," said Dr. Engelhardt. It won't go away until you open up and accept what happened."

Buck reached out and took Carrie's hand. "It's all right, Bucky. I'm right here. Just talk and Dr. Engelhardt and I will listen."

Buck sighed and slowly began. "I remember the awful blast from the buzz bomb. It was so loud, and then I was flying through the air. The blast blew me into the street and I must have hit my head because I couldn't focus."

Here he paused and Dr. Engelhardt said, "You're doing fine, son. Keep going."

"Then there was the pain. I think I was bleeding from my mouth. I'm not sure. But I know I was covered in blood from my belly." He paused again and Carrie squeezed his hand.

"That piece of glass was sticking out of my belly and I wanted to pull it out, but I didn't have the strength to move my hands."

"What was going through your head, Buck?" said Dr. Engelhardt. "At that moment. What were you thinking?"

"Carrie! I pictured her face and I knew I was going to die and never see her again. Never hold her again. I—" At this point, tears were welling from his eyes and Carrie wiped them away saying, "Shh, shh, darling. I'm right here."

"Anything else Buck?" asked the doctor.

"I'm so ashamed," he said. "I tried to picture my kids' faces but I couldn't."

"Why are you ashamed, Buck?"

"They're my kids! How could I not know their faces?" said Buck.

The doctor put his pad down and looked straight into Buck's eyes. "Buck, you almost exsanguinated right there in the gutter. How many transfusions did it take to fill you up with blood again? Do you know when people donate a pint of blood how weak they get? Now think of all the blood you lost. It's not just the body that gets weak, Buck. Your blood feeds your brain and it was starving for food. I'm a little surprised you could even think of Carrie."

Buck nodded accepting what Dr. Engelhardt told him.

"OK, we're getting somewhere, son. Now, tell us what else you remember."

"Not much, doc. I woke up in the London Free Hospital and they told me I had been out for over five days. When I woke up, I didn't know where I was or remember much about what happened."

"What were you thinking when you were lying in that hospital bed, son?"

"That somebody had to tell Carrie. I needed to see Carrie."

"What else, Buck?"

He was having trouble holding his emotions in check. "The band. I was worried about the band. What would happen to them."

"At a time like that, why were you worried about a band?"

"I was their CO. I had responsibilities, doc!"

"Not to yourself? Not to Carrie? Not to your kids?"

"Well yes, of course, but these guys depended on me. I didn't want to let them down."

"Do you think they were worried that you were letting them down?"

That took some thought. "No, I guess not. I was the CO, but we were more like brothers—all of us."

"And I suppose none of them came to see you in the hospital and during your convalescence?"

"No, no, they all came. It was so good to see them—every one of them," said Buck.

"All right, son, let's try something. You game?'

"Sure, doc, whatever you say."

## A CHANGE OF KEY

"You were terrified that you would lose Carrie and never see her again. That about sum it up?"

Buck nodded. "OK, face her, Buck. Take your hand and touch her cheek." Buck did as he was told. "Now wrap your arms around her and hold her—tight." Again Buck complied.

"Does she seem real to you, son?"

"Well of course she does, doc."

"So you didn't lose her. She's right here—now. In the present. Is that right, Buck?"

"Yes."

Dr. Engelhardt leaned back in his chair. "So you see? Whatever you feared back then never came to fruition. You didn't die. You didn't let anyone down. Carrie's right here and I tell you something, Buck, I'm a pretty shrewd observer—and I'm not sure I've ever seen more love in a woman's eyes than I am seeing right now."

Carrie hugged Buck even harder. "The past, Buck. Sometimes it grabs us by the nuts—sorry Carrie—and twists them until our whole being gets contorted like an ill-made pretzel. But that can only happen if you let it. You have to fight it, son, you have to leave the past behind or you are going to have a lot of trouble enjoying the present and your future will look pretty dim. Let it go, Buck. Let it go."

Buck's hand was at his mouth and he couldn't fight back the tears which Carrie wiped away with a tissue. "But doc—"

"There are no buts here, Buck. You kept all this bottled up for so long, this was bound to happen. But now you've let it out. All of it. Your fears, the pain, the doubts—you've shared them with your wife and with me. I'll bet you a shiny new quarter that this is going to go away now. You know, Buck, I have some patients who have been with me for years. Years! Why? Mostly, they just need someone to talk to. I'm going to see you one more time, because I think that's all that will be necessary. See, you have someone to talk to, and she's beautiful and loving and she's your ear, Buck. Don't ever hold anything back from her and you will be fine. Oh, and that new saxophone? Don't let it trigger you.

## A CHANGE OF KEY

It's not a land mine and believe me, I've seen up front and close what one of those things can do. It's just a hunk of metal. Pick it up. Play it. Let it be your friend, not your source of fear. Conquer your fears, son, and you'll be amazed how good life will be."

"All right, doc. Let's see what happens," said Buck.

"Good. That's what I want to hear. Now, hey, it's late and I've got a wife and some grandkids in my house who want to see their Pop Pop—so the two of you get out of here. And Buck? You have my number. Anything you need to talk about, you just call me."

Buck stood and extended his hand to Dr. Engelhardt, thanking him profusely for listening to him and reassuring him that he would be fine. Back in the car, Carrie embraced him and said, "I love you, I love you—and I love you. I believe in this doctor, honey. I believe you—us—everything is going to work out perfectly."

Buck kissed her and said, "I don't know what I would do without you, Carrie. I don't even know who or what I would be without you."

"Good, because you're stuck with me forever, unless I die of hunger, so you better feed me pretty quick," she said.

"What would you like?"

"Let's go up to 86th Street and find a nice German restaurant. It'll be like the time we went to Luchow's on your birthday."

"German it is." It was after nine when they got to a place called *Jaegemeister* which meant hunting master in English, so Buck assumed it was some kind of a steak house. He was right. He let their waiter make suggestions and then followed his lead by ordering what he thought they would both enjoy. Over dinner Carrie could tell that he seemed a lot more relaxed, the worry lines all but faded from his face. The meal was excellent, and they finished stuffed like one of the pheasants that was on the menu. They held hands on the ride back to Queens and after checking on the kids, who Rachel had put to bed, Buck said, "Come Mama, I'll walk you home."

## A CHANGE OF KEY

"Walk me home? Benjamin, I live two houses down from you. You think I need a bodyguard to make sure I'm tucked in?" said his mother. "You go get some sleep. I'll scream if a robber comes up to me. They'll hear it back in Brooklyn."

Buck showed her to the door, kissed her good night and thanked her for taking care of the kids. "Everything all right, Benjamin?" she asked.

"I'm fine, Ma. I'm going to be just fine. Not to worry."

"Since when doesn't a mother worry?" She hugged Buck and was out the door.

That night, Buck and Carrie made love once before the two of them, mentally exhausted from the session with Dr. Engelhardt, fell asleep in each other's arms. Buck's sleep was dreamless and the following morning, he woke up refreshed and relaxed. Maybe, thought Carrie, his recovery has started.

.....

At half-past nine the following Monday morning, Cindi Kay found her way in the mammoth RCA Building to Buck's office. She introduced herself to Kelsey Burton and said that she had an appointment. Kelsey buzzed Buck and told him his appointment had arrived. Buck came out of his office, saw Cindi and opened his arms to her. Then he led her into his private office.

"Some digs you have here, Buck. Quite a step up from those barracks we used to stay in."

"You bet. Everything first class around here, Cin. And this is what I want you to be a part of," said Buck.

He then went over the details of the contract she would sign with RCA. "Basically, Cin, you would be an employee of the label. You'll have a regular salary, say twenty thousand to start."

Cindi, who had just lit a cigarette, almost choked on the smoke. "Did you say—"

"Yeah, that's to start. For that, you will commit to making three albums for us, with us holding an option for a fourth, based upon the success of the first three. Once the option runs out, you can decide at that point what you want to do. After an album sells a thousand units, you will receive royalties for each additional sale. The label maintains ultimate control over content on your albums, but as I have explained to the other artists I have brought on board, I will never impose anything on you without your input. We work as a team, here, Cin. It's not a dictatorship. What do you think?"

"You were a pretty damned good CO in the Army, Buck. Everyone trusted and respected you—and you gave me that big break when you got me into the band. I'm not going to start doubting your word after all that. Where do I sign?"

Buck laughed. "Don't you want to run it by Tony first?"

"Nah, he gave me his blessing and made me promise not to leave him when I become a big star. What can I say, Buck? I love the guy like crazy."

"Great. I'm going to have legal draw up the contracts and they should be ready in a few days. Let's go down and meet the orchestra."

When they got to the rehearsal studio, Chuck Fein shouted, "Jumpin' Jesus in boxer shorts! It's Little Sis!"

He laid down his bass fiddle and came to Cindi. "Chucky you big bear! Gimme your best hug!"

So petite was Cindi that it looked like Chuck's arms could wrap around her twice. She kissed him and patted his face. "You look great, Chuckie. Civilian life seems to suit you," said Cindi.

Then the rest of her Army bandmates came up to her and hugged her: Noni, Pete, Tony. Bill Dwyer and Al Rovitz also were thrilled to see her and hugged and kissed her. There was such a joy in seeing each other again. That soldierly bond hadn't faded since their discharges. For Buck, the bond was particularly strong. When he was laid up in the hospital, it was Cindi Kay who went out and bought another Victorian doll for little Laura to replace the one destroyed in the bomb blast. She sat by his side every day holding his hand. Chuck had called her 'Little Sis' and that's how every player in the band regarded her. They were protective of her and had the utmost respect for her talent.

Next, Buck introduced Cindi to Kip Roman. "Kip? Meet Cindi Kay. She's our next star. I'd like you have her sing for us.

**A CHANGE OF KEY**

If we don't have any charts for what she wants to do, I'd like you to write them soon as you can. Then to Cindi he said, OK, hon, what would you like to sing?"

"Do you have an arrangement of 'It might as Well be Spring?' she asked.

The song came from a Rodgers and Hammerstein film musical called *State Fair*. Margaret Whiting had a big hit with the tune, but covering other singers' material was part of the business. "I don't have a chart for that one, Buck, but Kenny? Do you know the tune?"

Kenny Ferraro, who had been the piano player in Buck's civilian band was a veritable encyclopedia of popular music. He had a thousand songs in his memory and in his fingers. "No problem, Buck. Cindi, what key?"

"How's F?"

"Got it. I'll give you four as an intro."

Fran Michaels walked into the studio as Kenny played the intro to the song. She looked at Buck who nodded towards Kenny as if to say, 'Watch.'

Cindi Kay had always been a powerful singer, but somehow in the intervening months since Buck last heard her, she had become mesmerizing. Her delivery was flawless, eliciting every ounce of the wistfulness and longing for love that the lyric contained. Then she asked Kenny if he knew "My Funny Valentine," the same song Buck had heard Chet Baker sing at Bop City.

"How's G, Kenny?" asked Cindi.

"You got it. You'll get four to set it up," he said.

It was a completely different song from Chet Baker's version. She made the lyric weep. She found its soul and strolled it around the block, never letting go of its hand. When she finished, Chuck Fein said, "Holy balls! Little Sis can still bring it, Buck!"

Fran Michaels said, "She's magnificent, Buck. Who is she?"

"Go ahead, Buck, tell her how we met," said Cindi.

"Cindi was my vocalist in the Army Band. We're thinking about signing her up at Victor."

"What's to think about? Get her name on a contract pronto," said Fran.

"Cin? What do you have up-tempo for us to hear?" said Buck.

"What about 'Swinging on a Star, Buck?'"

"Terrific." The Jimmy Van Heusen and Johnny Burke song had debuted in 1944 in the Bing Crosby film, *Going My Way*. It won the Oscar that year as Best Original Song. Crosby owned the song but lots of singers had covered it. He was backed on the Decca recording by the Williams Brothers Quartet, but Cindi would be singing it bare bones.

"Eb Kenny?" asked Cindi.

"Easy peasy, kiddo," said Ken Ferraro.

As Cindi sang, Fran Michaels looked at Buck in amazement. She mimed writing on a piece of paper as if to tell Buck to sign her right away. He knew all along he wanted her, but Fran's approval sealed the deal.

When she finished, Kip Roman came up to Buck and said, "Christ Almighty, Buck, this kid is all energy. I'm talking about as high voltage as I've ever heard."

Buck took Fran aside and said, "I love this girl, Franny, and I want to sign her—but not if it's going to upset you."

"Me? What are you talking about, Buck?"

"Honey, we're going to have to spend a lot of studio time with her like we did with you. We're also going to have to do a big publicity roll-out. I don't want you to think we're shunting you aside. If you feel that way, I'll find another label that would gladly snap her up."

"Buck, you are absolutely the dearest man I know—except maybe for Pete. You're always more concerned about others more than yourself. Do you think I believe I'm the only female vocalist working for RCA? You want to sign the best, because let's face it, the better they are, the more LPs they'll sell and that means more money for everyone concerned. So don't you worry about it. And if you need me to help in any way, you just let me know."

"Thanks, Franny. I'm glad I can count on you. Now, later on today, come up to the office. I want to talk about the next album."

"About one Buck? Pete said he wanted to take me to lunch like a good husband."

"Perfect. See you then."

Then he huddled with Kip and Kenny to talk about Cindi Kay. "I tell you Buck, she's wonderful. Phrasing, intonation, emotion—it's all there in that one tiny package. She's a can't miss star in the making," said Kip.

"She's like a younger version of Fran, Buck," said Kenny Ferraro, "but just as talented. I'm with Kip. She can't miss."

Buck beckoned to Cindi who was sitting on a stool smoking. "Verdict's in, Cin. We want you for RCA Victor under the terms we talked about earlier. What do you say?"

She hugged Buck and said, "Yes! Oh absolutely yes! And then she kissed him on the cheek and said, "Thanks for giving me this shot, Buck. I won't let you down."

"Hey, Little Sis, you married or what?" said Chuck Fein.

"Sure am," she said, wiggling her ring finger.

"Well, damn," said Chuck in feigned disappointment.

"But you would have been my second choice, Chucky!"

"That's OK, doll, second place ain't so bad."

She blew a kiss towards Chuck and then returned to the office with Buck.

## CHAPTER SIXTEEN
### *"These Kids are Great" August 1946*

By August, Carrie was growing larger by the day. She was frequently exhausted and so Buck made it his business to leave the talent scouting to Al and Bill so he could stay home at nights and take some of the burden off of her shoulders. Bevvy would also come by and help with basic chores with Rachel providing meals for the family several nights a week.

"I feel bad, Mama. You have the two girls to cook for and you still spend your time cooking for all of us," said Carrie one afternoon when Rachel brought over two large casseroles which were enough to feed the family for at least two days.

"What? You're not one of my girls?" said Rachel.

"Yes, but—"

"But, but, but. Children are always full of buts. You're not 'like' a daughter to me; you *are* a daughter to me. You've given me two wonderful grandchildren and a third on the way. So there's no such thing about troubling me to cook for my family. It's my pleasure. Now come here and give me a hug."

Carrie embraced Rachel and said, "Why can't my own mother be like you, Mama?"

"Eh, people give what love they have inside of them. Maybe she didn't get a big enough supply to give you. By the way, you talk to her maybe?"

"Not much. I call every few weeks. She never initiates a call to me. I don't even remember the last time I saw her. Maybe four, five months ago."

"And your Papa?"

Carrie laughed humorlessly. "I'm sure he would need permission from my mother to call me."

"Eh, I wore the pants in our family too, you know. My husband let me be the boss, but I never really ordered him around or anything. We worked together on everything—but I had the stronger hand. He was a fine man and a good provider. I wish you could have met him."

# A CHANGE OF KEY

"Me too. Maybe Buck takes after him?"

"No, darling. Benjamin is his own man. He was very young when Louis passed. He developed into the man he is today by working hard and maybe listening to his mama now and again."

Rachel hugged Carrie again and left her with the food, returning to her own home. Carrie didn't know what she'd do without Rachel helping her out.

By nine o'clock that Tuesday evening, the children were asleep and Carrie and Buck sat on the sofa, Carrie's feet elevated on a pillow on the coffee table. Buck had tuned in the console radio to *Arthur Godfrey's Talent Scouts*. The show had started in July and was an immediate hit for the CBS network. Each week, 'talent scouts' would present performers they had discovered who would compete against each other, though no prize was ever announced. The winner would be determined by an 'Applause Meter' that would allegedly measure the volume of applause from the audience viewing the radio program in its studio. Each show presented four or five contestants: singers, comedians, instrumentalists, even some jugglers.

Buck and Carrie exchanged opinions on the performances, some rating higher in their estimation than others. For the third act of the night, Godfrey announced, "Well, now, folks, we have for you a group of young people we think you're going to really enjoy. Here to sing the old Tommy Dorsey theme, 'I'm Getting Sentimental Over You,' let's hear it for The Quinns."

The group, four brothers and a sister, produced a perfect vocal blend tightly harmonizing the lyric—and they did it without the benefit of musical accompaniment. "Jesus, Carrie, if they can sing like this *a capella*, imagine what they would do with music behind them."

"What are you thinking, darling?" asked Carrie.

"I'm thinking I just found my backup singers—if we can get them."

The Quinns didn't win the Talent Scouts that night, but as Buck told Carrie, "There's more than one way these kids can come up winners."

## A CHANGE OF KEY

The next morning, Buck was energized. He said to Kelsey Burton, "Kel, contact CBS, find out who the producer of the *Arthur Godfrey's Talent Scouts* is. Find out if The Quinns have an agent. If not, get a phone number and call them. Get them over here—all of them—as soon as possible."

"Wow, Buck, something big brewing?" asked Kelsey.

"I hope so. I've got an idea going around my brain I want to see if I can make something of."

"I'll get right on it, Buck. By the way, you have a visitor in your office. He said he wanted to surprise you," said Kelsey. "He was very hush-hush."

"Morning mysteries. Just what I need," said Buck.

And it was exactly what he needed. Sitting on the sofa in his office was his old friend and idol, Tex Beneke. "Well lookee here, if it ain't ole' Buck Fisher," said Beneke in his folksy Texas drawl. He stood and shook Buck's hand, then embraced him and said, "How you getting' on, Buck?"

"Fine, Tex, just fine."

"Can't grease the axles on this old jalopy, Buck. Tell the truth."

"Mostly fine. A few ups and downs, but I'm almost fully recovered. Almost," said Buck.

"I tell ya, Buck, it was like gettin' punched in the gut twice. I was down in Oklahoma leading a Navy band when we got news of Glenn. Between you and me, I cried like a baby when I heard. He gave so many of us our big break and he was a good friend—or as good a friend as he'd let anyone be. Glenn could be a cold fish at times, but he was different with me. He could let go. Then just a few months later I opened a copy of *Stars and Stripes* and you were all over it—and that was the second punch. Don't mind tellin' ya, Buck, I prayed for you every day. For your recovery."

"Thanks, Tex. That means a lot to me. You know, I once told you that you were my musical idol. After I heard you play, I wanted to *be* Tex Beneke—but the job was already taken. I confess I copied a lot of my playing style from you."

## A CHANGE OF KEY

"That's right kind of you to say, Buck. I'm flattered. Now how 'bout that little gal of yours?"

"Well, Carrie and I have two kids and she's going to give us our third one sometime in late September."

"Well I'll be! That's just great Buck. Happy for you."

"Now tell me, Tex, what brings you up here?"

"Well, I work for these folks, Buck."

"Come again?"

"When I got back from the war, Helen, Glenn's wife, contacted me about leading what they call a 'ghost band.' It was gonna be an officially licensed band by the Glenn Miller estate and I would be the leader. I had my doubts at first. I had led two bands in the Navy, but this was different. I wanted to learn more about leading a big band before I took on the job. But Helen was insistent and we put together an outfit that mimicked Glenn's Army Air Force outfit—complete with big string section. The estate signed us up with RCA for a number of albums and we'll be touring all over the country, keepin' the Miller name and sound alive."

"Did you get your old bandmates back?" asked Buck.

"I had Paul Tanner for a bit, but he took a studio job out on the coast," said Tex.

"Yes, I ran into him in the airport in Chicago when he was headed out there."

"I also got Bobby Nichols from the Army Air Force Band. He's just a kid but he can play the hell out of the trumpet. I'm afraid Jerry Gray snapped up a bunch of the guys I played with and the others went solo, became studio players or just gave up the business. I did get Henry Mancini on piano and as my chief arranger."

"I got back five or six of my own from the civilian band. I wish it could have been more, but like you say, everyone kind of scattered during and after the war. But wait until Carrie hears that I saw you! You know, Tex, if it wasn't for her, I never would have met you."

"Why's that?"

## A CHANGE OF KEY

"The first time I heard you at the Hotel Pennsylvania, I was so intimidated by you that I wanted to junk my horn and go back to learning how to be a butcher. She's the one that went up to you and brought you to meet me."

"I remember that. Boy howdy, that little gal could sing," said Tex.

"Well, now she's a full-time mom—and she loves it. Doesn't miss the hassle of touring one bit."

"Smart little gal too," said Tex laughing.

They spent another half hour talking, exchanging stories. "I never figgered out how come the Navy needed a base in Oklahoma where the biggest body of water is a lake for trout fishing," said Tex, "but when you read about what those swabbies went through at places like Iwo and Okinawa, I wasn't sorry to be there," said Tex. "Now, ole' pal, I gotta get to a meeting upstairs. If ya don't mind, when I'm back here, I'll stop in to see you again."

"That would be great Tex. You take care, hear?"

The two men shook hands and embraced again and then Tex left Buck alone in his office. Almost immediately, Kel buzzed Buck and said she had news. Buck told her to come in and she sat down, steno pad on her lap.

"What's the news, Kel?"

"You've got a meeting with the Quinns—all five of them—tomorrow at one. I spoke to Tim, he's twenty-five and the oldest in the group and he was very excited about meeting with you. There's three other brothers, Terry, twenty-three, John, twenty-one, and Bill, who's a fraternal twin with Betty, both nineteen."

"That's great work, Kel. Would you call down to the rehearsal studio and get Kip up here for a few minutes?"

"I'll call down now."

Fifteen minutes later, Kip was sitting in Buck's office. "What's up, boss?"

"Kip, you know how we talked about someday having a group of back-up singers?"

"Yes, you told me that when you interviewed me."

"I am hoping tomorrow you can meet that group. Their called the Quinns—a family act. Look, Frannie has already laid down the vocal track to 'Dream.' The Quinns are coming in tomorrow to meet with me. Can you have a vocal chart by then for all five of them. Fran will still sing the lead, but I want a real warm background vocal behind her. The string and reed parts are fine as is."

"What about the key, Buck?"

"What's it written in now?"

"Bb."

"That's right in the middle. It shouldn't be a problem for their range. OK, get me something fantastic—like always."

.....

The next day, the Quinns showed up promptly at 2 PM. They were so well-scrubbed and clean-cut that for a moment, Buck wondered if perhaps they were Mormons. He welcomed them into his office got them seated and then began. He noticed that Tim Quinn walked with a pronounced limp.

"Did you serve, Tim?"

"Yes sir. Marine. I got hit in the knee during the Kwajalein invasion. They tried to fix it, but they said it would never be the same, so they discharged me with full disability."

"Glad you made it home alive, Tim."

"Thank you, sir," he said.

"I heard you kids on Arthur Godfrey and I think you are terrific." He then explained who he was and what he was doing at Victor. "I've put together a fantastic orchestra and we've signed up some terrific performers, adding more each few weeks. I'm looking for a back-up group that can work behind soloists, who can harmonize, sight-sing, and be part of our team here at RCA."

It was Tim Quinn who responded. "You know, Mr. Fisher, we've always been sort of a self-contained act. Our songs alternate in featuring one of us on the lead vocal."

"I understand, Tim, and in time, we just might be able to make albums with you as the headliners. But for now, I need backups. We'll pay each of you eight thousand dollars a year to start—more later the more you do work for us." That got their attention. In a time of post-war recession, eight thousand dollars must have seemed like a small fortune to them. For a group that had never had a professional gig before, in fact it was a small fortune.

"Mr. Fisher—"

"Buck. It's Buck."

"All right, Buck. Can you tell us just a little more about the job?" asked Tim Quinn.

"I can tell you what it's not. We don't tour. Everything we do is right here at RCA or at one of the downtown studios. You won't have to be here every day, but when we're ready to rehearse a particular number, you all will need to be here. There's also a restrictive clause in the contract which says you are the exclusive employees of RCA Victor. No more free-lancing, no more talent shows. In a manner of speaking, you belong to us. Now, you may have some questions and you may want to think things over for a few days. That's OK with me. But we do want you all to come down to the studio now so we can hear you on a number or two. But first, questions?"

It was John Quinn who asked, "Do we have any input as to what goes on during a session?"

"That's a good question. We all work cooperatively in this division. We are always open to any suggestions our performers may have and if they're good, we incorporate them into the sessions and the recordings. But understand this: someone has to make the tough decisions. That's me, and to a slightly lesser degree, Kip Roman, our Music Director who you will be meeting soon. Thus far, I have not heard a single negative word from anyone we work with. Personally, I'm a man of my word and our musicians can attest to that—and I have a staff who are equally dedicated to keeping everyone happy and doing what they do best. That answer your question, John? Oh, and one more thing. Can you guys sight sing?"

"We're all highly trained," said Terry Quinn. "We can sing anything that's down on paper," added Betty Quinn.

"And yes sir, you answered my question and it does sound good to me," said John Quinn.

"All right, then. Let's head down to the studio and see what we've got."

Buck introduced the Quinns to the orchestra, to Fran Michaels and to Kip Roman.

"Got that chart ready, Kip?" asked Buck.

"Sure do, Buck." He handed sheets of vocal music to the five Quinns and then made sure the orchestra was ready to go.

"We're going to have you sing back-up to Fran on 'Dream.' She's already laid down her vocal, but I want to hear you sing with Kip's new chart. Do you need a few minutes to review the music?" he asked the Quinns.

"No, Buck. We're good to go," said Tim Quinn. "We love the song, especially the Pied Pipers' version. Whenever you're ready, let's do it."

Kenny arpeggiated the first chord and the orchestra joined in with warm strings for eight bars. Fran stepped to the microphone and began the vocal. Underneath the melody, the Quinns provided a smooth background that rather than hiding the melody, enhanced it. They followed the crescendos that Kip had noted in the score, and when the number came to the end, all six voices hit the final chord in an emotionally perfect fermata.

It was Kip Roman who said, "That was just terrific, kids. Really solid harmonies."

Cindi Kay had been observing the rehearsing and Buck said to her, "Cin? Could you do us a favor and do 'Swinging on a Star' for us? I'd like to see what these kids can do underneath something a bit more up-tempo."

"Sure, Buck. No problem," said Cindi.

"Buck? I didn't write anything for the group underneath the song," said Kip.

Tim Quinn then said, "It's no problem, Mr. Roman. We'll do it just like the Williams Brothers did it underneath Bing Crosby—except we'll add Betty to the mix."

Kip looked at Buck who shrugged and said, "Let's do it."

## A CHANGE OF KEY

Again, it was perfection. At the end of the song, Kip was all smiles and he said, "I guess I don't have to write anything down; they nailed it on their own."

Then John Quinn said, "Mr. Fisher? I don't know if the band knows the tune, but we do something real special on "It Don't Mean a Thing if it Ain't Got That Swing."

"We have the chart from my civilian band in the book. Fran? Still remember it?"

"Sure, Buck. There aren't really that many words to the song," she said.

"After the bridge we do something really neat with the return to the melody," said John.

Kip smiled and said, "Let's see what happens, Buck. Can't hurt to take a listen."

Then Kip said, "OK, strings, lay out. Brass and reeds, kick it in the ass and let's make it swing."

Buck had heard a lot of music in his lifetime, but he never heard anything quite like the rendition he had just witnessed. The band kicked off the melody, Fran sang the vocal and then moved to the bridge. When the second chorus of melody began, Fran laid out and the Quinns took over. To his utter astonishment, each of the five Quinns took a scat chorus, culminating with all five singing in counterpoint with each other. It was something that Johann Sebastian Bach would have been amazed at, so intricate was the interweaving of voices. After the final scat chorus, Tim nodded at Fran who did one more round of melody before the band took the song out.

"Holy shit!" said Noni Furillo, and that about summed up the band's feelings about the number.

By that time, scat singing was fairly accepted amongst jazz performers, but no one had ever done anything like this before. The contrapuntal complexity simply blew everyone in the band out of their socks.

Kip opened his mouth to say something, but he thought better of it, closed his mouth and sat down in his chair by the piano.

## A CHANGE OF KEY

As for Buck, he was all smiles because he knew he had struck gold. "Fran?" he said, "What did you think of that?"

"Really want my opinion, Buck?"

"Naturally."

"If it's not too late and the LP hasn't been pressed yet, I'd like to recut that track and add these kids to it. Same thing for 'Dream.'

"You sure you don't mind?" asked Buck.

"Our versions are fine, Buck, but with these kids, they'll be further out there than anyone has ever heard before. I say let's do it."

"Kip?" said Buck.

"Call Jack Merrill, tell him what we've got here and if he can get an engineer down to 26$^{th}$ Street by Wednesday, we can redo the tracks."

Before he called Jack, he wanted to make sure the Quinns were on board. "Well, kids? Want to be a part of this lash-up?"

The five Quinns looked at each other and one by one, they nodded in agreement. "Where do we sign, Buck?" asked Tim.

"Tomorrow, my office. We'll make it official."

Back in his office, selling Jack Merrill on the idea was the easy part. "You're not going to believe what these kids can do, Jack. They will be perfect backing up anyone we hire," said Buck.

"I believe anything you tell me, Buck. You're doing one helluva job with your division. Just keep it up."

"Once we cut a master, I'll bring it up here for you to hear, Jack."

"Great. Let me see what Phil Flagler or Whip Elliot have on their plates. If either one is free, I'll send them downtown to redo the tracks. I'll get back to you in thirty."

Then Buck called down to Kip in the studio and said to him, "Kip, by next week I want ten charts, five each for Fran and Cindi. Work the Quinns into the arrangements. We've got five jewels here, Kip. Let's use them to the max."

Then he called Bill Dwyer. "Bill, got a sec?"

"Need me, Buck?"

## A CHANGE OF KEY

"Yeah, come to the office. Wanna talk to you," said Buck.

When Bill arrived, Buck said, "These kids, Bill, I discovered them just by chance when Carrie and I were listening to that Arthur Godfrey show.

"I catch it now and again," said Bill.

"No. Now it's part of your permanent homework. I want you to listen every week. You hear something good, you tell me right away and we'll pursue them, just like we did the Quinns. Who knows what we'll discover?

"No problem, Buck. We just got a new radio and Cathy loves to listen to that show."

# CHAPTER SEVENTEEN
*"You Had Better Sit Down" September 20, 1946*

The balance of the summer had gone well for Buck and his department at RCA Victor. Thanks to Buck's efforts, the label had signed such musical luminaries as Don Redmond, Coleman Hawkins and Dinah Shore. He was also lucky enough to get Fletcher Henderson to sign. Henderson had been one of the main arrangers for the Benny Goodman band, but as the leader of his own group, he was looking for a contract with a big label.

Henderson led his own band in the 1920s and he along with Don Redman was responsible for the alignment of the swing band into different sections: reeds, bones, trumpets, rhythm. He was often seen as the pioneer who served as the bridge between the Dixieland era of jazz and the Big Band era. He was largely responsible for the success of the Goodman band. He was also a brilliant piano player and arranger and Buck wanted to add him to the label to work with Kip Roman on charts for the RCA Studio Orchestra. Buck remembered the meeting he had with Henderson.

"I'm too old to stay up late playin' gigs at all hours, Buck. I had my shot at leadin' a band and I made me some money. But tourin' again? Nah, this is a young man's business now. But if you need an arranger, I'd be delighted to come to work for you. Pity you don't play that horn of yours anymore. I tell ya, Buck, I never heard anyone blow such a sweet tenor—and I heard 'em all."

"I'll offer you a hundred a week plus another hundred for every chart you turn out. I'll want you to sit in and listen to some of our singers before you start so you can get a feel for what we're doing."

Henderson had done some figuring in his head and he said, "That's a fair piece of change, Buck. I'd be happy to come and work for Victor."

On a trip to the West Coast, Al Rovitz had heard Lena Horne singing with the Billy Eckstein Orchestra. She had recorded for RCA in the early 1940s but left the label to make films in Hollywood. But because of the Production Code in Hollywood, she had been pigeon-holed into shows with all Negro casts, not being permitted to be in interracial relationships in films. This relegated her to small speaking parts and singing roles. Buck wanted to resign her for the Victor label and give her the solo career she deserved. It took weeks of long-distance negotiation, but finally, she said, "Honey, if you can do all you say you can do, I'll come back to RCA in a heartbeat."

And so Buck Fisher was putting together a line-up of stars for RCA Victor that easily rivaled Columbia's and Capitol Records. As far as LP sales were concerned, Victor had some big hit-makers on its roster. Fran Michaels' album had been released in late May and according to *Billboard* magazine it was in the Top 10 of album sales for over twelve weeks. Its early sales were over 65,000 units—a phenomenal run for a new performer, which meant Frannie was earning royalties on nearly 15,000 album sales.

Cindi Kay's LP was coming together nicely and would be released by late September. It was called *Little Miss Powerhouse*. Everything was going fantastically for Buck.

And then suddenly, it wasn't.

.....

Carrie's due date was September 28th. She had been seeing Dr. Meyers frequently during the pregnancy and had been assured that all was well. On the morning of September 20th, a week early, Carrie woke up in terrific pain. Her moaning woke Buck up and he jumped out of bed to tend to her. The sheets were streaked with blood. Alarmed, he called Rachel and told her what was happening.

"Benjamin, get Carrie to the hospital at once. Call the doctor first—but hurry," said his mother. "I'll call the girls and we'll get there as soon as possible. Don't worry, Benjamin. Everything is going to be fine. This happens with women sometimes."

In the car ride, she was in great pain and kept clutching her stomach. "Soon, babe, I'll have you there soon." He drove up to the Emergency Room entrance and left the car in a No Parking Zone, not caring about a ticket and then he ran into the hospital calling out for a doctor and a wheelchair. An orderly immediately responded and he and Buck got Carrie out of the car. They signed in and got Carrie into a bed in the maternity ward. She was in terrible pain.

Forty minutes later, Dr. Meyers came hurrying into the ward and spoke to a frantic, Buck. "She's in labor right now, Mr. Fisher. We're going to get her into a delivery room as soon as we can prep her. Don't worry. We'll take care of everything. You just stay in the waiting room and we'll keep you informed."

"Bucky!" cried Carrie.

He rushed to her bedside and clutched her hand. "It's going to be fine, darling. I'm going to be right here. Don't worry about a thing. Dr. Meyers is here now."

"Bucky I'm so scared!"

"Shh! Shh! Doc says there's nothing to be scared about. You're in good hands."

Five minutes later, Carrie was wheeled away into an operating room. He could hear her calling out, "Bucky!" as they took her down the hall. Buck had never felt so helpless in his life.

Rachel, Arlene and Bevvy showed up a half hour later. "Benny! Tell us what's happening," said Arlene. "Cathy Dwyer has the kids, so don't worry. But tell us."

"I don't know. They took her into surgery but I haven't heard anything yet. Look, I have to call into the office. Can you stay here for a few minutes? There's a phone booth in the lobby and I'll be right back."

"Benny, we're not going anywhere. We're staying with you until this is over," said Bevvy.

Buck found the phone booth and called Kelsey. He explained what was happening and asked her to inform Bill, Al, and Jack Merrill. "Also call down to Kip and explain I that I might not be in for a while. A few days in any case. I'll let you know what's happening as soon as I know."

Buck, his mother and sisters, sat silently on the sofa in the waiting room. Every so often, Arlene of Bevvy would hug him and try to reassure him. Each time the double doors leading to the waiting room swung open, Buck leapt to his feet expecting to see Dr. Meyers, but it was always another doctor, a nurse or an orderly.

An hour turned into two hours and then into three. By eleven that morning, Benny's stomach was growling in hunger. "Benny, I'm going to go down to the cafeteria and get you something to eat," said Arlene.

"Sis, I couldn't eat a thing."

"Yes you can. You have to. You need your strength, darling. I'll get you something small—but you have to get something into your stomach," said Arlene.

"All right, thanks, sis."

She kissed him and gave a knowing look to Bevvy indicating that she should take care of him in her absence.

Three hours into four, then five and still no word. Buck thought he would lose his mind if he didn't hear something soon. Finally, at a little before five in the afternoon, Dr. Meyers came into the waiting room. Her surgical scrubs were stained with blood and she wore a grim expression on her face.

The four of them jumped up when the doctor entered and waited anxiously for the news.

"You had better sit down, Mr. Fisher," said the doctor.

He felt as though he was losing his balance and he reached out for the arm of the sofa to steady himself. Buck and the family sat on the sofa facing the doctor, who had pulled up a chair to talk to them.

First, let me tell you the good news. You have a daughter, Mr. Fisher. Just under eight pounds, healthy, and doing just fine. She's in the nursery now and you can see her soon."

"There's some bad news too," said Dr. Meyers.

"Carrie! What's wrong with my wife!" He felt overwhelmed and the tendrils of fear and grief were creeping up his spine to his mind.

The doctor, who looked exhausted, said, "I'm going to try to keep this as simple as I can. Carrie's placenta—that's the sack in which the baby develops inside the uterus—it was blocking the opening in the cervix that the baby has to pass through in a normal pregnancy. It's a condition called *placenta previa* and there's no way to know a woman has it until she's ready to deliver. You say Carrie was bleeding overnight?"

"Yes, the sheets on our bed seemed soaked with blood," said Buck.

The doctor nodded. "Well, we had to deliver the baby via caesarian section. That means we made an incision in her stomach and delivered the baby through that opening instead of the normal way. Mr. Fisher, Carrie lost a tremendous amount of blood. We've spent hours trying to stanch the flow of blood—but with limited success. We think we have it under control, but can't be a hundred percent sure."

"What else, doctor?"

"Two things. First, there was too much damage to the uterus, so we had to perform a hysterectomy. That means we had to remove Carrie's uterus. As a result of that, Carrie can never have children again. Second, because of the huge amount of blood loss, Carrie has slipped into a coma."

"A coma?" said Rachel, alarmed at the sound of the word.

"Yes, it's the body's defense mechanism. It shuts down all the systems to the bare minimum so it can heal. It's a very deep sleep."

"How long do they last, doctor?" asked Bevvy.

"There's no set number. Hours, days—maybe never."

"What are you saying!" cried Buck.

"What I'm saying, is we might lose her." The words hung in the air like an anvil ready to drop from the sky onto his head.

"No! No! I can't lose her!" Buck wailed, tears pouring from his eyes.

"Look, she's young, strong and basically in good health. We will monitor her every minute of the day. She's already received four units of blood and we'll be transfusing her more until we know the bleeding has stopped. If we have to go back inside to find out the source of any further bleeding, we will. Now, I suggest you all go home and rest."

## A CHANGE OF KEY

"No! I'm not going anywhere! Can I see my wife?"

"Mr. Fisher, she won't know you are there. She's in a deep coma," said Dr. Meyers.

"I don't care. I must see her!"

"All right. Look, I'm going to arrange for a private or semi-private room for her. There will be an extra bed so if you need to sleep, you can lie down next to her. I will be back first thing in the morning. I'll go make that room change and send an orderly to come and get you."

Buck fell back on the couch, head in his hands, great heaving sobs emanating from deep within him. Arlene and Bevvy sat on either side of him and held him.

Each time he tried to compose himself, he lost it again his face awash in tears. This was not the strong brother they had known their entire lives. This was not the powerful force in American music. This was not the Army veteran who himself had been in a coma. This was nothing more than a little boy, hurting, clinging to hope, lost and at the mercy of whatever god was supposed to look after decent people.

"Benjamin?" said Rachel.

He looked up and saw his mother standing over him. "Listen to me, my son. Carrie is a fighter. You have to be one too. She will come out of this. Asleep or not, she will feed off of your strength. I believe that she will know you are there. So go to her. Be strong, and with the help of God, she will return to you. Now, before you go to see her, why don't we go down the hall and see your new daughter and my new granddaughter?'

He was reluctant to leave, but Arlene and Bevvy helped him stand and they all went to see the baby. She was in the nursery under a light. A nurse explained that it was standard procedure to keep the baby warm. "My wife nursed our other two children, nurse. What happens now?"

"Don't worry about that, Mr. Fisher. We will bottle feed her until your wife recovers. Then she can start to nurse her."

The nurse brought the baby to the window, all wrapped up in a pink blanket and fast asleep. "Oh, Benny," said Bevvy, "she's gorgeous. She looks like Carrie."

At that, he started to cry again until Bevvy hugged him and said, "Honey, Carrie once told me that she would never, ever leave you. That's how much she loves you. She'll be back. I promise."

"Benjamin? You go to Carrie now. We'll go home and be back in the morning. Try to get some sleep, my son."

Buck nodded and hugged the three of them. When they had taken the elevator down to the lobby, he went back to the waiting room where an orderly was waiting for him. "If you'll come with me, Mr. Fisher, I'll take you to your wife's room."

The doctor had procured a semi-private room, but the other bed was vacant. Buck pulled up a chair and sat next to Carrie's bedside. There was an IV stand next to the bed with tubes leading to Carrie's left arm. One dripped blood, the other dripped a clear saline solution, a third had a bottle that Buck assumed was some kind of nutrient to keep her strength up. Her eyes were closed and she looked so peaceful. He took her hand, bent over the bed and kissed her on the lips.

"I'm right here, Carrie. I'm not going anywhere. Would you like me to talk to you, my darling? I don't imagine you can hear me, but I need you to know that I won't leave your bedside."

Carrie looked so terribly pale, and Buck imagined it was from the loss of blood. He fought back the tears as he sat next to her, trying to show the strength that his mother said he needed to find. At around midnight, he dozed off in the chair, but when a nurse came to check Carrie's vital signs, she said, "Use the bed, Mr. Fisher. I'll bring you a blanket."

Buck's sleep was fitful and he was sure he had a string of nightmares, none of which he could remember the next morning. At 6 AM another nurse whose shift had just began, came into the room to take Carrie's temperature and check her blood pressure.

## A CHANGE OF KEY

"Mr. Fisher? I'm going to change Carrie's drips. That's how we're feeding her, but I'm going to bring you a breakfast tray. Would you like that?"

He hadn't been aware of how hungry he was, but he felt it now and thanked the nurse for her kindness. Eggs, toast, bacon and ham, none of which had been prepared with presentation in mind, filled Buck's stomach. He needed to stretch his legs and walked back to the waiting room. At about ten that morning, the elevator opened and Chuck Fein hurried off the car and came up to Buck, throwing his arms around him.

"Talk to me, buddy," said Chuck.

"I don't know what to say, Chuck. No one knows when and if she will come out of the coma."

"She will. I just know it. Bill and Al are on the way up. They were just parking the car. Some of the other guys will be by during the day. Kip gave the orchestra the day off. No one really felt like playing today anyhow."

The elevator opened again and Chuck said, "Oh, here's Little Sis." Cindi Kay hurried to Buck and hugged him. She could see how distraught he looked and she said, "Come sit by me Buck." He did as she asked and she took his hand.

"Remember how I sat with you in the hospital in London? I knew then that we weren't going to lose Buck Fisher. You can bet we won't lose Carrie either. Now tell me, what can I do to help?"

"Oh, Cin, have any miracles up your sleeve?"

"You don't need a miracle. You need time. She needs time. Give me your mom's number. I'll call her and tell her to bring some changes of clothes for you, a toothbrush, comb—anything you need. I'm going to come here every day after work to check on you. Tony sends his best too."

By that time, Bill and Al had arrived. He told them the same thing that he told Cindi and Chuck. The news was grave, but they both expressed hope. It was Bill who said, "Buck, you take as much time as you need. Kip has everything in hand, and the orchestra will be back at work tomorrow. Jack Merrill called and said he'd get here sometime towards evening."

"Thanks, fellas. You're the best friends a guy could ask for."

"All right, we know you want to get back to Carrie, so we'll take off now," said Al. I'll check with Arlene later to see if there's any progress. As the two of them were leaving, Pete McCormack along with Fran Michaels got off the elevator and came up to Buck. Franny hugged him and Pete asked if there was any news.

"Nothing yet. I spent the night here last night and will again tonight. I'm not going anywhere until Carrie wakes up."

Fran glanced wide-eyed at Pete and the look said it all: 'if she wakes up.'

They sat for a while with Buck but they knew he wanted to sit by Carrie, so they said their goodbyes and said they'd be back to see him the next day. When they all left, Buck returned to Carrie's room and resumed his seat by her. Her breathing was regular and unless he was mistaken, there was slightly more color in her cheeks. Probably from the constant infusion of blood.

Dr. Meyers showed up at about half past ten to check on Carrie. She examined the chart and said to Buck, "Her vital signs are fairly strong, Mr. Fisher, so that's a good sign." "Dr. Meyers, I'm not going home any time soon, but I want to see my children. Can my sisters bring them by—just for a short visit—here in the waiting room?"

"We usually don't permit little children up here, Mr. Fisher, because it sometimes upsets the other patients. But if they bring them to the main lobby, you can spend some time with them there."

"All right. I'll ask my sisters to bring them by later this afternoon. Thank you, doctor," said Buck.

"Did you eat anything, Mr. Fisher?"

"Yes, the nurse brought me some breakfast earlier."

"Good, but make sure you eat a good lunch. Maybe take your children to the cafeteria and have lunch or dinner with them."

## A CHANGE OF KEY

He nodded and when the doctor left to finish her rounds, he went back to Carrie's room. He took her hand and kissed each finger. "We have another daughter, my love. She's big—almost eight pounds. She's doing just great—and you will be soon. The hospital had to fill out a birth certificate so they needed a name. I told them Katharine Carol Feinstein. We can call her K.C. or maybe Casey. How does that sound, darling? I think it's cute. Casey. Maybe if she becomes a famous singer or something, she'll go by Casey Fisher. Wouldn't that be nice?"

He wiped away more tears with a tissue he took from the box on the small night table and blew his nose. "Mama and the girls were here yesterday, and this morning Chuck Fein, Bill, Al, Pete, Franny and Cindi all came by to check up on us. They all send you their love and wish you a speedy recovery. The doctor says you are doing OK and that was very good news, darling."

Buck knew he was just chattering idly but maybe Carrie could hear his voice in her sleep and know that he was by her side. Nurses came in and out with regularity checking vitals, replacing fluid bottles and making notations on charts.

A little after one, Jack Merrill showed up at the hospital. He hugged Buck and said, "How's she doing, fella?"

Buck could barely get the words out. "She's holding her own, Jack, but no signs of coming out of the coma."

"Come sit down next to me," said Jack.

Clearly exhausted, physically and emotionally, Buck did as Jack asked. "First, let me tell you this, Buck: I want to put your mind at ease about something. No matter what this costs, the hospital stay, the doctors, the surgeries, the medicines, everything—RCA is picking up the tab. You won't have to shell out a red cent. Secondly, and this is very important, Buck, you take as much time as you need. I know you tend to work your ass off at anything you undertake, but this is different. I don't want to see you at 30 Rock. Not until Carrie is all better. I don't just mean out of the hospital. I mean you stay at home with her until she's back on her feet and she can take care of herself. I mean it, Buck. Your family comes first—and don't give me any argument."

## A CHANGE OF KEY

Jack Merrill had been a friend to Buck for many years but this gesture of generosity surpassed anything Buck had known in the past. A single tear dropped from his left eye which he quickly wiped away before he said, "I don't know what to say, Jack. Thank you."

Jack grabbed his coat and got up to leave, but then he said, "You go sit with Carrie now. I'll head back to the city and talk to the orchestra and tell them what I expect of them—what you expect of them. And remember, don't worry about a thing."

Jack left and Buck returned to Carrie's bedside. He continued the one-way conversation with her that he had had the night before. He was too emotionally drained to even cry anymore as he looked at his beautiful wife, lying there inert, lost in some kind of a medical neverland. Buck glanced at his watch—the watch that Carrie had bought for him years ago. Arlene, Bevvy and his mother would be there at noon with Eddie and Laura. He missed his children terribly, but at the same time, he dreaded having to try to explain to them why their mommy couldn't come home to them.

They met in the lobby and walked the short distance to the cafeteria where they found a table off to one side. Arlene got on line and ordered lunch for everyone. Buck hugged Eddie and Laura and kissed them tenderly. It didn't take long for the question to come. It came from Laura.

"Where's mommy, daddy?"

"She's upstairs, sweetheart. Mommy is feeling a little sick right now, but we all hope she'll get better real soon and come home to us."

"Can I see her, daddy?"

"No angel. The doctors gave her medicine to make her sleep. But I tell you what we can all do after lunch," said Buck.

"What's that, daddy?" asked Laura.

"Well, you know you have a new baby sister named Casey. Would you like to see her?"

"A sister! Oh yes, daddy. Can Eddie come too?"

Always thinking of her big brother, thought Buck.

## A CHANGE OF KEY

"Of course, baby girl. Casey is Eddie's new sister too."

They ate mostly in silence. Arlene could see the strain evident on Buck's face, but neither she nor Bevvy had any idea how to ease his pain. Playing the waiting game must have been torturous for him. But what else was there to do?

They finished eating and took the elevator to the floor with the nursery. The family stood in front of the window and a nurse held the baby up for all of them to see. Then she came out and said, "Mr. Fisher, if you gown up and cover your head, you can hold your daughter. We do that just as a precaution. She's doing beautifully."

Even at eight pounds, Casey felt light as a feather in Buck's arms. She brought her close to the window where his children could see her. They smiled at Buck and after bouncing her in his arms for a bit, he returned her to the nurse for her feeding. Then he rejoined the family outside the nursery.

"I've got to get back to Carrie. Can you take care of the kids?" asked Buck.

"We've got them, Benny. We're going to take turns staying at your house. We think it's best that Eddie and Laura be in their own place that they're familiar with. Is that OK?"

"Sure, I'll give you money to stock the fridge and pantry."

"Benny, stop it! We don't need your money to take care of our niece and nephew. They are dear to us and we'd do anything for them—and for you. So stop worrying and get back to Carrie.

Day after day the ordeal continued. Dr. Meyers came every day and reassured Buck that Carrie had not taken a turn for the worse, but neither was there any improvement. Buck felt as though he had lost fifteen pounds, not through any particular effort, but because he had no appetite at all. On the eighth day while sitting at Carrie's bedside, Buck completely lost it. He sobbed uncontrollably as he held Carrie's hand. He thought of how much love he had for this woman and how the thought that Carrie would never wake up was more than he could bear.

He was mortified at the thought that a nurse would come in and see him crying like a child who had lost a favorite toy. But he just couldn't stop. His entire body was wracked with paroxysms of fear and grief. He clutched Carrie's hand so tightly, he was afraid he would hurt her.

And then she clutched back.

"Nurse! Nurse! Please, come in here!"

The nurse came flying through the door and said breathlessly, "Mr. Fisher, what's happened? What's wrong?"

"She gripped my hand. I felt it. I swear, I felt it!"

The nurse checked Carrie's pulse and blood pressure. She knew that what he had experienced could have been nothing more than muscles contracting. But there was always a chance that it was more.

As Buck stared at Carrie's face, he noticed that there seemed to me a fluttering eye movement behind her closed eyelids.

"Oh! Oh my!" said the nurse. "Let me see if I can find the doctor." She went to the nurses' station had paged Dr. Meyers STAT.

"Come on, babe, please, come on!" implored Buck.

Then he heard a low moan come from Carrie. Low, but unmistakable. And then, her beautiful blue eyes opened and flitted around the room examining her surroundings.

"Bucky?" she said. Her voice was raspy, the result of her throat being so dry. Then her eyes focused on Buck and she smiled wanly at him. "Bucky?" she repeated.

"Yes, darling, yes. I'm right here."

"Where?" she asked, disoriented from eight days in a coma.

"You're in your own hospital room, sweetheart. You've been asleep for a long time, but everything is going to be all right now. We have a daughter, a beautiful, beautiful daughter."

"A daughter?"

"Yes, love. Her name is Katharine Carol Feinstein—but we'll call her Casey, if that's OK with you."

"Casey. I love it," she said. At that moment, Dr. Meyers came rushing in and said, "Well, look who's back! With a small light she examined Carrie's eyes, rechecked her pulse and blood pressure and examined the IVs that were still in Carrie's arms. Both arms were almost completely black and blue because every three or four days, they had to change the site of the catheters.

"Carrie? I need you to listen to me," said Dr. Meyers. "It's important that we get you up and walking. Your muscles are going to feel very weak, so your husband and an orderly will be with you every step of the way. Later today, if you feel up to it, I'm going to have your baby brought to you so she can start to nurse. Do you think you can handle that?"

"I would like that. I want to see my baby," said Carrie.

"And you will—but only after you walk a little. I'll tell you what, Mr. Fisher, how about you walk her down to the nursery where she can at least see Casey. Then we'll get her back here and bring the baby along shortly after that. Dr. Meyers lifted Carrie's hospital gown up so she could examine the stitches from the C-section. "This looks good. There's no seepage and the area isn't red, which indicates that there's no infection," she said.

Carrie groaned a little as she tried to move. "I'm going to have the nurse come and help get Carrie cleaned up a bit before we get her walking. Why don't you go to the waiting room and we'll bring you back in when she's ready? Before Carrie nurses the baby, I'm going to do a vaginal examination. I have to make sure that the bleeding has stopped completely. You probably want to wait outside for that too," said Dr. Meyers.

Bill Dwyer was in the waiting room when Buck came out of Carrie's room, an unasked question on his face. "She's awake, Bill. She's back," And he lost it again. Bill hugged him and said, "Thank God Buck. Thank God. This is just the greatest news. "I'm going to call Cathy with the news. Do you need anything, Buck?"

He dabbed his eyes with his handkerchief and said, "I think we're OK. But thanks. Can you tell the guys for me?"

"Of course. They're going to be as excited as I feel right now. Any idea of when she can come home?"

"The doctor hasn't said anything about that, but I don't imagine it will be in the next few days. She still has to get quite a bit stronger."

"Well, she's been through a helluva lot, Buck. But as long as she's doing well, that's all that matters. I'm going to head for 30 Rock and let everyone know."

"Can you call up to Jack Merrill for me, Bill?"

"Definitely. He's been calling every day for updates. I'll let him know what's happening."

"Thanks again. For everything."

Dr. Meyers had completed her examination of Carrie and she came to get Buck. "It's looking very good, Mr. Fisher. I believe she's out of the woods, but we're going to watch her very carefully over the next few weeks. Now, this is Tommy, he's an orderly, and he's going to walk with you and Carrie. Limit it to about ten minutes at first. If she can handle that, we'll increase it after dinner."

Buck and Tommy escorted Carrie to the nursery where she had a chance to see Casey for the first time. "Oh, she's beautiful, Bucky! When can I feed her?"

"The doctor says by this afternoon, you'll be nursing her."

They walked back and forth in the corridor, Tommy steadying her by her elbow, and Buck holding her other hand. "Any pain, love?" asked Buck.

"No. No pain. Everything kind of aches—my back, my legs, but no sharp pains," she said.

Tommy said, "That's because you haven't moved those muscles in about eight days, Mrs. Fisher. Once they loosen up, the achiness will disappear."

Another seven minutes of walking and Carrie felt she needed to lie down again. "All right, darling, we'll go back to the room now and I'll sit with you."

After Tommy excused himself, Carrie took Buck's hand and said, "Bucky? Do you still love me?"

Buck's jaw dropped and he said, "Sweetheart, why would you even ask such a question?"

"I put you through so much. And the family too. They must all hate me," she said, the tears beginning to flow.

## A CHANGE OF KEY

"Carrie, darling, I love you more now than ever before. Mama, the girls, Bill, Al, everyone in the band—they all love you so much and have been praying for your recovery. But believe me when I say that none of them could love you as much as I do at this moment."

She settled back on the bed and took a sip of cold water that the nurse had left on the bedstand. Then she took Buck's hand.

"Kiss me, Bucky?"

"With the greatest of love, darling." He took her in his arms and kissed her with a passion he never thought he would feel again.

"Are you hungry, Carrie?" he asked.

"Yes! I feel like I haven't eaten for days."

"Well, you haven't. Other than the stuff that came out of an IV bottle, you haven't had anything solid for about eight days. So I will have the nurse bring you some lunch—but I want you to eat slowly."

…..

Each day over the next week, Carrie got stronger. She was still very emotional, but she seemed happiest when she was nursing Casey. Buck was with her almost constantly, although she insisted that he go home and take a shower and play with the children. He did, and he returned that same evening. Dr. Meyers saw her every day and finally announced that she could come home. It didn't take long to pack Carrie's few things in a small travel bag. Tommy showed up with a wheel chair. "I don't think I need that, Tommy. I can walk on my own now."

"Sorry, Mrs. Fisher, but it's hospital policy. All discharged patients who have had a surgical procedure must be taken out of the hospital in a wheel chair. Can't change the rules, even for you."

"All right. I wouldn't want to get you into any trouble. Can I hold Casey as you wheel me down to the lobby?"

"Of course you can. Just hang on tight."

Buck held Casey as Carrie got into the car. Then he handed the baby to her. "OK, family, off we go to home at last."

## A CHANGE OF KEY

Since it was Arlene's turn to watch Eddie and Laura, she was in the house when Buck, Carrie and Casey arrived. She had laid out a nice lunch spread which everyone devoured. "Can I ask Mama and Bevvy to come over to see the baby?" Buck asked.

"That would be wonderful! I'm so eager to see them!" said Carrie.

Following her light lunch, Carrie nursed Casey and then excused herself to lie down and rest. Buck cleaned up, put the kids up for a nap and then joined Carrie in bed. He held her closely, kissing her lightly and stroking her hair.

"I'm beyond words to tell you how glad I am to have you home," said Buck.

"I remember so little of what happened, Buck. Is this how it was for you in England?"

"Yes, you don't remember your thoughts while you're in a coma. But that's all over with for me and you. We have a beautiful new daughter, two wonderful kids—and it's all good from now on."

"I hope so darling. I really do." Then she fell fast asleep.

## CHAPTER EIGHTEEN
*"It Takes Time" October 1946*

For the next week, Buck did as Jack Merrill had ordered: he stayed at home and helped Carrie reacclimate in every way he could. He minded his two older children as Carrie tended to Casey. It had become a daily routine for Rachel to deliver food to the house so Carrie would not have to bother cooking. His sisters also either came or phoned daily, each visit accompanied by new playthings for the three kids.

But something was off. He couldn't quite put his finger on it, but Carrie was acting very differently. She simply was not herself. She cried often at the slightest things, and on several occasions, she shouted at Buck—something he had no recollection of her ever doing before. Once, after he had made breakfast for the children, he was about to do the dishes when Laura started screaming from the hallway. She had fallen and scraped her knee. As Buck was putting a bandage on it, Carrie had gone into the kitchen, saw the dishes in the sink, and exploded. "Why the hell aren't these goddamned dishes done! Can't you do anything around here?"

Buck couldn't even find the words to respond to the accusation, so he kept silent and went into the kitchen where he finished cleaning up. "Would you like me to make you breakfast, darling," he asked.

"I don't want any goddamned breakfast. What the hell is wrong with you?"

Then she broke down in tears as she rested her head on her hands bent over the kitchen table. She looked up at Buck and there was this haunted expression on her face—yet another thing Buck had never seen in her before.

This went on for days and days, Carrie alternating between screaming at the children or at Buck. When not nursing Casey, she hid in the bedroom where she either slept or cried. Finally, Buck knew he had to do something. He came into the bedroom early one evening to find Carrie sitting on the side of the bed. She looked up and said, "What do you want?"

"We need to talk, darling."

"Why?" There was a bitterness in her tone that stung like a wasp.

"Why? Because you're not yourself. Because something is wrong and I have no idea what it is. You scream at the kids, you scream at me, you sulk, you sleep constantly—this isn't normal, Carrie."

"There's nothing wrong with me. Not a goddamned thing!" she said.

This time, Buck's tone matched her own: "Yes! There is! And we'd better face up to it before things get a lot worse than they are."

"So what do you want me to do about it? This is me," she said.

"No! It is most definitely not you—not the Carrie I have loved for years and years. And you'd better realize that. I'm calling Dr. Meyers in the morning and we're going to see her. This has to stop," said Buck.

"More doctors? Haven't I seen enough doctors? Haven't they done enough to me?" Again that acerbic tone.

"What they did was save your life, Carrie. Admit it or not, it's the truth. So we're going and I don't want to hear any argument about it."

"Fine. Whatever you say. Now get out!"

That felt like she had punched him in the gut, but he did as she asked. And for the first time since they were married, they slept apart, Carrie in the bedroom and Buck on the sofa. He didn't sleep very much at all; he spent most of the night staring at the living room ceiling wondering what was going on. Carrie was hurting, of that he was certain. But so was he. Buck had always been very sensitive, even growing up, and Carrie's accusations and remarks hurt him to his core. There had to be an answer to what had caused such a change in Carrie. Maybe the doctor would know.

## A CHANGE OF KEY

Buck was up early and dressed and started making breakfast for the children. He checked on Casey who was sleeping soundly in her crib. He was as quiet as he could be as he poured cereal into bowls and scrambled eggs in the cast iron skillet on the stove. By eight, both Eddie and Laura were awake and Buck helped them dress, wash their faces and brush their teeth. Carrie was still asleep.

At a quarter past eight, Buck called Dr. Meyers' office and got the secretary. He explained the problem and stressed how worried he was about Carrie. He was told that the doctor could see her at eleven that morning. He immediately called Rachel and asked if she could mind the children for a few hours while he took Carrie to the doctor.

"Something is wrong, Benjamin?" she aksed.

"I don't know, Ma. I can't understand it, but there's something wrong with Carrie. I don't understand the way she is acting. We have to get to the bottom of this."

There was a slight delay at Dr. Meyers' office so it wasn't until close to noon that Buck and Carrie got to see her.

"Mr. and Mrs. Fisher, how are we doing?" said Dr. Meyers.

When neither Buck nor Carrie answered right away, the doctor said, "All right, let me rephrase the question: what's wrong?"

That was Buck's cue. He explained in great detail what had been going on with Carrie. The episodes of anger, the crying jags, the constant lassitude, the loss of appetite He left nothing out. Carrie sat silently through Buck's explanation.

"And Carrie? What do you have to say?"

"I don't think it's as bad as he says it is. It's just that I'm tired a lot. Nothing more."

The doctor spent a few minutes writing notes on her pad until she put her pen down and faced Buck and Carrie.

"What we have here is a case of post-partum depression or PPD. It's not uncommon, but we really do not know the cause. It's a curious condition, that's for sure."

"What do you mean, doctor?"

"Some mothers have it for the first child—and then never again even if they have five more kids. Sometimes the first birth is totally free from it—and then it will hit for the middle child, but not for the third child. Carrie? Am I correct in assuming that you didn't go through this for your first two children?"

"Well, a little bit, but not like this," said Buck.

"How would you know? You weren't even there when Laura was born." Carrie's angry response was very telling and the doctor scrawled some more notes on her pad.

"I was in the Army when Laura was born, doctor, so no, I don't know how she was."

"There! See?!" said Carrie.

"All right, let me explain some things. Though the cause of PPD is mostly a mystery, there have been some successful methods of treatment. For one thing, Carrie's hormones are all unbalanced now. The fetus really sucks them out of the mother's body, so we can treat her with some estrogen to get her back in balance. I can also prescribe an anti-depressant. These will for the most part prevent mood swings and keep Carrie on an even keel. But the third thing is counseling. There are groups of new mothers, many of whom are gong through the same thing as Carrie. Sharing the experiences with others has really proven to be helpful. I can give you the names of some groups that meet right at Queens General. But if that isn't successful, then I strongly recommend individual counseling. Carrie needs to open up about what she's going through—and with no offense, Mr. Fisher, sometimes the husband is not the right person to talk to."

Having seen a psychiatrist for himself, Buck knew that it could also help Carrie. "Do you have a referral for a therapist, doctor?" he asked.

"Yes, of course. I have several female colleagues who are mothers and have been through this themselves. They've had some really wonderful results in one-on-one counseling, but if Carrie would prefer a group, she leads those too."

"How long does this condition last, doctor?" asked Buck.

## A CHANGE OF KEY

"I wish I could give you a timetable on this. For some women, it could be a few weeks. For others, it could last for a year—or more. It's a very case-by-case thing. Your job, Mr. Fisher, is to be supportive, helpful, and above all, patient. She's going to have more episodes and it's inevitable but you'll be the whipping boy. Let it roll off your back, knowing what's causing it and that it's not her real self shouting at you."

Buck had already been through some of that and he wasn't looking forward to repeat performances. But if that's what it took, he would endure it.

"There's one final thing I want to talk about," said Dr. Meyers. "It's another of those things that therapists handle best, but I have had enough women who underwent this to know what happens. As you both know, we had to remove Carrie's uterus during the delivery. In many cases, because a woman can no longer have children, she feels inadequate—as if she isn't a woman anymore. Even if a couple didn't want to have any more, it still gets into her head that she is less than a woman. This too can affect their moods and the overall severity of the PPD."

Neither Buck nor Carrie had anything further to say or ask the doctor. "I would like to see you back here in two weeks, Carrie. My secretary will give you the referral numbers for the group and for the therapists I recommend. Let's show some optimism here and believe that this will work itself out."

They rose, shook hands with Dr. Meyers and went back to the car. On the drive home, Carrie was silent until she suddenly broke down into tears. Buck pulled the car over to the curb and held her in his arms. "I'm sorry, Bucky, I'm so sorry. I don't know what's the matter with me and I've been so unfair to you and the kids. Please, please don't hate me!"

Buck held her tightly and said, "My darling girl, we now know what's going on. It's not your fault. As for taking things out on me, I know that's not my Carrie yelling at me. It's someone else. My Carrie will be back in time—just as she came back from those awful eight days."

Buck hoped his tone sounded the right sympathetic note.

Carrie couldn't stop wailing, no matter how hard Buck tried to comfort her. "I made you sleep on the sofa! I'm horrible! How can you say you love me?"

"Carrie, Carrie, it's OK. That was the different Carrie. Not the one I love and who I know loves me," he said.

Still the tears flowed unchecked. "Are you going to leave me, Bucky? Please don't leave me!"

Now Buck wanted to cry. The thought of leaving this woman who he had devoted his life to was an absurdity. Everything he had done, had achieved, had wanted—it was all centered around Carrie. "I will never, ever leave you, Carrie. You are my life. Our family—it's what we are all about, darling. Nothing will split us up."

"Promise? Promise Bucky?"

"You have my word. And I never break my word," he said.

"No matter what I do or say, please don't sleep away from me again. I was so lonely last night!"

"No, darling. That bed is ours, and I'll be there with you every night for the rest of our lives."

Buck dried her tears and continued the drive home. She clung to him on the whole ride. At home she hugged Eddie and Laura, took Casey from Rachel's arms and sat with her in the arm chair, just holding her and staring at her.

That afternoon Carrie called the number Dr. Meyers had given her for the group sessions with new mothers. The meetings were Thursday evenings in a conference room a Queens General Hospital. She planned on attending that Thursday evening and though she was still somewhat skeptical, she owed it to Buck and her children to try anything that could help her overcome the effects of the PPD.

Weeks went by and though now and again Carrie had episodes of sadness and weariness, Buck had to admit that she did seem better. Perhaps the other mothers had given her suggestions for dealing with PPD. Or maybe there was a natural healing process going on. He did notice that after an outburst, she seemed very aware of what she had done—and she apologized for her behavior.

After nine days, Buck felt secure enough in Carrie's well-being for him to return to work. It was something he both wanted and needed to do. He double checked with Carrie that she would be all right and asked Rachel to stop in to check up on her during the day. "She seems OK, Mama, but you know, she can still use some help."

"Leave it to me, Benjamin. I'll take care of her," said Rachel.

.....

Buck's first stop at 30 Rock was Jack Merrill's office. Jack, always a friend first, a boss second, greeted Buck warmly said, "How is she, Buck? Everything getting back to normal?"

"Some rough spots, Jack, but it's going to be fine." He explained about the PPD and Jack said, "Yeah, Margie had that with our second one. It was tough, but it just went away in time."

"Glad to hear that. Now tell me what I've missed," said Buck.

"I heard the two tracks with the Quinns backing Fran. Fantastic! Buck, those kids are amazing. I asked Kip to write more charts incorporating them but he told me you already asked him to. I listened to some of the new arrangements that he wrote for Cindi. He added flute to the charts—his copyist Pammy Wendorfer playing. She's quite a performer in her own right. And as for Cindi? Her album is doing great so all the new charts will be for a follow-up album for her. Fran's is still in the top ten according to *Billboard*. And here's something that may please you: General Sarnoff is really happy with your work—and the money you're making for RCA."

"I didn't even know he noticed what we're doing," said Buck.

Jack laughed. "The general? He notices everything. And I do mean everything."

"I'll be sure to tell Kip what a great job he's doing. By the way, I gave him the title of Music Director. And with Fletcher

## A CHANGE OF KEY

Henderson on board as an arranger, the orchestra has really come alive."

"Great. Now here's what I want you to do next. Get together with Fran and start putting together a playlist for her holiday album. Do that soon. We'll have to rush to get it into production for Christmas. How are Al and Bill doing scouting around for talent?"

"I'll find out when they meet with me later today."

"Good, good. Just keep me posted all along the way. And send my love to Carrie."

In his office, he had Kelsey call down to the rehearsal studio and ask Fran to come to the office. Twenty minutes later, she was seated on the sofa sipping a cup of coffee.

Fran asked after Carrie and was relieved to hear that things were returning to normal. "It's great to have you back, Buck. You're the hand that rocks this cradle and Kip is great—but everyone knows that you're the boss."

"Well, our first order of business is to nail down a playlist for your holiday album. Tell me what songs you'd like to do. Nothing's written in stone but we'll get a general idea."

"Well, if I had my choice, Buck, I'd rather do serious songs instead of fluff like 'Jingle Bells.'"

"OK, so let's hear what you want, Franny."

She took out a list from her pocketbook and told Buck her choices: "'O Little Town of Bethlehem,' 'Silent Night,' 'Santa Claus is Coming to Town' as an upbeat number, 'Carol of the Bells,' 'I heard the Bells on Christmas Day,' 'Have Yourself a Merry Little Christmas,' 'I'll Be Home for Christmas,' 'Sleigh Ride' also upbeat, 'Swinging on a Star,' 'The Holly and the Ivy,' 'The Bells of St. Mary's' and finishing with a Shubert sounding 'Ave Maria.' After that last cut I figured I'd do a simple voice-over saying, 'Merry Christmas, everyone.'"

Buck looked at the list and nodded. Then he said, "Franny, I would like you to hear something. Got some time?"

"Sure, Buck. What do you have?"

"It's something very special, Franny. Wait till you hear."

## A CHANGE OF KEY

Buck cued up a well-worn 78 RPM record and played it on the Victrola he kept in his office. For three minutes they listened and at one point, Fran put her hand on her mouth in surprise.

"My God, Buck, what was that? It was an absolutely gorgeous melody."

"It's not a Christmas song, nor is it a song specifically for Hanukkah. But here's the thing: when I was a kid in Sunday school, the rabbi used to tell us that in the *shtetels* of Eastern Europe, especially those where czarist *pogroms* were frequent occurrences, the children sang the song at Hanukkah to keep their spirits up in light of the oppression the Jews experienced. It's about learning their alphabet. But there's something haunting and very spiritual about it that I have always loved."

"But Buck, what language is that?" asked Fran.

"It's Yiddish, Fran. The language of the Jewish people of Europe. The name of the song is 'Oyfn Pripetshik' which means 'On the Hearth a Fire Burns.'"

"The song simply weeps, Buck. It's beautiful."

"What if I had it written out phonetically? Would you take a crack at it?"

"Whoa, Buck, I've sung in Italian and I've done *Carmen* in French. But Yiddish, Buck?"

"Would you be willing to try?"

"I'll give it a shot, but don't be surprised if I make a fool of myself."

"You? Never. And I'd never let that happen."

"Now, I love this list. I see you singing solo on 'Oyfn' and 'Ave Maria.' But for the others, I would like Kip to write arrangements with vocal and orchestral backgrounds. That will give it a beautiful, full sound for each track. What do you say?"

"I'll go down to the studio now and give Kip the list and tell him what you want."

"Tell him full speed ahead on this. We only have a few weeks to get this into production for the holiday season. In the meantime, I'll get that phonetic version of 'Oyfn' to you."

## A CHANGE OF KEY

Once again Kip Roman proved himself to be a worker of minor miracles. By the following Tuesday, the orchestra was down at 26th Street rehearsing and then recording Fran's Christmas album which was given the title *From Me to You: Christmas with Fran Michaels*. Buck told the art department that they had three days to come up with a proper cover for the LP. They too did a wonderful job. A fully decorated Christmas tree in the background, artificial snow everywhere, mistletoe, and Fran in the foreground sitting on a huge red ornament that looked like it belonged on some giant's 100-foot-tall tree. Paul Jennet was brought in to do the shoot and his 8x10s in color were fantastic.

Kip's arrangements for the Quinns singing behind Fran were wonderful—particularly in "Carol of the Bells" where the five siblings somehow managed to sound like an entire carillon. "I'll Be Home for Christmas" captured the pathos of the song perfectly, as did his poignant chart for "Have Yourself a Merry Little Christmas."

During the rehearsal for "Oyfn Pripetshik," it was Mendel Cohen, the first violinist, who helped Fran with her pronunciation. "My Dahlink, it's a very guttural language. You should feel like you're going to spit on someone when you pronounce the words."

"Thank you, Mendy," said Fran. "Can we run it again, Kip?"

The arrangement was so moving, Fran's performance so emotional, that after they ran it again, Mendel Cohen had to wipe the tears from his eyes. "Please forgive me, everyone. I-I-I lost so many family members over there. This song. The children sang it—on the way to the gas chambers. I'm so sorry. Please excuse me for a moment." Mendy left the stand and went into the hall where he composed himself. The orchestra, shielded from the horrors he must have seen, was, nevertheless, sympathetic and supportive of him. When he returned, his fellow string players patted him on the back and he nodded at Kip indicating that he was ready to play.

Even though the recording session only lasted for three days, there was no compromise in the quality of the album. Whip

**A CHANGE OF KEY**

Elliot had the orchestra, Fran and the Quinns balanced in one take. Then they laid down the master.

The following day, Buck brought a freshly pressed LP and the mock up of the album art to Jack Merrill's office. "Buck! What do you have for me?"

"I'd like you to play this LP, Jack. Right now. If there are any changes to be made, I need to know right away."

Jack looked at his watch and said, "OK, I've got time before my next meeting. Cue it up and let's give a listen. He did more than just listen. His smile after every track showed Buck that he was thrilled with the LP.

"Jesus, Buck, you did all this in three days?"

"Well, you can thank Whip Elliot for most of it. And Kip Roman for his arrangements."

"Fantastic. Just fantastic. What's next, Buck?"

'We have a few groups lined up that we're going to record soon, and Al and Bill are constantly out there checking on groups and soloists. My aim is to build the catalog of the label with a wide variety of talent."

"Well, keep it up, because I tell you, Buck, the money is rolling in. We've already made a fortune between Fran and Cindi and this holiday album should set new records. And Perez Prado? He's already sold 48,000 albums in Mexico alone, and we haven't even gotten them into the other Central and South American countries. We're thinking of releasing one of his songs as a single. It's called "Mambo #5" and it's got a great sound."

"By the way, Buck, that Oyfn song? I never heard anything like it. I was really moved by it. It's a great inclusion on the album. "

"Thanks, Jack. It was a stretch for Fran, but she really hit it—and Mendy Cohen in our string section, he helped her with the lyrics. He's got stories you wouldn't believe."

"Gotta go meet with the general now. Keep me informed on production," said Jack.

They shook hands and Buck returned to his office where Kelsey had a dozen slips of paper with calls he needed to return.

## A CHANGE OF KEY

It had been a long but very productive day and Buck headed for home satisfied with how well his department was functioning. He hoped he would feel that same satisfaction when he got home to Carrie.

Her recovery from depression had been spotty with episodes of great happiness followed by funks that she did not seem to be able to recover from. Everyone said it would take time but that it would eventually work itself out. Buck went through his days with his fingers crossed.

# CHAPTER NINETEEN
*"Welcome to America" December 1946*

On the morning of December 12$^{th}$ with Buck and Rachel in one car and Arlene in the other, they were finding parking at Newark Metropolitan Airport. It was the only airport in the metro area that handled international flights. They found spaces in the lot and moved to the terminal where they awaited the arrival of Mila Sadowsky and her daughters, Zofia and Agnieska. Rachel's cousins had finally gotten visas to travel to America and since Buck would be sponsoring them, there should be no problem in their entering the country.

They would have to clear U.S. Customs, but considering their backgrounds, they would not be arriving in America with too many possessions. The flight on a Douglas DC-3 took many hours with several stops with the flight originating in London.

Rachel was nervous about meeting her cousin but Buck reassured her that it would be fine. They had an apartment waiting for them in Fresh Meadows and once they settled in, Bevvy would get the girls, 9 and 6, registered for school. Since Rachel had never seen her cousins, she inked a small sign that had their names on it and they held it up behind the gate area where passengers would walk to get their luggage and then go through customs.

The flight was a half hour late and it was full, so clearing customs took nearly an hour. Mila Sadowsky spotted the sign and carrying her smallish suitcase, came up to Rachel and hugged her. "I glad to see you *kuzyn!* These my children Zofia and Agnieska." The two little girls, both blonde with striking green eyes, hugged Rachel, then Buck, then Arlene. "We glad to come America," said Zofia.

"Well, we're very glad you are here. Welcome to America!" said Arlene.

"You are aunt to us?" said Agnieska.

Arlene thought it best not to get too deeply into the second cousin once removed thing, so she simply said, "Yes. I am."

"*Ciotka* Arlene. I like!" said the little girl.

## A CHANGE OF KEY

"And you are *wujek* to us?" said Zofia.

Buck assumed the word meant uncle, so he said, "Yes, Uncle Buck. That's me."

The girl struggled with the word, finally smiling and saying, "Onkele Buck. I like!"

"Let's find the cars. We'll come to our house and have some lunch. Then the girls will take you to your new apartment," said Buck.

"*Dziekuje!* I thanking you," said Mila Sadowsky.

"*Prosze!* Please. I soon learn the English speak better."

"*Drodzy* Mila, don't worry. You will learn soon," said Rachel.

For the balance of the ride, Rachel and Mila spoke in Yiddish, with the two little girls joining in the conversation when they could. At the house, Buck helped unpack from the car's trunk the three small battered suitcases that had been provided by ORT. Buck introduced the two little girls to their *kuzynow* Eddie, Laura and little Casey.

"*Piekne dziecko!*—Beautiful baby!" said Agnieska.

"And this is *ciotka* Bevvy," said Buck.

Bevvy had laid out lots of food for everyone and their new cousins ate with gusto. Buck watched the girls eat as if they hadn't had a good meal in years—which was probably the case. He also noticed that as they were eating, he spotted the numbers tattooed on the arms of all three of them. Carrie saw them at the same time and gasped. "Oh, oh dear!" she said.

Mila followed her eyes and said, "Is numbers from Bergen-Belsen. They did to all prisoner, even babies. No one was excepted."

Rachel said, "Mila, you must try to forget what happened there. What you saw. You are going to have a new life here in America."

"Can never forget. Must never forget. Such things I saw—all saw."

Then in Yiddish, Mila explained how her Children's Medical Clinic which treated both Jewish and German children, had been closed by the Nazis. She had been arrested for daring to put her hands on an Aryan child. Two other doctors and four nurses were all sent to the camps. She never saw any of them again.

Because she was a doctor, at Bergen-Belsen she was allowed to treat the Jewish inmates. But since she had almost no medicines and even bloody bandages had to be reused, most of her patients died. When Rachel explained what she had just been told, Carrie and the girls turned pale and lost their appetites.

Even though Mila had been trained at the University of Krakow, one of the oldest and most prestigious universities in Europe, she would not be permitted to practice medicine in America unless she took a lot of courses, did residencies and passed a national exam, which would be difficult until her English skills improved. But Rachel was determined to find a job for her. Maybe Bevvy's doctor boyfriend had a Polish colleague who could use a Polish speaking receptionist or nurse.

After lunch, Buck and Arlene took the Sadowskys to their apartment in Fresh Meadows. The building was a four-story part of a complex of similar buildings just off of 188th Street and 68th Avenue. The apartment was on the second floor. When they entered, Mila was startled to see that the apartment was furnished. Buck had purchased living room furniture, a small kitchen table with four chairs, beds for the girls in one bedroom and a queen-sized bed in the larger of the two bedrooms for Mila. Dishes, towels, silverware, cleaning products—a fully stocked refrigerator and freezer and cabinets that served as a pantry also full of dry goods and basic cooking products. Before they got to the apartment, Buck showed them the neighborhood—where the food market was, the post office, the school the girls would be attending, things that they could not even imagine having just a year earlier.

In the best English Mila could muster, she said, "I cannot make thanks enough for what you do for us."

"We're family now." Buck had had the phone company install a wall phone near the kitchen. "If you need anything, you

**A CHANGE OF KEY**

just call Rachel or me and we'll be here to help you." He took down her number to give to Rachel, kissed the three of them goodbye, and with Bevvy, returned to his house.

"Think they'll do all right, Buck?"

"It will be hard at first, until they learn more English, but compared to what they have been through, this must seem like heaven."

.....

Things started to move rapidly at RCA. Al and Bill met with Buck and the topic of the conversation was the burgeoning Rhythm and Blues movement in popular music. Bill had been up to Harlem to the Apollo Theater and he caught some acts that he said were terrific. Shortly thereafter, RCA signed the Cardinals, The Four Falcons and the Five Drumbeats—a group with a female lead backed by a quartet of Negro singers whose harmonies were amongst the tightest Buck had ever heard. They also had their eyes on some solo singers who showed great promise.

One morning, Kelsey buzzed Buck and told him that there was a Mr. Deauville to see him. Buck told him to come in, and the Mr. Deauville turned out to be Ronny Deauville, Tex Beneke's vocalist with his Miller-styled band.

"Ronnie! Come in and have a seat," said Buck.

Ronnie Deauville was a handsome young man of twenty-five who got his professional singing start with Glen Gray's Casa Loma Orchestra. He honed his craft singing in the Naval Air Corps during the war. He had been singing in top nightclubs like Mocambo in Los Angeles and El Mirador in Palm Springs. On a western swing with his band, Tex caught his act and offered him a job in his band.

"What brings you up here, Ronnie?" asked Buck.

"Well, as you probably know, I'm singing with Tex Beneke. We've been touring all over and the band is a big success. So many people still enjoy the Glenn Miller sound, we're sold out everywhere we play."

"That's great news." But something in Deauville's expression said otherwise.

## A CHANGE OF KEY

"Or is it?" asked Buck.

"Don't get me wrong, Buck. I love Tex. In fact, everyone who's ever worked with him loves him. He's a real gentleman and he's very generous with his players."

"And this is a problem?"

"No, no. It's not a problem—for now. But you know, Buck, Sinatra, Haymes, Bob Eberle, they all started out with big bands but were able to move into solo careers. I was wondering if that might be in the cards for me."

"You want to leave Tex?" said Buck.

"Not right away. I have a contract for another year or so, but once that's up, I would like to try for a solo act. What are the chances that Victor would hire me?"

"It's possible, Ronnie, but you have to understand, Tex is a good friend. I don't want to be accused of raiding his band and leaving him in the lurch. But I can't imagine Tex standing in the way of someone wanting to make a career move."

"No, I would never do that to him, Buck. Like I say, I love the guy."

"Let me ask you this: does Tex hold an option on your contract?"

"Meaning?"

"You say you are under contract for the next year and a half or so. Let's say he holds a year option on the contract. If he wants to, he could exercise that option and keep you for another year. I'm not saying that would happen. I think the world of Tex and I can't see him holding back talent for his own purpose."

"Neither can I," said Deauville.

"Let's do this, Ronnie: first, this conversation is confidential. I won't mention it to anyone here at Victor. You come and see me once that contract is up and I think we can bring you on board the label and develop your solo career. No promises right now, but I'm always looking towards the future."

"That's fair enough Buck—and thanks." He stood up, shook Buck's hand and left the office. Buck jotted down a few notes, put them in a manilla folder, and filed it in his desk. Then

## A CHANGE OF KEY

he buzzed Kelsey. "Kel? Could you call up to Jack Merrill and ask if he's got fifteen minutes for me?"

"Right on it, Buck."

Five minutes later she buzzed him and said, "Go right up."

"Buck! What do you need?" said Jack when Buck was seated in his office.

"We have a problem, Jack."

"Oh? I thought everything was going so well," said Merrill.

"Yes, but that's part of the problem. We have lots of acts now and they're all ready to start cutting albums. The problem is we don't have enough studio time for all of them. With the exception of Franny's Christmas album, it usually takes a good two weeks to record a fourteen-song album. The rehearsal studio here isn't state of the art so it's not suitable to cut an album. Downtown is fine—but we're backed up for months, and it's hard to build this label if we can't get music out to the public."

Jack thought about it and said, "I see what you mean. Let me ask you, Buck, we recorded your band at Webster Hall. Would that work to ease some of the load off downtown?"

"The industry has moved forward so quickly, Jack. There would have to be significant modifications made over there to get a good quality for recording LPs."

"What about Carnegie Hall? I think the New York Philharmonic is on hiatus for the holidays. From what I hear, Artur Rodzinski is off in Europe on vacation or conducting some orchestra over there. I'll call their management and see about availability."

"We'll still have to move a lot of equipment to both spaces if these LPs are going to be of the highest quality," said Buck.

"Let me huddle up with Whip, Tommy Taylor and Phil Flagler to see what they would need. Once we can secure the spaces, we'll start trucking the gear over. Your job, Buck, is to make out a schedule so everyone gets time in one of the three spaces. Leave yourself a day or two leeway in case we have to redo some tracks."

## A CHANGE OF KEY

"That works for me, Jack. Once you tell me what you got, I'll do the scheduling."

"Oh, and there's one more thing. Shirley has a manilla envelope on her desk waiting for you. Pick it up. I think you'll know what to do with it."

Back in his office, he opened the envelope and stared in absolute astonishment at a pile of checks, each one made out to every member of the orchestra, plus Bill, Al, Kip, Fran and himself. RCA had given a bonus of $500 to each member of the orchestra. Bill and Al got $2000 each, as did Fran and Kip, and his check was a bonus of $5000. He could scarcely believe it.

He called Al and Bill and told them about his conversation with Jack. "Do you want us to take a break from scouting?" asked Bill.

"No, let's not do that. Besides, not everyone you go to see will pan out. So keep up the scouting missions."

"Roger that, boss," said Bill.

"Ugh. Sounds like we're back in the Army. Now, get Al and come down to the office. We have some, umm, Christmas presents to give out."

The three of them went down to the studio and one by one, they called out the names on the checks. No one in the orchestra expected a bonus—especially one as large as they had just received. When Pammy Wendorfer picked up hers, she burst into tears and hugged Buck.

"Merry Christmas, guys. And Chuckie, a Happy Hanukkah to you!"

…..

That night as in the previous five or six nights, Carrie seemed to be growing ever stronger. She was very affectionate to Buck and the children and talked about how happy she had been during the day. Now and again a brief cloud would cross her face and her eyes grow dejected. At those times, Buck would reach out, put his hand on her cheek and gently say, "Shh, shh." That was sufficient to bring her back from wherever she had wandered. Then he would hug her and all was well again.

## A CHANGE OF KEY

When they got into bed that night Carrie said, "Bucky? Casey is over a month old now."

"Yes, darling, I know."

"Well, that means we can make love again, doesn't it?'

"Technically, yes. But only when you think you are ready, darling."

"I'm ready. Would you make love to me tonight, Bucky?"

"Anything to please you, love," said Buck.

"Bucky? Would you be gentle with me?"

"Am I ever anything else, Carrie?"

"No. Never. You are the sweetest, most caring man I could ever imagine. Being loved by you is so special. Now come hold me and make me happy," she said.

For hours, Buck did everything in his power—everything he knew—to make Carrie happy. Her first climax released an incredible amount of tension from her and she wanted to scream in ecstasy. The next several were not quite at that intense level, but she was content to have Buck inside her binding their bodies together. She kept murmuring, "I love you, Bucky, I love you, I love you." And as for Buck, he was reasonably certain that the Carrie he loved with his whole heart was back.

.....

The next night, Buck asked if Carrie would mind clearing and doing the dishes because he had something he had to take care of. "Of course, darling. Go do what you need to. I'll be here when you get back."

Buck didn't go far. In fact, he went to his home's basement, taking with him the Selmer soprano sax. He figured he might as well give it a try and see if he had anything left inside of him. He moistened the reed, fastened it to the mouthpiece by the ligature and blew a few notes. Like all Selmer instruments, the soprano was lightning fast in its key action and the tone was perfect. That was unusual in a soprano. It was the rare instrument that was in tune with itself in different octaves. Usually a player had to make lip adjustments every time he hit the octave key because the soprano tended to be a hair flat in the upper register.

## A CHANGE OF KEY

This was especially noticeable in the curved version of the soprano sax, but to a lesser degree in the straight instrument.

At first, he experimented with scales in all the practical keys, sharps and flats. Then he played arpeggios, but what he really wanted to do was to see if he had any jazz chops left. He started riffing on the old Jimmy Lunceford tune, "Uptown Blues," and he captured the wailing sound that Jimmy Smith so ably had got out of the alto sax, which Buck had to admit, had a lot more balls than a soprano. He handled the ad lib sax solo and then did the trumpet ride. In all, the solos were about 96 bars of the song. When he finished, he realized that he wasn't even breathing heavily—but then again the soprano sax required a lot less air than the tenor. Nevertheless, he resolved to keep playing.

The next number he tried was "Riffin' Away," a big hit for Buck's civilian band that was written specially for him by Johnny Blair and showcased his amazing tenor playing with 112 measures of sax solo over riff patterns in the rest of the band. It was shocking for Buck to realize that so much of his playing was still in his fingers. They almost moved over the keys on their own. He guessed it was similar to riding a bicycle. Once you knew how, you didn't forget.

Buck played four more songs, all with intricate solo passages. Finally, he felt that his lip was a little sore. The mouthpiece for the soprano sax is small compared to the tenor and it requires much more compression of the embouchure. It was enough for the night. He took the horn apart, patted it as he would a favorite pet, and closed the case.

When he came upstairs, Carrie threw herself into Buck's arms and said, "Oh sweetheart, I am so proud of you! You sounded fantastic! Are you all right?"

"Yes, hon. No pain, didn't even lose my breath. In fact, it felt good to play again."

"This is just great. I can't wait to hear you play some more," she said.

But that night, Carrie remained awake long after Buck had fallen asleep. She wanted to make sure that there was no triggering

## A CHANGE OF KEY

in Buck's mind, having played his instrument at long last. But Buck slept soundly without even the slightest whimper.

Maybe Dr. Engelhardt was right on the money when he said it would take time for his memories to fade into the background of his brain. If she had to stay up every night to protect him, she would.

And she had to admit that the group sessions she had attended were working for her too. It was comforting to know that other women experienced the same PPD that she had—and in some cases, much worse. She had promised Buck that she would be better, and just as he never broke a promise to her, she would extend that same courtesy to him.

# CHAPTER TWENTY
*"Meet Johnny Mercer" January 1947*

Buck felt that 1946 had been a memorable and successful year. He was a new father, his wife seemed to be fully recovered, he had begun to build a formidable array of performers for the RCA Victor label. The money was flowing into the corporate headquarters from record sales both in America and internationally. And that was just the beginning.

His dear sister Arlene married his friend Al Rovitz. The ceremony was at Temple Emanuel in Manhattan and the reception at the Plaza, though not in the huge ballroom. There were about a hundred and fifty guests at the wedding and Arlene looked simply beautiful. Bevvy was her maiden of honor and Carrie and Cathy Dwyer her bridesmaids. Buck and Bill Dwyer were Al's groomsmen. Al hired a seven-piece combo from the RCA Studio Orchestra to provide music for the reception. Fran Michaels and Cindi Kay, though guests, agreed to sing some songs with the band.

Arlene and Al had been lucky enough to find a lovely three-bedroom home on Fresh Meadow Lane and 48th Avenue—a mere two blocks from Buck's and Rachel's homes. It was Stavros Nikolaides, the same realtor who had found a home for the Dwyers, who located the house for Mr. and Mrs. Rovitz. Bevvy had helped set the home up with Arlene and with the wedding present Buck gave the couple, they could furnish it as lavishly as they wanted to.

In the middle of December, Buck asked Carrie if she felt strong enough to host a small New Year's Eve party at their home. "Ten, maybe fifteen people, darling. I'd like to do something nice for all of those who have really helped us."

Carrie didn't have to give it a second thought. "That would be so nice, Bucky. What would you want me to cook?"

"No, no, no, I think we'll have it all catered in. Maybe a turkey and deli meats. There's a real nice kosher deli up on Northern Boulevard. You won't have to do a thing."

## A CHANGE OF KEY

"That's no fun, sweetie. I want to try my hand at some hors oeuvres."

"That's fine. I'm sure Mama and the girls will bring things too."

As far as parties go, it was a great success for several reasons. Mostly, it was the gathering of good friends: Bill, Al, Pete and Fran, Noni, Chuck, Kenny, Kip—even Eddie Holberg from the old Bensonhurst neighborhood came with his wife, the former Ruthie Levy who grew up with Buck and Eddie back in Brooklyn. Only Cindi Kay could not be there because she promised Tony that she would perform at his club for New Year's Eve. Buck had also invited Kelsey Burton and her husband, but she said he was still very self-conscious about his artificial leg, so he preferred to stay at home. Buck understood and said, "That's OK, Kel, maybe next year he'll be ready."

The food and champagne flowed, there was music, and great company. Bill's kids got along perfectly with Buck and Carrie's and April, Bill's oldest, rode herd on the youngsters to keep them in line. She was extremely mature for a twelve-year-old. Mila Sadowsky and her daughters also came, and even in just a few weeks, the three had made great progress in learning English. When Buck asked how they had accomplished so much, Mila said, "We listen American radio. Good to learn that way."

At about a quarter to midnight when everyone was eagerly awaiting the arrival of the New Year, Al Rovitz took his champagne flute and clinked his spoon inside it, the gesture calling for everyone's attention. Buck expected that Al was going to offer a toast to success in the New Year. He was wrong.

"Sorry to interrupt the fun, folks, but as I look around here tonight, I think there's someone missing, but by next year, I hope to see that omission remedied. Arlene? Come on over here. You're on, sweet cheeks."

"Well, as you all know, Bevvy and I have the most wonderful nieces and nephew in the whole world. So we wanted to return the favor. Bev? Buck? You're going to be an aunt and uncle!"

Bevvy screamed and ran to her sister to hug her. Buck did the same, as did Carrie. Rachel was beyond speaking. She just sat and smiled like she had just won the Irish Sweepstakes.

Buck and Bill congratulated Al and in his mind, Buck was thinking, 'Wow, the wedding was early in December. They sure didn't waste any time!' but he was thrilled for his big sister who probably had the biggest heart of anyone in the family. He went up to Arlene and hugged her tightly. "I love you sis, and I'm going to be the best uncle a kid ever had."

"Love you too, Benny. I'm so happy!"

In the corner of the living room stood an antique grandfather's clock that Carrie just loved. She found it in a shop in a store in Ridgewood, a very German section of the city. It had all the craftsmanship of an old-world masterpiece. At precisely midnight, it struck the hour. Everyone shouted "Happy New Year!" Buck hugged and kissed Carrie, there was much back-slapping and kissing, and after another hour, the party wound down.

New Year's Day was a Tuesday and everyone had the day off on Wednesday. Benny was looking forward to watching the Rose Bowl between the Fighting Illini and UCLA Bruins, but the house would have to be returned to its normal neat state. Rachel had already begun to clear dishes and wrapping up leftovers.

"Ma! No! Go home. Bevvy? Take Mama home. I'll do the clean-up."

"What, I shouldn't help my son with this mess?" said Rachel.

"You're the greatest, Ma, but it's late. So I'm throwing you out!"

He winked at Bevvy who had retrieved their coats from the bedroom. She helped her mother into her coat and kissing Buck and Carrie goodnight, they both left. The kids had fallen asleep before midnight and April Dwyer was very helpful in helping Carrie tuck them in bed.

"That April is some kid, Carrie. What is she, twenty-five?"

## A CHANGE OF KEY

"Twelve, darling. But you're right, she's really something. Cathy and Bill have done a heck of a job raising her."

"Yeah. I hope we can be as good. Now, you head to the bedroom and I'll get this stuff put away. When I get there, we can snuggle. OK?"

"I feel guilty about leaving you to clean up the mess, Bucky."

"It's really not that bad. Go ahead. I'll be in soon."

Soon turned out to be two hours later, but Buck was determined to leave nothing for Carrie to do in the morning. He even took the carpet sweeper from the front closet and made sure that he swept up every remnant of the meal that didn't make it into someone's mouth. By the time he was done, the house had the orderly appearance that both he and Carrie loved.

In the bedroom, he put on his flannel pajamas since it was quite chilly, and slipped into bed next to Carrie, who looked to be fast asleep.

"Bucky?"

"Right here."

"Hold me, love."

He wrapped his arms around her and soon they were both fast asleep.

Having had a good night's sleep except for Carrie having to get up once to nurse Casey, she seemed invigorated the next morning. "Mr. Feinstein?"

"Yes, darling?"

"What do you say we start the new year off right?"

"You mean—"

"Exactly—now come to me."

.....

It was back to work on Thursday and Buck wrestled most of the morning with scheduling. Without knowing if they could get Carnegie or Webster Halls, there would be a very long backup in getting new LPs out to the public. Complicating the problem were the reports that Al and Bill had filed for the month of December. Bill was super high on a R & B group called the Four

## A CHANGE OF KEY

Kings and Al was touting a young vocalist named Peggy Dillon. If they were as good as they say, there would be the whole process of getting them under contract, having Kip or Fletcher write charts for them with the orchestra, rehearsing, and then getting them studio time for recordings. Just when Buck thought his brain would pop out of his ears, Kelsey buzzed him and said Jack Merrill wanted to see him right away.

"Sounds serious, Kel," said Buck.

"Actually, Jack sounded pretty excited so your guess is as good as mine," she said.

When he walked into Jack Merrill's office, Jack stood, and said, "Buck, meet Johnny Mercer!"

Sitting on Jack's sofa was a living legend. Johnny Mercer was one of the greatest lyricists of all time. His list of hits was simply enormous including such standards as "Goody, Goody, "Ain't We Got Fun," "Jeepers Creepers," "Hooray for Hollywood," "You Must Have Been a Beautiful Baby," "That Old Black Magic, "Acc-Cen-Tu-Ate the Positive," and during the war, "G.I. Jive." The list of his hits could fill a book and he had already won an Oscar for "On the Atcheson Topeka and Santa Fe," which he wrote with Harry Warren supplying the music.

The pride of Savannah, Georgia, and a descendent of Confederate Generals and American Revolutionary Generals, he was also a distant cousin of General George S. Patton. He stood and shook hands with Buck saying, "Well ah'll be horn swaggled if it isn't ole' Buck Fisher! Ah'm delighted to make your acquaintance" Mercer had this instantly recognizable Georgia lilt in his voice.

"Johnny and I go back all the way to 1928 when he first got to New York. I got him his first job writing lyrics for Miller Music. What was it, Johnny, fifty bucks a week?" said Jack.

"Hah! That would have seemed like all the money in the world back, then. It was twenty-five bucks—and I was glad to get that. Ah was livin' on oatmeal and breadsticks I stole from Horn and Hardart back then. But you, Buck, why hell, son, you shot right to the top so fast. Everybody I worked with knew all about you and that tenor sax of yours. Ah mahself said a prayer for ya, when we heard what happened over there in England."

"I don't know if you know it, Buck," said Jack, "but back in 1942, Johnny founded Capitol Records along with Buddy DeSylva and Glen Wallichs. Buddy used to write songs with Lew Brown and Ray Henderson. They had a big Broadway hit with *Good News*. Show ran for a long time."

"Right," said Mercer, "then ole Buddy got more into the production side of things. Jack tells me what you're doing over here for Victor. Helluva deal, according to Jack. Wish I could steal you away to the west coast," joked Mercer.

"Hey, pal, no poaching! Buck's destined for even bigger and better things here," said Jack.

"You know, Johnny, my arranger, Kip Roman, just wrote a chart on one of your songs for one of our biggest stars, Fran Michaels—'Day in, Day Out.' I wonder if you would like to give it a listen," said Buck.

"Ah say let's do it!" said Mercer.

"Mind if I tag along too, Buck?" said Jack Merrill.

"That would be great, Jack. You know, Johnny, I've got a number of the guys from my civilian and Army band in the orchestra. It's so great to have the same guys with you day after day instead of journeymen popping in and out of the group."

"That civilian band. 'Tween you and me, Goodman had nothing on you guys. And he even recorded a number of my songs. You could really bring the swing."

"Thanks Johnny. Those were great years."

They took the elevator to the rehearsal studio and most of the band members immediately recognized the somewhat chunky, gap-toothed form of Johnny Mercer.

Fran Michaels had a look of terror on her face, afraid that she would have to sing in front of the great man. But that's exactly what was going to happen.

"Folks," said Jack Merrill, I'm sure you all recognize Johnny Mercer. Kip? I hear you have a new chart of one of his songs. I'd like Fran to sing it for him, if you don't mind."

## A CHANGE OF KEY

Fran's gulp was almost audible. Buck sidled up next to her and whispered, "He's the nicest guy you'd ever want to sing for. You've played before tougher audiences, believe me."

"Well, here goes nothing," she said.

Kip counted off four and the orchestra launched into a semi-swing version of "Day in, Day Out."

Usually the song was done in a slower tempo, with a more torch-songish feel. But Kip's arrangement gave it an entirely new flavor—and Fran walloped the lyric in a masterful performance. When Kip took the orchestra out, Mercer leapt to his feet and applauded loudly. Then he said to Fran, "Gal, you could be another Maggie Whiting. That was just spectacular." Then in a stage whisper he added, "You ever move to California, you look me up at Capitol. I'll sign you up in a second."

Fran, blushing, thanked him and said, "Mr. Mercer, coming from you, that's quite a great compliment. Thank you."

At the piano, Kenny Ferraro played the first few bars of "G.I. Jive." Mercer laughed the hearty laugh he was famed for and he grabbed the microphone and regaled the orchestra with the novelty song that rang true with so many soldiers during the war. When he finished, the entire orchestra stood and applauded, except for the fiddlers, who rapped the back of their bows against the body of their instruments as was the custom.

"Why Ah thank y'all very much. That was very pleasant—and thanks to you, sir," he said to Kenny Ferraro.

Then to Jack Merrill, Mercer said, "You know Jack, Ah think Buck is onto something here with this idea of a studio orchestra that can back any kind of a performer. It surely does work for you. Ah'm gonna think on it flyin' back to L.A. We sure have plenty of musicians on the coast who might like permanent studio work."

Then Buck interjected, "But that's the difference, Johnny. These are all contract players. They work for the label with not a free-lancer amongst them. We pay them well—so well that none of them think of jumping ship. See? That's the difference. I never have to go in search of players because they're already right here."

## A CHANGE OF KEY

"Ah see what you mean, Buck. Well, ya sure have given me lots of food for thought. I have to head back now, but it was sure enough a great pleasure meeting you and seeing your work here. And Jack? It's always grand to see you too."

When Jack and Mercer left, Fran came up to Buck and gave him a sock on the arm. "You might have warned me, Buck! Christ, I thought I would soil myself!"

"He loved you, Franny. You know, Johnny Mercer hobnobs out there in California with a lot of Hollywood types—Crosby, Astaire, Gable—Cary Grant. I wouldn't be a bit surprised if he drops your name to them and that you get a call from some agent out there."

"Oh come on, Buck," said Fran.

"What, you never heard the song 'You Ought to be in Pictures?'"

"Sure I've heard it. But that's not me, Bucky."

Buck sighed and shook his head. "Franny, you are the most beautiful woman I have ever seen. In my entire life, I don't expect that I'll see anyone who approaches you for beauty. And your voice? Well, you heard what Johnny Mercer said about it, and you know what I think of it. Some studio out there could build entire movie musicals around you."

"Oh, so now you think I'm Judy Garland or Shirley Temple?"

"No, Fran. Better than both of them. You are one in a million and I think the albums you will make for us are just the beginning. They're selling like hotcakes and Jack has mentioned to me the possibility of arranging a one woman show at Carnegie Hall."

"Jesus, Buck, your killin' me! I'm not that good, for crying out loud."

Buck put his hands on Fran's shoulders and looked right in her eyes. "Yes you are! Don't let anyone ever tell you differently. From the day you auditioned for the Johnny Blair Orchestra, I knew that you were more than special, more than just talented. You had a charisma that made your every move as a

# A CHANGE OF KEY

singer into a consummate performance. Maybe it was your operatic training—the acting part of it to go along with the singing—but I tell you, Franny, you're going places you never dreamed of."

Fran hugged Buck and said, "Thanks for believing in me, Buck. But let's just see what happens."

"Hey! What's going on over there with my wife?" said Pete McCormack.

"What do you think? I'm stealing her from you," said Buck.

"Oh, OK. But can she be home for dinner?"

Buck sighed and said, "Oh, here. Take her."

Pete and Fran kissed and Buck was so happy to see his two dear friends so much in love. It reminded him of how much he was still in love with Carrie. And that he was eager to get home to her and his children.

**A CHANGE OF KEY**

# CHAPTER TWENTY-ONE
*The One That Got Away: February, 1947*

As 1946 came to an end, Buck reflected on what he had done. Both Fran and Cindi had delivered certified Gold Records for RCA. The list of performers under contract for LPs had grown almost exponentially and everyone from Jack Merrill to David Sarnoff were thrilled with the amount of money that was pouring into to the RCA coffers.

Buck had convinced Jack to completely refurbish the rehearsal studio to bring it up to state-of-the-art standards so that LPs could be made right on site. There were now four separate sites where RCA artists could record. That didn't even include the west coast studios in Los Angeles where singers and instrumental groups could record without having to trek all the way to New York City to cut LPs.

On the personal side of his life, Buck couldn't have been happier if some Hollywood script writer had penned its course. Arlene had delivered a beautiful seven-pound son in August—ten days late, but not enough to cause alarm. Al was over the moon as a father and Buck as godfather held little Jonathan during his *bris*. Buck was a little squeamish about it so he turned his head when the rabbi performed the actual circumcision. Al had dipped his finger in Scotch and put it in the baby's mouth, essentially getting him drunk so the pain would be minimal. Carrie was equally thrilled and she was determined to be just as good an aunt to Jonathan as Arlene and Bevvy have been to Eddie, Laura and Casey.

There was no vestige of Carrie's post-partum depression remaining. She was happy, content, and seemed to enjoy every day. Naturally there were moments when running a household with three young children and all the other responsibilities of homemaking would overwhelm her, but it was at times like those that Buck was there to support her and help out.

One day after rehearsal, Chuck said, "Buck? Got a sec?"

For just an instant, Buck sensed that this could be very bad news, that Chuck was leaving the orchestra. He was wrong.

"Sure, Chuck. What gives?"

"You still have that name and address of that jeweler you went to when you got the ring for Carrie?"

"Sure. Morris Horowitz on 47$^{th}$ Street. That's where Al got Arlene's ring too. How come?"

"Oh, nothing. Nothing at all."

"Uh huh. Keeping secrets now, Chuckie?"

"Ah, shit, I'm gonna ask my girlfriend to marry me," said Chuck.

"Girlfriend? Who the hell even knew you had a girlfriend? When did all this happen?" said Buck.

Chuck laughed and said, "What, you think I don't have a life outside this studio? I've been seeing her for about eight months. A nice Jewish girl. My mother approves—and she hates everybody."

Buck was delighted and flabbergasted in equal parts. "Well, Jesus, Chuck, I'm thrilled for you! What's the gal's name"

"Becca. Well, Rebecca. Rebecca Smulovitz. She's from Williamsburg. A friend of my mother's introduced us. A real *shidduch*, but hey, sometimes those arranged deals work out. She's a great girl, Bucky. Teaches elementary school and plays violin like that Isaac Stern kid. Went to Manhattan School of Music to become a music teacher. Decided she likes little kids better—which is good, cause I wouldn't mind a passel of them crawling around my house."

"I couldn't be happier for you. I'll write Morris Horowitz's address and phone number down for you. You be sure to mention my name and he'll get you a terrific deal."

"One more thing, Buck."

"OK, shoot."

"When we set a date, and I hope it will be soon, will you be my Best Man?"

"Chuck, my dear friend, it would absolutely be an honor to stand up with you."

## A CHANGE OF KEY

"Thanks, Buck. We sure have been down a few roads together," said Chuck.

"Wait till I tell Carrie! She's going to go crazy!"

.....

One of the downsides of all the good things going on in his life was the fact that Buck kept sending Bill and Al out on road trips. Especially now that Al had an infant son. For that reason, Buck decided to relieve them of some of the burden by flying out to the coast to check out some performers.

Buck was a little uneasy about breaking the news to Carrie, but his trepidation was needless. "I know you have to do this for work, sweetheart. It's OK. How long do you think you will be gone?"

"Two days travel there and back and three days in L.A. A total of five days, darling. Then I promise I will hurry home to you."

Buck's flight out of Newark had him departing at 9 A.M. With stops, the Pan Am 307 Stratoliner would get him to L.A. by four that afternoon. The plane was comfortable and extremely solid, because it had been constructed on the same airframe as the famous B-17 heavy bomber which wreaked havoc on the Third Reich during the war. Buck, ever the nervous flyer, noted that the effects of air turbulence were barely discernible on the big aircraft.

Kelsey had booked Buck into the Beverly Hills Hotel. It was the hotel frequented by Hollywood actors and actresses and some of their more secretive liaisons had been fodder for the tabloid newspapers that dealt in sensationalism. Much to his surprise, a number of people recognized him and wanted to shake his hand, including the desk clerk. It had been so long since he had performed publicly that he was sure he was all but forgotten. Not according to the reaction he got from the people scurrying in and out of the lobby. After he had put his things in his room on the second floor of the hotel, he needed to find someplace to eat. He sat down on a sofa in the lobby and picked up a magazine called *L.A. This Week*. It was similar to what *Cue* magazine was to New York. It listed restaurants, clubs, concert venues and movie

## A CHANGE OF KEY

theaters in the area with a host of information about times, prices and addresses and phone numbers for reservations.

As he perused the magazine, a gentleman sat down next to him and said, "Mind if I sit down and shake your hand, Buck?"

It was Clark Gable.

Buck, startled by the presence of the superstar right next to him, stood up to shake his hand. "Hey, none of that, pal. Just think of me as a fellow warrior who loved what you did for the boys over in England. I flew with some of those boys and big as the Flying Fortresses were, they could take a severe beating—along with the ten men flying them."

After the death of Carol Lombard, Gable's wife, in 1942, he enlisted in the Army Air Force. The commanding general, 'Hap' Arnold wanted to assign him to a photographic unit, but Gable, perhaps distraught over the love of his life, preferred combat. He got out at the rank of Major, but during the war he flew many combat missions for the 351st Bombardment Group earning himself a Distinguished Flying Cross and an Air Medal.

"What brings you to our fair city, Buck?" he asked.

"Oh, I work for RCA Victor now scouting and developing new talent and getting them down on these new LP records."

"Miss playing?"

"Every minute of the day, Mr. Gable."

"Bullshit. It's Clark. Comrades in arms and all."

"You were in the thick of the flak and the Luftwaffe. I was leading a band," said Buck.

"I know. I heard you in a concert in London just about a week before you got hurt. I hope you're doing all right now."

"Thank you, yes. The recovery was slow, but I hardly have any recollection about what happened. I'm trying to keep it in the past."

"Yeah, that's a good idea. The things I saw in the tail gun spot in a B-17, well, I know what you mean about forgetting it. You make a movie, the blood is all fake. You fight in a war, it's as real as it gets. You know, Buck, even before the war, I liked your music. Carole loved it too," he said, referring to his wife.

## A CHANGE OF KEY

"Makes us even. I like all your films. I think my favorite was *Mutiny on the Bounty*. And if I may say, I think you got robbed on *Gone with the Wind*."

"Yeah, well, me and Olivier must have split the vote. Robert Donat? Come on! Don't get me wrong, I did like him in *Goodbye Mr. Chips,* and the makeup was as good as Orson Welles' in *Citizen Kane,* but I don't think his role was all that big a stretch. But keep that under your hat, Buck, we're not supposed to speak poorly about our colleagues in the profession."

"I understand. Doing anything lately?" asked Buck.

"I just finished a film called *The Hucksters*. You ask me, it's a piece of shit, but we're supposed to put on a brave face and say how wonderful it was to be involved with such a masterpiece." Gable laughed and said, "If you ever run out of bullshit back in New York, just let me know, because this town manufactures it by the ton."

"Say, you wouldn't happen to know of a decent restaurant in town, do you?" asked Buck.

"Sure, try Musso and Frank Grill. Joint goes back to before prohibition and lots of big names eat there. Shit, Scott Fitzgerald has a regular table, so does Gary Cooper."

Buck laughed and said, "I'm not looking to collect autographs; I'm just hungry. Would you like to join me?"

"Damn. I have a goddamned meeting with some big shots at Metro, otherwise, I would love to. Say, wait here a sec. I won't be a moment."

Gable went over to the registration desk and asked to use the phone. He was gone for about five minutes and when he returned, he said, "Buck, when you go there, you tell them who you are. It's all on the house."

"No, that's not—"

"Sure it is. It's on my tab—so eat and drink all you can handle. And it's really my pleasure. Now, I better get cleaned up and make my meeting. They're trying to get me for something called *Homecoming*. It won't shoot until next year but my agent wants me to get my name on the contract now. I told him to go fuck himself. If I don't get to read the shooting script, I don't sign anything. Once you put your name in writing, these jackasses can make you look like a real idiot and you have no say in the matter. Gonna set them straight but good tonight. But you go and enjoy yourself."

Buck thanked Gable, still stunned at the man's generosity. But then he remembered how he himself had treated other veterans and he had a better understanding of why Gable was doing what he did. He shook hands and Gable left for the elevators.

The desk clerk had ordered a cab for Buck and twenty minutes later he was being shown to a seat in Musso and Frank Grill. It was an elegant place that absolutely wreaked with celebrity. When he gave his name at the desk, the Maître d' knew who he was, not just because Clark Gable had called ahead, but because Buck was—or had been—world famous as a musician.

"Such a pleasure to have you with us this evening, Mr. Fisher. Anything you want tonight is complimentary."

Buck's table was towards the rear and a middle-aged waiter who might have been with the establishment from the day it opened brought him a menu and took his order for a Manhattan. The menu was fairly typical for a steak house: a variety of steaks, chops, ribs, and seafood. Buck laughed to himself when he tried to imagine Myrna Loy picking up a sticky rib with her fingertips and eating it trying not to soil her makeup.

He settled on the chicken pot pie for dinner because it reminded him of the ones his mother made when he was a boy. But when he placed his order, the waiter said, "I'm terribly sorry, Mr. Fisher, but the Chicken Pot Pie is only available on Thursdays. Please excuse me for a moment."

He returned with the Maître d' a few minutes later. "Mr. Fisher, we usually don't prepare that dish on any other day but Thursday, as I'm sure Mr. Plummer here has told you. But I will speak to the chef personally and ask if he can make an exception"

Clearly the power of a famous name could open a lot of doors—especially at Musso and Frank's. The Maître d' came back

## A CHANGE OF KEY

to the table and said, "Our chef would be honored to prepare the dish for you, Mr. Fisher. But you will have to give him about thirty minutes to do so. In the meantime, the drinks are on the house so enjoy them while you wait."

When the meal came and he started to eat, Buck wondered if he was being disloyal to his mother, because the pot pie was beyond anything Rachel Feinstein had ever made. Maybe it was the touch of white wine or the quality of the chicken. He didn't know. What he did know was that every bite was a wonderful experience.

He finished his meal with a slice of New York cheesecake—which he found ironic since he was about as far from the city as he could get—but it was as good as anything he had ever tasted at Junior's on Flatbush Avenue.

After a quick cab ride back to the hotel, Buck went to his room, undressed and fell asleep almost immediately, the long and tiring day behind him.

…..

The next evening, Buck was scheduled to go to the Hollywood Bowl to hear a young singer named Mario Lanza. The concert venue on North Highland Avenue in the Hollywood Hills was world famous for its architecture and acoustics.

It was Bill Dwyer who tipped Buck off about Lanza, whose real name was Alfredo Cocozza. Bill said that the buzz around town was that the young man was going to be a huge singing and film star—a Fred Astaire without the dance. His training had been operatic but, in his concerts, he mixed arias with popular tunes.

Buck had a fifth-row seat just off the aisle. For the concert, Lanza would be backed by the Hollywood Bowl Symphony Orchestra under the baton of Leopold Stokowski. Lanza began his program with *Vesti la giubba,* the tragic aria from Leoncavallo's *Pagliacci.* The crowd was absolutely enthralled by the performance. He then switched to a string of popular tunes from Jerome Kern, Cole Porter and even one by Johnny Mercer. He finished the first act with a masterful performance of *Largo al*

# A CHANGE OF KEY

*Factotum*, Figaro's comic aria from Rossini's *The Barber of Seville*.

In addition to being musically versatile, Lanza was movie-star handsome. At the end of the performance, Buck made his way backstage but was stopped by two security officers. He showed them his business card from RCA Victor and one of the guards recognized his name immediately. "I'll see if Mr. Lanza will talk to you now, Mr. Fisher."

He returned and said, "I'll show you to Mr. Lanza's dressing room."

Buck knocked on the door and Mario Lanza said, *"Entrare!"*

Lanza was at his dressing table using cold cream to remove the stage makeup that prevented glare from the dozens of lights used in the performance. "Well, Mr. Fisher, what can I do for you?"

Buck explained why he was in Los Angeles and what he was hoping to achieve for the Victor label. "We think you could be another Frank Sinatra if you wanted to," said Buck.

"I do enjoy popular music, Mr. Fisher, but my heart is with opera. I've been studying since I was sixteen. I don't mean to boast, but Koussevitzky said I had a voice heard only once in a century. I don't know if that's so. That honor probably belongs to Caruso, but it was very flattering to hear, you must understand."

Lanza spun around in his chair and said, "I don't know if you are aware of it, Mr. Fisher, but Lewis B. Mayer has signed me to a seven-year deal at MGM. He wants me to make a lot of pictures, some with me singing popular music, others more operatic."

"Would that interfere with you signing with us to make records?" asked Buck.

Lanza laughed and said, "No, it wouldn't, but I'm afraid you are a bit late."

"Meaning?"

"I've already signed with RCA—but with their Red Seal division. That's where all the long-hairs record and they felt it was better suited for me to sing opera for them than try to be just another pop singer. I'm committed to at least four albums with the label holding an option on a fifth."

They chatted for a few brief minutes longer and then they shook hands and Buck caught a cab back to the Beverly Hills Hotel. He couldn't help but think that his trip to the coast was a bust.

Over the next two nights, he checked out a rhythm and blues group and a jazz trio. Neither of the groups particularly excited Buck. No, Lanza was the big fish—and he was the one that got away.

He couldn't wait to fly home the next morning and even the prospect of a flight that sucked the energy right out of him, he didn't mind, knowing he would see his family soon.

From Chicago's Midway Airport, Buck called Jack Merrill and told him the trip had been a flop—particularly in his pursuit of Mario Lanza.

"Don't worry about it, Buck. He's still going to make money for RCA even if it's not in your division. Anyone else good out there?"

"Not for us, Jack. They'd be better suited to small west coast labels until they develop more."

"That's fine. Again, not to worry. There are still plenty of fish in the musical sea for us to go after. We'll talk when you get back."

Buck's flight was called soon thereafter and he boarded the plane realizing that they would all have to work a lot harder to find performers if they hoped to keep pace with Columbia and Decca.

When he finally arrived home, as exhausted as he had felt in months, he kissed Carrie, kissed the children and asked her if she minded if he went to sleep early.

"My love, you look totally out of it. You go sleep and I will be there soon to hold you. You can tell me all about your trip tomorrow. For now, you need rest."

Carrie was right, and sleep came easily to Buck that night.

# CHAPTER TWENTY-TWO
*"Tragedy Hits When You Least Expect It" June, 1948*

Over the previous months, Buck had summoned the courage to move up from his soprano saxophone to his tenor. It required much more air and the embouchure was wider, which distended the facial muscles much more than the soprano did. He started slowly at first, maybe twenty or thirty minutes of scales and arpeggios. Gradually, he advanced to actual songs requiring considerable jazz improvisation.

As when he first started noodling with the soprano, Buck was surprised at how much music remained in his fingers. He even experimented with the 'new' sound of bebop, particularly the rising triplet figures that seemed to leap into the upper register. Initially he was uncomfortable with that type of jazz. Riffing off of chords instead of melody was alien to him. More than a decade earlier, his teacher, Freddy Constantine, stressed the importance of knowing how to read chords and master the associated scales with them. He had made a career of expanding the melodies of songs, embellishing them, creating intricacies that no other tenor player had ever attempted. Now, with bebop melody seemed almost superfluous.

He remembered when he had heard Charlie Parker and realized that the melody to a song as familiar as "I Got Rhythm" was completely buried in the improvisation on the chordal structure of the piece. Parker and later Dave Brubeck had told him the same thing: they did not want to be trapped by the confines of melody. They were experimenting with much more sophisticated musical possibilities.

The important thing was that he enjoyed playing. Even before Jack Merrill hired him at RCA, he had mentioned the possibility of Buck recording an LP with a quartet or quintet. As Buck's fingers flew over the keys, he wondered if that was possible. After all, he had helped quite a number of artists gain fame and national recognition with their albums. Maybe there was still a market for a big band retread whose famous days were years behind him.

It certainly was something to think about and he would talk to Jack about it first thing Monday morning. Unfortunately, it would have to wait—for a long time.

"Bucky! Help!"

Buck heard Carrie shriek and took his sax from around his neck, put it in its stand and took the stairs two at a time to the first floor. Carrie was shaking—and Laura was lying prone on the floor.

Buck swept Laura up in his arms and laid her down on the couch. "What is it sweetie?" he said to his six-year-old daughter. "Tell daddy."

Carrie was unsuccessfully fighting back tears and Buck said, "Carrie, tell me what happened. Tell me everything. What did she do, trip or something?"

"Hurts daddy!" said Laura, clutching her right leg.

"Shh! Shh, sweetheart. Daddy make it all better," he said, gently massaging her leg.

"Buck, Laura was sitting on the couch coloring. I told her to come to me and when she stood up, she immediately collapsed. I thought it was funny at first, so I went to her and picked her up. But it was as if she couldn't support herself on her legs. She collapsed again."

"OK, let's remain calm. Maybe it's just a cramp or a sprain. Tell you what, get on the phone and ask if Bevvy can come over."

Bevvy heard the alarm in Carrie's voice and was at the front door two minutes later. "What happened, Buck?" She saw Laura lying on the couch crying and she went over to the child stroking her hair. "What's wrong, sugar? Tell auntie what happened."

"Hurts, Auntie Bev. Lots."

"Well, we'll just have to make it better. Don't worry, sweet girl, we'll fix this right away." She looked at Buck and Carrie, an unasked question on her face.

## A CHANGE OF KEY

She took Buck and Carrie aside and said, "What's going on? What happened.?"

Carrie explained that Laura just collapsed. Her leg wouldn't support her. "Was there any kind of trauma, Carrie? Did she bang the leg against the coffee table or chair leg?"

"No. Nothing like that. She was just walking towards me and then she collapsed. I don't know what to do," she said, now in full crying mode.

"OK, let me call Jerry," said Bevvy. Dr. Jerry Rosen was now the Chief of Neurology at Queens General Hospital. He and Bevvy had been dating for several years and Buck had the feeling that an announcement would be coming soon. He was a brilliant doctor who was making a reputation for himself in the field of neurology. He already had published several articles in prestigious journals like the *New England Journal of Medicine, Journal of the American Medical Association,* and even two in the British journal, *The Lancet.*

Fortunately, he had office hours that day and when Bevvy explained the problem, he said, "Get her here right away. We'll take a look and see what's going on."

Rosen's office was on Queens Boulevard in Forest Hills. It took about twenty-five minutes for Buck, Carrie, Bevvy and Laura to get there. Rachel had come over to mind Eddie and Casey. They found parking a block from the office, but when Laura stepped out of the car, she again collapsed, crying and holding her leg. Buck lifted her up and carried her into the office. There were five other patients in the office, but when the Nurse saw Laura's condition, she said, "I apologize, folks, but we have a medical emergency here and this child has to be seen immediately."

She brought them into an examination room and Buck laid Laura down on the examination bed. Dr. Rosen came in a few moments later, kissed Bevvy and Carrie, and shook hands with Buck. Then he went to the examination table and said, "Well hi there, sugar bear. What's happening here? Tell Uncle Jerry so we can fix you up."

## A CHANGE OF KEY

In the last two years, Rosen had been to so many family functions that the children already thought of him as their 'uncle.' He had no objections to the honorary title. "Can you stand up for me, lambchop?"

He picked Laura up from the bed and placed her on the floor—where once again she promptly collapsed. Placing her back on the bed, Dr. Rosen said, "Buck, Carrie, we have to admit her. There are a lot of tests we have to run that I just can't do here in the office. I'll call ahead to the Emergency Room and tell them you're coming. That way they will admit her quicker. We'll get her into the Children's Wing. I don' know about room availability yet, so she might be in a ward. It's not important. We'll be running tests all day. Hopefully she will only have to stay overnight. Or maybe an extra day."

Carrie was now crying, and Bevvy's face also glistened with tears. "Listen, you two," said Jerry Rosen. "Keep it together. We don't know anything yet. It could be absolutely nothing. Try not to let Laura see you go to pieces. It won't help. You can stay with her when she's in the ward, but you won't be able to go with her when we do the tests. Don't worry. I will be with her every second."

"She loves you, Jerry. As long as you're there, I think she'll be OK," said Bevvy.

"Thanks, Jer. Love you oodles," said Carrie, but then she saw something in Rosen's face that was there for a fleeting moment and then vanished. Bevvy gave him a questioning glance, but he shook his head slightly. Then he motioned Bevvy to stay behind when Buck and Carrie took Laura to the hospital.

"What's wrong, Jer?" asked Bevvy.

"Honey, don't say anything yet—not a word—but I have kind of a bad feeling about this. I've seen it before—many times—and it could be quite serious. I'm telling you now so you can prepare yourself, but still, let's wait till I've done all the tests. "I'm going to call a cab for you to get you home."

"No, have it take me to the hospital. I want to be with Buck and Carrie."

## A CHANGE OF KEY

"That's fine. I'll get to the hospital as soon as I clear up all these patients. Probably early this afternoon."

At Queens General, from the Emergency Room, Laura, in a mobile bed and escorted by Buck and Carrie, was taken to a children's ward that had eight beds. The Nurse in charge of the ward was a very pretty young woman, perhaps not that long out of Nursing School.

She glanced at the chart and said, "Well hello, Laura! I'm Nurse Penny—like the coin—and I'm going to look after you until you're all better. I hope you like storybooks because I have lots of them to read to you."

Then to Buck and Carrie she said, "Mr. and Mrs. Fisher, I'm going to bring two chairs in here so you can sit by Laura's bedside. I'll be here until midnight so every two hours, I will be checking her vital signs. Everything will go down on the chart for Dr. Rosen to see. That button by the head of the bed? Anything you need, just press that button and I'll be here right away."

Then she looked at the chart carefully and said, "Oh, excuse me, but this says that Laura's name is Laura Feinstein. Is she not yours?"

"My husband's real name is Feinstein. His stage name as a professional musician is Buck Fisher."

"Wait, THE Buck Fisher---the one my parents rave about and listen to on old 78s?"

"Yes, Penny, that's me."

The expression on the young woman's face said it all.

"Oh wow! Well, we'll just have to make sure we take extra special care of this pretty girl, won't we? I'm going to find her something for dinner, but first, I have to draw some blood for the lab. I'll use a very thin needle, but you know, kids and needles don't really go together well, so you might want to hold her while I get the blood."

Laura was weeping constantly, but Buck didn't know if it was because she was terrified or in awful pain. He glanced at his watch and said, "Carrie, I have to call Jack Merrill and tell him what's going on. Then I'll call Bill and Al."

## A CHANGE OF KEY

At that moment, Bevvy walked in and said, "Don't bother calling Al, Benny, I already called Arlene and Mama and she'll fill Al in. Go make your call, Ben, and I'll sit with Carrie."

Buck left for the lounge where there was a phone booth. Carrie was barely holding it together and he was glad he didn't have to witness Penny drawing Laura's blood. His baby was in such pain, it was tearing him up inside. Even though the needle was a mere pinprick, Laura cried out in anguish and Bevvy and Carrie both soothed her. "That's such a brave girl, Laura!" said Penny. "All over."

Exhausted from crying, Laura fell into a fitful sleep. Bevvy motioned to Carrie to come out into the corridor. "Honey, you have to be strong now," said Bevvy. "Don't let Laura see you lose it. Jerry will be here in about an hour, but he said they won't start the battery of tests until the morning. Maybe by noon we'll have an answer." She hugged Carrie and brushed the hair from her eyes. Carrie was visibly shaking so Bevvy hugged her tighter and got her to sit down, pulling the other chair up next to her.

Buck phoned Jack at 30 Rock and explained what was happening. "Jesus Christ, Buck! Is Laura going to be all right?"

"We don't know anything yet, Jack. Bevvy's boyfriend is a neurologist and he'll be here soon."

"You call me as soon as you know anything. And Buck, you stay out as long as you need. I'll tell Bill and Al to keep doing what they're doing. I swear to God, Buck, tragedy strikes when you least expect it, but we have to have faith that it will all work out in the end."

Jerry Rosen didn't arrive until close to five that afternoon. "I'm so sorry, but I had more patients than I thought and they took longer than I expected," he said.

"That's OK, Jerry," said Buck. "You're here now."

He pulled Laura's chart from the rack and perused it. "So far the vitals seem normal. But we'll know a lot more tomorrow when we start tests tomorrow. Why don't you all go home now. I'm going to order up a slight sedative for Laura and she'll sleep through the night. And Penny's on duty until midnight."

# A CHANGE OF KEY

"No," said Buck. "I'm not leaving my daughter alone all night. What if she wakes up and no one is here? Bevvy, you take Carrie home and I'll spend the night right here. I'll grab something to eat in the cafeteria."

"Buck, that's not necess—" said Rosen.

"It's done, Jer. I'm staying."

Rosen glanced at Bevvy who nodded slightly, knowing nothing was going to change Buck's mind.

Then to Carrie, Buck said, "Babe, tell the kids I'll see them tomorrow. And you get some rest."

Still in tears, Carrie came into Buck's arms and he hugged her tightly. "It will be OK, darling. You'll see."

But he didn't see his children the next day—or the day after or the day after that. Buck refused to leave Laura's bedside other than to clean himself and change into clothing that Carrie brought for him. Bill Dwyer came the fourth morning and when he saw Buck, he said, "Holy Shit, Buck! When was the last time you ate anything?" He looked like he had lost fifteen pounds.

"Oh, hey Bill. I don't know. Mama sent somethings for me to eat but I wasn't hungry."

"Buddy, you losing your strength and getting sick isn't going to help Laura. Cathy's been going over to Carrie every day and doing food shopping for her. Carrie will be here soon, by the way. I just wanted to know how you're doing. I have to get to the office and I'll keep everyone up to date on what's going on."

"Thanks, Bill. You're great."

"Least I can do, Bucky. You take care of yourself—and get some goddamned food into you."

Nurse Penny was on duty and she said, "Mr. Fisher, we have to get Laura up and walking around. She shouldn't lie in bed day after day. We don't want her getting bed sores."

"I understand. How can I help?"

"Jonah is the Orderly on duty. He's going to help me with Laura, but you can be right here and walk next to her."

They lifted her out of bed and got her on her feet. Laura winced when she put any weight on the leg. Buck was horrified when he looked at her leg. The right foot was turned in at a bizarre angle. It reminded Buck of the way Igor's foot looked in some Frankenstein movie he had seen as a kid. He wanted to cry when he saw how Laura had to shuffle with her foot at that awful angle. After about ten steps, she started to cry from the pain.

"It's all right, honey," said Nurse Penny. "Just a few more steps, OK?"

Three more steps were all she could manage. As she took the fourth step, she collapsed, "Up you go, Missy," said Jonah as he picked her up and carried her back to her bed. "You did great, Laura, just great," he said.

Carrie arrived at eleven with Bevvy. "Everything OK at home?" asked Buck.

"Yes, Benny. Mama is with Casey. She walked Eddie to school and will pick him up at three if Carrie isn't home yet. Jerry should be here any minute."

Carrie sat next to Laura and held her hand. Seeing her daughter lying in a hospital bed was overwhelming for her, but as Bevvy had instructed, she kept her emotions in check.

That is, until Laura said, "I want to go home, Mommy."

Bevvy jumped in and said, "Soon, honey lamb, soon. Eddie and Casey miss you so they want you to be all better when you see them."

Then Dr. Rosen came into the room, kissed Bevvy and Carrie and shook Buck's hand. "How's our big girl doing today?" he said, tousling Laura's hair. He checked the chart and then said, "How about we leave Penny here with Laura and we go someplace to talk?"

They went to the lounge where they drew up chairs into a small circle. Jerry opened up a file folder and perused it for a few moments. When he looked up, his expression was dour, not the jovial look that was always on his face. They braced for what they expected to be very bad news.

"OK, we've run all the tests—and there were a lot of them. The news, I'm afraid, isn't great."

Carrie clutched Buck's hand. "Go on, Jerry," said Buck.

## A CHANGE OF KEY

"At first, we thought Laura had something called flaccid paralysis. It's a neurological condition which affects the muscle tone and the nerves that go to a particular limb. Let me ask you a question. Laura is toilet trained?"

"Yes, of course, for some time now," said Carrie.

"Does she go alone—I mean with the door shut?"

"Yes, naturally. It's how we taught her."

"And you're sure she washes her hands thoroughly?"

Buck said, "Well, we don't check her hands whenever she comes out of the bathroom, but we've taught her to do that and have no reason to believe she doesn't. Why?"

"Just checking something out," said Rosen.

"So this—"

"AFP. That's short for Acute flaccid paralysis."

"So this AFP—you said at first you thought that's what it was. But now?"

Dr. Rosen was silent for a few moments. Then he said, "It's more than that."

"Let's have it, Jer," said Buck.

"It's polio."

That did it for Carrie. She gasped and burst into tears. "No! No! Not my baby!"

Bevvy hugged her, and said, "Tell us Jerry. What can we do? What's the treatment?"

"It's a strange disease. Poliomyelitis is caused by a virus. It's been around for a long time. You may remember that it was FDR who founded the March of Dimes to find a cure for Infantile Paralysis—that's another name for it. Eddie Cantor gave it the name March of Dimes—but despite millions collected for research, there's still no cure for it. Most of the literature suggests that it's spread by ingesting infected fecal material. That's why I asked about Laura and toilet training. If she didn't wash her hands and sucked her thumb or something, it could have gotten into her system. We found traces of the virus in Laura's stool sample, but it could have gotten there in other ways."

"Jerry, what's going to happen to Laura?" asked Buck.

"At this point, there's no real way to know. It can go in any number of directions." Said Rosen.

"Such as?" asked Bevvy.

"If it's degenerative, she could lose the ability to walk. If it's paralytic polio and it infects the central nervous system, we could lose her."

"No!" shrieked Carrie.

"Jerry, I noticed when Penny and the orderly tried to walk her, her right foot is turned in at a strange angle. Is that part of it?"

"Yes, Buck. It's rapid onset polio. One day it's not there, next day, well, it's there in spades."

"Give us the different scenarios, Jerry," said Buck.

"OK. If the disease is in its mildest form, it goes away in a week or so. But Laura's already past that point. If it's limited to the extremity or extremities, and it doesn't attack the central nervous system, the disease will be localized in that area. It most likely will degenerate further. Laura's muscles will atrophy and that foot turning in could become more acute. Worst case is if that's the variety of polio she has, she may be in a leg brace possibly for the rest of her life."

Carrie put her head in her hands and wailed uncontrollably.

"Now, let's talk about what we can do and more positive outcomes," said Rosen.

Having absorbed what they were just told, Buck didn't see any positive things in Laura's future. But despite that, he said, "Talk to us, Jerry. What can we do?"

"First off, I'm now Laura's doctor. I'm going to be with her through every step of this disease from observation to testing to retesting to treatment. I want you to know, I'm going to stick to her like a fly to flypaper."

"Thank you, honey," said Bevvy, "we're all counting on you."

"Next, Laura is going to need extensive physical therapy. It's going to be long—and it's going to be painful for her, but essentially, she's going to have to learn to adapt to that leg being the way it is and learn a new way of walking. Remember what Churchill said about blood, sweat and tears? Well, absent the blood, there will be plenty of sweat and tears. Look, I can't sugar coat this and I don't think that that's the way you want me to go with this. You, Buck, Carrie, Bevvy—the whole family is going to have to be strong for Laura. If she see's you're discouraged, she'll be discouraged."

"Where will this therapy take place?" asked Buck.

"Two places. Right here in the hospital where we can monitor her closely, and also at home. On a daily basis, or at least five days a week, we will send a physical therapist to your home to work with her. Look, if the disease plays out and goes no further, the damage she now has is as far as it will get. We can keep our fingers crossed for that, because if it spreads, well, we've talked about that."

Then to Carrie he said, "Carrie? You have a big job to do in all of this."

She looked at him with a confused expression on her face.

"Buck, Carrie, I'm not a parent, although someday I hope to be." At that point he glanced at Bevvy who smiled surreptitiously. 'But I've observed enough kids to know that some of them can be cruel little shits. They don't know any better and I guess that's why we call them kids. But if Laura comes home with a contraption on her leg, your children might make fun of her. And even if they don't, other kids will. Casey's too young, of course, but Eddie? You'll really have to teach him the right way to act. And if she can return to school, I guarantee you kids will make fun of her. Hell, I've worn glasses since I was five years old. Know how many times I was called 'four eyes' growing up? And that was just for a pair of pink-rimmed specs. This is a whole other ballgame."

"No problem there, Jerry. Eddie absolutely adores Laura and he thinks of himself as her big brother who is her protector," said Buck.

"Good, that's good. Carrie? You're going to have to be supportive of her—I mean a hundred percent. She's going to cry, be in pain, not want to do anything—you're the one at home and you must take charge. This poor little girl is going through something you can't even imagine. We all have to be on her side. Buck? You and Carrie will be instructed on how to massage the leg in a tub in hot water. Sometimes the affected neurons will regenerate. She might regain more movement and feeling in the leg---over time. This is no quick fix."

Buck was holding Carrie in his arms and he said, "We'll do it, Jer. We'll do whatever it takes. I'll quit my job if I have to. I'll hire a nurse to come every day to help Carrie."

"Whoa! Slow down, Buck. One step at a time. I'm going to keep Laura here for another few days for observation and to get her used to the therapy. We will also fit her for a brace that will be a big help in getting her up and about. At first, that brace will hurt like hell, so be patient."

"Thanks Jerry. It's a lot to absorb, but at least we know what the problem is and how we have to deal with it," said Buck.

"I'm going to go sit with Laura, darling. Maybe you should check in at work?" said Carrie.

"Good idea. Bevvy, let me get you a cab."

"No, no, Benny. We came in separate cars. I had a feeling Carrie would be staying the day. And hon, you need to go home and shower and sleep."

"She's right, Bucky. I will be here with Laura all day. Maybe you could pick Eddie up at school and sit with him while he does his homework."

"Right. Yeah, I can do that."

Carrie drew him close and said, "My darling, you look exhausted. Please, for me, sleep for a few hours. We're going to get through this. You'll see."

That was quite a reversal. Usually it was Buck who was in a position to reassure Carrie that all would be well. Now, she had taken charge. He kissed her with great ardor, and went to call Jack Merrill.

"Buck? Tell me. What's the verdict over there?" said Jack when he answered Buck's call.

"It's polio, Jack."

Silence. Then, "Good Christ! Buck, I am so sorry. What can I do? What does the doctor say?"

For the next twenty minutes, Buck explained everything they had been told. Repeating the information didn't make it any more real for him. It all seemed like a nightmare.

"Listen to me carefully, Buck. Laura's treatment is on us. If you hire a nurse, we'll pay for it. You need a wheelchair? We'll pay for that too. If you have to build a ramp up your steps to get a wheelchair in or out, that's on us too. I was talking to General Sarnoff the other day and he said to me, 'Buck Fisher is an incredible asset to RCA. The shareholders are getting rich largely because of him. You do whatever it takes to keep him happy.' Now I don't care when you come back to work, but Buck? I think you should. You need to get your mind on other things. You have to have an escape valve from all you're gong through. Take your time, but believe me, Buck, it will be good to see all your friends—like the ones who keep calling me to ask if I'd heard anything."

"Thanks, Jack. "I'll talk it over with Carrie and let you know."

"Good. Love to Carrie and a big hug and kiss for Laura from me."

**A CHANGE OF KEY**

# CHAPTER TWENTY-THREE
## *Picking up the Pieces: July 1948*

Buck took another two weeks to help Laura settle in at home and to be there to support Carrie in her new role as primary care-giver. Laura had ben fitted with a heavy brace and as Jerry Rosen had suggested, at first it would be very painful. Eddie cried the first time he saw Laura in her brace, but then he brushed away his tears and went up to her to kiss her on her cheek. "Love you, Lore," he said.

After giving her some lunch and putting her in bed to rest, Buck and Carrie sat at the kitchen table and went over the schedule they would be living by for at least the foreseeable future. Mondays, Wednesdays and Fridays, Warren O'Brien, the Physical Therapist, would be at the Fisher home by ten in the morning to work with Laura. Five days a week, Eunice Jefferson, the Registered Nurse, would be there to assist Carrie.

Warren O'Brien was a young man in his late 20s who walked with a distinct limp. When he saw that Buck noticed it, he smiled and said, "Okinawa, Mr. Fisher. I finished my studies on the G.I. Bill when I got out. I was a football player in college—half back. That's not in the cards anymore, so I thought I'd go into something to help others—others like me."

"Do you think you can help her?" asked Carrie.

"Mrs. Fisher—"

"Please, call me Carrie."

"All right. Carrie, why don't you bring her in here for a visit? No time like the present to get started."

Just then, the doorbell rang and in walked an enormous Negro woman who introduced herself as Eunice Jefferson. She had a face as round as a basketball and a smile that featured the whitist teeth Buck had ever seen. She reminded him of Hattie McDaniel who played Mammy in *Gone with the Wind*. Carrie had just brought Laura into the living room.

"Mmm, mmm, mmm! Jes look at this beautiful chile! Well, little honey, what's your name?" asked Eunice.

Laura was a little shy in the presence of such a formidable woman, but she said, "I'm Laura."

"Well you come on over here and give us a big hug," said Eunice.

As Warren O'Brien watched carefully, Laura made her way to Eunice and hugged her, her head barely above the woman's waist. "Well, thas a lot better, init, honey? Oh, we gonna be great friends, you just wait and see."

Warren introduced himself to Eunice and he said, "How about I start working with Laura and you take Carrie into the kitchen and talk to her about your role here."

"Now das a right fine idea. Come on with me, honey and we'll have a nice talk."

"Mr. Fisher, I'm—"

"Buck. Please, just Buck."

"All right, Buck. Today I'm going to do a diagnostic on Laura. I will be checking her range of motion in all her limbs. I'll be jotting down notes, but don't be concerned. We have to establish a base line of her movements to chart her improvement over the weeks. This is going to take time and at first, it will seem like nothing is happening. But believe me, the more we can get her up and about and keep her moving, the quicker her recovery might be."

"Might?" said Buck. "That indicates doubt. It doesn't sound very reassuring."

Warren shook his head and said, "You're right. There are no absolutes with this disease, Buck. I've worked with patients whose recovery was truly remarkable. Others, not so much. Still others, none at all—but my job—all our jobs, really—is to keep good thoughts and stay the course with the treatment.

"You're going to see things you don't understand and hear lots of crying, but in time that's going to get better. A lot of it depends on how Laura takes to the therapy regimen. Plan on my being here for quite some time."

In the kitchen, Carrie had made a pot of coffee and she sat with Eunice at the table drinking it and discussing what Eunice

## A CHANGE OF KEY

called 'the plan.' Big as she was, there was a gentleness to her that was very reassuring.

"You like to cook, honey?" asked Eunice.

"I cook every day, but honestly? I'm not all that creative about it and I keep promising myself to buy some cookbooks to learn how to make some more interesting things. I just never seem to have the time."

"Well, honey, Ahm from Baton Rouge and I got cookin' in ma genes. Outside of nursin', it's my favorite thing in the world. Why shucks, I raised me five healthy boys on my cookin' so I musta been doin' somethin' right."

"Five boys?"

"Yes ma'am. One's a professor at Howard University, two are in the construction business together, next one down the line is an accountant and t'other is in the Air Force. He wanna be a pilot but Ah keep tellin' him to keep his feet on the ground. Safer that way."

Carrie poured coffee for Eunice and put out a plate of cake, which the nurse gobbled up with alacrity.

"Now, honey, Ahma tell you how this all works. First is that Ahm not your typical nurse. Ah don't come here, sit around all day doin' ma nails and five times a day take yo child's temperature. No ma'am. Ahma hands on nurse. Ahma be comin' here for quite some time until that chile is better. When Ah is here, ahma gonna cook for you, clean for you, mind the house if you gots to go shoppin'. Ahma never gonna intrude, but dis fambly gonna be my responsibility. Together, we's gonna get that chile back to where a chile her age need to be."

"I scarcely know what to say, Eunice," said Carrie, still not sure of what Eunice Jefferson's role was.

"All you gots to say is that we on a mission and you, that handsome husband of yours, me, and Warren, we's gonna do our job and be successful."

Carrie started to cry and Eunice said, "Now, now, Ladybird, come on over here and Ahma give you one of my special hugs."

## A CHANGE OF KEY

It was comforting for her to know that Eunice would be there virtually all week long both as a nurse and as her companion.

Eunice wrapped her arms around Carrie and held her head to her huge bosom. "There, there, Ladybird, no cryin' in front of the little ones. Das a rule."

Carrie dried her eyes and shook her head.

"Now, let's us have a look in that big fridge over dere and see what Ah can whip up for yo dinner tonight. Ah have to ask ya, is there any kind of food you and these chillun don't eat?"

"No, they pretty much eat whatever I put on the table. Buck's not fussy at all."

"You like seafood? Like shrimp?"

'Oh, we love shrimp and it's Eddie's favorite."

Eunice laughed her hearty laugh and said, "Heh, heh, you got a fish store anywhere around here, Ladybird?"

"Yes, on 46$^{th}$ Avenue. It's just a couple of blocks away."

"Oh, das good. How 'bout you leave me to look after little Eddie, and you go gets me two pounds of big shrimp. And a couple boxes of white rice. I see you gots butter, so we OK there. Ahma need some nice tomatoes too and some flour. That Pillsbury white flour is real good."

"What are you making, Eunice?"

"Heh, heh, Ahma make you a nice *Etouffee*."

"I've never heard of that," said Carrie.

"Well, it oughta be made with crawdaddies, but I ain't supposin' you can find them up here in the North."

"What in the world is a crawdaddy?"

"Heh, heh, crawfish, honey! They looks like tiny lobsters but mmm, mmm, they's good eatin.'"

"All right, I'll take the car and be back in just a few minutes," said Carrie

"Good. Ahma look after everything here," said Eunice.

In the meantime, Warren was working with Laura in the living room. Buck had pushed the arm chairs back to give sufficient room for him to work. At first it was very slow-going. Laura was not used to the brace yet, and every step clearly caused her pain. Five steps were about all she could handle, but Warren said, "This is going to seem like the hardest thing you've ever done, Buck—watching your little girl struggle like this. But I promise you, each day it's going to get better." Then to Laura, he said, "OK sweets, let's try again."

With the help of a cane in her left hand, Laura was able to stand up. Warren got down on his knees and said, "Good, now come to me, honey. One step at a time."

Tears streaming down her face, Laura took very tentative steps. "Daddy?" she cried out in alarm.

"I'm right here baby. I'll catch you," said Buck.

"Come on, Laurie," said Eddie, using his pet name for her. "One more step. You can make it."

One foot in front of the other, slowly, laboriously, but Laura made her way across the room where Warren caught her.

"That was super-duper, Laura! Good girl!" he said.

Buck wasn't so sure if it was good or not, but he understood the importance of positive reinforcement so his daughter didn't become discouraged. And so he added, "That's my baby girl! Great job, hon!"

At that point, Eunice came into the living room and said, "Ma turn, boys. Ahma check some vitals and mark 'em down on this chart. Dr. Rosen say when he be by?" she asked.

"He comes by every couple of days," said Buck.

"Well, he the best there is, so this chile in the best o' hands," said Eunice.

"All right, I'm off now," said Warren. "I'll be back on Wednesday." He patted Laura's cheek and said, "You did great today, hon. It will get easier—I promise."

As he was exiting the front door, Carrie had come back from the Bohack with several large paper bags of groceries. Eunice said, "Ladybird, you takes them to the kitchen and Ahma put this little beauty in her bed for a nap. "Mr. Buck? You carries her and Ahma tuck her in."

Buck scooped her up, took her to her room and put her in her bed—a special hospital type bed with railings to keep her from accidentally rolling off in her sleep. Then he went out to play checkers with Eddie.

"Ladybird? You want me to feed the lil' chile or you gots it?"

"Oh, I'll feed Casey. That's OK."

"Good, then. Ahma start dinner for this fambly. Won't take but a few minutes."

An hour later, the entire house was filled with the aroma of cooking seafood, in a sauce made of butter, flower, and crushed tomatoes.

Buck came into the kitchen and said, "Wow! That smells fantastic. What is it?"

"*Etouffee*, Mr. Buck. A Cajun stew that Ah think you gonna love."

Eunice found a huge pasta bowl that had been a Christmas present years earlier from someone who Buck couldn't remember. She ladled a huge mound of white rice into the bowl and then scooped the stew on top of it. It looked as good as it smelled.

"Awright, folks, Ahma gonna go now and leave you to your fambly."

"Absolutely not!" said Buck.

"Sit down, Eunice. You're going to have dinner with us," said Carrie.

"Mr. Buck, Ahma just the hired help around here," said Eunice.

"Actually, you already feel like part of this family. So sit down and tell us all about yourself."

"You folks right kind. All my family be down south. Feels nice to be part of somethin'."

For the next hour, everyone ate with gusto—including Laura—as Eunice regaled them with stories of her life in Louisiana. She didn't pull her punches and said what it was like to be a Negro in the South.

Buck then talked about some of the discrimination his band had faced as they toured the South years ago. "It wasn't just against Negroes, Eunice. They sure as hell hated Jews down there.

## A CHANGE OF KEY

One time we had to change hotels because one of my players had a name that sounded 'too Jewish.'"

"Times is gonna change, Mr. Buck. Already started. My oldest boy was in the Navy durin' the war on a cruiser. He had a college degree from Grambling, but the only job he could have was clearin' dishes from the officers' mess. Why, heck, back then, Negro boys couldn't even fight alongside white boys. A real pity. A bullet don't care if you white or dark. But a dark chile always treated like second-class. But see? Now the President, that Mr. Truman, with one stroke o' his pen, he integrated the armed forces—all of them. So there's good things on the horizon. They jes takes time, is all."

"Wow! You don't have to worry about any of that here, Eunice. I didn't even realize you were a Negro," said Buck.

"Heh, heh, heh! You leaves me in stitches, Mr. Buck, I won't be able to get ma work done. Heh, heh, heh."

Eddie said, "This is really good. Can we have it again?"

"Why chile, Ah made you enough for three days, so sure you can have it again."

"Now, Mr. Buck, Ladybird, after I help you clean up, Ahma check Laura's vitals one more time and then Ah be on ma way."

"Eunice, please!" said Carrie. "You're a Registered Nurse, not a maid. I can do my own dishes. Good Lord, you've done so much in one day."

"Well, then, Ladybird, Ah be back tomorrow to look after this beautiful chile—and this fambly."

That night in bed as they snuggled, Carrie could tell that something was bothering Buck.

"It's just so hard to see her in pain, darling. I keep thinking, 'why her?' What did she do to deserve this? Why not me? Why not some murdering sonofabitch instead of an innocent child?"

"Oh, darling, who can answer such questions? You, me, we both would have welcomed this disease if it could have spared Laura. But, love, life doesn't work that way—and if you try to come up with answers, you'll drive yourself crazy. Laura *will* get better. It will be a long haul, but it is going to happen."

Buck held her tightly and just shook his head. Not having an answer was eating at him.

"Bucky, when I was a teenager, a friend of the family lost their seven-year-old son in a car accident. A car came around the corner too fast and hit him. He died instantly. At the funeral—and I'll never forget this—the rabbi gave this long spiel about how everything that happens—even the death of a child—is part of God's plan. At the time, I thought, 'what bullshit!' What kind of a God let's that happen? I think it's what turned me off to religion—a rabbi spouting cliches trying to comfort a family grieving over such a horrible loss. There's no point in blaming it on God or anyone else. Laura's polio happened, it's awful—but it's not going to break us."

Buck at that moment realized that it was Carrie who was now the strong one. A complete turnabout in roles—and he couldn't remember when he had loved her more.

"I love you, Carrie."

"Then prove it, Mr. Feinstein."

And he did.

.....

By Monday of the next week, things had settled into a routine with Warren and Eunice. Both had become indispensable parts of the Fisher household. The children absolutely adored Eunice who always did something special for them. Carrie relied on her in so many ways, and so generous, so giving a person was Eunice Jefferson, that anything she did came naturally to her. She was both a nurse and a caretaker of the family.

As for Buck, he now had to return to work. That first morning was so hectic, he hardly remembered any of the details. First, he went to his office where Kelsey hugged him—and then gave him a huge pile of correspondence and reports that he had to deal with. Then he went up to Jack Merrill's office. Jack came around from his desk and embraced Buck. "Tell me everything, Buck. How is she doing?"

## A CHANGE OF KEY

Buck explained the rigorous regimen of physical therapy that Laura was undergoing and that everyone was trying to be upbeat about the possibilities of a full recovery for her.

"You think it's really possible, Buck?"

"I don't know, Jack, but if the worst of it is that she'll have to wear a brace for the rest of her life, at least she'll have that life."

"True, true enough. Just remember, anything else you need, you be sure to tell me. Now, do you have some time to go over figures with me?" asked Jack.

"Sure. What do we have?"

"It's all good news. We reissued Fran's Christmas album this year and it exceeded last year's sales by far. As for Cindi, well, Cindi's got two gold records under her belt and I want you to get to work on a third LP for her. So far every group or soloist that you've signed has made money for us. Lots of money. General Sarnoff is fully aware of the success you've had here. He also knows what's going on at home and he calls me every few days to ask me if there's been any progress. He really cares about who works for him. Which is why, my friend, he's giving you a raise."

"What? A raise?"

"You're moving up, Buck. You're now making seventy-five thousand bucks."

"Jesus Christ!" said Buck. "Carrie's not going to believe this."

"You've earned it. But we can't rest on our laurels. We're kind of in a war here, Buck. Us, Capitol and Decca are fighting for talent wherever we find it. Then there are these dozens of tiny little labels that gobble up talent that we could do a much better job of promoting. Bill and Al have done yeoman's duty in scouting out talent—and by the way, they're both getting raises too, but I'll let you break that news to them.

"Music is changing, Buck. A lot. I keep hearing about a new style—mostly down south—but it's getting lots of buzz. They're calling it Rockabilly—whatever the hell that means. I want Al and Bill to do some research, find out some names and go scout them out. If they're good, let's sign them. We need to stay way ahead of the crowd on this one. From what I hear, this is going to be big."

"We'll get right on it, Jack. If it's got promise, we'll be in the thick of it."

"Good. Go see your orchestra now—and make sure you send my love to Carrie and the kids."

…..

When Buck got down to the rehearsal studio, he was swamped by his friends who had missed him and were worried about him. It was Chuck Fein who said to Kip Roman, "Hey Kip, take a break so Buck can tell us all what's been happening."

"Sure, Chuckie. We all want to know," said Kip.

Buck pulled up a chair and for a half hour, told the orchestra everything he could about Laura and her condition. Everyone knew that she had polio; Bill had kept them all apprised as he found out more information. But Buck explained about her treatments, the prognosis, how Carrie was doing—everything.

Fran Michaels came up to Buck and kissed him. "Oh Buck, we've all been frantic. I called Carrie several times, but nobody seemed to have any details. Tell her if she needs me to watch the kids if she has to take Laura to the doctor, I'll gladly do it."

"You're a sweetheart, Franny. We need to start talking about another LP. Can you come up to the office later this week?"

"For sure." She kissed him again and then Kip Roman came up to him. "Buck, would you like to hear some of the new arrangements?"

"Absolutely, Kip. I'll just sit over here and you go do what you need to do."

The first song Kip had arranged, Buck recognized immediately. It was a song called "My Foolish Heart" by Victor Young and Ned Washington. It was from a film by the same name that was universally panned. Even the song got raspberries in the music world as being too syrupy and cloying. But Buck had a soft spot in his heart for the melody. It was incredibly romantic sounding and the lyrics spoke to both the longing and the tenuousness of wartime romances. Kip's chart was a sweeping, lush tour de force which was perfect for Fran Michaels. After the orchestra ran through the chart, Buck called Fran over and said, "Do you know this one, Franny?"

"Yes, Buck. It's a fantastic melody."

"Would you try it out for me now?"

"Love to."

The strings with Pammy Wendorfer doubling the melody on flute did an eight-bar intro. Then Fran came in. Even from the first two lines of the lyric: "The night is like a lovely tune/Beware my foolish heart," Buck knew that he had just heard another winning number. Fran had become this amazing stylist who never just sang words. She sang emotions. The most interesting part of the arrangement was that the orchestra played as written, but Fran's delivery was more *rubato*. That is, her phrasing was not always strictly on the downbeats. This created a halting quality to her singing, as if she were actually choked up by the beauty and pathos of the words.

When the song ended, there was dead silence in the rehearsal hall until Chuck Fein said, "Holy shit! Fuck me twice if that isn't the greatest thing I ever heard!" Then the orchestra began applauding and Buck hugged Fran saying, "Honey, we *must* get this song recorded right away. I don't care if we release it as a single and put it on your next album later—but this is a hit if I ever heard one."

Then Kip said, "You know, Buck, Franny is also a helluva jazz singer."

"She sure was with my band, Kip. I don't imagine she's lost it since then."

"She hasn't. So I wrote a jazz chart for her. No strings, just the big band."

"Really. And what chart is that?" asked Buck.

"Now don't go getting all mad or anything," said Kip.

That made Buck laugh. "Kip, you've turned out seven gold records so far. You think I'm going to get mad over a jazz chart?" "I have to admit, Fletcher helped out a lot on this one. He's got so much big band experience under his belt, his suggestions really made the band swing," said Kip.

At that moment, Buck was thrilled that he had signed Fletcher Henderson to an arranging contract. He'd be sure to make even more use of him in the future.

"OK, then. Guys? You know which one," said Kip.

Kip counted off a quick four and Kenny Ferraro did an eight-bar intro a la Count Basie. Then the band came in on the melody. It was a novelty song called "The Hucklebuck." The song had been around for almost ten years and Tommy Dorsey had recorded it both with Charlie Shavers and later Frank Sinatra on the vocal. He had difficulty in imagining the beyond-beautiful Fran Michaels singing the rather banal lyric—but then she came in with the vocal line and absolutely owned it. She even showed dance moves that Buck never knew she had when she was singing with his band.

Kip and Fletcher's chart captured the riffy, big band sound of half a decade earlier and despite how much Buck admired it and Fran's singing, there was a moment of sadness—sadness for a lost era of music and for how that music had catapulted him to international fame and great wealth. He thought, 'God how I miss being out in front of my band.'

When the song ended, Chuck Fein, irrepressible as ever, called out, "I dunno, Bucky, but I'd hire her!"

The whole orchestra laughed at that because they knew that Fran Michaels was on her way to becoming a superstar. At the time, though, he wasn't aware of how quickly that was going to happen.

**A CHANGE OF KEY**

# CHAPTER TWENTY-FOUR
*"Maybe It's Time" January 1949*

After six months of intensive Physical Therapy, several things had become very obvious to Buck and Carrie. The first was that Laura had made real progress. She was moving more fluidly in her brace and there was no longer pain at every step. But the second thing that was clear was that she would be wearing the brace for the rest of her life.

Jerry Rosen explained that though they hoped the neurons would regenerate, it hadn't happened. "Despite that, her recovery has been beyond our expectations," he said. "But because the muscles have atrophied so much, her foot has turned inward almost forty-five degrees from center. It looks like she has clubfoot, but she doesn't. That's a birth defect and not the result of polio—but the turning in of the foot is similar in both diseases."

"And there's no treatment that can correct it?" asked Carrie. "Not an operation?"

"No, Carrie. Clubfoot can frequently be corrected by placing the foot or feet in casts and later cutting the Achilles tendon and physically forcing the foot into its proper plane. But in clubfoot there's no neurological damage; in polio there is."

"What kind of life can she have with this, Jerry?" asked Buck.

"Look, let's get one thing straight—and I want the two of you to listen to me carefully. I have been over Laura's charts for months now. Except for her leg, she is the picture of a healthy little girl. You must get out of your head the notion that she's a cripple and will be compromised for her whole life. If you act that way, she will feed off of that psychologically and the damage will be significant. You have to think and act just the opposite: that she can have a normal existence in every respect. She can go to school—and college if she wants, and outside of becoming a professional athlete, there's nothing she can't be—if you assure her that she can."

## A CHANGE OF KEY

Another thing that was clear to Buck and Carrie was that Eunice Washington had more or less taken over the household. She did everything for the children, who loved her, and she made life so much easier for Carrie. When Buck handed her an envelope with a $500 bonus for Christmas, the woman cried like she had just lost a relative. "This so kind o' you, Mr. Buck. Ahma at a loss for words to thank you and Ladybird."

"Eunice, I think back over these last six months and I'd be the first to admit this house would have fallen apart without you," said Carrie.

Frequently Rachel would come over and she would have coffee and cake with Eunice while trading ideas for recipes. Buck was glad that his mother had a good friend, because with Arlene now married and out of the house—and Bevvy to be married in the spring, it could be quite lonely for her. Her cousin Mila also came by to visit with her once or twice a week. She had made wonderful progress in learning English and Jerry was able to get her a job as a medical secretary for one of his colleagues who also happened to be of Polish descent.

But Eunice was the rock. Her flair for Cajun and Creole cooking made Carrie think that she could have opened her own restaurant with that talent. One day, she said, "Ladybird, Ahma have to give the little chile some shots today. They's vitamins that Dr. Rosen say she needs once a month. Ahma use a real thin needle, but you knows kids and needles, so Ahma need your help for this."

"That's all right, Eunice, she'll be fine," said Carrie.

"Das not all, Ladybird."

"Oh?"

"Ahma have to draw blood every month. Dr. Rosen says they needs to see if there's any more of the virus in her. Ahma need your help with that too."

"When do you want to do it?"

"No time likea present, I say, so sooner we gets it over with, the sooner Warren can get back to doin' all his good work wit her."

## A CHANGE OF KEY

Laura was playing with Eddie, who had become her best friend and biggest supporter. When Eunice called her into the living room, Eddie said, "Come on, Laurie, I'll go with you."

"Little lamb, we gots some work to do today. Gots to give you some lil' shots and take some of your blood for Uncle Jerry. Is dat OK?"

"I'll hold your hand, Laurie. Don't worry," said Eddie.

"Why what a fine little man you are!" said Eunice. "We gonna do the blood first, little one."

"Just look at me, Laurie, don't look anywhere else," said Eddie.

Despite her wincing as the small needle penetrated her vein, she didn't cry. Neither did she cry after the vitamin shots. When the procedure was over, Eddie hugged her and Eunice said, "Now how 'bout a big hug for me?"

Carrie was so moved by the way Eddie and Laura interacted that she almost cried. And in her turn, Laura loved looking after Casey, who was now taking her initial steps. There was an atmosphere of contentment in the household and for the first time in a long while, Carrie had faith that everything would work itself out.

Busy as he was, Buck found time to go to the basement with his tenor sax several times a week and play. It was his escape from work, from the pain of watching Laura's recovery—from everything, really.

He played traditional jazz, then experimented with some of the newer styles, which he had to admit he was growing more comfortable with. He could usually manage an hour or a little bit more of practice before he wanted to play with the children before they went to sleep. Of the three, little Casey was the most attached to Buck. She clung to him, patted his face, and buried her head in his chest every chance she got. And Buck had a soft spot in his heart for her. Maybe because she was the most difficult of Carrie's births—one that almost cost her her life. But whatever the reason, Casey had Buck wrapped around her finger—and he loved jumping to her wishes.

## A CHANGE OF KEY

One night when he came up from the basement, Carrie said, "How did it go tonight, hon?"

"Oh, pretty good I guess," he said.

"Darling, it sounded great to me, I mean really, really great."

"Thanks, hon. I didn't know you were listening."

Carrie put her hand on Buck's cheek and said, "Maybe it's time?"

"Time for what?"

"Time for you to play for more than four walls in a basement. You're still the Buck Fisher I married, you know. And didn't Jack Merrill once tell you that you could do small combo work?"

"Yes, but I didn't think he was being serious, darling."

"Ever know Jack not to be serious?"

'No, not really."

"Just think about it, Bucky. It could be very good for you," said Carrie.

"I will. I promise."

....

The following Monday brought a shock to Buck that he never anticipated. When he got to the office, Kelsey told him that Fran Michaels had left a message for him saying she needed to see him as soon as possible.

"Uh oh, I don't like the sound of that," said Buck.

"Could be nothing," said Kelsey.

"Hon, in my experience, every time I think it could be nothing, it's always something. OK, call downstairs and ask her to come on up," he said.

While he waited, Buck tried to imagine what was on Fran's mind. His first guess was that she was pregnant. It had been nearly three years since Fran and Pete were married and maybe they were starting to think about starting a family. Or, maybe Fran was just tired of singing and wanted to take a break. She had been at it for months straight.

It was none of these.

297

## A CHANGE OF KEY

Fran came into the office, hugged Buck and sat down in the armchair opposite his desk. "Morning, Franny. What's cooking?"

She took a letter from her purse and along with a business card, slid it across Buck's desk for him to read. As he read it, his eyes opened wide and he said, "Whoa! This is big, Frannie."

The letter was from Milton Applewhite of Metro-Goldwyn-Mayer studio in Hollywood. Evidently he was a talent scout who, according to the letter, had been told by Johnny Mercer that there was this huge talent working for RCA. It went on to say that they wanted her to fly out to Hollywood to do a screen test and based upon the results, offer her a contract with MGM.

"I don't know what to do, Buck," she said.

"Well, first, have you discussed this with Pete?"

"Yes. You know Pete. He would swim an ocean for me so he said that if it's what I want, he's behind me all the way."

"Then what's the problem?" asked Buck.

"If it works out, I'd be leaving everything and everyone I know. Plus I'm under contract to you and I still owe you two albums."

Buck could see that she was rapidly becoming overwrought.

"Honey, we're already in the works for your next one, and as for the other one? Do you honestly think I would hold you back after all you have meant to me?"

She dabbed at her eyes and said, "I'm a singer, Buck. I don't know if I can act."

"Then what was all that operatic training about? When you sang *Tosca* did you just stand in one place and sing arias—or was there movement and acting involved?"

"Yes, but—"

"No, Franny. I have admired your singing for years because you just don't sing. Every time you step up to that microphone, it's a performance. Maybe you don't even realize it, but you act the songs you sing instead of just belting them out."

"Thank you for that, Buck."

"But Fran, there's something you have to understand. When I was out in L.A. a while ago, I met Clark Gable. You didn't know that, did you? Yeah, we had a nice long talk and he really went off on the studio system."

"I don't know what that is, Buck."

"OK, here's how it works. If you sign a movie deal with MGM say for five or six pictures, essentially, they own you. Unless you're a megawatt star like Gable or William Powell, they can tell you to be in any picture they want. You have no right of refusal. If they say they want you to do a specific role and you balk at it—they'll threaten to sue you for breach of contract."

"I still don't understand," said Fran.

"I'll be blunt: if Louis B. Mayer says he wants you to play the ass-end of a horse, you have to do it. You're under contract. If he says he wants you to play some half-naked Amazon warrior, you have to do it. You're under contract. Now, I assume Johnny Mercer talked about your voice, so maybe they will build scripts around your singing—but if at the last-minute Mayer says cut the song, then it's out. Don't think you're going to start out as the next Myrna Loy or Ava Gardner—or even June Allyson. You're going to have to pay your dues and it's not necessarily the glamorous life you think it is."

Fran sighed. "So what do I do, Buck?"

"You be smart. Any contract they might offer you, you have a lawyer review. Do not let them smooth talk you and say that it's just a boiler plate contract. If there's anything specific you want down in writing, you tell that attorney and he'll negotiate with MGM. If Mayer wants you badly enough, he'll let you have your way. If not, well, it's up to you how much you want to give in."

She nodded in understanding and said, "Thanks, Buck, it's a lot to think about."

"One more thing, Franny. And I'm not joking around here: if they tell you they want you to take your clothes off to see how costumes will fit, you tell them to go fuck themselves. There's a lot of sleazy people out there and I don't want you to get caught up in any of that. Oh, they might say, 'This is just procedure. The stills go nowhere.' Don't believe it for a second. Pictures like that always make it into the public view."

"Pshew! I never would have even imagined that, Buck. Besides, if I did anything like that, Pete would divorce me in a second."

"When do they want you there?"

"Two weeks."

"OK, then let's try to lay down some tracks between now and then."

Fran stood, moved to Buck and kissed him on the lips. "Bucky, in ten lifetimes, I could never imagine a better boss than you. I'll keep you posted on what's happening."

She left the office and Buck sat there thinking that if anyone could be the next great Hollywood star, it would be Fran Michaels. He also thought that Cindi Kay would now be moving into the number one slot as the label's premier female vocalist. And then, there was his own career he was thinking about.

....

That night over dinner Buck recounted his conversation with Fran Michaels. Carrie was not at all shocked by the news. "Darling, Fran's the most beautiful woman I've ever seen. There's not a movie star out there who can hold a candle to her. Plus, she's got a body that should be on a pedestal in a museum. As for the voice—well, you above all know how good she is."

"I don't know what we'll do without her, hon," said Buck.

"Sure you do. You've treated Cindi as the B Team for too long. She's fabulous and she's got the gold records to prove it. It's high time you started promoting her as the star she rightfully should be."

"I've never heard her complain, Carrie," said Buck sounding more defensive than he meant to.

"That's because the girl is an absolute sweetheart—not to mention the fact that you've made her pretty rich. If you ask me, if Fran leaves, Cindi should be performing solo shows not at her husband's little club, but on the big stage at Carnegie Hall or other theaters in the city. Backed by your orchestra, you're looking at sellouts every night."

"You're getting pretty good at this talent evaluation, Mrs. Feinstein," said Buck.

"Well, I was in the business for a long time, so yeah, I know a good thing when I hear it," she said.

Carrie was staring at Buck with an inscrutable look on her face. "What? There's more?" said Buck.

"Since you trust me so much with what people want to hear, there's a certain—"

"Carrie!" said Buck in a warning tone.

"Bucky, listen to me. You've convinced yourself that the music you love is dead and that no one ever wants to hear you play again. You are so wrong, darling. Why do I have to keep reminding you that you're Buck Fisher? No one was better than you, honey."

"Key word: was."

"No, wrong tense. Is. You're still a fantastic player and I know there's a ton of people out there who would snap up your records in a flash—just like they used to. You just have to convince yourself of the same thing and START. MAKING. MUSIC!"

Buck sighed deeply and then said, "All right, all right. I'll talk to Jack Merrill Monday morning and kick around some ideas with him. Fair enough?"

"More than fair. Oh, Bucky! I love you so much. So very much. I'll stand behind any decision you make. Just as long as you know that I only want what's best for you."

"I've never doubted that. Not even once. All right, how about we check some homework from our brilliant son and then practice walking with Laura?"

Buck was fully aware of months flying by. There had been several developments that had a direct effect upon his life. Most importantly, Laura had made such great progress working with Warren that by September they were ready to register her for school. Because of her condition, the Board of Education would provide special transportation for her to and from the local school, P.S. 177, named for William Prince, who evidently owned a tree nursery on the site during the Revolutionary War. At first, an administrator at 110 Livingston Street, the Board's headquarters, wanted Laura to attend a school with students in similar conditions to hers. Carrie was adamantly against that. "My daughter is not going to be segregated from other children," she told the administrator. "She does not need to think of herself as different, so she must be with other children without disabilities."

With the help of a cane, Laura was able to walk comfortably for up to fifteen minutes at a time. A major challenge was stairs. She was terrified that she would lose her balance and tumble down an entire flight. But with the help of ever-patient Warren, she proved she was up to the challenge. "You can do this, Beauty (his pet name for her), and I'll be right behind you to catch you if anything goes wrong. Let's try it."

It was difficult at first, but Warren, Buck and Carrie all knew that if she was going to live a normal life, or as close to normal as her disease would permit, she would have to learn to overcome the physical barriers that life put in front of her. More to the point, New York City elementary schools did not have elevators, so for her to be integrated into regular classes, she would have to learn to navigate stairs.

It didn't take long for things to go bad at school. In fact, by the end of the first day, Laura came home hysterical, absolutely beside herself crying.

"Honey! What happened?" said Carrie, drying her tears.

"Mama! They laughed at me! They made fun of me! They called my gimpy and cripple and kept pointing at my leg!"

"Ladybird," said Eunice, "Ahma look after her for a bit. Mmm, mmm, mmm, I don't know why kids gotta be so damned cruel." She took Laura to the kitchen and gave her a snack, sitting with her and holding her hand.

Eddie came home an hour later and the boy was angry beyond measure. Usually a calm and even-tempered child, he was full of fury that Carrie had never seen before.

## A CHANGE OF KEY

"I'm gonna sock those kids in the nose, I ever hear one of them make fun of Laurie." He had balled his fists and Carrie fully believed he would do just that in defense of his sister.

When Buck came home that evening, he was appalled at what had happened. "All right, I'll go speak to the teacher tomorrow, hon."

"The hell you will!" said Carrie, unable to contain her anger. "I'll go and believe me I'll straighten this out. You can bet on that!"

"Darling, it's best that you try to remain calm," said Buck.

"Bullshit! What the hell is the matter with you? Our daughter is humiliated and you want me to remain calm? You stay the hell out of this!"

In all their years together, Buck had never seen Carrie in this state. She was purple with rage and Buck was concerned that if she lost her temper, she'd hit someone and wind up under arrest. "All right, sweetheart, I'm on your side. Remember that," he said.

"Yeah, well, we'll see about that."

The following morning, Eunice arrived early to look after Casey. Carrie drove both Eddie and Laura to school. Eddie went into the schoolyard to be with his friends, and Carrie went to the front desk which was manned by parent volunteers giving directions.

"Excuse me," said Carrie, "but where can I find a Mrs. Morten, the first-grade teacher."

"Straight down the corridor, Room 113," said the parent.

Carrie found the room and knocked on the door and entered, not waiting to be asked in. Mrs. Morten was a woman in her mid-fifties, with silver hair and too much makeup. "Yes?" she said.

"My name is Carrie Feinstein and my daughter Laura is in your class."

"Yes?" she repeated.

"My daughter is recovering from polio and she wears a leg brace. Some of your students have been belittling her—and it better stop!"

## A CHANGE OF KEY

"Mrs. Feinberg—"

"Feinstein."

"Oh, sorry, Mrs. Feinstein, children will do what children will do. The novelty of name-calling wears off in time."

"So you condone that type of bullying?" Carrie's rage was building within her.

"Not at all, but you can't expect me to keep my eye on thirty-four students every second that they are in my charge, can you?"

"I expect you to do your goddamned job!"

"Now wait just a—"

"No! YOU wait! This is bullshit. How do I find the Principal?'

Mrs. Morten smirked at Carrie and said, "Right down the hall—Room 100. Have a nice day."

Carrie entered the office and asked to see the Principal. "I'm afraid she's very busy right now," said her secretary.

"I don't care if she's entertaining the goddamned King of England. Get her out here. Now!"

The door to the Principal's office opened and Mary C. Oppenheim stood there sizing up Carrie. "Won't you come in please," she said.

Miss Oppenheim, a hawk-faced woman in her late fifties said, "What seems to be the problem?"

Again Carrie explained what had happened with Laura, telling her how distraught the child had been when she came home the previous day. "This must stop, Miss Oppenheim. I already spoke to her teacher and she said there's nothing she could do—that kids are kids. That's not an answer."

"What would you have us do, Mrs. Feinstein?"

Carrie was incredulous. "You must be joking with me. You're the Principal, goddammit! You can go into that classroom and threaten those kids with the direst punishment if they ever do it again. And that's just for starters."

"So you think threatening children is the best course of action?" said Oppenheim.

"I'm not the educator! You are! You tell me what the 'best course of action' is!"

"I would suggest just leaving it alone. Let nature take its course."

"That's your answer? I can't believe this shit," said Carrie.

"There's no need for that kind of language here," said Oppenheim.

"Oh really? I'm just warming up. Do you have any idea what it's like to have a child with polio? Her pain? Her discouragement? Her feeling of hopelessness? And to have a bunch of snot-nosed brats damage all the progress she's made—you better believe I'm just getting started."

"I think you are overreacting to the entire situation," said Oppenheim.

Carrie sighed and stared her right in the face. "You better come up with something. And quick!"

"Is that a threat, Mrs. Feinstein?"

"Oh yes. It most certainly is. You don't know who I am, do you?"

"I have no idea."

"No, you wouldn't. My husband is Buck Fisher, and unless you've been living under a rock for the last decade, you ought to recognize that name. I don't like trading on his name, but if you don't fix this—pronto—I will go to the *Daily News, New York Mirror* and the *New York Times*. How would you like reporters crawling all over this place asking questions about why the principal and teachers condone bullying of a handicapped child?"

"You wouldn't dare!" said Oppenheim.

"Wanna bet? You just try me and see what happens. My daughter comes home in tears even one more time and I'll bring this goddamned place down around your ears. You got that? And believe me, if I have to go the Mayor, he'll be next on my list."

Oppenheim tapped on the desktop for a few counts, a scowl on her face. Finally, she said, "I think you have made yourself clear, Mrs. Feinstein. I will talk to Laura's teacher and I will personally speak to the children in her class."

"Thank you." As she turned to leave, Carrie said, "Remember—just one more time!"

Buck came home a little after five that evening. "Hello, Eunice. Carrie home?"

"She out back, Mr. Buck. Jes sittin' there for a while now."

When Buck went into the backyard, he did a double-take when he saw that Carrie was smoking a cigarette.

"Carrie!"

She took a final drag and crushed it out. "I'm sorry, Buck. First one in years. It won't happen again. I promise."

"What gives? You must still be pretty upset to start that again."

She hugged Buck and said, "I'm calm now—and I'm sorry about the smoking. I just needed to settle my nerves. I swear it's the only time I did it. Here, you can take the pack and throw it out."

"Babe, tell me everything. Don't leave anything out."

"First hold me, Bucky. Tell me everything will be OK."

Carrie told Buck of his two conversations at the school. "You threatened them?" he said.

"I sure as shit did. Did I do the right thing, Buck?"

"I'm proud of you, angel. All that matters is that it doesn't happen again," said Buck.

"I love you, Bucky. But you better talk to your son. He's talking about busting kids in the nose if they bother his sister again."

Buck laughed at that. "Eddie? He wouldn't hurt a fly, darling."

"Yeah, well, he's a lion when it comes to protecting Laura."

"I'm glad they are so close, Carrie. Reminds me of how I was with Arlene and Bevvy. I wish you would have had a brother or sister to grow up with."

## A CHANGE OF KEY

"I do have sisters—now. Besides, if I had them back then, I wouldn't have grown up to be the spoiled brat I was."

"You're perfect, darling," said Buck. He kissed her and with his arm around her waist, they went back into the house.

A CHANGE OF KEY

# CHAPTER TWENTY-FIVE

*"What Does This Mean?" March 1950*

So many things were happening musically by 1950 that Buck could hardly keep up with the changes. The biggest change was that Fran Michaels had signed a contract with MGM for three films and an option on a fourth. She insisted in her contract that she be permitted to sing in every film and was reassured that the studio was writing scripts around her singing ability.

Pete McCormack had moved to Los Angeles to set up house with Fran and had found regular work as a studio musician in the same place that Paul Tanner worked. In fact, it was Tanner who recommended Pete to the leader. "He was Buck Fisher's lead alto for seven years. That should be all you need to know about him." He wasn't making as much money as he did at RCA, but Fran's contract at MGM more than made up for the deficit.

Her first film was set at a small midwestern college and it was called *Coed Cutie*. When she called Buck to tell him about it, she said, "I feel so silly, Buck. I'm nearly thirty years old and they have me playing a nineteen-year-old college junior. I do get to sing four songs, though, so that's the good thing. It's not exactly *Wuthering Heights,* but it's a start."

In fact, the reviews were fair to middling, but the critics noted a "new and formidable young actress named Fran Michaels whose future is as big as a mountain. Watch out Jo Stafford—this girl is a comer!"

Her second film was called *The Caliph of Baghdad* and it was a costume film in which Fran had to wear baggy silk trousers and a skimpy top that showed off her bare midriff—complete with a jewel in her navel. It was a musical knockoff of a 1911 play that was turned into a Hollywood romp of a comedy involving mistaken identities, an evil vizier and a handsome prince. It also had lots of singing in the harem, which showcased Fran's voice. Again the reviewers touted her as a rising star who in time would eclipse a lot of other big names.

## A CHANGE OF KEY

Carrie and Buck had gone to see that one at the RKO Keith's theater in Flushing.

Carrie laughed at every joke but said, "Honey, this is the dumbest thing I ever saw---but good God Franny looks sexy in those costumes."

When Fran called, she said, "It was a riot making that movie, but Pete sure was unhappy about all the kissing scenes I had with the co-star. He's a young actor named Robert Wagner and oh my God is he handsome!"

Buck had replaced Pete in the studio orchestra with Danny DeMaestri, a young Juliard graduate who played alto, clarinet, flute and piccolo and oboe. That opened up some new possibilities for Kip Roman for new arrangements—with paired flutes.

There had been no repetition of bullying at Laura's school and both she and Eddie were thriving. Casey was at the stage where she was putting words together, making near sentences, and showing love for everyone who held her. All was going well for Buck professionally and for the family in general.

And then it wasn't.

Buck came home on Wednesday, March 15th and instantly knew something was wrong. With a trembling hand, Carrie handed Buck an envelope with the return address The United States House of Representatives.

"Buck? What could this be?" asked Carrie.

"No idea, hon, let me open it and we'll see."

What he saw caused Carrie to gasp in fright. It was a subpoena from the House Unamerican Activities Committee. The powerful congressional committee was created to root out Communists in the State Department, the military and other spheres of American life.

The power of the committee was magnified by the "Red Scares" that followed World War II and the rise of Communism as Stalin gobbled up independent nations in Eastern Europe adding them to his Union of Soviet Socialist Republics.

And at the same time, Stalin had increased his sphere of influence in the Far East., attempting to ally with some nations in

**A CHANGE OF KEY**

Southeast Asia. There was good reason for fear and that fear had begun to dominate every aspect of post-war America.

Immediately following the war, the world divided as the allies who once fought for the same cause, now were bitter enemies. The United States had formed NATO with other Western European nations as a way of stemming the tide of Soviet incursion. For its part, the Soviet Union was looking to ally the socialist republics as an opposing force to NATO.

It was George Orwell of *1984* fame who coined the term "Cold War' to define the standoff between the two great powers. Now that The USSR had the hydrogen bomb, the idea of a full shooting war was all but unthinkable, but the nations pecked at each other initiating espionage plots to destabilize their enemy. Winston Churchill had described the "Iron Curtain" that had descended dividing Europe and enhancing the possibility of future conflict.

"Bucky! What do they want from you?" Carrie had that frantic tone in her voice.

"I have no idea, honey. This is a mystery."

Just then the telephone rang and it was Chuck Fein. "Buck, you're not going to believe this shit, but I just got summoned to D.C. for some goddamned reason."

"Me too, Chuck. You don't know what this is all about?"

"No idea."

"When do you have to appear?" asked Buck.

"Tuesday, March 28$^{th}$, 10 AM.," said Chuck.

"Me too. OK, we'll take the train to D.C. together and sort this out. It's all bullshit, if you ask me," said Buck. "Some politician trying to make a name for himself."

But it wasn't. For a few years now, an ugly term had entered the language: 'McCarthyism,' taking its name from Senator Joseph McCarthy, the junior senator from Wisconsin. McCarthy hag gained notoriety by saying that he had in his possession the names of Communists in the State Department, the Defense Department and the Hollywood establishment. The accusations were all either made up or disproven, but the damage had been done. The careers of many actors, directors, screenwriters had been ruined and they had been 'blacklisted,' making them unable to find work.

Some courageous newsmen had branded the House Unamerican Activities Committee the most ironically named government organ in history since their practices were absolutely unamerican. One of the country's basic principles of justice was the presumption of innocence—and the burden of proof upon the state to prove guilt. "Innocent until proven guilty" was a privilege afforded even the most hardened criminals until a jury of their peers had spoken.

But the HUAC had turned that principle upside down. Now, those accused of Communist ties had to prove their innocence—something infinitely more difficult to do.

The list of the accused read like a 'who's who' of American society and included such names as Charlie Chaplin, Aaron Copland, Dashiell Hammett and even Albert Einstein. Now, Buck Fisher and Chuck Fein found themselves on that list.

.....

On the train ride to D.C., Buck and Chuck discussed how they would act under interrogation. "I'm not taking any of their bullshit, Buck. They want to accuse me, they better goddamned have some proof or I'll tear them new assholes."

"Try to stay calm in there, Chuck. Just be truthful and it will all work out."

But calm wasn't in Chuck Fein's nature. In the committee room he faced ten members of the House of Representatives—five from each party. There was nothing friendly in their demeanors. They wasted no time in going on the offensive.

"Mr. Fein, are you represented by counsel today?"

"No I am not. Don't want it, don't need it."

"You understand that you are under oath and the penalties for perjury are extremely serious."

"Yeah, so?"

"On November 20$^{th}$, 1936, you attended a meeting of the *Friends of Worldwide Labor.*"

"Yeah, so?"

"Were you aware at the time that this organization was a Communist front whose avowed aim according to its constitution was the overthrow of capitalism?"

"Look, fellas, let me save you a lot of time and effort here. In case you don't remember, 1936 was the middle of the Depression. Millions out of work—including my grandfather, who in case your notes don't show it, was an out-of-work steel worker. He asked me to go to the meeting because he thought that if it had something to do with labor unions, it could help him get a job to feed his family. And from the looks of it, it doesn't look like too many of you went hungry in those years."

That prompted laughter in the gallery and the chairman of the committee banged his gavel to restore order. "This is not a time for levity, Mr. Fein," he cautioned.

"Oh no? That's pretty funny because this whole thing is a bunch of crap. I go to one meeting at the request of my grandfather and all of a sudden I'm a threat to the free world? Come on fellas, you're gonna have to do a lot better than that."

Another representative then said, "And are you saying you went to no other meetings of this organization?"

"Hell no. I was bored out of my mind. A bunch of speechmakers who thought they could remake the world out of a basement in Brooklyn. With no offense, they were about as useless as you guys and this committee."

Once more the chairman had to rap his gavel to quiet the crowd.

"May I ask what you did during the war?" asked the congressman from New Jersey.

"I spent four years in the Army, the last one in Europe, entertaining wounded troops in hospitals all over the country. Four years of my life. Any of you gentlemen serve?" Since most were sixty or older, the answer was obvious.

"And what was your security clearance during the war, Mr. Fein?"

"What the hell are you talking about? I played bass fiddle in the Special Services Band. Why the hell would I need a security clearance? You think our musical charts were Top Secret? Sheesh. You guys are really something, you know?"

The questioning went on for nearly an hour with many of the questions intentionally rephrased to try to trip him up. Sensing that there was nothing there, the chairman said, "Mr. Fein, you are free to go but understand that you are still under subpoena and can be recalled to testify should any other information turn up and be forwarded to this committee."

"Yeah, sure, sure. Whatever you say. It's been fun, fellas. Have a nice day."

…..

Buck had been informed that he would appear before the Senate Internal Security Subcommittee or SISS. The committee was chaired by Senator Pat McCarran, a Democratic Senator from Nevada. In addition to McCarran, there were five senators each from the Republican and Democratic parties.

"Mr. Feinstein, or if you would prefer, Mr. Fisher, all of us on this subcommittee are fully aware of who you are and what you did during the war—the millions of dollars in war bonds you helped to sell. I have a copy of your service record here and it is most admirable," said McCarran. "Purple Heart, Bronze Star, Distinguished Service Medal—and a full disability for your wound. Most impressive. No one is here questioning your loyalty."

"Why then am I here?" said Buck.

"It is, perhaps, your hiring practices that we are here to question," said the senator from Kansas.

"Meaning?"

"Were you not aware that Mr. Charles Fein was associated with a Communist front group when you hired him and that he attended a meeting of that group which was later shown to be subversive?"

"You have your information wrong, senator."

## A CHANGE OF KEY

"Oh? How so?"

"When I met Chuck Fein, he was already part of the Johnny Blair Orchestra—the musical group that later became the Buck Fisher Orchestra. So in fact, I never hired him."

"Yes, but—"

"However, senator, when I was put in charge of the Army Special Services Band, I did request that he be transferred from Fort Dix to Camp Polk, Louisiana. My reason for that request was simply his talent as a musician. I never asked any of my players what party they belonged to or who they voted for. When I was recuperating from my injury, it was Chuck Fein who watched over me every day in the London Free Hospital."

"Not even if they belonged to the Communist Party?" asked Senator Herbert Lehman, the New York State Democrat.

"Senator, Mr. Fein has already discussed with me the fact that he attended a single meeting in the mid-1930s. I am sure you are privy to his testimony to that effect. To accuse a man of being a Communist on such flimsy ground is to also condemn the 75,000 actual members of the Communist Party in that decade. It is wrong, and more to the point, it is unjust. You are tampering with a man's good name, senators. A man who enlisted after Pearl Harbor and served his country with honor for four years."

"Like you, Mr. Fisher?" said Senator Russell Long of Louisiana.

"No, senator. He enlisted. I was drafted. I wouldn't presume to compare myself to him or his patriotic act, nor would I compare it to anyone else who signed up."

"No one is impugning your honor here, Mr. Fisher," said McCarran.

"I think you are wrong, senator. The very fact that people like me and Mr. Fein are summoned here to defend ourselves against charges which I frankly find absurd, is in fact besmirching our honor."

"Our job, Mr. Fisher, is to protect the United States from Communism—not to protect your honor," said Senator Millard Tydings of Maryland.

## A CHANGE OF KEY

"You protect neither, senator, when you falsely accuse innocent Americans. Does not the Ninth Commandment say, 'Thou shalt not bear false witness against thy neighbor?'"

"False witness, Mr. Fisher?" said Russell Long.

"What would you call it, senator, when you violate our rights under the Constitution? I'm no expert, of course, but unless I have misread both the fifth and sixth amendments, neither of us was apprised that we could have counsel, nor has there been a presentation of evidence by a grand jury."

"That is for heinous crimes, Mr. Fisher," said McCarran.

Buck was losing his patience. "Senator, you are essentially accusing Mr. Fein of treason if you brand him as a Communist—and what of me? Is guilt by association now the norm in this country?"

"For a musician, you are very eloquent and well-informed, Mr. Fisher," said Senator Lehman.

"Well, even a musician can have an education, sir."

At that point, Senator McCarran said, "I believe we have the testimony we need, Mr. Fisher. However, I must remind you that should we need to recall you upon the revealing of any additional evidence, by law you will be compelled to answer that subpoena."

"Understood," said Buck.

"Good. The witness is now excused."

On the return train ride back to Penn Station, Chuck said, "Fuck 'em. Fuck every last one of those pompous bastards. I really put it to them, Bucky. They got nothing from me 'cause there ain't nothing to get. I'll bet you a double sawbuck that we never hear from those pricks again."

He was correct. Though McCarthyism reared its ugly head all across the country and grew more and more insidious as Joseph McCarthy became more powerful, neither Buck nor Chuck Fein ever had to appear in Washington, D.C. again.

# CHAPTER TWENTY-SIX
## *"It's Starting Again!" June 1950*

Sunday, June 25th was replete with sunshine and the promise of a long, languid summer. Buck had helped Carrie pack a picnic basket for lunch and then they headed out to Coney Island for a day at the beach. On the way, he drove through Bensonhurst to show the children where he grew up.

At 1415 West 8th Street, he pulled to the curb and said, "This is where I grew up with Nana and Auntie Arlene and Beverly."

Carrie said, "This is where I fell in love with your father, kids," and she leaned over and kissed Buck on the lips.

"Eww! Ma! That's disgusting!" said Eddie.

Carrie laughed and whispered, "He still thinks the stork brought him to us."

Coney Island was jammed by eleven in the morning with sunbathers on blankets and swimmers romping in the surf. At first, Laura was leery about walking on the beach because her heavy brace sank into the sand. As Buck led her by the hand to the water's edge, he could sense many eyes watching him and his child. Fortunately, no one said anything. They only ventured out a few feet into the water and since it was low-tide, no breakers threatened to knock Laura over.

"The water tickles, daddy," she said.

"Feels good, doesn't it?" said Buck.

Just then, Eddie came whisking by and plunged into the water up to his waist and he splashed with a joy particular to the young. He swam for a bit before coming up to Buck and Laura. "I'll take her, daddy. Don't worry, I won't let anything happen to her."

He took Laura by the hand and Buck stood a short distance off watching his children just to make sure they were safe. His pride in how Eddie always looked after Laura almost brought tears to his eyes. They were so special together with not a trace of sibling rivalry. Most of that he attributed to the seeming unending supply of affection that Carrie was capable of. She had always been demonstrative in her love towards Buck, but it was different with her children. She was like a lioness protecting her cubs if anyone or anything threatened them.

Back on the blanket, Carrie had unpacked sandwiches and bottles of juice for the kids. She also had packed two bottles of Miller High Life for Buck and herself. Buck helped feed Casey and he thought how glorious life was, his family, his job, the sunshine—even a beach crowded with happy people. All things considered, he was a very lucky man.

Unfortunately, Buck's personal 'era of good feeling' came to an abrupt end when the family returned home to Queens late that afternoon. Buck unpacked the car and got the kids inside. Casey was the most exhausted of the three so he put her down for a nap. Eddie and Laura wanted to get cleaned up from the day at the beach. Buck had installed bars in the shower so Laura could steady herself and there was also a small seat in the shower in case she got tired of standing while maintaining her balance.

In the downstairs shower, Eddie claimed that he had sand "in places I don't want to tell you about, daddy," so a long shower was imperative.

Carrie said, "I'm going to fix dinner, hon. You go busy yourself. Watch the news or something."

Buck had purchased a television set late the previous year. The novel device had tremendous entertainment possibilities which Buck was quick to note. At the time, there were four TV networks: NBC, CBS, ABC and the Dumont network. NBC was also owned by the RCA corporation so he thought of it as his 'sister company.'

Buck settled into his easy chair and tuned the set into the *Camel News Caravan,* the nightly round-up of world and national news. The news reader on the show was John Cameron Swayze who had done voice-over work for the *Camel Newsreel Theatre* before the advent of the new medium.

As Swayze reported the top story of the day, Buck looked on in horror and he exclaimed loudly, "Jesus Christ! It's starting again!"

Carrie came rushing into the living room and said, "Bucky? What is it?" She could read the alarm in his face. "What happened?"

"Good God, Carrie, North Korea invaded South Korea across the 38$^{th}$ parallel."

As Swayze reported it, the North Koreans had sent close to 75,000 troops into South Korea through what was supposed to be a 'demilitarized' zone. The South Koreans had only lightly defended that border and they had no tanks or heavy artillery to repel the invasion.

President Truman immediately had ordered American naval and air force units to come to the aid of South Korea. But even the troops that Truman had ordered to the country were quickly overrun by the Communists because they too were undersupplied. Both the 8$^{th}$ Infantry Division (Pathfinders) and the 2$^{nd}$ Infantry Division (Indian Head) were overrun with both divisions losing their colors to the Communist onslaught.

"The North Koreans have already captured the South Korean capital of Seoul," reported Swayze, "and there are tens of thousands of refugees leaving the city heading south, clogging the roads and preventing the movement of troop reinforcements."

Buck shook his head and rubbed his temples. "Another goddamned war, Carrie. More death, more young Americans to be sacrificed—and for what? Korea is what—8000 miles away from us? What the hell are we even there for?"

Carrie rubbed Buck's shoulders and said, "At least you won't have to go, darling. You've done your part. It's now others' turns."

"I'm not sure that makes me feel any better, Carrie. There still will be more death."

Buck switched channels to the *CBS Evening News* hosted by Douglas Edwards. He had been a regular on CBS Radio as a newscaster since 1942 and he took over the television broadcasts as soon as the medium gained a foothold with the American listening public. Edwards had access to the same information as

## A CHANGE OF KEY

had Swayze, so the reporting was basically the same. Truman was ordering General Douglas MacArthur to take charge of all allied troops in Korea to combat the Communist invasion. According to Edwards, it would take weeks or longer for American forces to arrive in Korea, basically leaving the two beleaguered divisions to fend for themselves.

"You know, Carrie, this country keeps making the same goddamned mistakes," said Buck.

"What do you mean?"

"After the First World War, what did we do? Cut our armed forces so much that Bulgaria had a bigger army than we did. And our navy was reduced to a tenth of its size. Remember how I told you that at Camp Polk some troops had to train with broomsticks because we didn't have enough rifles? Well it's the same thing all over again. The war just ended five years ago and once again we cut down our army and navy—even though we were supposedly in a cold war. Now, we don't have enough ships to transport soldiers to Korea to relieve those combat divisions. They're as good as gone."

"Well, General MacArthur should be able to do something over there, no?" said Carrie.

Buck snorted. "Despite all the press, Carrie, that egotistical bastard wasn't all that respected by his troops. They called him 'Dugout Doug' on Corregidor. Then FDR goes and gives him the Medal of Honor—for what? For escaping the Philippines on a PT boat leaving his entire army to be captured and slaughtered. Even Truman jokingly called him 'the new emperor of Japan.' No, hon, this war is going to be long and every bit as bloody as the last one."

"What about the orchestra, Bucky?"

"What do you mean?"

"Will they put back the draft?"

Buck had to think about that for a minute. He remembered how the draft decimated the big bands in 1942 and it could happen again.

The thought of losing his men to war was unbearable.

## A CHANGE OF KEY

"I think most of them are above the draft age limit. Others have already served, and we may have a few 4-Fs in there too. Let's hope for the best on that score, Carrie."

All that summer the news of the conflict flooded the airwaves both on radio and television. Places like Inchon and the Pusan Perimeter were everyday fodder for news along with the Chosin Reservoir, Pork Chop Hill and other distant battlefields in a country that few Americans could even point to on a map.

In 1950 MacArthur, to his great credit, gambled with amphibious landings at Inchon that completely surprised the North Koreans. Shortly thereafter, the U.S. 8$^{th}$ Army invaded North Korea and their army started to disintegrate. But when the U.N. forces reached the Yalu River, the People's Volunteer Army of Communist China counterattacked and invaded Korea, once again nearly obliterating the 8$^{th}$ Infantry Division and forcing the American Army to retreat.

The back-and-forth conflict went on for months, but when the Americans and their allies finally got the upper hand, MacArthur, against orders, announced his plans to invade Communist China, which prompted President Truman to fire him, replacing him with General Matthew Ridgeway.

Truman declined to run again in 1950 and Dwight D. Eishenhower, America's five-star general who commanded all forces in Europe during the war was elected president. He vowed to go to Korea and bring an end to the conflict.

Eventually, the war and all its horrors faded in the American consciousness and it was replaced in nightly news reports about other, more current events.

But it was always on Buck's mind.

Fortunately, the RCA Studio Orchestra lost no one to the draft and they continued making LPs featuring both established stars like Cindi Kay and new discoveries who were rising rapidly in the musical world.

One night in early October, Buck was playing with his children on the living room floor when the phone rang. Carrie answered it and poked her head into the room.

## A CHANGE OF KEY

"Buck honey? A General Travis Burton on the phone for you?"

Buck picked up the phone and said, "Trav? Is it really you?"

The last time Buck had seen him, he was Colonel Travis Burton and he was in command of Brooklyn's Fort Hamilton, the post Buck had been assigned to with his band after their return from Europe. It was Travis Burton who had informed Buck that he had been elevated to the rank of an acting Lieutenant Colonel. The two had worked together not only as military colleagues, but as good friends as well.

"It's me, Buck. Great to hear your voice."

"Well, Colonel sir, how can I help you?"

Burton laughed. "You mean Major General Burton, don't you?"

"Holy cow! Two stars! Congratulations, buddy! But Trav, something tells me this isn't just a social call."

"No, it's not, Buck."

"Well, you can't draft me again, I'm a 4-F for sure," he said.

"No, we can't put you back in uniform, but there's something else you can do for us, Buck, and believe me, it's very important."

"Anything. You know that," he said.

"Careful, Buck, you haven't heard what I'm asking."

"OK, Trav, lay it on me."

"You've probably read that this Korean thing has turned into a real cluster fuck. Back and forth, up and down that goddamned peninsula, MacArthur fired, Ridgeway trying to get a handle on things—and the body bags keep getting filled up. There are an unbelievable number of casualties, Buck. We have hospitals in Manilla—but that city is still rebuilding since it was almost destroyed in the war. We also have hospitals in Guam and of course at Pearl."

"You're getting at something, Trav. Why all the suspense?" said Buck.

## A CHANGE OF KEY

"First let me say that General Lawton Collins—he's the Army Chief of Staff just in case you haven't kept up on things—he's already talked to General Sarnoff over there at RCA and has his blessing for the project."

By this time, Buck was laughing. "What project, Trav? You keep beating the same dead horse."

"How would you like to spend ten days in Hawaii with Bob Hope and a bunch of pretty girls?"

That shocked him into silence. "Want to give me that again, Trav?"

"We want you to go to Hawaii with your orchestra and entertain the troops at the hospitals there."

"The whole orchestra?!" Buck really was speechless at that point.

"The whole shebang. We'll fly you out there on a brand new Lockheed Super Constellation—first class all the way. We'll send a Transportation Company to your studio to pack up all your stuff and move it to Floyd Bennet Field. You won't have to do a thing. You'll be there for ten days. Hope will front the show and you'll back up his singers. By the way, that pretty little girl still in touch with you, the one that sang with the Army band?"

"Cindi Kay works for me, Trav. She's selling records by the bushel for us."

"Maybe she'd like to come too."

"I'll certainly ask her," said Buck.

It was a lot to think about, but finally Buck said, "Look, Trav, what do you need me for? I'm just a guy who used to be a musician. Nobody remembers me."

"Don't kid yourself, Buck. General Collins remembers you from your War Bond tours. He even met you at a base in Wisconsin. Buck, he asked for you personally."

"Look, Trav, I can't do anything until I speak to Carrie. I've got three kids, you know."

"Buck, my friend, I know more about you than you can imagine. Now tell me, how's your little girl doing?"

"You know about Laura?"

## A CHANGE OF KEY

"Oh hell, Buck, what do you think the FBI does all day—look for Communists? As a routine they do a background check on anyone who will perform for the troops. They've already done it for everyone in your orchestra. So tell me, how's she doing?"

"It's been tough, Trav. Years of physical therapy, but she's getting around very well. She might be in that leg brace for the rest of her life, though."

"Damn. That's a tough break for a little kid, Buck. I wish her all the best." Buck said, "Thanks. That means a lot to me."

"Oh, by the way, how's my niece doing working for you?"

"Your niece?"

"Well, my niece by marriage. She married my nephew and she tells me you're a great boss."

"Wait, wait, Kelsey Burton is your niece?"

"Sure is. Beautiful, isn't she?"

"She's more than that, Trav. My office would fall apart without her. She's great."

"All right, look, I've got a meeting to get to. You talk to Carrie, talk to your orchestra and I'll call back in a few days. I hope you can do this, Buck. There are a lot of young kids with awful wounds who could use a little cheering up."

When Buck ended the call, Carrie was standing in the living room, arms crossed and foot tapping impatiently. "Going to tell me now, Bucky, or do I have to wait?"

Buck explained the substance of the call with Travis Burton. He looked less than enthused. "I just don't know what he needs me for, Carrie. Hell, Les Brown still leads his band and I know for a fact he's worked with Bob Hope before."

"The general asked for you, Buck. I keep telling you that you're Buck Fisher and no one has forgotten about you."

"Even if that were true, how am I supposed to just leave you and the kids for ten days?"

"Honey, we will be fine. Eunice will be here, Warren still comes three days a week, the girls live close by and Mama is right next door. Plus, Cathy Dwyer is right down the block in case I need her help. Of course we'll all miss you and I wish I could be there in Hawaii with you. I'm told Hawaiian girls are the most beautiful in the world so I'd like to protect my man from their roaming eyes."

"None are as beautiful as you, Carrie," said Buck.

She kissed him on the lips earning another, "Ewww, Ma!" from Eddie.

"I don't know, Carrie, I don't want to disappoint Travis. Hell, because of him I have a full disability from the Army and that huge check we get every month is his doing."

"Then you owe him, Buck. Time to clear your marker."

"I love you, Carrie. I don't want to be away from you for ten days."

Carrie sighed, hugged Buck and said, "Why Mr. Benny Feinstein, I love you too—and we've been through worse times. Like a war? I'll be right here when you get back. And Buck? All those boys over there sure will be grateful that you showed up."

That night, Buck's sleep was restless. Perhaps memories of the war and his own stay in the hospital were circulating in his mind. Carrie woke up when she heard him muttering in his sleep. His face was soaked in sweat. She took her handkerchief and wiped away the sweat—or maybe they were tears, and said, "Shh, shh, my love. I'm right here and nothing can hurt you." She nestled his head against her breasts and held him until he fell asleep.

…..

The next morning at the studio, Buck broke the news to the orchestra. "If anyone doesn't want to make this trip, I will understand, but I have to know right away because I will have to fill your chair with a replacement and that's not going to be so easy to do in the time we have."

It was Chuck Fein who spoke up. "Listen, Bucky, Rebecca will have my ass for going, but where you go, I go. And as for the rest of you sonsabitches, the way this man pays us and takes care of us—every last one of us—we owe him. So I'm gonna be real pissed off at anyone who backs out of this. Except for the guys who were with us in Europe, none of you are old enough to remember the faces of those kids we entertained in hospitals. For a lot of them, it was the last time they smiled before—well, before they cashed in their chips. We owe something to these kids too."

"Holy shit, Chuckie, who knew you were such a speech-maker," said Tony Tancredi. "Maybe you should run for office or something."

"You got a wife like mine, you better learn to speak or she'll talk you to death before you can get a word in edge-wise," said Chuck. "Besides, all politicians are assholes."

As it happened, Cindi Kay was in the new studio on the 18$^{th}$ floor working on some new material with a piano accompanist. Buck took the elevator to the studio and walked in as she was running through "There's a Small Hotel."

She saw Buck and stopped the song, went to him and hugged him. "What brings you down to the dungeon?"

"Can I talk to you for a moment, Cin?"

"Sure. Come let's sit. They pulled up two folding chairs and Cindi took a Chesterfield from a pack and lit it. She took a long drag and said, "What gives?"

Buck explained about the trip to Hawaii and that General Burton had asked for her specifically to go along. Her single word reaction said it all, "Wow!"

"What about the LP I'm working on, Buck?"

"It's just for ten days, Cin. And like it was in England, a lot of what we're going to see isn't going to be pretty."

"Yes, but those guys really appreciated what we did over there, Buck. Let me ask you a question: will you be playing with us or just swinging a baton? It would be great to see you out in front again."

"I've been practicing a lot, Cin. I would like to try to play," said Buck.

"Buck Fisher rides again! I love it! Count me in—assuming my husband doesn't threaten to divorce me. When do we leave?"

"November 15$^{th}$ out of Floyd Bennett."

## A CHANGE OF KEY

"Jesus, that brings back some memories, doesn't it?"

"Yeah, some not so great. So we have a little over two weeks to get ready. I will need you with the orchestra to practice—but most of the songs are the ones you already know from the Army band. I'll bring a trunk load of charts and you can pick the ones you like best."

"Great, I'll be there in the morning. And Buck? Don't worry, you'll be terrific."

He kissed her and said, "Bright and early tomorrow, Cin."

"Yes sir, colonel sir," she said, throwing him a mock salute.

.....

Buck stopped in to see Jack Merrill and explain about the trip to Hawaii. It was hardly necessary. As usual, the tendrils of the RCA grapevine found out things before official announcements.

"General Sarnoff already briefed me, Buck. He thinks it will be great publicity for the label and at the same time, it will be good for those boys in the hospital. Here's something you might not know: there is a possibility that one of the shows you do with Hope will be televised on the NBC network."

"Really?"

"Yeah, one of the shows from the deck of an aircraft carrier."

"You're kidding."

"No, you're scheduled to do a show on the USS Kearsarge. She's one of those big Essex class carriers. She arrived too late for World War II but her planes have been flying combat missions over North Korea for months. She'll be in port for a refit before she goes back to Korea. Those ships get plenty beat up over there."

"It's not going out onto the water is it, Jack?"

"No, Buck. She's tied up at a pier—and you don't even have to worry about U-Boats."

"Well, that's a relief."

"Is Carrie going to be OK while you're gone, Buck?"

## A CHANGE OF KEY

"She has it in hand, Jack, and there's lots of help close by if she needs it. Ten days will fly by so we're not too worried."

"Good, great. I'll have travel details ready for you by Monday. Do a good job out there, Buck. The General will be watching every minute of it."

.....

The Pan American Lockheed Super Constellation was leaps forward from the DC-3. Spacious by comparison and faster, the plane had been leased to the Air Force and was used for ferrying VIPs from place to place. It was one of the new generation of commercial aircraft flying internationally.

Though it was categorized as a long-range aircraft, the itinerary called for stops at Chicago's Midway Airport and a long layover at Los Angeles International Airport. The final leg would be to Hickham Field in Oahu. The orchestra would then be bussed to the Royal Hawaiian Hotel on the beach in downtown Honolulu.

"Helluva lot better than sticking us in Schofield Barracks, Bucky," said Chuck Fein. "I sure have had a bucketful of barracks life," he added.

Because of the time difference, the flight between L.A. and Oahu seemed the longest. Cindi sat next to Buck and despite the fact that she had been provided with a pillow and blanket, she fell asleep on Buck's shoulder.

She woke a few hours later, looked out the window at the endless expanse of the Pacific Ocean and said, "Oh, Christ, I need a cigarette. At least it's not like that awful ride to Greenland when we all thought we were going to crash into the Atlantic." That memory was still fresh in everyone's mind.

"Yeah, that's about as scared as I've ever been," said Buck, remembering the harrowing ride in the 'Fightin' Filly,' the B-24 that ferried the Army band to England. The plane had lost an engine and smoke filled the entire cargo area of the aircraft.

At 4 PM local time, the Super Connie touched down at Hickham Field. There they were met by a man who introduced himself as Bill Adler. "Hello Buck, *aloha* and welcome to Hawaii.

## A CHANGE OF KEY

I'll be producing the show you're doing with Bob Hope so I'm the point man for all your questions, logistics and so forth."

"Please to meet you, Bill. What's our schedule for hospital shows?"

"We've got you doing six hospitals in seven days. Your group will have a full day off before rehearsal day with Bob. Then Saturday night is the show on the Kearsarge and by Sunday, you're back in the air."

"I have to get these kids ready for what they're going to see, Bill. How bad is it?"

"It's bad, Buck. Those guys in your orchestra who were with you in Europe? They've seen the horror up close. It's pretty much the same here. A lot of these guys were in hand-to-hand combat with the North Koreans or the ChiComs. I hate to say it, but a lot of the guys you'll be playing for aren't going to make it."

"We've seen our share of that, Bill. I just need these young guys to understand that no matter what they see, they have to gut it out and like we used to say in the Army, 'continue to march.'"

"I hear you, Buck. I was 1st Armored Division and we were right in the thick of the shit all across Europe. To me, horror is pulling a charred corpse out of a Sherman tank that took a direct hit from a German Tiger."

"I understand. Really, I do. Listen, do you have a place where I can gather the orchestra together and fill them in on the schedule."

"Yeah, sure, Buck. The busses should be here in about forty minutes, so you can have some time with them. Let me show you the mess hall and then you can get your troops together."

"Troops. Shit, Bill, it's been a long time since I heard that term."

"It stays in the blood, Buck. OK, follow me."

Buck met with the band and laid out the schedule, taking time to explain some of the unfortunate sights they would be seeing. "You will be doing a show within spitting distance of the USS Arizona. She's resting on the bottom of the harbor—with

## A CHANGE OF KEY

over 1100 souls still inside her, so remember, respect at all times. If the soldiers and marines you see want to talk to you, take the time and give them attention. It's the least we can do for them. Any questions?"

Chuck Fein said, "Listen. We saw things in Europe that would straighten out the curl in your pubic hairs. I imagine we're going to see the same things here. You get emotional, turn your heads. Don't lose it in front of them and don't show pity to these guys. They don't want it. They want you to treat them like regular Joes. Don't be afraid to talk to them."

Bill Adler popped his head into the mess hall and announced that the busses had arrived. "OK, fellas," said Buck, "let's mount up"

The ride to the Royal Hawaiian Hotel took about thirty minutes. It was one of the oldest hotels on Waikiki Beach. Its pink façade housed a six-story, 400 room edifice. It was as luxurious as any of the big-name hotels Buck had played with his band in the States. During the war, the War Department had leased the entire hotel and used it as an R & R site for military personnel, mostly Navy and especially submariners in from thirty-day patrols beneath the oceans.

Bill got everyone settled in and then said to Buck, "How about we meet in an hour, you me, Bill Dwyer and Al Rovitz. We can go over any and all details and take care of whatever you need."

One topic of discussion was Bob Hope. Buck wanted to know what he was like and how the orchestra should act towards him. "I can say this about Bob, his real-life persona is virtually the same as his on-screen one. He's the nicest guy in the world. He did so many USO shows during the war that Congress gave him a medal. Tell the guys not to hound him for autographs, but otherwise, just go about your business and if he talks to you, don't act star-struck. He'll always say, 'Call me Bob.'"

The orchestra was served a sumptuous meal in one of the banquet rooms of the hotel featuring Hawaiian specialties like poi and roast pig. Exotic drinks were served in half-pineapples. The hotel had even provided some entertainment—a troupe of eight beautiful girls with distinctive Eurasian looks dancing the hula to Hawaiian melodies.

"Jesus Christ, Buck," said Chuck, "how 'bout we hire these babes for the orchestra? They are gorgeous with a capital G!"

Cindi put on a pretend frown and said, "Hey Chuckie, I thought you wanted to marry me!"

"That's OK, Little Sis, there's plenty of old Chuckie to go around."

After another hour or so, the players retired to their rooms for a good night's sleep before the performances began the following day.

First stop on the mini-tour was the Tripler Army Hospital. The facility had treated thousands of wounded Marines and Army personnel during the war. Now once again, it was dealing with the broken bodies and scarred souls of young men who fought in both the blistering heat and unimaginable cold of the Korean War.

For Buck, being out in front of a band with a tenor sax in his hand was beyond cathartic. As the group did the swing charts that had made him famous, he felt as if he were home. It started during the rehearsals leading up to the trip to Hawaii: a sense that once again he was one with his instrument—that it responded to every musical nuance he put into it.

And now, fronting the band, talking to the soldiers and Marines, and most importantly, hearing them respond so enthusiastically to every song the band played, it was astounding to him. But even as he played, he once again understood that music—great music—endures. Not every wounded soldier was a nineteen or twenty-year-old. There were a lot of grizzled veterans in the audience who had either stayed in the service when the war ended, or reenlisted to fight this one. They knew who Buck Fisher was and were thrilled to hear him play again.

Playing the charts that Johnny Blair had written so long ago brought back memories of his friend, mentor and business partner. His death on an operating table as surgeons attempted to remove a huge tumor from his stomach was a personal blow to Buck. He had grown unimaginably wealthy because of Johnny Blair, but even more importantly, the music world lost a great talent who truly had his finger on the pulse of musical trends.

When Buck introduced Cindi Kay, the audience responded as earlier audiences had: they whistled, stood up (those who could) and applauded raucously. She looked beautiful in a floor-length gown—topped by a sailor's 'Dixie Cup' hat. She strode onto the stage, grabbed the microphone and said, "Any of you swabbies wanna swing tonight?"

The response was predicable: their shouts of approval answered the question. "OK, then, fellas?" she said, turning to the band, "Hit it!"

Buck launched the band into "It Don't Mean a Thing if it Ain't Got That Swing." Buck took ninety-six bars of amazing and creative tenor solo. Then Cindi did a terrific scat chorus on the melody which got some of the patients up and dancing—even with casts on their arms.

Buck then slowed it down with the beautiful Kip Roman chart on "It Might as Well be Spring." Cindi Kay—the little WAC that he and Bill Dwyer had caught at the Officers Club at Camp Polk and who had joined Buck's Special Services Band, had become a consummate professional. Her delivery captured the aching quality of young love perfectly.

Next, Buck did a duet with her on "You're the Top," and he was surprised that both he and Cindi remembered all the little shticks that they used to add to the song.

More Swing, more ballads, more cheering, and the show came to an end. At its conclusion, a soldier in a wheelchair made his way to the impromptu bandstand.

"Mr. Fisher?"

"Yes, how can I help you?"

"Master Sergant Danny Boyle, sir. I saw you play at the U.S. Army Hospital 804 in Shropshire during the war. I was in the 101$^{st}$ at Bastogne. That's where I got it in the leg. They patched me up pretty good and I stayed in. Got this second one at Pusan. I just wanted you to know how much it meant for the guys to hear you today—and how much it meant to all of us back then."

"Well sarge, believe me when I say that it's an honor to be here. You guys, you're the best this country has," said Buck.

"I was still in the hospital when I heard what happened to you in London. I want you to know that every swingin' dick said a prayer for you. I'm glad you made it home."

"Thank you, sarge. As far as I know, maybe it was those prayers that helped me survive and gave me the opportunity to play for you fellas here."

Master Sergeant Danny Boyle was unable to stand, but he still snapped a perfect salute to Buck. Almost as an instinctive reaction, Buck brought his feet together and returned the salute crisply.

As Boyle began to maneuver the chair to leave, Buck said, "Wait, wait just a second, sarge. I want you to meet someone."

Then he called out to Cindi, "Hey, Cin, got a sec?"

Cindi, always a bundle of energy came bounding over and said, "What's up, Buck?"

"I want you to meet someone, Cin. This is Master Sergeant Danny Boyle formerly of the 101$^{st}$ Airborne Division—and a survivor of the Bulge who heard us play in England."

Her face lit up with her million-dollar smile and she bent over to embrace Danny Boyle and kiss him tenderly. "You get well real soon, OK sarge?"

"You bet, ma'am." And then he wheeled himself back towards the mess hall for chow.

For just a second, there was a sadness in Cindi's eyes that Buck couldn't help but notice. "What is it, Cin?"

Cindi sighed deeply. "I almost feel guilty about telling him to get well quickly, Buck. They'll just send him back to that meat grinder and who knows what will happen then? It's just one more war with boatloads of dead and dying."

"He's a lifer, hon. He knows the risks. Guys like him—totally forgotten and taken for granted back home—they're the ones who keep us free. We can never do enough for them."

## A CHANGE OF KEY

The next day saw the orchestra at Naval Station Pearl Harbor. Bill Adler was there with a Lieutenant Commander Arleigh Ingersoll who was the Navy's liaison officer. He took the entire orchestra down to the embankment where they could stare across the harbor to Ford Island where the Arizona lay buried in the mud.

"If you look carefully," said Commander Ingersoll, 'and if the sun is just right, you can see what looks like a rainbow on the water. That's fuel oil from Arizona's bunkers. It leaks out a few drops per minute and the Bureau of Ships estimates that it will bleed like that for the next fifty or sixty years."

Cindi gasped and tears welled in her eyes. Chuck Fein wrapped his arm around her shoulder and drew her close. "It's OK, Little Sis, I want to cry too."

"Only the Arizona and the Oklahoma were unsalvageable," continued Commander Ingersoll. "Every other battleship was raised, repaired, upgraded—and lived to give the Japs hell before the war ended."

It was a somber moment for the orchestra—both for those who had served in the war, and for those too young to have been there. There was very little talking amongst the players. Overall, it had the feeling of being at a wake and silence and respect were the orders of the day.

"You'll be playing before about three hundred patients," said Commander Ingersoll. A lot of them are ambulatory—but many will be there in wheelchairs and even a few on gurneys. I know I don't have to say this, but try to bring them a little happiness. These guys need it—badly."

They all nodded in complete understanding.

The orchestra met the Commander's expectations—and then some. The patients absolutely fell in love with Cindi, who blew kisses to them after each song she performed. She really remembered how to work a crowd. And they clapped along in rhythm to Buck's solos.

When Buck brought the show to a close, there were so many cries for "More!" that he said, "OK, fellas, take out "One o'clock "Jump" and let's floor 'em with it." He was happy to give these men an encore or two.

All the first chairs got to take solos with Buck's being the lengthiest—just as Johnny Blair had written the chart ten years earlier. At the conclusion of the song, Ingersoll took the microphone and said, "How about we give a huge hand to Buck Fisher and the RCA Studio Orchestra!"

The audience willingly complied and Ingersoll said, "Sorry Buck, but these guys have to get back to their rooms for meds, therapy and then chow. I know they wanted to hear more, but we're on a tight schedule. We have to move a bunch of them out of here quickly because we've got a whole raft of new casualties coming in from Korea."

"Understood. Will you be with us for the next show? I think we're at the Naval Hospital in Aiea Heights."

"Yes, I will. I'll be with you right through Bob Hope's Saturday night show on the Kearsarge. I have to run now, but I'll see you tomorrow."

The U.S. Naval Hospital, Aiea Heights was a massive building with all the personality of a tire factory. Fortunately, the band would be performing outdoors in the balmy Hawaiian sunshine.

The concert was scheduled for one that afternoon because as Commander Ingersoll had said, "We can't make it later in the afternoon because every day at about four, we get thunderstorms. Don't ask me why, but you can set your watch by them."

Almost none of the sailors and marines that they played before were ambulatory. The wheelchairs were lined up with military precision and each patient had been equipped with a canteen of ice water. Every row had an orderly at the end just in case any of the patients experienced distress. There were even some off-duty doctors and nurses who had eschewed sleep in favor of getting to hear Buck Fisher and his orchestra perform.

In some ways, that third performance was the most gratifying of the series. Some of the patients had their arms in casts up to the shoulder or in slings, so they couldn't applaud—but they could stomp their feet in appreciation and they were as vocal as any of the other crowds.

Buck had instructed the orchestra member to mingle with the sailors and marines after the show and it was Cindi who led the way. Some of the sailors were so young and had no idea that she was a recording star. Others knew very well who she was and told her that they owned her LPs. That always prompted a kiss for them from the lovely Cindi Kay.

Then the following day was the show aboard one of America's newest aircraft carriers. The USS Kearsarge seemed gigantic. At 820 feet in length and 36,000 tons, the massive ship could handle almost ninety aircraft and it seemed like a floating city manned by just under 3,000 sailors and officers.

The show would take place in front of the ship's massive superstructure or 'island,' located midway on the flight deck on the starboard or right side of the vessel.

Bill Adler scurried around making sure that every detail was in order before the telecast began. With the exception of a small duty section, the entire crew and compliment of officers plus local Hawaiian officials would be the audience for the show.

Bill had introduced Buck to Bob Hope who acted as if they were old friends. "That was some band you had, Buck, and you even raised more money in war bonds than I did," said Hope.

Buck thanked Hope and then made a suggestion which he was certain would be declined. "Bob, my band has an arrangement of 'Thanks for the Memory,' that I used to sing with my civilian band with my wife, Carrie Collins. My vocalist now, Cindi Kay, knows the song perfectly and I think it would be really fun if you sang it with her. She even knows the patter you did with Shirley Ross down to the last syllable."

Hope thought about it for a bit before he said, "OK, Buck, let's do it. It should be fun."

The show would begin at 2 PM so that it would be broadcast live during prime time back in New York City. Frank Barton, Hope's announcer, did the introduction underneath a long roll on the floor tom-tom by Tony Tancredi. Then the band began

## A CHANGE OF KEY

to play "Thanks for the Memory," in an instrumental version as Bob Hope took the 'stage.'

He did a fifteen-minute monologue replete with jokes—many about his best friend, Bing Crosby. "Yeah, Crosby wanted to be here today, but he threw a five iron into a pond when he blew a shot and said he needed to fish it out." A few more jokes at the expense of his friend Jerry Colonna had the audience clutching their sides.

Then Hope said, "Fellas, we brought you something special today. You might remember that just a few years ago, he was even more famous than, well, than Crosby. Then he went on to serve his country and emerge a hero. Let's here it for Colonel Buck Fisher and the RCA Studio Orchestra!"

The crowd was on its feet instantly applauding before the band even played a note. Then Buck led them through three swing numbers including his famous, "Riffin' In" which Johnny had written for him and which sold a million 78s. The response from the crew was unbelievable.

Then Hope came back out and said, "Got another surprise for you. Cindi Kay? Come on over here." The crew whistled and threw their hats in the air when Cindi appeared. She took a bow and Hope took her by the hand. "This gorgeous gal and I are gonna do a song from way back in 1938. In fact, it won the Oscar that year as the best song of the year—'Thanks for the Memory.' Of course, it won the Oscar—but I didn't. They leave that to Crosby and his Father O'Malley character. Humph. I'm gonna have to tell my agent to get me a part as a priest! So here goes. Miss Kay?"

"Mr. Hope? Ready if you are."

It was perfect. Cindi could have been Shirley Ross singing. And Bob Hope knew just how to insert a funny line into the bitter-sweet lyric. At the end of the song, they took hands and bowed theatrically to the crew, who loved it.

Bob Hope was effusive in his praise.

"Now how about that!" said Hope. "Not only is she a knock-out, but boy can she sing! Don't worry, fellas, we've got some more beauties on tap for you right now."

## A CHANGE OF KEY

Then Hope introduced the June Taylor Dancers who Hope had borrowed from the *Jackie Gleason Show*. The troupe of sixteen long-legged dancers did an elaborate tap routine as Buck and the orchestra backed them with "Anything Goes." Buck was pretty sure that the sailors had more appreciation for the incredibly shapely girls than they did for the music, but, boys will be boys, he thought.

Hope reintroduced Cindi who did a few ballads with the full orchestra and then some up-tempo songs with the jazz band. The two-hour show was over before Buck realized how quickly the time had gone by. Bob Hope thanked everyone involved and gave a special thanks to Buck Fisher.

"You boys going back out there, you make sure to stay safe," said Hope, and once again, thanks for the memory." Buck brought the orchestra in with the theme song and the broadcast came to an end.

Early the next morning, the gear was packed and the orchestra boarded a TWA flight for the first leg of the journey home. There was a brief layover in Los Angeles and an even shorter one in Chicago. There they had to change planes for the last leg of the trip.

It wasn't until 8 PM that the flight touched down at Newark International Airport. Buck, Bill and Al grabbed a cab to Queens and by nine that evening, buck opened the front door to his home and was greeted by cries of 'Daddy!' as his three children were the first to greet him.

It was a little past their bedtime, but Carrie had acceded to their pleading to stay up late to see their daddy.

After the obligatory hugs and kisses to Eddie, Laura and Casey, he enfolded Carrie in his arms and kissed her passionately.

"Ugh!" said Eddie. "Again?"

Buck laughed and said, "My son, there will come a time when this will be one of your favorite things in the world."

"Not me, Pop. I'm gonna be a bachelor," said Eddie.

Buck simply stared at him as Carrie giggled and he said to her, "Where does he get this stuff?"

337

## A CHANGE OF KEY

"Television, I imagine. Now come and tell me everything that happened. I'll fix you a plate."

That night in bed while locked in each other's arms, Carrie said, "Was it very difficult, darling?"

"Most of it was all right, but the memories it brought back were difficult. The terrible injuries—the boys you just knew weren't gong to make it, the ones who had lost limbs. I thought I had seen the last of that in Europe, But this war? It's no different than any other. Slaughter is the same no matter what part of the globe it happens on."

"No more, darling," said Carrie. "Ten days without you is more than I ever want to be apart again. Now come and surprise me."

And he did. Three times.

A CHANGE OF KEY

# CHAPTER TWENTY-SEVEN
*"Get 'em Under Contract" February 1951*

Though he was fairly exhausted from the lengthy flight from Hawaii, Buck was back at work on Monday morning. After getting another pile of mail and messages from Kelsey, she told him that he should "straighten your tie. The General wants to see you."

Buck had only met David Sarnoff once and that was on the day he was hired. Now he was told that the great man had sent for him as soon as he came in.

His first inclination was to think, "Oh shit, what did I do now?" But at the same time, he thought there was no time like the present to find out if it was bad news, so he took the elevator to the rarified atmosphere where the General had his office.

He was greeted by Sarnoff's secretary who asked him to have a seat while she informed the General that he had arrived. Five minutes later, she opened the door and ushered Buck into Sarnoff's palatial office.

"Buck! Come on in and grab a seat" said Sarnoff as he came around from his desk to shake Buck's hand. "Get you something to drink? A bagel maybe?"

"No, sir. I'm fine. I had breakfast with the family before I left for work."

"Good, good. Let me tell you why I've asked you to visit with me this morning. I saw the show you did with Bob Hope on that ship and it was spectacular. Bob called me himself to say what a pleasure it was to work with you and the orchestra. And I also got a call from George Marshall, the Secretary of Defense, who said every hospital commanding officer sang your praises for the shows you did for the soldiers, sailors and marines. It really gave them the morale boost they needed,"

"That's very nice of him to say. General. He's a very busy man," said Buck.

"Oh, he said more than that."

"Sir?"

## A CHANGE OF KEY

"He said he wished he could put you back in uniform, but your disability status means you aren't even in the inactive reserve anymore."

"Honestly sir? I'm very glad about that."

"I understand, Buck. But he also said if this damned war lasts a long time, he might call on us again. That is, you again."

"If it comes to that, you can count on me, General."

"Good, good. Now I would like to talk to you about a few other things if you have time," said Sarnoff.

"Sometimes, Buck, my head spins with all the changes that are happening in entertainment. We believe that television is going to replace radio very soon as the major form of entertainment that Americans will follow. We're gearing up to produce inexpensive television sets that we envision every American having in their homes. At some point, we're going to move you over to the production side of TV. You'll learn from the ground up and believe me, you're going to be integral to our plans. But that's a little bit down the road. For now, I want you to know you're doing a fantastic job with the record label. But there's where we have a bit of a problem."

"What problem is that, General?" asked Buck.

"To put it bluntly, music is a mish-mash right now. There are all these styles which not only compete against each other, but influence each other as well. You've got rhythm and blues which kind of grew out of swing' you've got gospel, country western, blues, this rockabilly stuff and now out in Cleveland, there's a young Disc Jockey who's calling what he plays rock n' roll."

"Pardon me, General, but I'm missing something here. Why is this a problem?"

"It's a guessing game, Buck. Which style will dominate? And that means who do we go after for the label? Do we sign artists from each of these splinter groups or concentrate on one area? If we guess wrong, the other labels will swamp us and we'll never rise to the top again. Besides, there must be a hundred of these nickel and dime labels that release one song by a soloist or a group and then the label folds."

## A CHANGE OF KEY

"So what's the plan, General?" asked Buck.

"I'm going to leave that up to you, Buck. But my one order is this: get 'em under contract. All styles, groups, singles, instrumentalists—all of them. I want you sending Al and Bill out to really find us new talent. When you can, you go hear the ones they recommend. But get their names on paper."

"But sir, everything has to go through the Legal Department for contracts."

"The hell with that, Buck. You tell Bill and Al to travel with contracts in their pockets. If they like what they hear, sign them up. Just leave blank how many albums we'll guarantee them until we see if their music takes off."

"But what if some of the people we sign up don't pan out?" asked Buck.

"That's inevitable," said Sarnoff. "Nobody bats a thousand. But if we even hit on thirty or forty percent, we're going to make a fortune. So go mobilize the troops and bring me back hit-makers."

"We'll get right on it, General. I won't let you down," said Buck.

"You never have in the past, Buck, and I know you'll continue to do great things for us."

As Buck rose to leave, Sarnoff said, "By the way, Buck, what are you driving these days?"

"My Oldsmobile from the time they sponsored our radio show."

"Not anymore. There's a brand-new Cadillac Fleetwood Sixty Special sedan waiting for you in the garage. A little present for you because you went out to Hawaii for those kids in the hospital."

Buck was stunned. "I don't know what to say, General. Thank you very much!"

"It's the least we can do for you, Buck. Think nothing of it." Sarnoff tossed him a set of keys and said, "Congratulations again, Buck. Now go get 'em." Back in the office he had Kelsey call Bill and Al and told them to drop everything and come meet with him right away. Ten minutes later, the three were huddled up in Buck's office.

"What gives, chief?" said Bill.

At some length, Buck recounted the conversation he had with General Sarnoff. "He wants results, fellas, and he wants them quickly. Al, what did you find out about this rockabilly stuff?"

"It's kind of strange, Buck. Basically, it's a hybrid."

"Of what?" asked Bill.

"Take one part country one part rhythm and blues, one part bluegrass—that's where the billy comes from for hillbilly music—and mix it all together and it comes out as this new style they're calling rock n' roll," said Al.

"Any names of note?" asked Buck.

"Some. I keep hearing about Billy Adams, Johnny Cash, and a group called The Saddlemen fronted by a guy named Bill Halley," said Bill.

"And I'm going up to Harlem Friday night," said Al. "I have a line on a guy whose name is Ellas Otha Bates. How's that for a name? But he goes by the stage name of Bo Diddley and I hear he's really something."

"OK, good. If he's as good as they say, get him down on paper, Al. And Bill? You're off to Nashville to do some scouting. We have an RCA Nashville label which is strictly country, but if you think there's anyone good, sign them up and maybe they'll be part of this new wave of styles," said Buck.

"Got it, chief," said Bill.

"Speak to Kelsey and she'll make all the travel arrangements for you. And Bill? If some of these country performers can maybe cross over into standard popular singing, use your judgement and sign them."

Two days later, Al met with Buck. "I saw this Bo Diddley guy at Paris Blues on Friday, Buck. All I can say is I never heard anything like this before. It's these driving rhythms that make it so different from the jazz we're used to—it's not even close to bebop. I spoke to him after his set and in his words, "We rockin' n' Rollin here."

**A CHANGE OF KEY**

Buck said, "That's what that Fried guy in Cleveland is calling it: rock n roll."

"I asked him about signing with us and he said that right now he's with Chess Records," said Al.

"Who the hell are they?" asked Buck.

"One of these peanut labels. He's not very happy with them. Again in his words, he said, 'Dey keep recordin' whole albums o' my music, but they don't release shit. I needs me a label that'll promote my music—this kind of music.' I think he'll sign if we make it attractive enough. I don't know, Buck, maybe you should go talk to him?"

"Good idea. He's still at Paris Blues?" asked Buck.

"Yeah, but you have to hurry. He got offered a steady gig in Chicago at the 708 Club—so if you don't want to schlep all the way out there, I'd get to him soon."

Buck called Carrie and told her he'd be home late and not to wait up for him. He then had Kelsey make a reservation for him at Paris Blues. He felt a little self-conscious about driving a big Cadillac through Harlem which despite its famous night spots like the Cotton Club, Savoy Ballroom and Apollo Theater, was still an almost all Negro enclave and a depressed area.

Buck listened with great interest to Bo Diddley's set and he knew what Al was talking about: it was very new stuff. The use of the guitar as the lead instrument was certainly unlike anything he had ever heard. Even Charlie Christian with the Benny Goodman Sextet in 1939 played mostly rhythm behind Goodman's clarinet, though he got plenty of solo time himself. But this went far beyond that. Bo Diddley *was* the band with all the other instruments simply backing him up.

After his set, Buck knocked on the tiny dressing room door and when he was asked in, he introduced himself. "Weeelll," said Diddley with a distinct southern drawl, "we gots Buck Fisher here. A real pleasure, Mr. Fisher. I took to admirin' your playin' way back when. You could outblow Prez, Hawk and Ben all put together. How can I helps you, Mr. Fisher?"

"Buck. Call me Buck."

## A CHANGE OF KEY

"Awright then, Buck, what brings you up to Harlem middle of da week like this?"

"You. Al Rovitz spoke to you a few days ago about coming to work for RCA. I'm here to offer you that gig. You know, when I was listening to you play, you reminded me a lot of Louis Jordan."

Diddley laughed and said, "Truth be told, I admire Louis a lot. Ain't nothing he can't do with a saxophone and that group o' his."

Louis Jordan had been a top performer all through the 1940s. Along with Ella Fitzgerald, he was the vocalist in Chick Webb's band. But he left the band and formed his own group, the Tympany Five. It wasn't the small combo jazz of Goodman's sextet or Shaw's Gramercy Five. It was heavily rhythmic with Jordan as the only soloist. At the same time, He did all the lead vocals but the other members of the group added humor and harmonies to each number. They were incredibly popular and after the big bands died, he was the influential force in jazz.

"So you borrowed from Jordan?" asked Buck.

"Not zactly. I never sang any of his songs, but the idea that the rhythm section be just as important as all them saxes and horns, he showed it could work and I just ridin' his coattails."

"It's a very new sound, Bo, and we think it's going to be the next wave. We'd like to get you in on the ground floor."

"What dat mean, zactly?"

"I know you're with Chess Records right now," said Buck.

"Hell wit 'em, Buck. I don't owe dem shit. I made all the albums I gonna make for them. They got no hold on me anymore cause they don't do shit for me."

"Then we're prepared to sign you to a four-album deal with an option for a fifth. We'll promote you, get you radio time and our sister television network, NBC, is going to feature a number of variety show that we'd like you to appear on. We're not Chess Records, Bo. We're huge, and as vice-president of the label, I stand by any promise I make. If this rock n' roll is going

# A CHANGE OF KEY

to be as big as we think it is, we see you as one of the leaders of this new sound."

"You know, Buck, I gots a steady gig comin' up out west. I don't want to let those folks down none."

"That's fine. Look, I have some of the finest players in the business working for me who will be your back up players on piano, bass, drums and even on rhythm guitar—Buddy Scraggs. Maybe you've heard of him."

"Buddy? Who ain't heard of him? I did some stuff wid him years back. So ole' Buddy be workin' for you dese days."

"Yes, and he's terrific. So here's how it works: an album has about 12-14 songs on it. When you have sufficient material, you let us know and we'll bring you to New York. It might take a few days to lay down the tracks in the studio, but believe me, it'll be worth it."

"Das no problem, Buck. I can gets me a sub at the 708 Club if it come to that."

"Then how about you come to the RCA building Monday morning and we'll sign the contracts," said Buck. "By the way, if you think you need an attorney with you, that's fine by me."

Bo Diddley extended his hand and said, "Buck, ma handshake is ma lawyer. You do your part, I do mine and everybody happy."

"It's a deal."

Buck left Paris Blues confident that he had just added another star to the RCA Victor universe.

**A CHANGE OF KEY**

# CHAPTER TWENTY-EIGHT
## *Buck Fisher Rides Again: March 1952*

1951had been a banner year for Buck. He was pleased with all that had happened. There was great success in building the RCA label and the list of performers was growing including such stars as Dinah Shore and Perry Como and a handsome young singer named Eddie Fisher. Another young performer they signed was an eighteen-year-old singer named Eydie Gorme, who had been the girl singer with Tex Beneke's band but who now wanted to pursue a solo career.

At Bill Dwyer's suggestion, they had signed a young gospel singer named Sam Cooke who was looking to make his mark in the new genre of rock n' roll.

The label had also added such notable instrumentalists as Don Redman and Ruby Braff and a young tenor player named Sonny Rollins. For the Latin American market, Buck negotiated a contract with a timbale player/band leader named Tito Puente, who would be a perfect compliment for Perez Prado on the label.

There were also a few very notable moments, one of which was very amusing. One morning in July, Kelsey buzzed Buck and told him he had a visitor. Buck told her to show him in, and that visitor turned out to be Artie Shaw.

Buck was cordial, inviting Shaw to sit down and offering him a drink, which he declined. Buck had a clear memory of when Shaw had stopped by to hear his band play in the Palm Room of the Hotel Pennsylvania—and then tell him that his band stank. Considering the amount of money Buck had made with that very band and the number of gold records he had accrued, he was inclined to remind Shaw of the insult.

It proved to be unnecessary because Shaw said, "You know, Buck, I was wrong about you and your band back in 1940. I was full of myself back then and I was an arrogant shit. I looked down on every other band, no matter how successful they were just because they weren't my band."

## A CHANGE OF KEY

Buck sensed Shaw wanted to say more so he didn't respond to his opening remarks.

"Dorsey, Barnet, Woody Herman, Glenn Miller, I thought none of them could hold a candle to me or my group. Not even Goodman, who just loved to be called 'The King of Swing.' Truth is, they were all great. Even Glenn, who I used to make fun of—he was the smartest of us all. He knew exactly what the public wanted—and he gave it to them. His band didn't swing like the others—not even like yours—but he made a zillion bucks doing what he did best. Sad that he died serving his country when he didn't even have to go."

"I have no hard feelings, Artie," said Buck. "I got what I wanted from the business, and though I do miss playing a lot, this job keeps me plenty busy. But let me ask you, what brings you here?"

"Well, after I walked out on my band in the middle of a set that night, I was kind of *persona non grata* in the business. Nobody thought I was stable or trustworthy enough to want to bring me back. I felt like a real shit for putting so many of my guys out of work, but I just had had enough. So I kicked around Mexico for a while, heard some interesting music. When the shit hit the fan, I enlisted in the Navy and spent two years leading a band that toured every shithole in the Pacific. When I got out, I guess they figured they could trust me enough to let me lead another band—but after a year I got tired of it. I got tired of everything. Hell, I've been married six times, but I'm just not that easy to get along with."

"You know, Artie, I also played clarinet in my band—mostly Dixieland stuff. Well, back in '41, someone gave me a copy of your 'Concerto for Clarinet.' I gotta tell you, I couldn't touch it. I never played half those notes in that upper register. Then I heard you play it and I thought it was a masterpiece."

"Thanks, Buck. Early on I thought I'd be a symphonic player, but it just didn't turn out that way. Plus, they only pay peanuts. Back then I was conducting the orchestra for the "Burns and Allen Show." They were making five grand a piece a week—

and I was clearing sixty thousand a week. But it's true what they say about money not buying happiness."

"So are you looking to play again?" asked Buck.

"I'm not sure. I know I don't want to be back in front of a big band again, and besides, they're for the most part as dead as my Uncle Heshie. But a small group might be something I could like. If I put one together, what are the chances RCA would rehire me to do some recordings?"

"I wouldn't rule it out, Artie, but there could be a lot of 'ifs.'"

"Such as?"

"How committed would you actually be? You say you 'found' yourself in the Navy playing in places like Guadalcanal. Does that mean you seriously want to be a musician again?" said Buck.

Shaw laughed. "Good question, and as long as I'm bearing my soul, I have to be honest. I won't be able to answer that question until I put a group together and see what happens."

"That's fair enough. You get your group together, and let me know every step of the way how it's going. If you think you're ready, we can talk recording contracts," said Buck.

They shook hands and Artie Shaw left the office. When he was alone, Buck thought about the irony of the role reversal. When Buck started out, Shaw was already a legend in the big band world. His 1938 recording of "Begin the Beguine" catapulted him to stardom after he had kicked around for two years with his band going nowhere. Then he gave it all up—only to come to Buck to see if he could get back into it.

"Wait till I tell Carrie," he said aloud. "She'll die laughing."

.....

In early December, Buck was visited by his old friend and musical idol, Tex Beneke. He had promised to drop in for a visit the next time he was in town and there he was in the outer office waiting for Buck. The two friends embraced and Buck said,

## A CHANGE OF KEY

"Come on in Tex and make yourself at home. What brings you back to the city?" Buck asked.

The very fact that Beneke hesitated was proof enough for Buck that something was wrong. Tex was always the most affable, friendly guy he knew. As quick with a smile as he was with his fingers on his tenor sax, that smile was barely there now.

"Want to talk about it Tex?" said Buck.

"Long story, pal," said Beneke.

"For you I'll make time. Let's have it," said Buck.

"You know, Buck, when I got home from the Navy, Glenn's wife wanted me to take over his band. You know that. So I did—string section and all, just like the Army Air Force Band. But by 1949, the big band business was so bad, I had to get rid of the strings."

"OK, I get it so far. Keep going."

"Well, we did mostly Glenn's charts from the civilian band. We had Hank Mancini on board as our arranger and he's done great things—but still, it was still the Glenn Miller Orchestra. After a few years of that, I wanted to do some different things—musically, you know? But the Miller estate clamped down on me and said I was limited to do Glenn's music as long as my band had the Miller name."

"I have a feeling I know where this is going," said Buck.

"So after a while, our relationship grew so rancorous that I wanted out of the contract. I told Helen that she could find someone else to front Glenn's band. I'm afraid that wasn't very pleasant. At one point she called me a traitor to Glenn's name and we haven't spoken since. Now it's the Tex Beneke Orchestra and I figured everything would by hunky-dory. We toured a lot and believe me, Buck, the crowds loved us. We played a combination of Glenn's charts and a lot of our own pieces. I still didn't have the guys from Glenn's band, but the musicians I hired were all great players. The section work is tight and the sidemen who take solos are terrific. Everyone of them could be a star if that's what they wanted."

"But these are all positives, Tex. What's the problem?"

# A CHANGE OF KEY

"RCA said they would record and promote albums of my band and they keep waltzing me around the dance floor but not coming through with their promises. Then, to make things worse, Herb Hendler—you know him, Buck?"

"Sure, I know Herb. A & R man for Victor."

"Yeah, well he's the guy who signed Glenn to his last contract with RCA, he signed up Ralph Flanagan and his band too. When Hal McIntyre left Glenn and started his own band backed by Glenn, Flanagan was his pianist and arranger. He also did charts for Charlie Barnet and Sammy Kaye. So all of a sudden he's the big star with a big band that copies the Miller sound—and I get left out in the cold. All the promotion is about Flanagan's band, not mine."

This was all very troubling to Buck. Tex Beneke was a superstar as a player, singer and musician. He was largely responsible for the universal success of Glenn Miller's Orchestra. Now to be shunted aside by RCA Victor—in his mind it was just plain wrong.

"Want me to see what I can do, Tex?" said Buck.

"Tell ya the truth, pardner, I just came up here to spout off. I think it's gone too far. I know Victor isn't gonna all of a sudden start producing my band's records. I think it's best that I leave the label. Already been some snooping around from a rep from Decca, but I think there's an even better deal for us with Coral Records. They're not all that big, but they guarantee me that I'll be the lead act on their label and all their promotional efforts will go into my band."

"I'd really hate to lose you, Tex," said Buck.

"Well, you may lose me from the label, but you'll never lose me as a friend. So I guess it's up to the lawyers now. I'll have mine call over to the Legal Department here and I have a feeling they won't object too much if I leave."

"I'm going to ask some questions upstairs, Tex. I don't know if it will change anything, but I want you to know this door is always open to you. Whatever happens, you've got a friend right here."

## A CHANGE OF KEY

Tex shook hands with Buck and said, "See ya at the chuckwagon, pard," and then he was gone.

A final surprise for Buck had happened during Christmas week. There was a light knock on his office door and when it opened, there stood Fran Michaels. She rushed to Buck to hug and kiss him and then she sat down on his sofa beckoning him to sit next to her.

"My God, Franny, I didn't think it possible for you to look any more beautiful than you already are, but what can I say, Hollywood must agree with you because you look absolutely gorgeous!" said Buck.

"Tell me everything, Bucky. How are Carrie and the kids? How's little Laura? How's Casey?"

"Whoa, honey. Slow down! Everyone is doing fine. The kids are in school, even Casey is in kindergarten. Laura is getting around so much better, it's even shocking to her physical therapist. Eddie is already eleven and he's decided he might want to be a doctor so he can cure people like Laura. Those two are peas in a pod, totally dedicated to each other."

"I'm so happy for you, Buck, and for them!"

"Now what brings you to New York?"

"MGM finally decided I can do more than play a college kid or an ingenue, so they have me co-starring in a film with William Holden called *New York Confidential*. I play this hard-boiled reporter for a city tabloid who goes after a corrupt mayor. It's totally opposite from the other characters I have played. I don't even get to sing in this one. So we're here shooting exteriors and stock shots. The 'offices' are all done on sets in Hollywood. They want it to have a real city feel, so they sent me here."

"How's Pete?"

"He's doing well. He's back in California working and minding the house."

"Are you happy, Franny?"

"Yes, Buck, I am. I make three or four films a year, they pay me unbelievable sums of money and Louis B. Mayer treats me like this fragile China doll."

## A CHANGE OF KEY

"So they delivered on everything they said they would?" asked Buck.

"Yes. When my first contract was up, I got an agent to represent me, so I had some say about what would go into the next one. And I learned from other actresses that if you don't put exactly what you want down on paper, they'll really screw you over. Or if you don't sleep with the producer, you don't get anywhere. I put a stop to that crap instantly."

"So did you put down that you wanted all these perks and to be treated like Bette Davis—you know, flowers and chocolates in your dressing room?"

Fran laughed and said, "No, nothing like that—and my dressing room is a trailer. No, I said absolutely no nude scenes, no hot love scenes and no smoking or drinking in any film I make. I have an image to protect, you know. Besides, Pete would absolutely murder me for any of those things. But if I'm going to play this tough dame in this movie, I have to at least look like I smoke and drink. Pete said as long as it's fake, he doesn't mind."

"How long are you in town for?"

"Right after New Years I return to California."

"Have dinner with us tomorrow night. Carrie would just love to see you."

"I can't tomorrow, Buck. We're doing night shots. But how about the night after?"

"Fantastic! Where are you staying?"

"The studio put me and the crew up in the Plaza—can you believe that!"

"Great, I'll be outside the hotel at six. That be OK?"

"Sure, Buck. It's a light day of shooting so I'll have plenty of time to get ready. What can I bring?"

"Yourself. That's more than enough."

"Yes, well, we'll see about that. Now, mind if I go downstairs and say hello to the gang? You can't imagine how much I miss them."

"I'll go with you. I can't wait to see their faces when you walk in."

## A CHANGE OF KEY

Buck wasn't disappointed. Chuck Fein spotted her first and said, "Well holy shit! Who's that gorgeous creature? Looks like one of my old girlfriends."

Fran laughed and said, "You missed your chance with me, Chuckie. Now get over her and give me one of your special hugs."

Ken Ferraro, Noni Furillo, Tony Tancredi and Kip Roman all lined up to hug and kiss her. "Wow! If I knew I'd get this kind of reception, I never would have left! It's great to see all of you."

Kip Roman had just finished a run-through of his new arrangement of Jerome Kern's and Oscar Hammerstein's "The Last Time I Saw Paris." The 1940 song had become a standard recorded by everyone from Kate Smith to Ann Sothern. When the orchestra had finished, Fran said, "That was divine, Kip. I love the addition of the flutes to the strings. Mind if I try it out with you?"

"That would be something, Franny. You know the lyric?" said Kip.

"Doesn't everyone?" she laughed.

As she sang the lyric which ached for the Europe of pre-World War II, Buck realized what a gigantic talent this girl still was. She owned every song she sang and her stardom was well-deserved.

She finished the lyric and the orchestra had a *ritornello* on the last sixteen bars, ending with a hushed fermata for the entire ensemble.

"Perfect, Franny. That was just exquisite," said Buck. She came over to him and kissed him. "Thanks, Buck. It feels so good to sing with you and for you. Is this for Cindi?"

"Yes, it's for her new album," he said.

"Don't worry, then, Buck, she's just fantastic and she'll make it a huge hit."

Buck picked up Fran at the Plaza and she had three huge bags of toys for the children that she picked up at F.A.O. Schwartz on 59th Street. "Didn't have to do all that, Frannie," said Buck.

"What, show up empty-handed for my nephew and nieces? Never," said Fran. "You know that wasn't ever going to happen, Buck."

**A CHANGE OF KEY**

Like so many others, Fran Michaels was a 'courtesy aunt' who always remembered the kids' birthdays no matter where she was at the time.

By seven, Buck pulled up in front of the house and helped Fran out of the car with her packages. Carrie answered the door and screamed and then hugged Fran like a long-lost sister. "Oh, God, I hate you, Fran! You look fabulous!" said Carrie.

"You look gorgeous yourself, babe," said Fran. "Now, where are your kids?"

As if on cue, Eddie, Laura and Casey came out of their rooms for hugs and kisses—and presents from Fran. "Oh, my God, they've grown so much!" she said.

"Well, dear, you've been away for a while and kids? They have a tendency to grow when you're not looking," said Carrie.

Buck took Fran's coat and started to take his off when Carrie said, "Sorry darling, you have to run out to Bohack and pick up a few last-minute items for us. Sorry, hon, but there are things we have to have."

"Carrie, you don't have to trouble for me," said Fran.

"Oh, it's no trouble for Buck. It's right down the block," she said, adding a wink that Buck caught out of the corner of his eye. Something was up, but he didn't know what.

Buck returned a half hour later and everyone came to the dinner table. Carrie had prepared an incredible meal of roast beef, baked potatoes, candied carrots and a salad. During dinner, Carrie couldn't help but notice that Eddie's eyes never once left Fran. She motioned for Buck to take a look and he saw his son's eyes riveted on the spectacular Fran Michaels. Kid hasn't even reached puberty yet and already he's got an eye for the ladies, thought Buck. But Eddie was no different than every other male of the species who couldn't help but gape at her.

As Carrie brought dessert to the table, Fran said, "So, Buck, I caught the show you did with Bob Hope. It was really fantastic."

"Yeah, we had lots of fun in Hawaii. I only wish Carrie and the kids could have been with me. It's a beautiful place."

# A CHANGE OF KEY

There was a pregnant pause when there was absolute silence at the table. Fran filled it by saying, "I'm going to cut to the chase here, Buck. You're missing out."

Buck was about to put a piece of cake in his mouth when he stopped and placed it back on his plate. "OK, Franny, you're going to have to explain that one."

"Buck, I saw every minute of that show. I watched the joy on your face as you played. It brought back so many memories—memories of what a fantastic player you were. Memories of how happy I was as part of your band. Why on Earth did you stop playing?"

"Well, the accident and all, and the new job keeping me busy and the family," said Buck, and even to his ears it sounded lame.

"Nonsense. Like they say on the set of cowboy movies, 'that dog won't hunt.' Carrie and I were talking it over and—"

"Aha! So *that's* why I had to run out for a few last-minute items. You two were conspiring against me."

"*For* you, darling," said Carrie. "We both decided that you need to get back into playing—a lot. Not just once a year to entertain the troops."

"Come on, guys, big bands are dead," said Buck.

"Maybe, maybe not—but small groups are the thing of the future. Remember the fun you had playing with the Ice House Six?"

That was true. The Ice House Six had been Johnny Blair's idea. A small combo within the big band to play Dixieland music in case the audiences were on the 'oldish' side. "That was Dixieland stuff and yeah, it was fun playing it, but that's all as dead as big bands now.

"Not the point, Buck. If combos are the in thing now, start one—with you as the featured player. Don't tell me RCA wouldn't want to record what you do. You know they'd jump at the chance."

"She's right, honey," said Carrie. "You deserve to be back in the spotlight."

## A CHANGE OF KEY

Buck laughed and said, "Look at this: I'm being ganged up on by two beautiful women. That's pretty amazing, no?"

"Bucky, when was the last time I asked you for anything," said Carrie.

"An hour ago, when you sneakily sent me out to Bohack so you could hatch this plot," said Buck.

"I'm serious," said Carrie.

"Darling, when have I ever refused you anything?"

Carrie pulled a face and then said, "All right, all right, never. Then you'll do this—for me?"

Buck sighed and said, "I'll talk to Jack Merrill and see what he says. If he thinks it's worth a shot, I'll see what I can put together. But if he says it's a no-go, then that's it. Kaput. Fair enough?"

Carrie clapped her hands and said, "Fantastic!"

Buck looked at Fran and said, "And miss, how come you're grinning like the Cheshire cat?"

She got up from the table and came to Buck to hug and kiss him. "This is going to be great! And if you ever need a girl singer for the group, look me up."

"Not so fast, Franny, It's all up to Jack."

What Buck was unaware of was that Carrie had called Jack Merrill weeks ago suggesting that Buck get back into playing. "Honey, I'd love to see that happen, but it's up to him. He's got to be ready," said Jack.

The meal came to an end and Carrie had to get the kids ready for bed. Buck drove Fran back to the plaza and in the car, she commented on everything from the great dinner to how well Laura was walking. In front of the hotel, she said, "I can't tell you how wonderful tonight was, Buck. I miss you, I miss Carrie, the guys, the city. Everything. Sure I have a different life out there in Hollywood and it's got its benefits. But I want you to know that I will never, ever forget that it was Buck Fisher who gave me my first break—and that I love him very much for that."

She kissed Buck, hugged him, and as she got out of the car, she said, "Make that damned album already!"

## A CHANGE OF KEY

When Buck got home after eleven, Carrie was still cleaning up from dinner. She saw Buck and said, "Darling, don't be mad at me."

"Why would I be mad at you, Carrie?"

"You know, the whole playing thing. I only want you to do what you want. But—"

"Kinda knew there was a 'but' coming," said Buck.

"But I think it will be good for you. All that talent. Why waste it?"

"Sweetheart, I had my shot. Long time ago."

"Take another shot, darling. You're Buck Fisher. And don't you ever forget that."

"Come here," said Buck. He wrapped Carrie in his arms, kissed her on the lips and said, "Words can't begin to tell you how much I love you, Carrie."

"Actions speak louder than words, Mr. Feinstein," said Carrie. And she took him by the hand and led him to the bedroom where actions definitely spoke louder than words.

.....

The next morning, Buck went to Jack Merrill's office to broach the topic of forming a combo and recording some songs.

"Buck! What's the good word?"

"Well Jack, I need you to think back a long time ago when I first got out of the Army. You said my career as a player was over, but that in time, maybe I could get back into it. Well, I'm ready."

Jack laughed and said, "What the hell took you so damned long, Buck?"

"I don't know, Jack. I guess the timing had to be right. For me, at least."

"So how do you figure this plays out?" asked Jack.

"I'm thinking about a quintet. Sax, piano, drums, guitar and bass. I want to use the guys I've worked with in the studio orchestra and in my civilian band."

"Give me names, Buck," said Jack.

## A CHANGE OF KEY

"Kenny Ferraro on piano, Chuck Fein on bass, Tony Tancredi on drums and Buddy Scraggs on guitar."

"They're all top players, Buck. Now tell me about the music. Are you planning on just rehashing your big band songs for a small combo?"

"No, not at all, not at all. There's a lot of new songs out there and I've been practicing some of these new styles."

"That bebop shit?"

"Not exactly, but I've been borrowing some of their melodic devices but not their harmonies. I still solo close to the melody, unlike these bebop guys who go off on these rides that last for ten minutes and you have no idea what you're listening to. That's not my style."

Jack tented his fingers and thought for a few moments. Then he said, "All right, Buck. We'll give it a go. Put your group together, rehearse it until it's tight, and then I'll give it a listen before we record anything. If it's good, we'll do an album and promote it big time. Any suggestions for an album title?"

"As a matter of fact, Cindi Kay suggested one."

"Oh? And what's it called?"

"Buck Fisher Rides Again."

Jack Merrill roared with laughter. "I love it! It's perfect. 'Buck Fisher Rides Again.' Imagine that!"

## CHAPTER TWENTY-NINE
### *Starting from Scratch: April 1952*

Two days after Jack Merrill gave Buck the nod to go ahead, he went to the rehearsal studio and asked Kip Roman if he could talk to the orchestra for a few minutes.

"It's your orchestra, Buck, so go right ahead."

"Here's the deal, fellas, I need to speak to Kenny, Chuck, Tony, and Buddy. Join me next door for a few minutes. Kip? Can you give the orchestra ten or fifteen?"

"Sure Buck, no problem. Take fifteen, fellas."

In the lounge next door, Buck laid out plans for the Buck Fisher Quintet. What they would be doing, and the possibility for recording an album. "If we get that far, you guys will be getting royalties on top of your orchestra salaries. It'll be a separate contract with the label. But naturally the royalties depend on sales. If we're good, if we're special, we could make a lot of money."

"So how's this gonna work, Buck," asked Chuck.

"First of all, forget the name Buck Fisher Quintet. You guys are all superb musicians and I don't want you to think that our cuts are going to be me playing endless solos with you guys in the background. As a rhythm section, that's inevitable, but I want each of you to have a chance to solo too. Even you on bass, Chuck."

"Hell, I'll be another Slam Stewart," said Chuck.

"Yeah, but without the bow and the humming," said Buck, alluding to Stewart's distinctive musical style.

"And me, Mr. Buck?" said Buddy Scraggs.

"I've got something very special planned for you, Buddy. You know, way back in the late '30s, Charlie Christian was playing with Goodman and they put a microphone in front of him along with a small amplifier. He turned out some incredible solo rides. So then Les Paul comes out with that solid body Fender Broadcaster and everything sounds different. The guitar really becomes a solo instrument now. We're going to get one of those Broadcasters for you and I want you to get comfortable with it.

**A CHANGE OF KEY**

When you take your solos, it's going to have a really modern sound which is what we're looking for."

"Dat fine with me, Mr. Buck. I be wantin' to try out one of them electrified guitars for a while now," said Buddy. "Acoustic guitar just doan carry at all."

"I want to start Friday, fellas. I'm going to ask Kip to write some charts, but mostly, it's improvisational. You'll have the chords written out but that's about all. The songs will be standards, but we're going to give them a new wrinkle. Anybody have any questions?"

When no one had any, Buck said, "OK, ten o'clock on Friday."

Back in the rehearsal studio, Buck called Kip aside and explained what was going on. "So I need some combo charts for Friday, Kip. Just a melody line on a lead sheet for piano and one for me. Just chords for bass and guitar.

"I can do that, Buck, but what songs did you have in mind?"

"Ever here the Nat King Cole Trio doing 'Route 66?' I want to do that with the quintet. Write it out in concert Bb. Then, you know the chart you wrote for 'My Foolish Heart?' for Cindi? I want that one in F Major. That one's going to be nice and bluesy. Finally, for a first rehearsal, write one for 'A Cottage for Sale.' Concert C is good for that."

"That's two slow and one fast, Buck. Maybe you need another up-tempo song?"

"Any ideas?"

"I have one, but I'm not sure you're going to like it," said Kip.

"I'm listening."

"There's this pianist, his name's Thelonius Monk. Strictly bebop, but he has a song that I swear would be fantastic for you. It's called 'Straight No Chaser.' Rhythmically it's pretty complex, and it's going to be a real challenge for you on the solo ride, but if you're looking to move past the standard swing stuff, this is perfect."

## A CHANGE OF KEY

"I don't know the song, Kip, but if you write out the melody line, we can give it a try. Throw me a break and keep it in concert Bb. We can move it up or down depending upon how we do. I tell you what, Kip. Give the orchestra the day off on Friday so you can be at the rehearsal session. I want your input all the way."

Buck spent the next two days fretting about what would happen at Friday's rehearsal. Carrie reassured him each day saying, "It's just a rehearsal, darling; it's going to be fine—you'll see."

When Buck got to the studio on Friday morning, the other four members of the group were already there warming up with Kenny Ferraro noodling the difficult melody line of "Straight No Chaser."

Kip Roman, in his job as Music Director, explained the chart of "Route 66" to the band. "Just like the Nat King Cole recording, Kenny, you're going to take sixteen bars to set up the melody. Then Buck, you've got a chorus with the bridge, then back to the melody, then you've got your improv ride. It's about sixty-four bars."

Kip nodded to Kenny and the song began. When Buck came in with the melody line, his big tenor sound was as good as it ever was. After his ride, he returned to the melody, then to the coda and took the song out.

"That sounded pretty damned good," said Tony Tancredi.

"It was OK, but I want to try something different with it," said Buck. "After I take my solo, I want to trade fours with Buddy. I'll take the first four, and Buddy, you answer it. We'll do that four times, then return to melody and the coda."

"Das OK by me, Mr. Buck. I'm wid ya," said Buddy Scraggs.

The second run-through was much better. The trading fours reminded Buck of the 'sax battles' between Tex Beneke and Al Klink in some of Glenn Miller's swing charts. But the electric guitar gave the song the more modern sound that Buck was looking for.

## A CHANGE OF KEY

"How about we give it one more shot," said Buck.

Again Kip nodded to Kenny to kick off the song and the third run-through was a even better than the second. Chuck Fein's bass and Tony Tancredi's drums were absolutely solid behind Buck and Buddy, and Ken Ferraro's ad lib fills fit perfectly behind the melody.

Next up was "My Foolish Heart." Instead of a piano intro, Buck led off with a slow, rubato exposition of the melody. After the first two notes of the song, Kenny and Chuck provided a fill and then using an intuition common to all great players, they provided a rich textural background to Buck's solo. After Buck played the melody, Kenny did an improv chorus with it that was part blues, part bebop—and one hundred percent perfect.

"Shit, that was something," said Chuck.

As with "Route 66," they ran the song twice more, each time tightening it and getting more emotion into it, now that the players knew the chart better. Tony used his brushes on both the snare and the ride cymbal. That pianissimo percussion effect was subtle, but tonally, it added yet another dimension to the number.

"You guys want to take ten or keep going?" asked Buck.

"Hell, yeah, we should keep going," said Tony. This is a lot of fun."

"How about we do 'A Cottage for Sale?" said Buck.

Kip Roman said, "Buck, this is going to sound very unusual, but I really think you should do that song on alto. I just hear it in my head that way. I'd like to try it. It's in three sharps for the alto, but that shouldn't be a problem for you."

Buck went to his sax case and found an old Otto Link mouthpiece that he hadn't used in over a decade. He couldn't remember why he even had it, since he never owned an alto sax.

"Let me see if Danny DeMaestri left his horn here. He won't mind if I borrow it," said Buck.

He found DeMaestri's alto, a vintage Conn horn that had obviously been well-taken-care of. The action of the keys was smooth and fast. He wasn't certain about playing alto, but he trusted in Kip Roman's musical judgement and so agreed to try it.

## A CHANGE OF KEY

After Kenny's intro, Buck came in with the melody in the middle of the alto's range. In that register, it had an almost weeping sound that Buck milked to match the tone to the emotions of the song—a song about a failed marriage and a lonely, deserted home.

At the conclusion of the song, Chuck said, "Damn I wish Franny or Little Sis were here to do a vocal on that song. Kind of gave me the chills the way you played it, Buck. Gotta put that one on any album we do."

The second run-through was even better because Buck was more comfortable with the alto and he had adjusted his embouchure for the smaller mouthpiece.

"I say leave that one alone, Buck," said Kip. "I can't see it getting better than that. But you're going to need some chops for 'Straight No Chaser.'"

Since he was unfamiliar with the melody, Kip had written it out. It was in two sharps for the tenor and Buck could see it was heavily syncopated. Though it was in 4/4 time, the accents seemed to occur well off the downbeat. The first time he tried it, he lost it completely.

"Whoa! I sure screwed that up," he said.

"It's OK, Buck," said Kip. "Take it under tempo until you get the feel of that melody. In fact, how about you take some time and practice it on your own and I'll take the other guys through their parts."

"Good idea. I'm going to go next door and work on it for a bit." Buck took it extra slow at first until he assimilated the melody pattern. But he thought to himself, 'what the hell am I going to do with a solo on this thing?' After a half hour, Buck had the notes in his fingers and rejoined the band.

Before he started, he said, "Buddy, after I do the melody, I want you to take thirty-six bars of solo so I can get some idea of how it fits over that syncopation."

"Check, Mr. Buck. I got me some ideas," said Buddy.

Kenny had eight bars of intro before Buck came in with the melody. He decided to change up the sound by playing in a subtone rather than a clean attack. He just felt it would sound more modern, though he didn't know why.

Buddy Scraggs nailed the solo and as he had hoped, he gave Buck some notion of what a solo in the bebop piece would sound like. They played it again and this time, Buck found his comfort zone with the solo, utilizing the rising triplet figures that he heard both Charlie Parker and Sandy Adams use frequently in their rides.

When he finished, he said, "Eh. I can do better than that. Let's run it again."

"Look, Buck, if you're going to master this style, you've got to get away from the idea of eight to the bar. Bebop musicians like Parker—those complex runs they do that seem to go on forever—they're sixteenth and thirty-second notes. That's what is part of the uniqueness of that style. You're going to have to take a risk and try your solos that way," said Kip.

The switch from swing to quasi-bebop was, as Kip Roman had suggested, a big challenge for Buck, but as a polished and skilled musician, he quickly started building his melodic vocabulary to go with the style. On the third run-through, he said, "OK, Buddy, you take thirty-six, then Kenny, you take your thirty-six, then I'll bring back the melody and we'll take it out. Got it?"

"That one was pretty good," said Buck at the song's end. "OK, guys, let's call it a day and start again next Wednesday. Kip, let's talk."

"What do you think?" Buck asked.

"I think you're still the greatest tenor player I've ever heard. Even the Monk tune worked out OK in the end. But I think another problem we have is finding more material for the combo. If you don't mind, I'd like to try my hand at some originals in a modern style as well as some standards I think will work for you."

"Fair enough. Do what you can for the next rehearsal and I also want to run all these songs again."

"It's a deal. See you next week, boss."

At home that night, Carrie demanded every detail of the rehearsal. "Was it terrible, Bucky?" she said, hugging him.

## A CHANGE OF KEY

"No, darling. In fact, I thought it went pretty well. Kip thought it was even better than that. We're going to get together again next week and see what we can add."

Carrie's face was beaming with pride. "Oh darling, I told you that you could do this. One day I want to come to a rehearsal to hear you."

"Whoa! We're not quite at that point yet, sweetheart. I know I'm playing with great guys and all, but adapting my playing to this new style is going to take some time—and lots of practice. So how 'bout I let you know when we're ready for the public to hear us?"

"Whatever you say. Now come and eat. I'm starving and I hope you like tuna casserole," said Carrie.

After dinner, Rachel paid a visit bringing a freshly baked *babka* which was the kids' favorite cake. "Mama, if you keep bringing me all this cake I'm gonna get as big as a horse—and then your son will leave me."

"*Mamala,* you look the same as you looked twelve years ago—and that's after three children. So *essen* and be happy. Now, where are my grandchildren?"

"Kids! Nana's here. Come out and say hello."

Casey came tumbling out of her room and ran to Rachel to be enveloped in her arms. "Look how frisky you are, little one!" Next Eddie came to Rachel and kissed her saying, "Hiya Nana. How are you?"

For a moment, Rachel was caught off-balance. She looked at Carrie, a question on her face. Carrie laughed and said, "Yes, Mama, his voice is changing."

"What? When did this happen?"

Buck overheard the exchange and he piped in, "Ma, Eddie's *bar mitzvah* is next year. He's going to be thirteen. These things happen, you know."

Rachel just shook her head and said, "Where's my sweetheart?"

Laura, assisted by her cane, came to Rachel for the obligatory hug and kiss. "Oy! I could eat you right up!" she said.

## A CHANGE OF KEY

Then to Buck she said, "My son, this child is going to be very dangerous when she grows up. So beautiful!"

"Don't worry, Nana," said Eddie, "I'm her big brother, I'll take care of her."

Buck watched the scene with pride. The bond between his two older children was as strong as it had ever been—and both of them took it upon themselves to watch over Casey, who was the darling of the family.

Rachel stayed for a while and Buck asked her, "Ma? With Arlene and Bevvy both out of the house now, are you sure you're OK living alone?"

"So who's alone? Every day the girls call me. Sometimes twice a day. And Arlene is so close, she comes by a lot and takes me grocery shopping once a week. And then there's this luscious girl over here," she said, motioning toward Carrie. "Believe me, I don't ever feel alone.

"Don't worry, Pop, sometimes I run to Bohack for Nana too," said Eddie.

"And don't forget, he also mows my lawn," said Rachel. "He's such a good boy, Benjamin."

"Ma, I can get a gardener to do that. Eddie doesn't even mow our lawn." Said Buck.

"What, I should pay a gardener when I pay my grandson for the same thing? *Du bist meshuga* Benjamin."

"Don't argue with your mother, Buck. You can't win," said Carrie.

"Yeah, I can't win an argument with you either. Huh. Women. They control my life."

Carrie hugged Buck and said, "Swear you don't love it."

Buck sighed and said, "Of course I love it, but I can't admit it. I just wouldn't be the he-man I am if I owned up to that."

Carrie looked at her wristwatch and said, "In about an hour or so, we're going to see just what kind of a he-man you are, Mr. Feinstein." She winked at Rachel who nodded knowingly, put her coat on and bade everyone a good night.

…..

## A CHANGE OF KEY

The following Wednesday, the Buck Fisher Quintet met again for its second rehearsal. Buck had picked up a second-hand Buescher alto on 48$^{th}$ Street in Manhattan so he wouldn't have to borrow Danny DeMaestri's. Buck had to replace a few pads and adjust the action a little to make it quicker, but the overall sound of the instrument was high quality. And for sixty bucks, it was a real steal. He thought he would need it for just the one song the group had already rehearsed—but he was wrong.

"What do you have for us, Kip?" asked Buck as he set up his tenor.

"I have three charts, Buck. I have an original I wrote called 'Tempo de Bop,' and two standards—'Four Brothers' and 'Harlem Nocturne' and I think that works much better on alto than tenor."

"OK, what's up first?"

"Let's try 'Four Brothers.'" said Kip.

The song dated from 1947 when Jimmy Giuffre wrote it for Woody Herman's second band. That version featured incredibly intricate section work for Herman's reed players: Zoot Sims, Serge Chaloff, Herbie Steward and Stan Getz. The song was a big hit for that band, with each of the 'four brothers' taking eight bar solos in bebop style—three tenors and Chaloff on baritone in the upper register.

"Now," said Kip, "you're going to play all the parts which amounts to thirty-two bars of solo, then Kenny has the bridge melody and then you come in to take it out. I've written out those two bar coda passages that Herman's reeds played but the chords are there so you can ad lib it if you'd like. Remember, there's no intro to the song so you just come in after a four count and the rest of the combo will follow."

"OK, here we go," said Buck. He began to play the intricate melodic pattern which Kip had written in the key of D. That meant Buck was in E Major with its four sharps. The first time through, Buck had to stop the band because he missed several of the accidentals in the melody.

"Sorry, fellas, that one's on me. Let's try it again."

## A CHANGE OF KEY

The second time he nailed the melody—but he felt uncomfortable with the improv passages, so he stopped the band again.

"Take your time, Buck," said Kenny Ferraro. "This piece is a hot bitch—but you'll get it."

"Sure about that, Kenny?" said Buck laughing.

"Absolutely. Here we go again," said Kenny.

On the fourth run-through, Buck had it down. He was using a sub-tone more in line with the sound of Woody Herman's sax players and his solo after the exposition showed that he had adapted to the new bebop style of playing, if not completely, then mostly.

"Helluva job, Bucky," said Chuck "I like that you aren't using any vibrato. Sounds like Prez himself." Lester Young tended to avoid putting vibrato on anything.

"These notes move so fast, Chuck, there's hardly enough time to put a vibrato on any of them."

"OK, switch to alto Buck and let's run 'Harlem Nocturne,'" said Kip.

The song had been kicking around since 1939 when Earle Hagen had written it for the Ray Noble Orchestra. It had a pulsing rhythm behind the alto solo which had a haunting, blues quality to it. Kip was right about it being better on alto. The throaty quality of the horn evoked images of darkened Harlem streets, lonely people wandering home in the early hours of the morning and the glow of dim streetlamps in the fog. A single take was enough for Kip to say, "That's perfect, Buck. I can't imagine you doing it any better. Let's move on to the third chart."

"Tempo de Bop" was a simple eight-bar blues melody played *vivace* which made the solo section a real chore for someone still mastering the new style. First Buck had to get the melody itself into his fingers. Buck was playing in D so its two sharps weren't a problem. But Kip had created something with great rhythmic complexity beneath the melody. It had an almost herky-jerky feel to it. It was almost poly-rhythmic with Buck playing in four, but the rhythm playing in five underneath him.

## A CHANGE OF KEY

At the conclusion of the song, Tony Tancredi said, "Jesus, that was a real workout. Did we get it, Kip?"

"Not quite, Tony. Let's run it again."

Unlike the other numbers, "Tempo de Bop" took a good five run-throughs before the band really felt in sync with each other. But Buck had to admit, it was a terrific piece of music.

At the end of the session, Buck said, "Well, we've got seven charts, but we're still shy seven or eight tunes if we're going to turn this into an LP."

"I'm toying with a few ideas for originals, Buck, but I'd also like to know what songs you think you could adapt to move us away from a total swing sound," said Kip.

"I was thinking about a tenor version of "I Got it Bad and that Ain't Good." I loved how Johnny Hodges handled it on alto with the Duke. Maybe I could bring something new to it," said Buck.

"All right, that's one. But we need some up-tempo stuff to build those bebop chops," said Kip.

"What about "I Got Rhythm" in a scorching tempo," said Buck. "I heard Charlie Parker do it that way. I don't have his vocabulary, but I might be able to work with it," said Buck.

"Yeah, and it certainly doesn't have all that many chord changes," said Kip. "We'll work it out next time we rehearse."

"That will have to be in week or so. You have to work with the orchestra and Cindi for her next LP. And we'll have the Quinns for the backups.

"All right. Then let's make it a week from now and we'll see what else I can come up with."

**A CHANGE OF KEY**

# CHAPTER THIRTY
*"Miracles Do Happen" December 1952*

All through the summer and autumn of 1952, the Buck Fisher Quintet rehearsed, added songs to their repertoire and by early December, Buck felt confident enough to ask Jack Merrill to give the group a listen to see if it was worth it to release an LP.

Though none of the members showed it, they all were apprehensive. After all, they had rehearsed for months and they didn't want it to all be for naught, even though they had enjoyed every minute of playing together.

Jack came down to the studio at one o'clock on Wednesday, December 3rd. "I've cleared about two hours for you Buck, so show me what you have—the whole thing. I'm going to give it an honest listen and then I'll tell you what I think."

"Great, Jack. We'll play every number we've worked on," said Buck.

"There's one thing I want you to know, Buck. I know it's going to be good. I would expect nothing else from this talented bunch of guys. But whether or not it's good enough remains to be seen. If I don't think it's worth the money to promote it, it dies right here. But if I think it has possibilities, we'll back it a hundred percent—and I'm going to want to get you out in front of some live audiences too."

"You've always been honest with me, Jack, so I'd expect nothing less," said Buck.

"It's not just about honesty. And it certainly isn't all about money, though that's a consideration. It's about you, Buck. I will never release any single or album with your name on it if it in some way damages your musical reputation. You're one of if not the greatest player of all time on tenor sax. If critics are going to call you a washed-up has-been, I'll never let them do that to you. You mean too much to me personally to have them drag you through the mud."

"Fair enough. Grab a chair, Jack and we'll get started."

"Good. Don't let me shake you, Buck, but I'm going to

sit here and take some notes while you're playing."

For the next two hours, Jack Merrill heard everything the quintet had to offer. Kip Roman counted off each song or simply nodded to the group and they instinctively knew how to begin. Jack Merrill sat stone-faced during the entire performance, but so intent upon the music was the quintet, that they scarcely realized that he was even there.

After they concluded the performance with "Tempo de Bop," Buck said, "Well, that's it, Jack. That's what we have."

Jack finally smiled and said, "I wouldn't have believed it possible, Buck, but you just made my head spin. Anyone ever tells you that you've lost a step in your playing, they'll have to answer to me. This was absolutely fantastic. Guys? You've done a helluva job with this man. Now, by next week, I want you to start getting things down on masters. I'm going to assign Tommy Taylor to produce and Whip Elliot to engineer the sessions."

"Now you're talking my language!" said Chuck Fein.

"I want these LPs in record stores by the second week of January, so you have a lot of work to do. Say, what was that name you suggested for the album?"

"Oh, that was Cindi Kay's suggestion: Buck Fisher Rides Again."

"That's it. I love it. OK fellas, I'm back to work. Great work. Truly great work. We're going to make a fortune from this."

.....

Since it was Buck's birthday weekend, Carrie had some special things planned for the family. Friday night Rachel agreed to watch the children so that Carrie could treat Buck to dinner and a movie. *New York Confidential* starring William Holden and Fran Michaels was playing at the Century Meadows theatre. Located on Horace Harding Boulevard, the movie house, which opened its doors in 1949, sat just under 2200 people and showed the same first run movies that the big Manhattan theaters were showing.

Carrie wanted popcorn and a Coca Cola, which Buck bought for her, but he said, "Just small ones, hon. Don't spoil your appetite."

## A CHANGE OF KEY

Carrie faked pouting, but then leaned over and kissed Buck on the cheek. "Always taking care of me, Feinstein. I guess I'll keep you."

Before the feature, there was a newsreel narrated by Lowell Thomas, a travelogue about Tahiti, a Daffy Duck cartoon and then coming attractions. By 7:15, the film began. *New York Confidential* was a very dark story. The mob had its hooks into the Mayor of New York City who muscled the City Council to pass all kinds of ordinances beneficial to mob properties. It also got the Mayor to get the Police Commissioner to have the department close its eyes to protection and gambling rackets and wink at its being suppliers of heroin for a population that was becoming increasingly reliant on hard drugs.

Fran played a reporter who uncovers the scandal and with a crusading editor played by Holden, they bring the Mayor's administration crashing down—but not without personal danger to both Holden's and Fran's characters.

It wasn't exactly *film noir* but shot in black and white, the film captured the seamy side of the city and the arcane and nefarious forces that controlled it.

When the film ended, the audience applauded—something Buck always found curious since no one on screen could hear it. But it was their way of showing how much they enjoyed the film—so Buck and Carrie clapped along with everyone else.

"Jesus, Bucky, she was fabulous!" said Carrie on the drive to Peter Luger's Steak House on Broadway in Brooklyn.

"I know. She said she would be acting against type, but who knew she could be so, well, so hard, so callous. I kept looking for my sweet, angelic Franny but I couldn't find a trace of her," said Buck.

"That just means her acting was great, darling. She completely became that character and she was absolutely believable in that role. I hope she does more like it," said Carrie.

"Yeah. I just hope Pete didn't flip out over those kissing scenes with Holden. They were pretty steamy," said Buck.

## A CHANGE OF KEY

"I'm sure Pete is super proud of what Franny did up there, and as for the kissing, you can bet that he knows it's all just an act," said Carrie.

Over a dinner of *chateaubriand,* Carrie talked about her plans for Buck's birthday party the next day. She had invited Bill and his family, Arlene and Al, Bevvy and Jerry, Rachel, Chuck Fein and Rebeca, Mila and the girls and of course, Eunice, who promised to bring some special Cajun dishes for the party. Cindi Kay would also be there, but she would have to leave early enough to make the ten o'clock show at Tony's club.

"Carrie, you're really going to a lot of trouble for this party. It's not that big a deal."

"What, my husband's thirty-eighth birthday isn't a big deal? Since when?"

"It just makes me feel like I'm getting old."

"To begin with, Feinstein, you're not getting old. Secondly, if you consider all the things you have done in life, all that you've accomplished in a short thirty-eight years, well, who wouldn't be impressed by that—or you?"

"So what time is this shindig tomorrow night?" asked Buck.

"Everyone should be there by six thirty. I want it to be early in case all the kids get tired and have to go to sleep. I ordered a really nice cake for you, hon, but can you pick it up at about a quarter to six? It's at Marguerite's. They say they can't have it ready until then."

"Sheesh, what is it, a wedding cake or something?"

"Nah, but it's the season. They are always busy this time of year."

"All right. No problem. I'll get the cake. They better spell my name right, is all I'm saying."

They finished the meal and Buck paid the exorbitant twelve dollars, but he had to admit the steak was perfect and having some private time with Carrie made it even better.

.....

## A CHANGE OF KEY

Birthday parties for him usually made Buck feel very silly. It was the kind of thing he thought was for little kids only. But the next night, he dutifully went for the birthday cake and when he returned home, he had to park down the block from the house because every available spot on 187$^{th}$ Street and 48$^{th}$ Avenue was taken.

'Dang,' thought Buck, 'shoulda bought a house with a damned driveway.'

Everyone had already arrived when Buck returned home which explained why so many cars were on the block. Buck greeted everyone warmly, and Eunice relieved him of the cake which she brought to the kitchen. Even though Buck saw some of his friends every day, there was a different feeling in seeing them in a social situation where the talk was not of record sales or recording sessions.

There was a stack of presents in the corner which Buck appreciated, but thought was completely unnecessary. The music business had been very good to him and he and Carrie had more money than they could spend in two lifetimes. But he also understood that friends and family wanted to show their appreciation for all Buck had done for them through the years.

Puzzled, Buck looked around and said, "Umm, Carrie? Where are the kids?"

She looked around the living room in apparent surprise. "Oh wait. I'll call them. Eddie? Almost time to eat."

Eddie Feinstein had grown like a weed these last two years and was now as tall as Buck. "Hey, Pop! Happy Birthday!" he said.

Then she called, "Casey? Come on in darling," and little Casey, all energy, all boundless enthusiasm came running to Buck for a hug and kiss.

"Is Laura asleep, Carrie?" asked Buck.

"Oh, no, not at all. She has a special birthday present she's been working on for you. Hang on and I'll call her. Laura honey? Daddy's home."

## A CHANGE OF KEY

And then, to everyone's astonishment, Laura came out of her bedroom and walked to Buck—without a brace and without a cane. There was a noticeable limp, but not overly pronounced. Everyone watched in stunned silence as Laura hugged Buck and said, "Happy Birthday, Daddy."

Buck hugged her tightly to his chest and his tears flowed unchecked down his cheeks. His daughter, victimized by polio given little chance to even survive, was now able to walk on her own. There could be no better birthday present than this. He could barely speak, so overwhelmed was he.

Aunts, uncles, friends all came to congratulate Laura on her amazing achievement. Jerry Rosen, Bevvy's husband who had been Laura's neurologist from the initial diagnosis of polio said, "All I can say, Buck, is sometimes miracles happen. I've dealt with so many cases of polio I've lost count. But I can't ever remember a patient doing so well in such a short period of time. It couldn't have happened without so much hard work on Laura's part."

"And don't forget Warren O'Brien," said Carrie. He's been with her every step of the way. He's part of the miracle."

"I wanted to surprise Daddy on his birthday, Uncle Jerry," said Laura.

"Well, honey, I'd say right now your old man is the most surprised man on the planet. We're all proud of you," said Jerry.

The rest of the night overflowed with joy not just for Buck's birthday, but for the happiness that everyone felt for him and his beautiful daughter. In time, they hoped, her limp would become less pronounced. The girl was so beautiful that any young man down the road would gladly overlook something as inconsequential as a limp to be so close to such a wonderful girl.

Eunice stayed to help clean up and as she did the dishes alongside Carrie she said, "Mmmm, mmm, quite a party Ladybird. And dat chile? Mmmm, mmm. I never seen Mr. Buck so emotional. But havin' my own kids, I understands how he feels. Sometimes I feels like she be one of my own. You know, dat Ima part of the family."

## A CHANGE OF KEY

Carrie paused in mid-dish and said, "Eunice, I love you dearly, but that's about the dumbest thing I ever heard! I mean seriously. You *are* part of this family—and don't you forget it. You're more a mother to me than my own mother ever was, and frankly, I don't know what I'd do without you."

"You a sweetheart, Ladybird. You always gonna have ole' Eunice to count on."

"Thank you. Now, I'll finish up here. Go home, rest, and remember how much all of us love you."

.....

Back in the studio Monday morning, Buck said to Kip Roman, "I have an idea. I heard a recording of Charlie Ventura with the Gene Krupa combo playing a tune called 'Dark Eyes.' He used a subtone throughout and it was a very distinctive sound. I think we can do something with that song, but in a more bebop style. Can you write out the piano line for Kenny and the chords for Buddy and Chuck and we'll see how it sounds?"

"I know that song, Buck. The chords are easy. It's got kind of an Eastern European sound. I don't know, I think maybe it was based on a gypsy song. Give me twenty minutes and I'll get something down on paper. Oh, and Buck, when you have a minute, can we talk?"

"Sure, Kip. Whenever you'd like." But it had been Buck's experience that whenever one of his players 'wanted to talk,' it was never good news. Maybe he just wanted to talk about a raise or something like that.

It took a half hour instead of twenty minutes, but Kip had the chart for "Dark Eyes' written out. The band ran it, but two minutes into it, Buck stopped it and said, "No good. I want this to be really up-tempo. Let's do it again."

The second time around Kenny Ferraro's intro was *presto* rather than *vivace*. The melody raced by in thirty-two bars and then Buck was off on his ride, a solo loaded with blazing thirty-second note runs featuring every bebop melodic trick that he had learned. Then he nodded at Buddy Scraggs whose fingers flew over another thirty-two bars of solo. Even Chuck Fein who had been playing double-time rather than a walking bass line, got to have a solo with the other rhythm instruments backing him.

When the song was over, Chuck said, "You trying to kill me, Buck?"

"You're too nasty to kill, Chuck, but you did a fantastic job on that solo. Kip? What do you think?"

"I think you'd be crazy to leave it off the album. We have to pick the fourteen songs we're going to lay down and then get them recorded."

"Good idea. Let's set it up now. And Kip? You wanted to talk to me?"

No time like the present for bad news, thought Buck. He hoped that it wasn't about Kip leaving the label. He had been so important right from the beginning, Buck didn't even want to think about replacing him. His arrangements were as much the stars as were the singers they backed up.

He brought Kip into the studio's office and said, "OK, Kip, what gives?"

"Well, I'm not sure how to say this, Buck, but—"

"Then just say it," said Buck.

"Well, I wonder if I could have a week off for the last week in January."

"Jesus Christ! Is that all? I thought you were going to tell me you were quitting," said Buck.

"And give up this job? This is my dream, Buck. No, it's not that at all," said Kip.

"OK, I'm all ears. So why the week off?"

"Pammy and I are getting married and we'd like to go someplace warm for our honeymoon. Maybe Mexico or Aruba or some place like that."

Buck just stared at Kip before saying, "Pammy Wendorfer? As in our copyist and sometime flautist? When did all this happen?"

That made Kip laugh. "We've been dating for over a year, Buck. I finally got up the nerve to ask her to marry me. When she said yes, you could have knocked me over with a feather."

### A CHANGE OF KEY

"Jesus, after over a year you would have been knocked over if she said no. But sure, you can have a week, ten days, whatever. Let's get this album done first so you don't have anything hanging over your head. And that way we can keep Jack Merrill happy."

The next week was notable for two reasons. The first was that true to his word, Jack had sent Whip Elliot and Tommy Taylor to produce and engineer the final recordings for "Buck Fisher Rides Again."

"You know, Buck, this is a lot easier than it was when we did all those sides for your band at Bluebird. With only five pieces, balancing the sound is a relative snap. And because we all want it to have that loosey-goosey jazz feel, I don't want to do too many takes. So barring any technical glitches, let's see if we can lay them down on the first shot," said Tommy.

"Yeah, tell you what. Let's do two cuts at a time. Then we'll play them back. If we're satisfied, we'll keep moving forward," added Whip.

"Just as long as we all agree it has to be the best possible product, I'm with you guys all the way," said Buck.

"You better be! Jack's already got the Art Department doing mock-ups for album covers and they're going to want to do a photo shoot early next week. He's going full-blast on production because he thinks this will be a sure-fire million seller," said Tommy.

One after another the Buck Fisher Quintet knocked off the songs they had prepared—and Buck felt the group was really hitting on all cylinders. He felt he was back fifteen years earlier when he first started out. He could always tell when he was 'on,' when he felt that every solo was the best he could give.

Whether it was the new bebop pieces or that achingly lonely sound of the alto sax on ballads, there was no question that Buck Fisher was back—and hadn't lost a thing as a big deal record label executive. No, Buck Fisher was home.

In three days time the sessions were completed and the masters sent to Jack for final approval. "Great stuff, Buck," said

## A CHANGE OF KEY

Jack. "I couldn't have asked for more. And I've put together an entire P.R. machine to get this out to the public," said Jack.

In fact, Jack had Buck booked for three consecutive nights on Martin Block's *Make Believe Ballroom* on WNEW radio. It felt like he had come full circle, because back in 1941, Buck had appeared on Jerry Marshall's *Milkman's Matinee* on WNEW and the air time led to a tremendous boost in sales of Buck Fisher 78s.

The show was to be a retrospective of Buck's music from his big band days to his current job at RCA—with plenty of plugs for the new album. Block's audience was huge and Jack was confident that the buzz Buck's appearance would cause would lead to huge record sales.

He was also booked for a Friday morning at WNEW on the Klavan and Finch show. Gene Klavan and Dee Finch owned the morning airwaves in New York radio. The two specialized in comic banter in between playing the most popular music of the day. So Buck's coming album would be plugged both in the morning and at drive time in the afternoon. Car radios had been around since the 1920s and by 1952, radios were equipped to play both the AM and FM stations—though AM radio was king.

And then there was the second piece of news that week. Carrie called Buck at his office and could barely contain her excitement.

"Whoa, whoa, slow down, hon. What's going on?" asked Buck.

"Sweetheart! They just announced the nominees for the Academy Awards! Fran got nominated for Best Actress! Can you believe it?"

"Holy cow! That's fantastic? Who else was nominated?"

"She's up against some heavy weights—Vivien Leigh, Katharine Hepburn, Eleanor Parker and Shelley Winters. But that's not the point, darling. This was her first serious film! I am so happy for her! What can we do?"

"I'm going to call her as soon as we get off the phone. And I'm going to send her the biggest bouquet of flowers that they make," said Buck.

## A CHANGE OF KEY

"Be sure to send my love too," said Carrie.

Buck gave Kelsey Fran's address and told her what he wanted. "Biggest, most expensive bunch that they have, Kel. And I want it there ASAP. Have them sign the card 'Congratulations and much love from Buck and Carrie."

"I'll get to it right away, Buck."

"Good, and then I want to talk to you later, Kel. Let's make it mid-afternoon."

"Sure. Problem?"

"No, no. Just have an idea I want to kick around with you," said Buck.

Buck's idea had been buzzing around in his head for months now. He had discussed it with Carrie and she thought it would be a great thing. But he had to get Kelsey's approval first.

It turned out that Buck had no need to call Fran Michaels. At about three that afternoon, she called Buck. It was Noon in California and she was home for the day after the morning's announcement.

"Buck! Good grief you sent me the whole Brooklyn Botanical Gardens! Thank you so much! They're gorgeous—and Thank Carrie too."

"We saw your film Franny and you were fantastic. It just blew us away, so we're sure you deserve that nomination and we can't wait until you make the next one."

"Well, I don't really have a snowball's chance in hell of winning. All the buzz is about Vivien Leigh in *A Streetcar Named Desire*. But believe me, it doesn't matter. Getting the nomination is more than enough for me."

They spoke for a few more minutes and Fran said, "Buck? I want you to know how much I love you. None of this—I mean none of this—would have been possible if you didn't give me that chance so long ago. I love you to pieces and will never forget how much you mean to me—and Pete."

"You're the best, Franny. I told you that ages ago and I haven't changed my mind. So once again, congrats and hurry up and make another movie!"

## A CHANGE OF KEY

After the call, Buck buzzed Kelsey and said, "Kel? Want to come in here for a few minutes?"

"On the way, boss." Two minutes later, she was seated on the sofa, steno pad in hand.

"What do you need, Buck?"

"Kel, I don't want to make you uncomfortable and be too personal, but you never talk about your husband. How come?"

Kelsey looked down at her pad, and when she looked up, there were tears welling in her eyes. Buck immediately came and sat next to her on the sofa.

"Talk to me, hon," said Buck.

"I don't know what to do Buck. No one seems to want to hire him because of his war injury. And he's so embarrassed by it he never leaves the house. He just mopes around, listens to the radio—and sometimes can't make himself get out of bed because he hates putting on the artificial leg."

"I love him, Buck, but I don't know how to help him. He's so distant. He stiffens up if I even try to touch him—and forgive me for all these details, but we haven't made love in months. He gets his disability checks, but I have to go to the bank to deposit them because he won't leave the house."

Kelsey was sobbing and Buck took her in his arms and said, "I have an idea, Kel. Maybe it would help. Listen to me and tell me what you think."

"I'll try anything, Buck. Because if this goes on for too much longer, I'm afraid I'll lose him."

Buck handed Kelsey a tissue and said, "Where do you live, Kel?"

"We have a place in Clinton Hill, downtown Brooklyn. It's a few blocks away from that school, Pratt Institute?"

"How about you invite me to dinner—soon. I think I can help."

"How?"

"Leave that to me," said Buck.

"Tuesday night is meat loaf night. I make it in advance so I just have to warm it up," said Kelsey,

"Good. Leave early that day and tell me what time to be there."

"We usually eat at six."

"Fine. I'll bring dessert."

Over dinner that night, Buck explained to Carrie what he had in mind and she said, "It's a great idea, Buck. She's a sweetheart and I'm glad you want to help her. But do you think he'll do it?"

"It's going to be tricky, but I can be pretty persuasive."

"You may have to be," said Carrie.

.....

At six o'clock, Buck showed up on Willoughby Avenue in Brooklyn. He knocked at Kelsey's door and she answered it, accepting the Junior's cheesecake he had brought for dessert. Kelsey showed him into the apartment and in the living room, he saw Joe Burton, Kelsey's husband.

Joe was a strapping six-footer, with a remarkable resemblance to Mike Douglas, the male vocalist with the Kay Kayser band. He extended his hand to Buck, though he remained seated. "Please to meet you, Mr. Fisher. Kelsey talks about you all the time."

"Buck. Please call me Buck."

Kelsey invited the two to the dinner table where she had set lovely place settings and the steaming meatloaf was already on a silver platter in the middle of the table.

Over dinner, the topics ranged from the Korean War to politics in general to their wartime experiences. Joe Burton had gotten out of the Navy as a Chief Petty Officer highly decorated for rescuing shipmates on the Intrepid after the Kamikaze hit. Joe tried to keep the bitterness out of his voice when he described that awful day, but it crept through.

Being polite, Joe said, "So how's work going at RCA? Kelsey says your always busy."

"Too busy, actually," said Buck. "I'm afraid I run your wife ragged at times," he added.

# A CHANGE OF KEY

"She loves the job and never complains," said Joe.

"I've been looking for more help for weeks now but oddly enough, nobody seems to want to work these days," said Buck, looking first at Joe, then at Kelsey, who knew for a fact that Buck was not looking for more help.

"What kind of work," asked Joe.

"Production Assistant in the studios. We have a lot of groups recording for us and we're using five different rehearsal studios. Each one has its own set-up. I need someone to be in charge of setting things up, moving things around as necessary, keeping track of studio time, moving the masters from the studio to production. And about a dozen other things. Kind of a jack-of-all trades job. It pays nine thousand plus benefits and that's to start. It's just strange that no one wants to take it on."

Buck thought for a moment and said, "Say, Joe, maybe you know someone who would want the job? A friend or someone?"

He looked at Kelsey whose eyes had opened to the size of dinner plates.

"Hell, I would do it, Buck, but I don't know if Kelsey mentioned it, but I've got a bum leg. Or rather, a bum half a leg?"

"Really?" said Buck, feigning surprise. "Wow, I never would have known."

"So I guess that rules me out," said Joe.

"Why?" asked Buck.

"Well, I can lift things all right, but I can't run around or anything like that. I wouldn't want to embarrass Kelsey by failing at anything. And I don't want a charity job where I just sit around doing nothing."

"You know, Joe, I almost got killed during the war. I didn't think I'd even live, no less work again. But when you have family and friends on your side, you'd be amazed with what you can accomplish. So what do you say? Want the job?"

There was total silence at the dinner table before Joe Burton said, "I'll take it, Buck. I'll do whatever you want—and I promise I won't let you down."

## A CHANGE OF KEY

Buck took a check and a fountain pen from his jacket pocket and wrote it out in the amount of $500 made out to Joseph Burton. "Here's an advance on your salary, Joe. Get over to Bloomingdales or Brooks Brothers—your choice—and get yourself three or four nice suits, some shirts and ties. Let Kelsey pick them out for you. Next Monday you come to 30 Rock prepared to work as a full employee of RCA Victor. Do a good job and you can move up the ladder."

"I don't know what to say, Buck."

"You can say it's time for cheesecake. And by the way, Kel, best meatloaf I ever had. Better than my mother's."

At the end of the evening when Kelsey showed Buck to the door, there were tears flowing down her cheeks. She hugged Buck and whispered, "I'll never forget this, Buck. You can't know how much this means to us. I love you!"

"He's a good man, Kel. He just needs a chance. Thousands of guys like him need a chance. I'll help whenever and wherever I can."

She kissed him on the cheek and said, "See you in the morning, Buck."

**A CHANGE OF KEY**

# CHAPTER THIRTY-ONE
*New Trends and Stardom Again—April 1954*

In March of 1954, Buck called a meeting with Bill Dwyer and Al Rovitz to discuss the progress of the label and what the future would hold for it. The meeting revealed that there were a lot of new trends happening in the music world.

"This rockabilly thing keeps growing, Buck," said Al. "When I was down in Nashville in January, I heard some amazing things."

"Like?" asked Buck.

"I heard a kid in a small club playing with drums, bass and rhythm guitar. His name is Duane Eddy and I never heard any sound like this. He gets this real twangy sound out of his guitar, partly due to reverb in the amps, and partly because he's playing on the bass strings of the instrument. You'll want to watch this kid. I don't think he's quite ready yet, but I'll wager he has a big future in this rock n' roll thing," said Al.

Bill then said, "I caught another kid—I don't think he was more than sixteen, playing drums. Jesus! Not only does he have every drum under the sun, but he plays every one of them on his songs. Kid's name is Sandy Nelson. I spoke to him and he's under contract to Imperial Records. I left him a card but he's another one that's going to be a star—either as a session musician or as one of those rock n' rollers."

It was then Buck's turn and he said, "I was listening to some Count Basie cuts on a jazz show on WNEW. It sounded so different from the way his band sounded in the '30s and '40s. So I called the station and spoke to Jerry Marshall. He told me that Basie has a new arranger named Neil Hefti who has completely altered the sound of that band. He's writing charts for a whole album of his songs for the band. I would love to talk to him and Jerry said he'd see if he could arrange it. If you get a chance, see if they've released singles to 'Little Pony,' 'Sure Thing,' and 'Why Not?' You'll barely recognize it as Basie's group. Jerry also said that back in the '40s Hefti was playing trumpet for Woody Herman."

"The Four Brothers band?" asked Bill.

"Yeah, the Second Herd. So I got Woody's number. He's out on the coast and I called him and asked him about Hefti."

"What did he have to say?" asked Al.

"He said he changed the sound of his band too and turned it into a real jazz band. He praised him to the hilt but said that right now he's leading his own big band."

"Where's he playing?" asked Bill.

"Some theater in Newark. I'm going Friday night to hear him," said Buck.

"Careful, Buck, if you're thinking of hiring him. You don't want to step on Kip's toes, you know. He's done great work for us."

"I understand, but with Fletcher gone, maybe he could use some help."

Fletcher Henderson was one of the truly great big band arrangers who had done some fantastic charts for Buck and RCA. His death in 1952 came as a shock to everyone in the music business.

"I almost hate to say it, Buck, but if I were a betting man, I'd put my money on this rock n' roll thing. I don't think it's going to be a fad kind of thing. It's going to have legs. Maybe we need to think about signing these kids and groups and developing them into moneymakers for us," said Bill.

"I think you might be right, Bill, but we have to keep the label diverse, so let's not neglect popular artists," said Buck. "OK, guys, keep doing what you're doing. Sign them when you think they have promise and let's move forward," said Buck.

It proved unnecessary to go to Newark to meet Neil Hefti because two days after their meeting, Kelsey informed Buck that Neil Hefti was waiting in his outer office.

She showed him into Buck's private office and the two men shook hands. Buck offered him a chair and something to drink which Hefti declined.

# A CHANGE OF KEY

"This is so strange. I was coming to hear you Friday night and here you are." Said Buck.

"Woody gave me a call and said you wanted to talk to me. You know how busy things get when you're doing a show so I figured this would be a more relaxing way to meet," he said.

"Well, where should I begin?" said Buck.

"Let me begin, then. You know, when I was with Woody, there wasn't a guy in that band who didn't envy you—and remember, we had some hot sax players. Sims, Getz—and later Al Cohn. But we knew you were just raking in the cash and turning out these million selling discs. And good as those four brothers were, Buck, none of them held a candle to your playing."

"Woody says you're the guy who turned his band into a real jazz outfit rather than a dance band that occasionally played some up-tempo things. How did you do that?" asked Buck.

"I think the key is in the section work. Let the sections be the stars. Sure, you have soloists, but take 'Four Brothers.' What's the first thing that impresses you about the chart? Jimmy Giuffre wrote these intricate figures for the sax section that just blow you away. The solos are terrific too, but the way the section works—like five fingers on the same hand, so together—that's what I try to bring to my charts. And Basie's sections are the strongest I've ever worked with so it was easy to show them off."

"So what made you want to lead your own band?" asked Buck.

Hefti laughed and said, "Well, it's just for now. There's really a very narrow market for big bands these days. Basie, Ellington, the Dorsey's are doing television, Tex Beneke is still working, but after that, it's kind of slim pickings. I'm doing it because it gives me a chance to play trumpet again."

"So do you have a label, Neil?"

"Sort of. I've done some stuff for Coral Records and Verve, but nothing too big. I like to keep my options open."

"Want to come work for me?" asked Buck.

"I had a feeling that was coming. But no, I don't think so, Buck. But I tell you what, I could write some charts for you on a freelance basis—both with strings and without. You could pay me on a per chart basis."

"What's your normal fee for a chart?"

"I get a hundred bucks for each one I write," said Hefti. "But if you want me to sign something, I'll only do it if it says I have to deliver at least four charts. After that, we'll see where it goes."

"Fair enough. Can't wait to see what you'll write for us," said Buck. They shook hands on the deal and Hefti took his leave, saying he needed to get to a rehearsal.

Buck had a splitting headache and he buzzed Kelsey and said, "Kel? You got any aspirin out there? My head's pounding like a bass drum."

"You better take three of them. Jack Merrill called you while you were with Neil Hefti. He wants you upstairs soon as you're free."

"Oy. What now?"

"Don't know. Here, swallow these. Buck? How's Joe doing? Is it working out?"

"He's great, Kel. He takes the initiative and does all that he's asked. He's worth every penny we're paying him."

"I'm glad to hear that. He's a lot happier at home. He's going to make a great father," said Kelsey.

Buck almost choked on the third aspirin. "He what?"

Kelsey smiled and nodded. "'Fraid so, Buck. Mid-December."

"I think I need another three aspirin. Jesus, Kel, my life is gonna fall apart without you. But, don't get me wrong, I'm thrilled for you. Come here and gimme a hug."

"You'll have me until the beginning of December. We'll worry about after that down the road. Now get up to Jack before he sends security for you."

When Buck entered his office, Jack's serious demeanor indicated that something serious was up. "Take a seat, Buck," said Jack. He took from his desk what appeared to be a heavy manilla envelope. Buck's first thought was that it contained many contracts that for one reason or another had kicked back from the Legal Department and now were invalid.

Jack dispelled that fear when his face broke out into a smile that illuminated his office. "This is for you, Buck. It took about six months longer than we expected, but, well—open it up," he said, handing the envelope to him.

Inside, Buck found a nine by twelve wooden plaque upon which was mounted a gold record. The inscription acknowledged that it represented the sale of one million albums of *Buck Fisher Rides Again.* In the study of his house, Buck had a "Look at Me" wall crammed with awards he had won—and six other gold records he had won with the Buck Fisher Orchestra. Also on the wall was his Honorable Discharge and his commission as an officer in the Army Reserve. But this gold record was special. It showed Buck that his career as a musician was anything but over. And Jack Merrill felt the same way.

"So Buck, congratulations on an incredible achievement. And General Sarnoff also sends his best wishes—and wants to know when you plan on cutting another album."

"Cripes, Jack, I've been so busy, I haven't even thought about another one," said Buck.

"Well, time to do more than think about it, kid. You know, strike while the iron is hot and all. But for now, take a few weeks to plan it out and then let's get you back into the studio," said Jack.

"All right, Jack. I'll meet with Kip and see what ideas he has for a follow-up."

"Great. And show this one to Carrie. I know how proud she'll be for you."

That was an understatement. When Buck showed Carrie the gold record that night she immediately burst into tears—but tears of joy.

"Oh, darling, I told you that you could do it. I knew your fans would flock to anything you played."

"I confess I had my doubts, darling, but yes, you were right. Now Jack and the General both want me to make another album."

**A CHANGE OF KEY**

"That's great, sweetheart! It will be just as successful as this one. I'm sure of it," said Carrie, hugging Buck.

It was strange—or maybe it wasn't strange at all that this woman who had been with him now for nearly fifteen years was still so in love with him—and he with her. They had experienced so much together, both happiness and near-tragedy, that the bond they felt now was possibly even stronger than when they both experienced young love.

The next day Buck announced the gold record for the Buck Fisher Quintet in front of the entire studio orchestra. "And I want to thank Chuck, Ken, Tony and Buddy and Kip for making it possible. It's just as much your award as it is mine."

"Hey Buck, maybe next time you can put my face on the album," said Chuck.

"The jacket isn't big enough for your face, Chuckie, but we'll see what we can do," said Buck.

The rest of Buck's week was spent scheduling rehearsal time for the many performers now under contract with RCA. In that area, Joe Burton had been a tremendous help. He had created an elaborate chart showing every Victor studio—including the ones in California, with dates and times for recording sessions. He had had cards printed for each artist and group. All he had to do was plug in the card under the allotted studio time and Buck knew exactly who was doing what where.

"Great job, Joe. Keep up the good work," said Buck. As an executive, Buck had taken the lessons he had learned as an Army officer and applied them to his civilian career. Complimenting his employees was a way to motivate them to work harder. He had encountered enough petty martinets in the military to understand that a leader like that just promotes resentment. Power went to their heads as soon as congress declared they were officers and gentlemen. On those few occasions when a member of his staff did something questionable, Buck was always tactful in talking over the problem with them. As a result, the entire division that Buck headed was a tight-knit group of friends all working towards a common goal.

# A CHANGE OF KEY

It was a smooth-running machine with its occasional glitches and surprises, but most of those surprises were good ones. One of the best happened in the third week of May. While Buck was poring over paperwork, there was a knock at the door and in walked Fran Michaels. An obviously pregnant Fran Michaels.

"Holy cow! Franny!" Buck came around his desk and hugged her, showing her to the sofa.

"Umm, Fran? Go off your diet or something?" said Buck, prompting a throaty laugh from Fran.

"Yep, been off it for about three months now," she said, patting her belly,

"Congratulations, Franny. This is great news," said Buck

"Mixed news, Buck. The studio has strict rules about pregnant actresses for insurance purposes. So I'm on hiatus until the baby is born, though I have three films scheduled for next year."

"Well what brings you back to New York?" asked Buck.

"Pete and I are moving back until the baby is born. Both of us want to be close to family when it happens, and there's no way they're moving to the coast—so here we are for a while."

There was a moment of silence between them before Buck figured it out. "Franny? There's something else, isn't there?"

"You can read me like a book, can't you, Buck?"

"OK, let's have it."

"I want to sing again, Buck. Don't get me wrong, I love the acting business, but singing is such a part of me. I haven't had a chance to sing since those first two movies I made at MGM. Oh, and once at one of Louis B. Mayer's holiday parties. I miss it so much. I was wondering if I could make another album for you."

Though it surprised Buck, he didn't have to think about it for more than a few moments. "You say the word and we'll do it, Franny"

Fran Michaels had already earned two gold records of her own for her RCA albums and she had made plenty of money for the label. The chance to have her make a third one was irresistible. And pregnancy notwithstanding, Fran Michaels was still heartbreakingly beautiful. Buck guessed it was true about how pregnant women had this glow about them.

"What does Pete think, Franny?"

"He's all for it. He says it would be better than me sitting around at home all day eating chocolates and watching Dave Garroway."

"OK, let's do this. Can you come back tomorrow morning at about ten and we'll meet with Kip Roman? Try to bring a list of songs you think you'd like to do. We'll free up some studio time to fit you in. Whatever it takes, I'll do for you," said Buck.

Fran got up and hugged Buck saying, "I love you, Buck. I've said it before, but I'll say it again—you are absolutely the greatest. I really mean that."

"For you the world, Franny. You know that. Now, plan on you and Pete coming to dinner next week. Wait till Carrie hears that you're moving back to New York. She's going to jump out of her skin with joy."

"Give her my love, Buck. See you in the morning."

# CHAPTER THIRTY-TWO
## *"Grief Comes in Threes:" July 1954*

It was a brutally hot day towards the end of July when Buck was glad to seek refuge in the fully air-conditioned confines of 30 Rock. He checked into his office, answered a few phone calls and then made his way down to the studio where Cindi Kay was rehearsing "I Have Dreamed," from Rodgers and Hammerstein's *The King and I*. The song was originally performed in the musical by Doretta Morrow, but not released as a single or on an album since, other than the cast album from the show. It was a beautiful ballad in a perfect range for Cindi, but there was something in the chart that was not clicking.

With Buck's permission, Kip had added two French horn players and an additional flautist to pair with his new wife, Pammy, to give a broader, more symphonic sound to the studio orchestra. After Cindi's second run-through, Kip sat at the piano shaking his head indicating his dissatisfaction with what he had written.

"What seems to be the problem, Kip?" asked Buck.

The young man, who had turned out so many fantastic charts for the label just shrugged and said, "I can't put my finger on it, Buck. Cindi's doing great on it, but the orchestra is off somehow. Maybe you could give a listen?"

"Sure. Run it and I'll see if I can figure it out with you."

Kip counted it off and the orchestra played the chart without Cindi singing. Then they did it again with her voice. Buck heard a few things that he could suggest.

"You know, Kip, I'm not sure if you're aware of the fact that Danny DeMaestri plays oboe in addition to sax and clarinet. He hasn't had any opportunity to play it yet, but I think if you add it to the reed line, it will really warm it up. Also, even though it's more of a mixing issue, I think the violins are too hot. They're fighting it out in the same register as Cindi's singing in. What if you drop them an octave—and maybe add some crescendos at the climax of the number. Really work the emotion of the song."

"I can do those changes, Buck. You think it's the answer?" asked Kip.

"Well, I've got one more thing. I love how you use the French horns, but I think you also have to drop them down an octave because they really stick out on top of Cindi's voice," said Buck. Make those changes and let me know how it works out."

"I apologize, Buck. I should be able to figure these things out myself. I don't know where my head is," said Kip.

"Hey, you are the Music Director of the greatest studio orchestra in the country and your charts have earned us a fortune. No need to apologize. Every now and again you need another ear for some input. Even Johnny Blair sometimes needed help with some of his charts, so it's nothing to be ashamed of. Anytime you want me to listen, you just call."

Then he called over to Cindi, "Hey Cin? Fantastic. Keep it up."

She blew him a kiss and went back to the microphone ready to do another take of the song.

Buck took a seat off to the side of the orchestra when Whip Elliot came out of the sound booth and said, "Hey Buck? Kelsey just called. She says she needs you upstairs immediately. She sounds really concerned."

That was a surprise since Kelsey was normally unflappable. But he left the studio and returned to his office. He could tell instantly that there was trouble. "What's wrong, Kel?"

"Oh, Buck, there's big trouble. I think you better get home quick as you can. Call home right away. Carrie called and she sounds absolutely distraught. I think something very bad has happened.

Buck's first guess was that something had happened to one of the children. That was enough to drive Carrie up a wall. In his office, he dialed his home number and Carrie picked up in one ring. She was still hysterical. "Honey, slow down and tell me what happened."

"Oh Buck! It's Mama. I went to drop something off at her house and I found her on the kitchen floor. Buck! She wouldn't

# A CHANGE OF KEY

answer me! I've called an ambulance and they'll be here in a few minutes to take her to Queens General. Please come home!"

"OK, darling, I'm on the way. Call Arlene and call Bevvy. Tell them what happened and to meet me at the hospital. I'll go straight there. You go in the ambulance with Mama."

"Please hurry, Buck. Eunice will look after the kids. said Carrie.

By Noon, the family had gathered at Queens General and Jerry Rosen told them to wait in the lounge until he had completed his examination and run some tests. That took another hour during which the family had very little to say. Their worried looks said it all. Buck said, "Arlene, I called Al and told him to get here right away. He's en route as we speak."

"Thanks Benny. I hope you don't mind, but I dropped Caroline off at your house. Eunice said it would be no trouble for her to watch the baby. She told me to go to Mama and that she'd handle everything."

"That's fine, Arlene. I'll take care of Eunice for her trouble."

At that moment, Jerry came into the lounge. His grim face told the story. "Rachel had a stroke. It was massive. She's on a respirator because she can't breathe on her own. Her limbs aren't responding to stimuli. We're running an EEG right now but from what I can see, her brain activity is extremely low."

"Give it to us straight, Jerry," said Buck.

"It's not good, Buck. Not good at all. I'd guess her chances are less than ten percent." At that point Bevvy ran to her husband who held her tight as she burst into tears. Al showed up just in time to comfort Arlene, who was also crying. But Carrie was the most emotional of the three. Rachel had truly been a mother to her and over the years, her estrangement from her own mother drew her even closer. There was a mutual love and devotion between them that was every bit as strong as Rachel's own daughters.

"Can we see her, Jerry?" asked Bevvy.

"Yes, hon, but she won't know that you're there," he said.

## A CHANGE OF KEY

"Let the girls go first, Jerry. Carrie? You go with them. Al and I will go up when you come back," said Buck, still in shock from the news.

"Sure. Follow me and I'll take you to her room," said Rosen.

The very sight of his mother brought back hideous memories of Carrie when she was in a coma. Intubated, unconscious, saline drip in her arm, and the incessant beeping of an apparatus whose function was a mystery to all but Jerry Rosen. Rachel's eyes were closed and only because of the respirator was she able to continue breathing.

Buck held her hand while Arlene brushed a strand of hair off of her forehead. Both Carrie and Bevvy lost it completely and hugged each other while they cried. Jerry stood in the background with Al, but after a short period of time he said, "I think that's enough for now. The nurse has to check her vitals. He took one last glance at Rachel's chart and ushered them back to the lounge.

Bill Dwyer was waiting there and he hurried to Buck and said, "Buck, what can I do? Can Cathy and I help in any way?"

Buck shook his head, but Bill could see that his eyes were glistening with tears. Bill hugged him and said, "Whatever you need, buddy. Just name it."

"Thanks Bill. I don't think anyone can do anything at this point, but maybe give Jack a call and inform him of what happened."

"Sure, Buck. I'll get right on it. There's a phone booth in the lobby."

"Listen everyone. No use in all of you hanging around here. Go home and I'll stay here. I'll call if there are any developments," said Buck. He kissed Carrie and said, "There's still a chance, sweetheart. Let's all hope for the best."

But this time, hope held none of the high cards. Buck sat at Rachel's bedside all afternoon and through the night. He held her hand and talked to her, though he knew she could hear nothing. His conversation was one-sided, but heartfelt. He told her what a great mother she had been and how much he,

# A CHANGE OF KEY

Arlene, Bevvy, Carrie and the kids all loved her. Every few hours he called Carrie up until eleven that night when he knew she needed to sleep.

Several times he dozed off in the chair interrupted only when a nurse came to check on Rachel and note her vital signs on her chart. At about midnight, the nurse assigned to her room brought a dinner tray for Buck and placed it on a chair next to him. He thanked her, but he had no appetite for food.

Just before dawn on July 19th, Rachel Feinstein passed away, Buck still holding her hand.

What had been a steady beeping sound from the machine at her bedside turned into a continuous tone. A nurse came rushing into the room, checked her pulse, listened to her heart with a stethoscope and she hurriedly called for the doctor on call for the floor.

He was a young second-year resident whose name tag read 'Wayne Albertson, M.D.' He repeated what the nurse had already done before turning to Buck saying, "I'm sorry, Mr. Feinstein. The stroke was just too massive to be survivable. Is there anything I can do?"

"Can she remain here until my sisters arrive? I know they would like to see her one last time, if that's permissible."

"Certainly. I'll inform Dr. Rosen. Once again, I'm sorry. Please accept my deepest sympathies." They shook hands and Buck headed to the phone booth where he made the calls to Carrie, Arlene and Bevvy.

An hour later the family had gathered at the bedside. Carrie said, "Cathy Dwyer came over to mind the children. I had to wait for her before I could get here."

"I understand, darling. Eunice will arrive by eight so we're covered," said Buck.

Buck, Jerry and Al stood together as Carrie and his sisters kissed Rachel on her forehead and said their goodbyes. At one point, Bevvy looked as though she would collapse and Jerry rushed to her for support.

"How about we all come back to our house and we'll make plans," said Buck.

"That's fine," said Jerry, "but where should we send Rachel? Where do you want the funeral, Buck?"

"There's a place on Queens Boulevard, Sinai Chapels. It's pretty big and I know some people who have used their services. They handle all the details."

"OK, Buck, I'll make the call and join you at the house in about an hour or so. Just let me do rounds and I'll come right after that."

"Sure, Jerry. Thanks a lot. See you in a bit," said Buck.

When the family had gathered, Buck said, "Look girls, there are a lot of things to go over. It's not going to be easy or pleasant, but we have to at least talk about everything. First, the funeral arrangements. It's going to be at Sinai Chapels. We'll have to make phone calls and inform people about the time."

"Buck? I already checked with them and Wednesday morning is what they suggest," said Al. "Oh, and I told them you don't belong to a *shul* and they said that's no problem. They have a rabbi on call at all times."

He looked at his sisters who both nodded. "OK, that works then. Thanks, Al."

"What about the kids, Buck?" said Arlene. "Do they know?"

"Yes. Before you all got here, Carrie and I sat them down and explained. Eddie and Laura cried, but Casey is still too young for it to fully register. Eunice took them to the park to get them out of the house."

"Laura took it the hardest, but she's my sensitive baby. I think she needs a lot of love right now," said Carrie.

"Next. Arlene? Do you know if Mama had a plot?" asked Buck.

"Yes, Benny. She kept a bunch of papers in her night table drawer and before I came here, I found a deed to a plot in Washington Cemetery on 20th Avenue in Brooklyn. That's the one not too far from the old apartment on West 8$^{th}$ Street."

"All right. I'll call them and make arrangements for the burial Wednesday afternoon, right after the funeral."

As was the Jewish custom, burial must happen as soon as possible, so the one-day delay was typical, allowing the family sufficient time to make arrangements.

"Buck? I also found a life insurance policy with her papers. I didn't even know she had one," said Arlene.

"All right. Can you call the company? They'll want a death certificate, I assume," said Buck.

"I'll handle that, Buck," said Jerry. "The hospital already has the paperwork. Both I and Dr. Albertson signed off on it."

"What about a will," asked Buck.

"Yes, that was there too. She named me as the executrix, Buck. I hope you don't mind," said Arlene.

"Not at all, hon. After all, you're the oldest."

"It's pretty standard, I think. Divides everything equally amongst the three of us."

"Well, you and Bevvy can take whatever you want from her house. Then we'll sell it and you and Bev can split the profits."

"No! Absolutely not, Buck! We were all her children. That house sale gets split three ways," said Bevvy.

"Bev, honey, I don't need the money. Really. You two took care of her for all those years. You deserve it."

"Bevvy's right, Benny. It was what Mama wanted—that all three of us share equally. Put the money in a college fund for the kids. That's what I'm going to do," said Arlene.

"All right. Whatever you want," said Buck, although he knew he was wealthy enough to send all three of his kids to medical school if that's what they wanted.

"Anything else, Buck?"

"Yes. We'll have to sit *shiva* Wednesday night through Friday night. If we were Orthodox, we couldn't do it on Friday night, but let's face it, none of us are terribly religious. Three days is more than enough. Al? Will you talk to the orchestra in case anyone wants to pay their respects and just tell them a few rules of the road?"

"Sure, Buck. I'm going to head over there now. Leave it to me."

Buck hugged his sisters and they gathered their things to leave for their homes. Eunice had returned with the children and Arlene took baby Caroline from her and she left with Bevvy who would drive her home.

When they were alone, Carrie said, "I'm so sad, Bucky. I miss her already. Darling? Do you think I should tell my parents?"

That was a touchy subject considering the non-relationship she had with both her mother and father. But having thought it through, Buck said, "If you don't tell them, they'll get their backs up about how you don't care. If you do invite them, they'll probably make an excuse not to come, but on balance, that's the better option."

"I guess you're right. You make your calls first and then I'll call home," said Carrie.

"I don't have that many to make. Eddie Holberg and I guess I should call the Bergmans, but I'm sure Rivka won't come."

"The love of your life?" said Carrie.

"You are the love of my life, darling," said Buck.

"Before me, I mean."

"Before you I was a stupid kid who was infatuated with the first girl who showed any interest in me. She turned out to be a real uppity bitch when she went to college."

"Well if she makes a play for you, I'll claw her eyes out. You're mine, Mr. Feinstein. Now, let's spend some time with the kids. They need some attention right now."

.....

At the rehearsal studio, Al interrupted a run-through and said, "Kip, I have to talk to the orchestra."

"All yours, Al."

Al explained what had happened and asked if any member of the orchestra wanted to pay their respects. Before anyone could answer, Chuck Fein came to the front of the group. He glared at them and said, "You all better listen up. Buck Fisher is like a brother to me. Hell, because of him, me, Noni, Tony and a lot of other guys didn't wind up in the goddamned infantry. So in a way, he saved my ass. That doesn't even include the cushy jobs he's given each one of us. We owe him. I better see every swingin' dick of you at his home for *shiva*. It's three nights, and anyone who can't make at least one of them better have a pretty goddamned good excuse why they can't be there. Anybody got any questions?

When no one said anything, Chuck said, "Good. I'll be there all three nights so I'll see you there."

Then Al said, "Look guys, I don't know how many of you here are Jewish, but there are just a few things you have to know about *shiva*. First, you bring something. It can be a cake, a box of cookies, a platter of cold-cuts—even a casserole you've made. Secondly, you don't ring the doorbell. You just walk right in. And third, you do not talk about the dead in a house of *shiva*. You can talk about the weather, sports, music, it doesn't matter. Just not the dead. I know that's hard, but that's the way it is."

Then Chuck added, "In an Orthodox Jewish house, they cover the mirrors, the mourners sit on hard benches, the men don't shave for a week and there's absolutely no sex. But to tell you the truth, Buck's about as religious as Petunia Pig. Eddie's *bar mitzvah* and sitting *shiva* are his two nods to being Jewish. So we'll all go along with the traditions."

Al then said, "All right, Kip. Sorry for the intrusion. I need to get back to my wife. It was her mother too, in case you didn't know." The funeral's Wednesday morning so if you want, you can give the group the day off. Up to you."

It was fortunate that Sinai Chapels was a large funeral establishment, because over a hundred people showed up at nine o'clock for the service. Rabbi Herschel Abelson had no idea who Rachel Feinstein was, so he asked Buck for some background on his mother.

"Look, Rabbi," said Buck, "with all due respect, I would prefer you not to talk about her. It just sounds absurd—like you're reading from a script. I and my two sisters will deliver brief eulogies. You stick to the funeral rite. Again, no offense intended."

"I fully understand, Mr. Feinstein. Your request is by no means unusual. I'll follow your wishes to the letter."

Unlike a Catholic requiem mass, the Jewish funerary rites were relatively brief. There were the obligatory prayers and a very brief sermon by Rabbi Abelson. Then Arlene, followed by Bevvy and Buck spoke about Rachel.

"Buck was too young to remember when we lived on eggs and grilled cheese sandwiches for dinner because there was so little money after my father died. But we never went hungry—and more importantly, we were happy. My mother was the Rock of Gibraltar in the family. The center of our world—and she held everything together," said Arlene, who by this time was choking back the tears.

Bevvy added, "My older sister, my brother Benny, and hopefully me—we are the decent hard-working and successful people we are because of our mother."

Though he was the middle child, Buck went last. "My sisters have said it all. But for me personally, let me say this: Mom never pushed me. She never tried to steer my life one way or another. She had only one thought in her mind: that I be happy. In that sense, Rachel Feinstein was the perfect mother. I have learned so much from her as has Carrie. If I could make a wish now, it would be that Carrie and I instill those very same values into our three children."

Rabbi Abelson then rose and asked the men in the chapel to rise as he recited *Kaddish,* the Jewish prayer for mourning. It was always recited at funerals, but not at the graveside. In Jewish tradition, *Kaddish* is never said alone. It requires a *minyan* of ten men. Buck was certain that there were at least that many Jewish men who rose to recite the prayer with the rabbi.

At the conclusion, the Rabbi announced the location of the burial. Buck expected just the immediate family to come to the cemetery, maybe one or two friends. He was astonished to see that there was a line of over thirty vehicles ready to follow the two limousines that would take the family to Washington Cemetery. His friends wanted to be with him at such a difficult moment.

Graveside services are usually quite brief, and the one for Rachel was no exception. Fifteen minutes culminating in everyone tossing a flower onto the coffin and it was over. The ride back to Queens was made in near silence, broken occasionally by Bevvy's sobbing. Jerry held her on one side and Buck on the other.

Arlene was stronger, and Carrie managed to hold it together with the redness in her eyes the only sign that she too had been crying.

Back at Buck's home, Carrie looked after the children and Eunice said, "Mr. Buck, we got a big gift here. I didn't read the card, but it sho enough got a lot of food on it."

It was indeed an enormous platter of cod cuts and cheeses accompanied by a giant basket of assorted fruits. The card read, "With My Deepest Sympathy and Care." Sincerely, David Sarnoff. The General certainly knew how to look after his key people.

The three nights of *shiva* went as smoothly as might have been expected. Every member of the orchestra came as did Jack Merrill on the second night. Chuck and Rebecca came all three nights with Becky helping Eunice in the kitchen.

Eunice Jefferson had become the major-domo of the household. The previous year she had moved into the basement apartment and had all but given up her role as a Registered Nurse in favor of devoting all her energies to the Fisher family. As she put it, "Dis ma family now, Mr. Buck. And Ima look over you all like a big ole' mother hen." She had offered to pay rent for her apartment but Buck refused saying, "With all you do for us, it would be a sacrilege to take money from you." In fact, Buck had upped her salary considerably.

The talk over the three nights had been of music, up and coming artists, sports, even politics, now that Dwight D. Eisenhower had been occupying the White House for the last two years. Naturally, no one spoke of Rachel Feinstein, though Buck and his sisters thought of her constantly.

## A CHANGE OF KEY

Fran and Pete came the first two nights and Buck was glad to have the opportunity to talk to his old lead alto player. Pete had made quite a name for himself as a studio musician on the West Coast and he had easily found similar work back in New York.

"How's my replacement working out, Buck?" asked Pete.

"He's fine, Pete. He even plays oboe so Kip has incorporated that into some of the ballad charts he wrote."

He also had a chance to speak to Fran for a few minutes. "Buck, I am so sorry for your loss. I wish there were more that Pete and I could do for you," she said.

"Just being here is enough, Franny. Now, tell me how the new album is going," said Buck.

"Well, I have a title for it. It's called 'Raising Standards.' I'm going to be doing a variety of former hits and newer numbers that have become standards in their own right. Kip is writing some wonderful charts and they're a combination of the full orchestra and the jazz band. It's really a wonderful mix, Buck."

"If it's as good as your other records, it's as good as gold already, Franny. If you don't mind, I'd like to stop down to a rehearsal or two to give a listen," said Buck.

"Why would I mind my old boss coming to here me sing? You and Carrie made me into the singer I am," said Fran.

"You were already that singer, Fran. We just brought it out a bit."

She kissed him and Buck returned to the other guests to thank each one of them for coming. There was a mountain of food and desserts that Buck would distribute to Arlene and Bevvy. He even implored Bill Dwyer to take some of the cakes and cookies for his children since Carrie and the kids couldn't possibly consume all the things that the orchestra members had brought.

At the end of the second night, Jack Merrill took Buck aside and said, "Listen, if you need another week or so to put your mother's things in order, take all the time you need. Bill, Al and Kip have things running smoothly."

"Thanks, Jack, I'll give it some thought."

## A CHANGE OF KEY

"A piece of advice, Buck. I've been through this same thing—three times. My parents and my grandmother. I found that getting back to work is a great palliative. It kept me from brooding and playing things over and over in my mind. But everyone is different, so you do what's best for you; the job is there whenever you come back to it."

By Saturday, with *shiva* over, Buck, Carrie and Eunice set about to getting the house back in order. Even the children helped with Casey gathering up her playthings and putting them in the large toy box in her room.

"Would you mind if I went back to work on Monday, darling," Buck asked.

"No, not at all. I think it would do you good. The girls said they would come Monday to start sorting out Mama's things. It might take a few days, but we can handle it," said Carrie. "We think the Salvation Army or ORT could use the clothes."

"OK, I'll be in my office all day. If you need anything, just call. If I stepped out, Kelsey will find me."

. . . .

Buck slipped back into the routine of work very easily. There was much to do and as Jack had suggested, the work kept Buck's mind on the details of the job, rather than his loss. But that loss was compounded two weeks later when upon returning home, Carrie handed him a letter with the return address, Beckman and Weisman, Attorneys at Law.

The substance of the letter was brief. It asked him to call at their office on Court Street in Brooklyn at his earliest convenience. Buck called Kelsey the next morning and said he would be in by noon.

The office of Beckman and Weisman was on the second floor of a somewhat shabby building on lower Court Street. A secretary asked him to have a seat while she informed Mr. Weisman that he had arrived.

Arnold Weisman was an elderly man, as bald as an egg and portly enough that the buttons on his vest bulged to the point of breaking.

## A CHANGE OF KEY

"Mr. Feinstein, a pleasure to meet you," Said Weisman, extending his hand across his desk.

"Thank you, but may I ask what this is all about?"

"Yes, of course. Forgive all the mystery, but we thought it best not to detail things in a letter rather than face-to-face, but as you are now here, I will tell you what this is about.

"Yes, please."

"You have been named as an heir in the will of Frederick Conovitz. In fact, you are the sole heir. I'm sorry to inform you, but Freddy died two weeks ago. I have been his attorney for nearly thirty years. I was best man at his wedding when I was still in law school. You may or may not know it, but Freddy had no family, no children—not even a cousin. Believe me, I know because we searched. He died alone and we only found out about his death when a housekeeper who came in once a month found his body in bed. She called the police and they found a copy of the will with our firm's name and phone number on it. That's how I learned of his death."

Fred Conovitz, who took the professional name Fred Constantine, had been Buck's saxophone teacher from the time he was eleven years old. Everything he knew about music and playing he learned from Freddy Constantine. Buck hadn't seen him in some time, but he still felt his loss profoundly.

"Freddy and I spoke once a week, sometimes more. We would get together for dinner every now and again at Katz's deli or Juniors. I don't know if you are aware, Mr. Feinstein, but he was so proud of you. He talked about you constantly as he followed your career. After you got hurt during the war, he called me and asked if your family needed any help. The man had a big heart."

"Nothing I have done could have been possible without Freddy," said Buck. "He made me the player I am."

"Yes, well, now let me tell you about the terms of his will. He had a life insurance policy worth twenty-five thousand dollars. You are the sole beneficiary. He also had bank accounts in five

## A CHANGE OF KEY

different banks in Brooklyn. They total nearly forty thousand dollars. Once again, you are the sole inheritor."

"What? You must be mistaken, Mr. Weisman," said Buck.

"No, not at all. Freddy's house was paid for. He lived simply, and he lived off of his investments. When he married Florence, she brought a lot of money to the marriage that she inherited from her father. They never spent much, never took vacations, but they were happy in each other's' company. He once said you were like a son to him. Oh, and by the way, according to the will, he also left you his instruments. It says here a tenor saxophone, a baritone saxophone, a bass saxophone and a curved soprano—whatever that is."

Those instruments were Freddy's prize possessions. The archaic bass saxophone was obsolete in modern music, but Freddy liked fooling around with it. Both the curved soprano and baritone were Selmer instruments with exquisite tone. Buck would treat them with the same love that his friend and teacher had shown towards them.

"Now, Mr. Feinstein, I have some papers for you to sign and if you will give me your bank account or accounts numbers, I will have the moneys transferred to you by the end of business tomorrow. The house is yours too, and you can sell it."

Buck signed the papers and thanked Mr. Weisman. Then he left the office. Money was not something that he needed; The fact was, he was one of the wealthiest leaders to emerge from the Swing era. Now, another sixty-five thousand dollars into his account could not make up for the loss of his dear friend.

When he told Carrie that night about the will and the loss of his friend, she held him and expressed her sadness at his loss. She had never met Freddy, but Buck had talked about him so much, she felt she knew him.

"Oh, boy, Bucky, we better be careful," said Carrie.

"How come?"

"Well, they say deaths come in threes. Or grief comes in threes. I forget which one."

## A CHANGE OF KEY

"They both mean the same thing, darling. But I wouldn't dwell on it. I don't expect anything else will go wrong this year," said Buck.

He was wrong.

On the evening of September 1$^{st}$, as the family ate dinner together, the phone rang and Eunice answered it. She came to the dining room and said, "Ladybird, dat call fo' you."

A few minutes later, Carrie returned to the table and sat stone-faced before picking at a few pieces of meat on her plate.

"Darling?" said Buck.

Carrie shook her head and Buck said, "Kids, if you guys are finished, how about you go and play for a bit."

When they had left the table, Buck repeated, "Darling?"

"That was my father. She'd dead, Buck."

Etta Chlumski, Carrie's mother who had scorned Buck because he wasn't wealthy enough to marry her daughter. Etta Chlumski, who never forgave Buck for getting Carrie pregnant before they were married. Etta Chlumski, who had all but ignored her daughter and her grandchildren for the last fourteen years had finally died.

"Are you all right, Carrie?" asked Buck.

"Yes, I'm fine. I don't know if I should feel guilty, Buck, but I feel nothing. No grief, no regret. Just nothing."

"Forgive me for saying it, hon, but she wasn't much of a mother to you," said Buck.

"Nothing to forgive. You're right. At times I think she hated me—hated us. Don't ask me why. You have been the ideal husband and father, not to mention the perfect son—all of which she could have had if she wasn't such a bitch. No, I'll shed no tears for her."

"So what's the plan?" asked Buck.

"Friday morning is the funeral in Brooklyn. I'll go to that."

"What about *shiva?*"

"Bullshit!" she said, rather vehemently. "Did they come for you? In all the time I was in the hospital and no one knew if

# A CHANGE OF KEY

I'd live or die—did they even once come to see me? Have they ever even met Casey? Do they even bother to send a birthday card to any of the kids? My father can sit *shiva* by himself—or with whatever big mucky-mucks he does business with."

"Sweetheart, I would never presume to tell you what to do, but I think you should at least think about it. I wouldn't want you to have any regrets later on. But it's up to you."

Carrie sighed and said, "Well, fuck. *Shiva* won't start until Sunday night. I'll go to that, but that's it. He can take care of her clothes and everything on his own. And Buck, you stay here with the kids. I don't want you to come—just in case I get into it with my father. Better you should stay away."

"Is that really what you want, darling?"

"Yes, Bucky. I need to do this on my own. Don't worry. I'll be fine."

Carrie could be the most emotional person Buck ever met, bursting into tears at the slightest provocation. But she also was one of the strongest women he had ever met. When she set her mind to something, there was no stopping her. So he thought it best to let her have her way in this.

"All right, love. You go, and we'll talk about it when you get home."

One year, three deaths. Were there any more surprises in store for 1954?

**A CHANGE OF KEY**

# CHAPTER THIRTY-THREE
*"This is the Big One!" December 1954*

Al Rovitz had spent a week in Nashville, Tennessee scouting out talent and signing five performers and acts to the RCA Nashville label. When he returned to work on Monday morning, Buck had never seen him so excited. He could barely speak.

"Whoa, slow down, buddy. What's going on?" said Buck.

"Oh my God, Buck, you have to book a flight to Nashville like yesterday. I saw someone that you just aren't going to believe. I'm telling you, this is the big one! RCA is going to make a mint off of this guy. I've never seen anything like this kid. Nobody has."

"Who? What? You haven't told me anything yet, Al. Who is this greatest thing since sliced bread that you're talking about?"

"Kid's name is Elvis Presley. I saw him perform at a club in Nashville. He sings, he plays a crazy guitar, he has moves that will get him banned in Boston, and he looks like a movie star."

"What the hell kind of a name is Elvis?" said Buck.

"How do I know? I didn't name him. But Buck, I promise you, he's the one."

"All right, so tell me about him," said Buck.

"Well, he's done some recording for Sun Records. A guy named Sam Phillips is producing them. He's got an agent named Colonel Tom Parker. I think he's the one who pulls all the strings."

"All right, Al. Tell Kelsey to book me a flight to Nashville first week in January. Where'd you stay when you were there?"

"The Hermitage Hotel. Real nice place. Classic Old South décor, real polite service and clean. I think you'll like it."

"OK, tell Kelsey to get me a room there too."

Then Buck went down to the studio to hear Fran Michaels record "Embraceable You" and "So in Love" from Cole Porter's giant hit show, *Kiss Me Kate*. Once again, the combination of Fran's voice, Kip's gorgeous arrangement and the latest in recording techniques had produced two terrific cuts for her next album.

After the second take, they rested for a few minutes and Buck said, "It sound terrific, Franny. We have to arrange a photo shoot for the jacket front."

"I know. They already scheduled it and said they would send the proofs to you once they have them. "

"I'm off to Nashville, so we'll talk when I get back."

…..

Nashville in January wasn't exactly a world where southern belles strolled down Broadway sporting big hats and parasols. Though not as cold as New York City or the entire Northeast, it was definitely top-coat weather. Buck had registered at The Hermitage and was shown to a spacious room with a number of amenities to appeal to even the most jaded traveler.

After changing his clothes, he grabbed dinner at the Capitol Grille, a restaurant that had been open since 1910. He had a dinner of pan sauteed trout almandine with sides of mashed potatoes and grilled brussels sprouts.

Following a dessert of peach cobbler, he hailed a cab which took him to a small club on Broadway in an area known as 'music row' for its many clubs and performing venues. He was shown to a table not far from the stage. At half past nine, the band took its place on the bandstand and an announcer said, "Ladies and gentlemen, Elvis Presley!"

Sitting by the side of the stage was a gentleman dressed in a white, broad-lapelled suit and a fedora, which he never removed. He was smoking a large cigar that Winston Churchill would have approved of.

For the next two hours, Buck sat enthralled as young Elvis Presley sang everything from gospel to this new rock n' roll and every style in between. It was not just his voice, which was as pure as any Buck had ever heard, but during the up-tempo numbers, his gyrations projected a sexuality that no other singer had ever attempted. And Al had been right about his looks. The young women in the audience practically swooned at his every movement.

While listening to Presley perform, Buck took the opportunity to eyeball the crowd closely. Their expressions were almost rapturous and at that moment, Buck realized that he was watching a kid who was going to turn the music world upside down. He concluded his show with the prayer-like song, "I Believe" which both Frankie Laine and Perry Como had recorded. He might be one of these new rock n' rollers, but Buck saw that his was a versatile voice.

At the end of the performance, Buck approached the stage to speak to Presley. He was intercepted by the man in the white suit who said, "Ah represent this young man, suh. How can Ah help you? Ma name is Colonel Tom Parker."

Though Parker was trying to affect a southern drawl, there was something not quite right about it. Buck detected a whiff of a foreign accent, though he couldn't place the nationality.

He introduced himself and handed Parker a business card. "Buck Fisher, ey? You that saxophonist everybody talked about some years back, right?"

"Yes, that's me. Now I work for RCA Victor and I would like to talk to you about signing this young man to a contract with the label," said Buck. "From what I heard tonight I'd say this young man has a big future ahead of him."

"Elvis, come on over here and meet this boy" said Parker.

Presley, sweating profusely from his vigorous performance wiped his brow on a handkerchief and extended his hand to Buck. "How you, sir?" he said.

"Just fine. I was just talking to Colonel Parker here about possibly signing you to a contract with RCA Victor."

"Oh, well the colonel handles all my business affairs, sir, so whatever he says, I'll go along with," said Elvis.

"How bout we meet tomorrow mornin' Mr. Fisher and we'll talk things over in my office. Here's my card. Let's say eleven o'clock?"

## A CHANGE OF KEY

Colonel Tom Parker's office was located a few miles from the Hermitage on Broadway on the second floor of a building, over a record shop. There was no receptionist so Parker said, "Grab a seat, Mr. Fisher. Anywhere'll do."

"What branch of the service were you in, if I may ask, Colonel Parker?"

That prompted a belly laugh, from Parker. "I never served anywhere, Mr. Fisher. Years back I helped Jimmie Davis become governor of Louisiana. He made me an honorary colonel in the Louisiana militia. Far as I know, there ain't no Louisiana militia—but I use the title anyhow. Been doin' some checkin' up. You were a real colonel, right?"

"Well actually an acting Lieutenant Colonel when I got out. My actual pay rank was Major. But my old boss told me that I was entitled to use the title colonel for the rest of my days."

"Ah see. So what kind of offer are we talking about with RCA?" asked Parker.

"We'd like to sign Elvis to a recording contract—probably the largest one RCA had ever offered anyone."

"Heh, heh, now you sound like a Yankee peddler. Gonna sell me some snake oil, Mr. Fisher?"

"I don't deal in snake oil, Colonel. I deal in the realities of the music business. I'm offering a six-album contract. We'll produce, market and distribute the albums all across the country. We'll also release singles on 45 RPM discs ahead of the albums to create the proper buzz. If they have the impact I think they'll have, Elvis and you are going to make a great deal of money."

"Pardon me if ah sound mercenary, Mr. Fisher, but what kind of money we talkin' about here?"

"Depending upon sales, up to fifteen cents per single. Maybe thirty cents an album again depending on sales. Do the math, Colonel Parker and see what a million selling single will bring you. If I guess right, this young man is going to make quite a number of million-selling records."

"And you're willin' to put all this down in writing all legal and nice?"

## A CHANGE OF KEY

"Absolutely. I have a contract with me, but if you'd like to have an attorney go over it, I'll be in Nashville for a few more days," said Buck.

"Ah don't think that would be necessary, Mr. Fisher. Ah assume you have the authority to make this kind of a deal."

"That's what I do, Colonel Parker. I'm head of the Artist Development Division at RCA. This is my job."

"Elvis gave me power of attorney for his legal affairs so Ah can sign the contract for him," said Parker.

"I understand, but I develop a personal relationship with every artist that we hire, so if it's all the same to you, I'd like to meet with Elvis personally and make sure he understands everything that he's signing up for," said Buck.

Parker looked at his watch and said, "Elvis will be along presently. Boy's never late and he should be here by noon," said Parker.

Sure enough, just before noon, Elvis Presley in blue jeans and a blue chambray work shirt showed up at Colonel Tom Parker's office.

"How you, Mr. Fisher," said Elvis.

"Just fine, just fine. I was talking to the colonel here about signing you to RCA Victor for six albums. The colonel thinks it's a really good deal, but I want to know what you think about it."

Buck then went over the details of the deal, the royalties per single and album, and the plans they had for promoting his music and getting his recordings onto the air and into record shops across the nation.

Elvis glanced at Colonel Parker who nodded almost imperceptibly. "Sounds good, Mr. Fisher. When do we start?"

"Well, we have a recording studio right here in Nashville. A lot of our artists on our RCA Nashville label record here. You can use that studio. I will talk to the sound engineers and see who's producing and schedule you in. Shouldn't take all that long to get started."

"Wonderin' if I could ask you a question, Mr. Fisher."

"Sure, go right ahead."

## A CHANGE OF KEY

"I have some friends that I would like to use as back-up singers on some of the songs I sing. They're called the Jordanaires. The boys started out as a gospel group, but they've sang behind lots of people and I really dig their sound. Think that's possible?"

"We'll certainly give them a listen and if the producer and music director at the sessions think its feasible, sure we can add them as background."

After that, Elvis signed the contract, as did Colonel Parker as his agent. The three men shook hands and Buck left the office knowing that he had just signed RCA's biggest money-maker ever.

Buck spent one more day in Nashville. He checked in at the RCA studio and spoke to the engineers and manager about scheduling recording time for Elvis Presley. They penciled him in for the first two weeks in February. The sessions would be at odd hours, but that was because studio time had already been allocated to other country acts that recorded for the label.

Dinner at The Standard restaurant at the Smith House and turning in early for a good night's sleep and Buck would be on a morning flight headed for LaGuardia the next day.

All that year, Elvis laid down numerous tracks at the RCA Nashville studio. After much deliberation, the executives at RCA decided to release his first song, "Heartbreak Hotel," as a 45 RPM single the following January.

Buck was livid about that decision and he stated his opposition to Jack Merrill.

"Jack, this is nuts! What do you want to sit on this kid's music for almost ten months? I'm telling you we're sitting on a gold mine and there's no reason to wait."

"I agree, Buck, but here's the thing. The label wants to do a lot of pre-release publicity on the kid. Get him performing, maybe some radio or TV time. Then when everyone's talking about this new kid, they'll release the song and follow it up with an album right after it hits. Do I agree? No. I'm with you on this, Buck. But Like everyone else around here, I answer to people above me in the food chain and this is their call."

## A CHANGE OF KEY

"It's a mistake, Jack. This kid is going to be the biggest thing in music since Louis Armstrong or Sinatra."

"Everyone here knows that you're the one who signed him. You'll get full credit when he makes it big."

"I thought my job was to make money for the label now—not a year from now."

"Patience, Buck, patience. It will all work out. You'll see."

Back in his office he had Kelsey locate Al Rovitz and ask him to come up for a few minutes. "Well? What did you think? Was the kid everything I said he was?" asked Al, almost breathlessly.

"He certainly was, or is," said Buck. Then he explained to Al about how the label wouldn't release his songs until early the following year.

"What? What the hell's going on here, Buck? This kid is gonna set the trend for the next decade."

"I know, Al, I know, but think of us as foot soldiers. We just follow orders."

All Al could do was shake his head in amazement. "I sure hope they know what they're doing, Buck. I guess they don't believe in striking while the irons are hot."

"Something like that. Well, let's just continue on with what we do every day. At least we know what we're doing."

That night he explained to Carrie the decision to hold off on releasing singles that Elvis Presley had recorded in Nashville. She was of the same opinion as Buck and Al. "You know, honey, I've been listening to the radio a lot and boy, this rock n' roll stuff is everywhere. Stations like WNEW are playing the kind of music we're more familiar with, but other stations, like WINS are playing strictly rock n' roll.

In the fall of 1954, WINS had hired Alan Fried away from his Cleveland station and brought him to New York City. Fried, nominally called the "King of Rock n' Roll' did much to make the format the dominant musical style in New York and across the nation. Soon joined by DJ Paul Sherman (the Crown Prince of rock n' roll) and speed-talking B. Mitchell Reed, the station was purveying music to an entirely new generation of teenagers.

The 1940s had its bobby soxers dancing in the aisles to swing bands like Benny Goodman at the Brooklyn Paramount, but the 1950s belonged to this new rock n' roll generation. Buck knew it, which is why he wanted to get Elvis into the public ear as soon as possible. He only hoped that RCA hadn't missed the boat with its decision.

A CHANGE OF KEY

# CHAPTER THIRTY-FOUR
## *"Just as We Figured"* May 1956

On January 27$^{th}$, 1956, RCA finally released Elvis Presley's first single, "Heartbreak Hotel." The song had been recorded two weeks earlier at the RCA Nashville studio. Its release had the impact of a hydrogen bomb. In twelve weeks, it was Number 1 on the Billboard Top 100 chart. Shortly thereafter it went gold selling its millionth copy.

Elvis Presley was everywhere—on the radio, in person concerts, television appearances on shows like the *CBS Stage Show* and *The Milton Berle Show*. There were also appearances on the *Steve Allen Show* and the much-ballyhooed appearances on Ed Sullivan's *Toast of the Town,* where as the myth had it, Presley could only be on camera from the waist up, because of his sexual gyrations. By April he was doing a two-week stint at Las Vegas' Frontier Hotel.

A recording session at RCA's New York studio produced hits like a cover of Carl Perkins' "Blue Suede Shoes" and Big Mama Thornton's "Hound Dog."

When Elvis did a live performance in La Crosse, Wisconsin, his stage gyrations prompted the local Catholic diocese to write to no less a personage than J. Edgar Hoover, director of the FBI, saying that Presley was a threat to American security because he was corrupting the morals of America's youth. All that did was validate the old P.T. Barnum maxim, "There is no such thing as bad publicity," because his record sales simply went off the charts after that.

During his stay in Vegas, he signed a seven-year deal with Paramount Pictures. Early on, Elvis had expressed interest in acting and by November, he was starring in his first film, a post-Civil War drama called *Love Me Tender*. In the film he got to sing the title song which also went gold.

At a concert he did at the Mississippi-Alabama Fair and Dairy Show, the governor had to assign fifty National Guardsmen to supplement the local police, so crazed were the crowds that

## A CHANGE OF KEY

attended the show. One critic opined that "no other musical performers besides Glenn Miller and Frank Sinatra have ignited such a wild response in America's youth."

Successful concert tours across America led to even greater record sales making both Elvis and Colonel Tom Parker very wealthy. Within months of the first record release, Elvis Presley had become a household name all across the country. Plus, there were Elvis fan clubs all around the world.

Jack Merrill summoned Buck, Bill and Al to his office for a conference. At the meeting, Jack revealed the extent of the profits that RCA Victor was realizing from Elvis Presley. Simply put, they were astronomical.

"I tell you, fellas, this is going down just as we figured. We knew this kid was going to break every existing recording record and he's well on his way. He's your boy, guys. You did an incredible job with this. Believe me when I say that come bonus time, you three will be well-taken-care of."

The three men thanked Jack but Buck sensed that there was more to this meeting than met the eye. "There's something else, isn't there, Jack?" he said.

Jack grinned and said, "After all these years, I guess you know me pretty well, Buck. OK, I'll tell you why else I asked you to this meeting. Upstairs, they are rethinking our line-up. This rock n' roll thing is without question, the future. Radio stations are popping up all across the country playing rock n' roll as their format—and their ratings are skyrocketing. Elvis has jump-started the entire movement and performers who were strictly country or rhythm and blues are making the crossover into rock n' roll."

"Carrie said the same thing to me a while ago. This 1010 WINS station is dominating radio in New York. Alan Fried is kind of the godfather of the format and his ratings are gigantic. Other DJ's are making big names for themselves too."

"That's just the point," said Jack. "I need you guys out there rounding up acts. Singles, male, female, groups, whatever. As long as they're doing rock n' roll, we need to bring them on board."

## A CHANGE OF KEY

"We're going to run into the same problem as we did several years back," said Bill. "These groups or singles release a single 45 on some obscure label, they get air-play for a week or so, and then they vanish. There's never any follow-up, even if that one single was a hit."

"I understand, Bill. But that just means that those people had no legs. Just like you knew Presley would be a lock for hit after hit and album after album, I want you to find us performers who we can develop into steady hit-makers," said Jack. "That's where the big money is at."

"You said they were rethinking our entire line-up. What does that mean, Jack?" asked Buck.

"We can't abandon all those fans who have bought our records on 78s, and our albums. You know, the ones who buy Sinatra, Shaw, Dinah, Fran and Cindi. Billboard calls them 'Middle of the Road' listeners—and there are hundreds of thousands of them. The trick is, we have to find the exact balance between new and old. It's going to require a lot of studying the numbers and deciding where to place our bets. That job falls to you guys. OK, anything else?"

"No, that about covers it, Jack. We'll get back to you with a plan very soon."

.....

Amidst all the many successes that Buck was delivering to RCA, things at home were changing rapidly. Eddie had started high school the same year he started to shave. Now and again, he would back talk Carrie—loudly. That would leave her both stunned and sad.

Buck had to explain it to her. "He's just cutting the cord, hon. He's flexing his muscles to show he's a man now and not so reliant upon his mother. It happens to every kid."

"I'm sure it didn't happen with you and Mama, Bucky," she said, a touch of despair in her voice.

"You would be wrong. Arlene used to have to be the buffer between the two of us. She would rein me in, sit me down and explain that I was being rude. Because I loved the both of them so much, I would always listen to her and apologize to Ma. I outgrew it eventually, but believe me, I was no angel."

"Where is my little boy?" said Carrie.

That gave Buck the biggest laugh he'd had in weeks.

"He's still there. He'll always be there, darling, and he loves you to the heavens. Boys his age just have to show it in a different way. He's not going to go all 'mushy'—especially in public because his friends would call him a sissy. So tread lightly with what we used to call PDAs in the army—public displays of affection. I remember one time we were at some big party, I forget the occasion, and Mama wet her fingers and tried to plaster down my cowlick—right on the dance floor! I wanted to die of embarrassment. He'd feel the same way if you did that or tried to straighten his tie—and never do that in front of girls," Buck said.

"Still love me Bucky?" said Carrie.

"No. I hate you. Now come here and let me show you just how much I hate you." He opened his arms and she came to him where she snuggled against him as he kissed her passionately on her lips.

"Don't worry, darling. I'll talk to Eddie," said Buck.

Buck thought it was best to deal with the problem sooner than later so he went upstairs, knocked on Eddie's bedroom door and said, "Hey Edd, how 'bout you take a ride with me?"

"Sure, Pop. Gimme a sec and I'll be right out."

Eddie came out of his room and said, "Need another minute. He went into the bathroom and when he came out, his hair was plastered down and he had sprinkled on Old Spice—a cologne that had been around since 1938 and which, in fact, Buck used frequently.

"Expecting to meet someone, Edd?" asked Buck.

"Nah, Pop, but you never can tell."

They took the Cadillac and drove toward Union Turnpike and Cunningham Park.

After some small talk about school and classes, Buck launched the first salvo. "So what's going on with you, kid?"

"What do you mean?"

## A CHANGE OF KEY

"Let me skip to the bottom line. Your mom is a little upset. She says you've been talking back to her. True?"

Eddie looked down at his fingers before saying, "Yeah, I guess so. Not a lot, though."

"Any particular reason?"

"I dunno, Pop. Sometimes she tells me things five times! I hear her the first time. Really. I do!"

"Anything else?"

"Sometimes she gets on me to clean my room."

"Is she right?"

"Yeah, but it's my room, Pop!"

"Oh? You paying rent on it?"

"No, but—"

"Eddie, let me tell you something. Your mother is the most wonderful woman I have ever met. To me, she's the perfect wife, and perfect mother. You have no idea how much she loves you, do you?"

"I know—and I love her too, Pop!"

"Ever tell her?"

"No, but—"

"How come?"

"I don't know," said Eddie.

"Sure you do, kid. You think it would make you look like a sissy if you told your own mother that you love her. Am I right?"

Eddie's silence said that he had hit the nail on the head.

"Kiddo, I want to tell you something else. I haven't checked, but I'm willing to bet that you've got hair on your nuts. Pretty soon, you're going to be thinking about girls all the time—that's if you aren't already thinking about them. So let me give you a piece of fatherly advice that I learned long before you were born. Girls and women like to know that you care. They like to hear nice things too. Contrary to what you might believe, a woman thinks it's very manly to hear a man say 'I love you,' and that goes for mothers too. Girlfriends will come and go—but take it from me: your mother will stand behind you for your entire life. That's what Nana did for me and what your mom will do for you."

## A CHANGE OF KEY

Eddie said nothing for a few minutes as he processed everything that Buck had told him. Finally, he said, "I'm sorry, Pop. I don't want Mom to be mad at me."

"Another thing that you'll learn, Edd, is that mothers can be incredibly forgiving. A big hug and an 'I'm sorry' can really work wonders. Look, none of us are saints. There will be times when you'll lose your temper. I know it's happened to me a lot over the years. The trick is to figure out why you get that way—and maybe defuse it before words come out that you'll regret."

"I get it, Pop. I'll do better. I promise."

"I know you will, son, but make sure your mom knows it too."

They drove home and Buck went to his study leaving Eddie to make it up with Carrie. He said what he had to and hoped that his son would learn from his words.

Of his three children, Laura was clearly the brightest. Her grades in school were nearly perfect. At one Parent-Teacher conference, her math teacher had said that her grasp of elementary algebra was like nothing she had ever seen in her career—and she had been teaching for thirty years. In fact, every teacher he met with lauded her and said they wished Laura could attend one of the City's specialized high schools like Brooklyn Tech or Stuyvesant, but unfortunately, at the time, those schools were not coed.

"But you're zoned for Bayside High School, Mr. Feinstein, and it's a grand place for an education. I think Laura will thrive there," said Miss Proski, her Chemistry teacher.

One night in bed, Carrie said, "You know, honey, I think it's some kind of compensation. Laura knows that she will never be exactly perfect in the way she walks, so maybe she feels like she has to be perfect in other ways. You can always find her reading when she's not doing something else. She reads more books in a month than I've read in my entire lifetime."

"Well, that's not a bad thing, darling," said Buck.

"No, but I'd like her to have more friends. Maybe she should become involved in some activities at school. I once asked her what she wanted to be when she grows up. She didn't hesitate for an instant. She said she wants to be an architect."

'Whoa. That's a tough profession for a woman to break into. It's really male-dominated," said Buck.

"I know, but I'm not going to discourage her if that's what she wants. Thing is, she'll probably change her mind five or six times by the time she's out of high school. She said her second choice was to be a doctor like Uncle Jerry so she could help children like her. That almost made me cry."

"She's a wonderful kid, Carrie. She gets that from you," said Buck. "And Eddie said the same thing about being a doctor."

"Us. She gets it from us, Bucky. Sometimes I don't think you're fully aware of what a great dad you are, or how much our kids look up to you. Fortunately, I'm aware of it—and how great a husband you are. So come over here and make love to me."

Buck happily obliged.

But the child that still had Buck's heart was little Casey. Maybe it was because her birth had almost cost Carrie her life. Or maybe it was because the little girl was very much like a puppy. She climbed all over Buck every chance she got, and when Buck sat on the couch, she snuggled next to him, simply needing that physical contact to feel safe.

Buck had no memories of his own father playing with him when he was a child. Maybe he was too young when his father died to recall it. He was determined that his children would have plenty of memories. He reveled in his opportunity to play with Casey, going over colors, shapes, doing simple jigsaw puzzles with her. Unbeknownst to him, Carrie would watch him and it would bring tears to her eyes, but they were tears of joy. Like Buck, she had no fond childhood memories of her parents ever playing with her.

…..

Following Jack Merrill's instructions, Buck and his team set about achieving the 'balance' in their lists of artists that the RCA label was looking for. Bill Dwyer had signed Eartha Kitt, a Negro actress and vocalist who gave the label two huge hits with

## A CHANGE OF KEY

"C'est si bon" (she was fluent in French), and "Santa Baby," a satirical Christmas song oozing with a love of materialism. Now, more albums were planned for her.

Al scored a contract with Ed Ames of the Ames Brothers singing group. The quartet had had major hits with "Rag Mop" and "Sentimental Me" and in 1956, they got their own television show. Ed wanted a solo career as well as remain singing with his brothers, so a contract was worked out to permit him to record as both a single and with the group.

Perhaps the biggest acquisition of all was a young, incredibly handsome singer named Eddie Fisher, one of the many performers to come out of Philadelphia. He had already hit it big with songs like "Oh My Papa" and "On the Street Where You Live" from the smash Broadway show, *My Fair Lady*. But the thing about Eddie Fisher was that he could master different musical genres. He also had a hit with a rock n' roll flavored song called "Dungaree Doll." Currently he was starring with his wife, Debbie Reynolds, on Broadway in a show called *Bundle of Joy*, so he had legitimacy about him as a pop standards singer.

In the meantime, Fran Michaels' album, "Raising Standards," had gone gold, giving her a third gold record. There was talk of bringing her to Broadway after her pregnancy and before she returned to Hollywood.

Cindi Kay was now a frequent guest on variety shows like *Toast of the Town* and *Arthur Godfrey's Talent Scouts*. One television critic said that Cindi was "Spunkier than Theresa Brewer with twice the voice."

Jack Merrill was both thrilled and impressed by the plethora of signings that Buck and his team had brought about. In fact, General Sarnoff sent a personal note to Buck thanking him for his great success—and the barrels of money he had earned for the RCA brand.

One night while driving home, Buck thought about his future wondering what else he could achieve at and for RCA. The answer was soon to come.

A CHANGE OF KEY

# CHAPTER THIRTY-FIVE
## *"Starring Buck Fisher!" November 1956*

"Sit down, Buck, and let's talk," said Jack Merrill. His tone was non-committal, but in Buck's experience, more often than not, when some one said, "let's talk," it was never a good thing. But this time it was.

"Do you know who Irving Levy is, Buck?"

"No, I don't think so. The name doesn't ring a bell. Who is he?"

"I've known him since he was a snot-nosed kid. Our families lived next door to each other in Prospect Heights. Well, let me enlighten you. In 1949 he opened a jazz club that he named Birdland. He picked that name to capitalize on the whole Charlie Parker craze, even though Parker only played there a few times. Seems he wanted too much money. Well, Irv's a smart cookie and he's turned the place into the most famous jazz club in the city—maybe even the country."

"And?"

"And I did some favors for him way back when and I also helped out his family when his father lost his job. So I called in a marker," said Jack.

"Meaning?"

"Meaning on Friday Night, November 30, the Buck Fisher Quintet is playing Birdland. We've got a publicity blitz working and this is going to be a huge event."

"What? You're crazy, Jack!"

"Why? You know the numbers on your album. I already handed you the gold record you earned. Obviously, you still have a huge number of fans. It's about time you put yourself out there live and stopped hiding behind a record jacket."

"And if I lay an egg?"

Jack stared straight into Buck's eyes and said, "First, when has Buck Fisher ever laid an egg? And second, do you think I would risk the good name of the label by putting out some wheezer at so visible a place as Birdland? Come on, Buck. You need to have the same confidence in yourself as I have in you."

Buck sighed and said, "How long a set are we talking about, Jack?"

"Give them ninety minutes. You go on at nine and by ten thirty you're packing up."

"Great. I can make a quick getaway," said Buck.

"Oh, and by the way, not to make you nervous or anything, but I've invited a bunch of critics to the show including Nat Hentoff at *Downbeat*."

"Oh Jesus Christ, Jack!" said Buck.

"Confidence, my friend, confidence," said Jack, smiling mischievously at Buck.

That night, Carrie said it was the greatest thing she had ever heard, the thought of Buck Fisher playing again for the public. Buck reminded her that he had already done that on an aircraft carrier in Hawaii.

"Yes, darling, but this is with all that new music and just a few pieces behind you. You have to admit it's very different."

"Yeah, that's what I'm afraid of."

…..

Buck had the feeling that the night of November 30th was kind of a rigged jury. Carrie made sure the entire family had reservations and many of the orchestra members had also reserved spots at Birdland. True, there were a lot of walk-ins and of course, the critics were also there, but still, it was nothing like an objective audience.

There was a line nearly around the corner at 1678 Broadway when Buck arrived. There was a temporary sign advertising the Buck Fisher Quintet attached to the awning that led to the entrance of the club. With Carrie on his arm and his tenor case in one hand, alto case in the other, he entered Birdland and was surprised at how roomy it was. The club was below ground and it could seat five hundred people in booths and at long tables. It had a fully stocked bar and there was even a special fenced in area for non-drinkers. The full stage could accommodate an entire orchestra, but tonight, there would just be five pieces.

Backstage, Buck found his friends warming up ready to give what they hoped would be one of the most impressive performances of their careers.

"Stay loose, partner," said Chuck. "We got this nailed."

"Hope your right, Chuckie. This could turn into another Nagasaki if we don't get it right."

At precisely 9 PM, an announcer said, "Ladies and gentlemen, Birdland proudly presents the Buck Fisher Quintet starring Buck Fisher!"

As the band took the stage, the entire crowd, minus a few expressionless critics, rose to its feet and applauded with unabashed enthusiasm. That did nothing to settle Buck's nerves, but there was no turning back.

Buck had selected as the first number, "No Name Jive," a swing number made famous by the Glen Gray Casa Loma Orchestra. After Buck played the melody, he took off on a solo that combined both swing and bebop figures—something that was stylistically brand new. It was a six-minute number that also gave Kenny Ferraro a chance to play thirty-two bars of bebop solo. Then Buck traded eights with Buddy Scraggs—another modification of an old swing trick. So new was the sound, that at the end of the song, there was a moment of total silence—before the crowd exploded into roaring applause.

The quintet followed up with "Route 66" and it was just as novel in its approach as the "No Name Jive." Kenny Ferraro played a sixteen-bar intro, then Buck did the melody and the bridge—and he was off on a seven-minute solo during which he explored every tonal and inventive characteristic of the tenor saxophone.

The third song slowed things down and it was one that Buck had wanted to solo on from the moment he heard Fran Michaels sing it years earlier: "My Foolish Heart." This time, Buck found the emotion in the melody without crowding it with all the notes of bebop. It was exhilarating, heartbreaking, and moving all at the same time. It elicited the same response from the audience as the first two songs had.

For forty-five minutes the audience sat enraptured at the artistry of the Buck Fisher Quintet. They took a fifteen-minute break during which time Jack Merrill came backstage and said, "Buck, you own them. This is just fantastic!"

The second set opened with Monk's "Straight, No Chaser." Buck changed his approach slightly for this song. It was more of a 'cool jazz' sound without the voluminous thirty-second note runs that both Charlie Parker and John Coltrane favored. And yet, it bore no resemblance to the swing sound of the 1940s. Buck had adapted to the progressive style of the 1950s and had turned the ninety-six bars into something amazing.

He switched to alto sax for "A Cottage for Sale," and once again he explored the deep emotions of the song, even absent the melancholy lyrics.

As had happened in the past, Buck could just tell when he was 'on.' The faces of the crowded club affirmed their appreciation of his ability to spin complex and inventive solos from simple melodies. Buck again felt 'one' with his instrument—that it was an extension of his body and soul, and he was willing to be even more daring in his solos than he had in the practice sessions.

As a tribute to Kip Roman's hard work, Buck ended the performance with his original, "Tempo de Bop." Every member of the quintet got to solo on the song with Buck's ninety-six bars the highlight of the number.

At the conclusion, Buck introduced the members of the group and thanked everyone for their generous response to the group's performance.

Carrie and the family crowded around Buck when he came out of the dressing room hugging him and raving about the performance. "Well, we'll see what Hentoff has to say. *Downbeat* comes out Monday morning."

But the critic for the Sunday *New York Times* entertainment section had filed his review directly following the

# A CHANGE OF KEY

show. His review read in part, *"The remarkable intonation, the flying fingers, the leaps and bounds of his solos showed why Buck Fisher was the premier saxophonist of his day—and any day."*

The *Daily News* critic was even more laudatory: *"If there were a World Series of saxophone playing, on Friday night I heard the World champion. Buck Fisher has retired the crown."*

Carrie had trouble understanding Buck's reluctance to believe the reviews. "Darling, why can't you see what everyone else sees? You think those critics would lie? Jeopardize their reputations? They came, they gave you a fair shake—and they decided that your talent was enormous. You knew that once upon a time, hon. What happened?"

"I don't know, Carrie. I don't understand it myself. But I think it was a stacked deck on Friday night. Hell, I practically knew everyone in the joint."

But if he had any doubt about the success of the concert and the Buck Fisher Quintet, those fears were allayed when Nat Hentoff's review came out in Monday's *Downbeat*. Hentoff said: *"When you've been around jazz as long as I have and seen all the great ones—Prez, Hawk, Webster, you would appreciate what I heard Friday last at Birdland. The legendary Buck Fisher, now appearing with a quintet rather than his big band, simply burned the place down with his playing. Fisher, the supreme tenor man of the Swing era, has now taken a leap forward into modern jazz. Accompanied by four remarkably skillful players, three of whom are alumni of his Swing days, Fisher explored the depths of his instrument like no one has before It would be a sin for him not to keep performing live."*

Hentoff, who was known for his critical analysis of music, often in acerbic terms, certainly had nothing but praise for the Buck Fisher Quintet.

Jack Merrill was simply beside himself after he read the reviews. He was on the phone to Buck early Monday morning. "Well, kid? What did I tell you? You were a smash! Not a single tepid review. Nothing but raves. You did it Buck! You did it! Tell the guys they were also fantastic."

## A CHANGE OF KEY

"I'm still in shock, Jack," said Buck. "I know it felt good up there and I think I hit all the right notes—but I'm glad the critics didn't have me for breakfast."

"Funny. Very funny. So let me ask you, what are you doing on the evening of December 23$^{rd}$?" asked Jack.

"Spending the night at home with the wife and kids, I suppose," said Buck.

"Bullshit. You'll be busy that night—playing Carnegie Hall."

Buck almost dropped the phone. There was dead silence until Buck said, "Now who's being funny?"

"No joke, pal. Some Hungarian piano player was supposed to appear that night, but she had to have her gall bladder removed and she's out until after the new year. So they called Bruce Baldwin at Red Seal and asked if anyone could sub, but his whole line-up is either booked or on vacation. So Bruce called me—and, well, you're it. We're going to do even more publicity for this one, Buck."

"But—"

"Forget it, Buck. It's a done deal. Now, you and the guys get your asses down to the P.R. Department for group photos and solo shots of you. We're going to put ads on busses, billboards, radio ads—the whole *megillah*. The place holds about 2800 people and we hope to fill it to the gills."

"You sure this is a good idea, Jack?" asked Buck.

Merrill laughed and said, "Oh, I forgot to tell you—we have the title of your next album. It's called 'Buck Fisher: Live from Carnegie Hall.' We'll be recording the whole show and then narrow it down to the best cuts for the two sides. I'm going to write the liner notes myself."

.....

For Carrie it was Hanukkah, Christmas and her birthday all wrapped up into one giant package. "I'm just so proud of you, darling, she said that night as they wrapped in each other's arms in bed. Imagine! Carnegie Hall!"

## A CHANGE OF KEY

"Don't get too excited, honey. Goodman was the first guy to play jazz at Carnegie all the way back in '38. Glenn played it in '39, so I'm kind of a late-comer to the party."

"Well, love, those two boys never got a chance to make love to me—as I'm sure you're going to do right now."

The next morning, 30 Rock was a hive of activity. True to his word, Jack Merrill had the P.R. Department going at full tilt. The first radio spot was heard that night on WNEW. By the next day, there were handbills on every lamppost and construction site plywood barrier in the city."

Jack had arranged an interview for Buck with Jerry Marshall on WNEW's 'Make Believe Ballroom." Marshall had taken over the show from Martin Block who had left the station in early 1954 when he moved to ABC. The interview lasted for a half an hour minus time for advertisements during which Marshall explored Buck's entire career from his beginnings as a Brooklyn-born sideman to his spectacular career as a big band musician to his military career and beyond. As the most popular station in all of New York City, the interview prompted immediate response from the listeners and in-person ticket sales as well as telephone reservations poured into Carnegie Hall.

The quintet still had a few weeks to practice before the 23$^{rd}$ of December. They added new material as well as the old favorites because Buck didn't want the show to merely be a reprise of the Birdland concert.

One surprise, or rather two surprises happened when Fran Michaels and Cindi Kay showed up at the rehearsal studio. "Let us each do a number with you, Buck. We don't want any kind of a billing or anything. It will be a great surprise for the audience when we come on," said Fran.

"What do you say, Buck? I always wanted to play Carnegie Hall," said Cindi, half-joking. "So now could be my big chance."

Buck looked at the other members of the group who all nodded. Chuck Fein said, "Hell, if I can't marry 'em, at least I can play for 'em."

## A CHANGE OF KEY

Cindi blew him a kiss and said, "Next life, Chuckie, next life."

And so the band got to work rehearsing and finding a suitable number for Fran and Cindi. "Remember guys, it's a live show so we don't want to be too perfect. Let's keep our playing on the loose side to give it a real jazz feel," said Buck.

After the first week of rehearsals, Buddy Scraggs took Buck aside and said, "Mr. Buck, I wantcha to know that you done everything you said you would do for me. Not a lotta white guys give a nigger like me the chances you did. Now here I be playin' Carnegie Hall—long way away from the Savoy Ballroom. I got me some money, I got me a steady job. You sho' kept your promises and I'll always give you my best."

"You're a major part of this group, Buddy. You help make it the success it is. I told you I'd never go back on my word and I hope I've kept my part of the bargain."

"Sho' 'nuf, Mr. Buck, sho' nuf."

.....

December 23$^{rd}$ was crisp and cold. Christmas lights had been strung all along 57$^{th}$ Street and the city seemed aglow with the spirit of the season. Carrie had taken the three children to see the tree at Rockefeller Center the previous week. Buck had come down during lunch to be with them—mostly to see the expressions of wonder and joy that he saw in the faces of his children—most especially little Casey. After lunch, Carrie took them to see the store windows in Lord &Taylor, Bloomingdales, and Bonwit Teller as Buck returned to work.

But now, they were across town standing in front of the grand entrance to Carnegie Hall watching as a line of people waited to purchase tickets. Jack Merrill was waiting in the lobby for him and he said, "Not quite a sell-out, Buck, but at least 1700 people with ticket sales still going on. Not a bad crowd at all."

The concert hall itself was a five-tiered affair with levels that rose six stories, with five of them devoted to seating. As Buck looked around the hall, he saw some empty seats in the upper-most tier, and some scattered empty seats on the orchestra level, but other than that, Carnegie Hall seemed crowded—and full of energy and anticipation.

A sound check had been run earlier in the afternoon without the quintet just to check the microphone and amplifier positions, but so legendary were the acoustics of Carnegie Hall that was not necessary to do the extensive balancing that was always required in the recording studios.

In a moment of self-doubt, Buck thought that maybe it would be best if the audience couldn't hear him. You can't pan what you can't hear, he reasoned. But no, there was no going back, so Buck kissed Carrie and the kids and headed backstage to meet the group.

At 8 PM, an offstage announcer said, "Ladies and gentlemen, the Buck Fisher Quintet!"

The curtain parted, the group bowed and Buck counted off the first number. He had selected Charlie Parker's "Ornithology" to open with figuring he'd play on bebop turf right from the start. Instead of Parker's throaty alto, he played it on the huskier sounding tenor—and he owned it. About twenty-four bars into the song, after Buck played the melody and launched into his solo, the audience was shouting enthusiastically. At one point, he traded eights with Buddy and then Kenny traded eights with Chuck. It was an innovative and brand-new arrangement of the Parker hit.

He followed it up with "Route 66" and once again the audience's response was thunderous. Buck's s solo was long, but everybody in the group got to take at least sixteen bars.

Next up was a Kip Roman arrangement of one of the very first bebop songs—Miles Davis' "Boplicity" from 1949. It was perfect for Buck's hybrid bebop/blues style. His solo was a creative gem without having to bust his fingers on the typical bebop runs.

After that song, Buck stepped to the microphone and spoke to the crowd. "Ladies and gentlemen, we have a very special surprise for you this evening. I'd like to bring out a young lady who got her start singing with my big band way back in the early

1940s. She went on to a career in the movies which garnered her an Oscar nomination to go with her three gold records that she recorded for us at RCA. Please give a special welcome to Fran Michaels!"

It was like setting off a stick of dynamite in Carnegie Hall. Every person in the hall jumped to their feet, whistled, shouted and applauded. Fran swept onto the stage wearing a floor length gown that showed off her exquisite figure perfectly while at the same time covering her pregnancy well. She hugged Buck and blew kisses to the audience.

Fran stepped to the microphone and said, "Thank you for that incredible welcome—and I want to thank Buck and the band—some of whom I have known since the beginning of my career, for letting me join them tonight. I'd like to do a song from my first album that Buck helped produce and that the wonderful Kip Roman arranged. It's the Rodgers and Hart hit, "My Funny Valentine."

Kenny did a soulful eight bar intro and then Fran, with her sugary alto voice that sounded like it came from an aged wine cask, presented the lyric. She found the heart and soul of the lyric and it was enough to make an audience weep in empathy. After the bridge, Buck played a Tex Beneke-like obligato behind her second chorus. More magic.

If an audience could lose its mind, it did so for Fran Michaels. Buck took the microphone and said, "Would you like to hear another one?"

The reaction was predictable and loud. Buck said, "How about something by the Gershwins?" If the shouts of glee from the audience were any indication, Buck had picked the right composer to show off her swing abilities. "Fran, let's do 'Nice Work if you can Get It.'"

The audience could see why Fran was an Oscar-nominated actress. She 'performed' the song rather than just singing it. Buck kept his playing subordinate to Fran's singing to give her a chance to shine. He took a brief sixteen bar solo and then Fran brought the song to its conclusion.

## A CHANGE OF KEY

When it was over, Buck said, "How about a huge hand for the very wonderful Fran Michaels?" Everyone in Carnegie Hall responded with a standing ovation for her. As she waved to the audience, Buck whispered, "Thanks Franny. You were just super."

"No, thank *you*, Buck. I love you!" She kissed him and swept off the stage.

There were four more songs in the first half of the program: "Straight, No Chaser," "A Cottage for Sale" on alto," and the most moving version of "My Foolish Heart" that anyone had ever heard.

He wanted to end the set on an upbeat note, so he had chosen "No Name Jive" to finish it.

Buck then said, "Folks, we'll take a short break and we might have another surprise for you in the next set.

The dressing room was crowded with well-wishers including Carrie, who had left the children in the care of Bevvy so she could see Buck. "You're doing fantastically, darling. They absolutely adore you—as do I." Then she saw Fran and ran to hug her. "Oh Franny, how wonderful you were!"

"Thank you, Carrie. I haven't had that much fun in ages. Just to sing with Buck's band again—it was amazing."

The second set opened with "Four Brothers" with Buck playing all the sax parts that Woody Herman's sidemen had played on the recording. Then he opened it up with a lengthy solo that once again demonstrated his facility on the tenor sax.

Two more numbers followed and then Buck again went to the microphone and addressed the crowd. "You know, folks, when I was in the Army, I had a lot of things happen to me—some good, and some, well, some not so good. But one of the best things was when one night in the Officers' Club at Camp Polk, Louisiana, I heard a young lady singing. I immediately brought her on board with the Army Special Services band as our girl vocalist. And she was fabulous. You know her as 'Little Miss Powerhouse,' Ladies and gentlemen, let's give a big hand to Cindi Kay!"

## A CHANGE OF KEY

Cindi, petite and gorgeous in a taffeta gown, came onto the stage, hugged Buck and said into the microphone, "Hi folks How 'bout we swing!"

The band launched into a really upbeat "It Don't Mean a Thing if it Ain't Got that Swing." Buck led off with the melody and then took ninety-six bars of mostly swing figures. Then, Cindi let loose with a triple chorus of scat singing that astounded everyone in Carnegie Hall. In the years since she left the service, Cindi had become an absolute master of the genre—and the audience loved it. When Buck raised his fist to indicate he was taking the song out, they moved to the coda and finished it with a fermata chord until Buck cut it off.

"Is it any wonder this gal has won two gold records—and is on her way to a third! How about we let her do another one?"

The audience's reaction said it all. This time, Cindi sang her signature tune, another Duke Ellington number "I Got it Bad and that Ain't Good." Little Cindi Kay could break your heart with the way she plumbed the lyric for its raw emotion. She completed the song, bowed to the audience and embraced Buck. Then she exited the stage leaving the quintet to finish its set.

There were five more songs before Buck wrapped up the show with his take on a song Neil Hefti had written for Count Basie, "Splanky." It was one of the freelance charts that Hefti had sent to Buck. The chart started with Kenny Ferraro doing a great imitation of Basie's two finger piano style. Then Buck presented the melody and his solo was a relaxed, bluesy piece of artistry that hearkened back to the Buck Fisher of the '40s, while still incorporating enough modern figures to avoid sounding too dated. Though the chart was a solid hit for Basie's big band, Hefti had miniaturized the song for the quintet that gave the whole group plenty of opportunity to solo. The song even ended with the typical 'three tinks' that Basie loved to do on piano.

Once again, everyone in Carnegie Hall was on their feet shouting "Bravo!" and "Encore!"

The quintet left the stage, but the audience refused to leave without an encore. Buck led them back out and said, "OK, you win. One more. Here's one that Dizzy Gillespie and Kenny Clarke wrote back in 1942 called 'Salt Peanuts.'" Though the song pre-dated the bebop era, it certainly had the feel of the style. It was played in a racehorse tempo that after nearly two hours of playing, was a challenge for everyone in the group. Buck's fingers moved as if they were in overdrive, speeding over the keys during his long solo. Kenny then played a bebop piano solo reminiscent of Lenny Tristaino, one of the stalwarts of the bebop movement and a master of improvisation. So fast was the song that Chuck Fein had to play in double time rather than in the walking bass style of the swing era.

The encore concluded and with it, the show. Everyone in attendance, including Buck, knew that it was an unqualified success. That much they could tell from the audience. But what the critics had to say was another thing. The morning papers would show what the 'experts' thought.

Jack Merrill had arranged for an after-concert dinner party for thirty people at Sardi's on West 44$^{th}$ Street. The restaurant was notable for its famous clientele of Broadway performers and film personalities, whose caricatures were enshrined on the walls. It was also famous as the birthplace of the Tony Awards given each year to Broadway shows and performers.

Vincent Sardi himself seated the group and he said, "Mr. Fisher, with your permission, I'd like to have Don Bevan do a caricature of you for our wall. About time you joined all the other personalities up there." Bevan had followed Alex Gard, the original caricaturist, and John Mackey as the resident artist at the restaurant.

Bevan came to the table and introduced himself. "This won't take too long, folks. Promise."

As Buck perused the menu, he looked up and saw Walter Winchell, syndicated columnist for the *New York Daily Mirror*, approaching his table. Winchell had the reputation as a gossip columnist who could make or break anyone's career from actors to politicians to national figures like Charles Lindberg who he publicly chastised for his appeasement of Hitler.

## A CHANGE OF KEY

"Caught your show at Carnegie tonight, Buck," said Winchell. "Terrific. Just terrific. Mind if I give you kudos in my next column?"

"Not at all—and thank you, Mr. Winchell," said Buck.

"Wow, honey," said Carrie. "Winchell! If he's impressed, everyone will be impressed."

Jack Merrill knocked his fork against his wine glass indicating that he wanted to say something. "I'm not one for making speeches," said Jack, "but I just want to say that what happened tonight was remarkable in every respect. I think we just got ourselves another gold record, but more importantly, Buck, you just showed the entire music world that you're at the top of your game. I know you're busy with all the other jobs I give you, but we're going to make sure you have plenty of time to make more music with the Buck Fisher Quintet. Now, let's eat!"

On the ride home to Queens that night, Carrie leaned against Buck as he drove. The children were asleep in the back seat and Carrie was on the verge of falling asleep herself. She said, "It's been a wonderful night, my darling. I'm so happy for you and the boys. They did such a terrific job tonight." Then she nodded off.

The following morning, all the New York papers reviewed the performance and the accolades were universal. Walter Winchell wrote, *"He's talented, he's personable, and his playing even with a smaller group brings us back to those grand days of Swing. In short, he is a musical marvel."* He had equally kind words for the rest of the quintet and Fran and Cindi.

Thinking about the night, Buck realized that he was out to prove something to himself—maybe to the world in general. He had met success in a number of different roles but he could not help but wondering, what was next for him?

A CHANGE OF KEY

# CHAPTER THIRTY-SIX
*"Coda" February, 1957*

After Buck returned to work the Monday after Carnegie Hall, he quickly fell into the routine of his job, signing talent, reviewing contracts, scheduling rehearsal and recording time, and working on a new album with the quintet.

There were scarcely enough hours in the day to accomplish the many duties that he had, but no one above him really pressed him on deadlines so if something was not completed in one day, it would wait until the next.

Things at home were a constant delight to Buck. Eddie was a senior in high school and he was applying to City College for the fall semester. One night at dinner, he announced that he wanted to be a lawyer. "That's great, kid," said Buck. Do well in college and I'll bet law schools will be falling all over themselves to admit you."

As he had predicted, Laura had decided against architecture in favor of becoming a doctor. She was still a few years off from graduating high school, but she was so bright that both he and Carrie were confident that she could do anything she wanted to. Her limp was barely noticeable anymore and unless one knew what to look for, it was hard to believe that she almost succumbed to polio. She enjoyed spending time with Uncle Jerry and talking about medicine with him. For his part, Jerry was thrilled to have such a young and bright niece who was anxious to learn everything she could about a myriad of subjects.

But Casey owned him. At nine years old she started flute lessons with Pammy Roman. "She really has taken to it beautifully, Buck," said Pammy one day after a lesson. "By next year she'll be sight reading Mozart and Vivaldi."

Buck had bought her a second-hand flute on music row in Manhattan but upon seeing it, Pammy said, "Can I make a suggestion, Buck?"

"Sure. Go ahead."

## A CHANGE OF KEY

"I know you got her an inexpensive flute to see if she would like it, but it's a closed-hole flute, and we used to call that the 'lazy man's instrument,' because the keys do all the work. What she should have is an open-hole flute. It forces her to have the right posture and keep her fingers perfectly positioned. Beside that, there really is no comparison in tone between an open and closed hole flute. I would recommend one made by Gemeinhardt. It will cost several hundred dollars, but I think Casey can be a wonderful player, so it's worth the investment."

"Thanks, Pammy. Whatever is best for her, she'll have."

And of course there was Carrie. The true center of his universe. At times he would lay awake at night marveling at the fact that he was still so in love with her. Nearly seventeen years of marriage—blissful years through triumphs and hardships—and his love had never wavered.

For her part, from nearly the moment she first laid eyes on Buck Fisher, she had staked a claim on him. He recalled the post-adolescent crush he had on Rivka Bergman, who had turned out to be a supercilious snob who felt a mere musician would never be good enough for her. No, Carrie was no Rivvy. Her affection was boundless for Buck and her children. Buck had given her absolutely everything she had ever wanted in life and now, with a few silver strands peaking through her lush blonde hair, her loving nature had not abated by one bit.

They made love often, mature, giving, mutually satisfying love, quite unlike the roaring passionate sessions of their younger days. Some nights he absolutely lusted after her wonderful body. Other nights they were content merely to hold one another and fall asleep in a loving embrace. No one could imagine that in the beautiful, mature and doting mother she had become, there once was a somewhat wild and free-spirited youth. Buck preferred her just as she was now, though he had loved her every minute of every day they had spent together.

One night, Buck found Carrie in her wicker chair in their bedroom, dabbing at tears in her eyes. Immediately, he was frightened. "Sweetheart? What is it?"

## A CHANGE OF KEY

"Oh, it's nothing Bucky. I just get sad sometimes."

"Tell me why," said Buck.

"It's Eddie. He wants to get an apartment close to CCNY when he starts college. He says the commute from Queens and back will take too long and he'll lose study time."

"It makes sense, darling. Can I tell you something?"

By this time tears were flowing freely down Carrie's cheeks. "Yes, please do."

"I know why you're upset. Yesterday Eddie was a baby in your arms and now—well, now he's on the verge of being a grown-up and you're sad because the time just seemed to fly by. I feel it too, darling. Face it: we're not twenty-four years old any longer, and we don't have our whole lives in front of us."

She hugged Buck and wept softly. "But, Carrie, look how far we've come. Look at all we have. We've done all this together and whether we like it or not, sooner than we can imagine, you'll be a mother-in-law with little ones calling you Nana."

She hugged him tighter and said, "Will you still love me if I get old, Bucky?"

He kissed her on the lips and laughed. "How many times over the years have you asked me this same question? And how many times has my answer been the same: I will go to my grave loving no one else in my life but you. And if you need me to repeat it every day, then I will."

"I love you so much, Bucky. So very much."

"And I love you, so let's just take joy in all that we've been to each other." He led her by hand to their bed—and found joy several times that night.

.....

Wednesday, February 13th started the same as any other day. Buck drove to 30 Rock, stopped to grab coffee and a cinnamon bun and took the elevator to his office. But when he got there, he knew something was very wrong. There was an almost panicked expression on Kelsey Burton's face.

"Kel? What's wrong?"

## A CHANGE OF KEY

"Better get upstairs Buck—all the way up. The General wants all hands on deck by ten this morning. It's in the boardroom. Do not be late."

When Buck got to the boardroom on the 65$^{th}$ Floor, his eyes sprung wide open as he saw that the head of every single major division of RCA was seated at the long table. Buck looked at Jack Merrill who merely smiled at him. The other department heads glanced nervously about at each other.

General David Sarnoff entered at a quarter past ten, said good morning and sat at the head of the table. For the next forty-five minutes, he went over the figures for last year which had finally been compiled by the Finance Department. It had been a very good year for RCA. Buck's division alone accounted for over eight million dollars in record sales. On the television side, the revenue was even more. Even the radio stations that RCA owned were pouring money into the company's coffers.

Sarnoff had praise for everyone involved in the company's tremendous success. Then he said, "I do have a few significant announcements to make. Bruce Baldwin will be leaving us to become the Chief Executive Officer at the Dumont Television Network. We're sorry to lose him at RCA Red Seal, but I know this is a great opportunity for him, so Bruce, I'm sure we all wish you a lot of luck. Next, we're going to be combining the Red Seal Division with Jack Merrill's RCA Popular Artists Division. It will all now be under the heading of RCA Records."

No one at the table aid anything, perhaps because they were expecting another shoe to drop. It dropped quickly when Sarnoff said, "Jack, you have the floor. The next announcement is yours."

Jack stood up and said, "I'll make this short and sweet. I came to RCA way back in 1925. I wasn't exactly a young man when I got here. I was already thirty-five years old and I've been here for thirty-two years. I talked it over with the General and I've decided now is the time for me to retire. I'm 67 years old, I have a nice place down in Florida and I'm getting damned tired of these New York winters. I'd like to spend more time with my wife and

## A CHANGE OF KEY

my grandchildren, and with the generous pension RCA has for me plus my social security, I'll have more than enough money to lounge around, play some golf and hit the beach every day."

Buck's hands were on the edge of the table in a death grip. How could RCA lose Jack Merrill? He was an institution at 30 Rock. And he was Buck's sponsor and friend. This was terrible news.

Jack continued, "I'm confident that the label is in great shape and it keeps getting better. We have an all-star lineup that the other majors would kill to have, and I believe it's only going to get better. So, I just want to thank General Sarnoff for the inspiration he provided me with for all these years and to let each of you know how proud and honored I have been to have worked with all of you."

Jack sat down and Buck's head drooped between his shoulders until General Sarnoff once again rose at his seat.

"So, my friends, we have a hole to plug up. With the two record divisions now combined, this is going to become a hugely important job. It will take someone very special to fill that position, and fortunately, he's sitting right at this table. Ladies and gentlemen, join me in welcoming the new President of RCA Records—Buck Fisher."

Buck wasn't sure he had heard correctly. He looked at Jack, who was now grinning like a jack o' lantern and he nodded at Buck showing that he had wind of this for some time.

Though he must have sounded tentative, Buck managed to say, "Thank you General. You have my word that I will do my absolute best to make RCA Records the envy of the music world."

"I know you will, Buck. We'll meet later this week and go over some plans together," said Sarnoff.

Twenty minutes later, the meeting broke up and Buck followed Jack to his office. "I've said this before, Jack, but are you absolutely out of your goddamned mind?"

"Here we go again," said Jack in mock exasperation. "Be honest, Buck, do you think I would have insisted that you become the president if I didn't think you could do the job? What a black

## A CHANGE OF KEY

eye that would leave me with. And Bill and Al are going to be vice-presidents working right along with you. I'll fill them in on their duties later today. Now look, I'm not out the door yet. We have a lot of talking to do over the next week or so and I won't go until I'm sure you're in the picture and you know what you're doing."

"Jack? You're sure about this?"

"Get the hell out of here and go tell Carrie the good news. And Buck? Congratulations. You are definitely the right guy for the job."

Buck called Carrie and asked if she could invite Arlene and Bevvy over that evening for dessert. He said he had an announcement that he wanted the family together for.

When Carrie asked him what the big secret was, he said, "Can't talk now, hon. I'll explain later. Oh, and ask Bill and Cathy to come too."

By half past seven, almost everyone meaningful in Buck's life was gathered in the living room of his home. Carrie, the three kids, his sisters and their husbands, and his closest friends. Neither Al nor Bill had revealed their promotions to their wives. Buck asked if they would keep it a secret until that evening.

Half-jokingly, Buck said, "I suppose you're all wondering why I called you here tonight."

"Darling," said Carrie, "Stop keeping us in suspense!"

"OK, OK. I wanted to tell everyone that my two best pals, Al and Bill have gotten two huge promotions at RCA Victor. They are now vice-presidents making more money than they ever imagined."

Arlene and Cathy screamed in unison and hugged their husbands. Jerry Rosen congratulated the both of them and Eddie said, "Way to go, Uncle Bill and Uncle Al!"

"Oh. And one more thing. He paused and let the silence hang in the air for just a few beats. "I've been named the new President of RCA Victor Records."

Now it was Carrie's turn to scream, "Oh my God! Bucky! Really?"

## A CHANGE OF KEY

"Yes dear. General Sarnoff announced it today."

She ran to Buck to be enfolded in his arms kissing him all over his face. Bevvy and Arlene could hardly believe it, but they knew how hard he had worked at RCA and they were thrilled for his success.

"So I just wanted you here so I could tell you that I'm not breaking up the team. Those two vice-presidents? They're still working for me, and we're all going to do great things together. Now, let's have some cake!"

The rest of the night was spent in a warm and congenial atmosphere. Friends, relatives, children—all together, all happy. What more could a man want?

When everyone had gone home and the children had gone to bed, Carrie sat on the sofa—and in typical Carrie fashion, began to cry.

"Honey?"

She waved him away with one hand while she wiped her eyes with a tissue in the other. "I'm sorry, sweetheart. I just can't believe how happy you've made me and how lucky I am that we've spent so much of our lives together. You know I don't think I deserve it, right?"

"You don't think you deserve Buck Fisher? Buck Fisher doesn't think he deserves you. You know, darling, I swear that each time I look at you, I fall in love with you all over again. So who's the lucky one?"

"Buck? Let's celebrate."

"Sure. How?"

She took him by the hand and led him to their bedroom. She smiled at him, and closed the door.